AFTER THE BADGE

Names: Addison Crissone
Title: After the Badge/Addison Crissone

Summary: A year after her brother's death and at the close of WWII in Belgium, Ruth DeVos has fought to forget the memories of her past. But when she is sent back to Antwerp on assignment with the newspaper, she is forced to face the darkness of war once again.

Subjects: | World War 2, 1939-1945- Fiction | Christian Historical- Fiction | Holocaust Fiction |
ISBN: 979-8-9914359-2-5

After the Badge

Addison Crissone

To all who are seeking victory.

Then this last summer, sadder now,
Did see him 'ere he died;
His right to live, to prove, then how
His head to fate reside.
There's many men who pledge their hearts
To answer freedom's call,
But few are they who freedom asks
To glorify their all.

And so when summer comes again
To warm our peaceful land,
The hills and fields and marshy glen,
The willows where they stand
Beside the stream and share our tears
For him who died to give
Fresh life to summer through the years;
He gladly died- and we live.

*A poem written by an
unknown RAF pilot in 1940*

PART ONE

NOUVELLE SÉRIE DE GUERRE

Brussels, Belgium

The Lord gave, and the Lord has taken away; Blessed be the name of the Lord.

JOB 1:21

CHAPTER ONE

NOUVELLE SÉRIE DE GUERRE
ANDREW

Ghent, Belgium

Bombs implode and gunfire erupts as gnashing Germans rush upon the ancient cobblestone streets to meet the Resistance men with a malice and vengeance that is both threatening and dangerous; but Andrew meets them with equal feelings of courage and faith, praying for the strength and valor to keep fighting.

The yellow badge still glints on his chest just as it has for over a year now, reminding him of the reason he fights.

He glances over his shoulder to ensure that the allied men and Jewish prisoners are still fleeing around him. They remain steadfast behind him, though struggling.

The prisoners are fearful and uncertain, their fear written across their pale and ashen faces, and he can see that each of them is thin and bruised. But for now, they are alive and breathing.

Soon, perhaps, they will be free.

The men in his troop are weary, tired, and injured; their eyes sunken and solemn as they await Andrew's command.

"Fight!" he urges them.

He faces the serene and tranquil waterways of the canal beside them. Planes soar over his head as men rush forward all around him, but he is reminded for a fleeting moment of the beach of his childhood.

Except this is not Vlissengen.

This is Ghent, Belgium.

The rush of gunfire and the stench of bombs hang thick upon the air that he breathes, leaving an unpleasant and repulsive taste upon his lips.

Nazi Germans march toward him, smoke and brass billowing from their rifles as they advance closer to the wounded soldiers belonging to the Resistance.

"Go!" he calls to the Jews behind him in a desperate final attempt to get them to safety.

But the Germans have gained control over the waterways; they have nowhere to go. The Germans have ensnared them—they have captured them at their weakest moment.

Behind him, awaits the dangerous and occupied city of Ghent; ahead, the daunting and ruthless Nazi troops in their gray uniforms and deadly bolt-action rifles poised for service.

The only way of escape is through.

He can taste the bitter sting of defeat in the air, but he knows that victory awaits him on the other side.

He swallows. He knows what he must do.

Father, this is it, isn't it? He prays silently, turning his face to the sky and setting his jaw.

All along, Lord, I have been a voyager across life's ocean; safe in Heaven's ark may I pass through a troubled world into the harbor of Eternal rest.

Bullets fall like rain as marching boots clap like thunder, but Andrew lunges ever onward, never stopping, though his fear only rises; and never does he doubt his destiny.

For a moment it is all the horrors of this world, the cry of gunfire, the stench of bombs and the bitterness of high explosives on the lips, the incessant drumming of weary legs and the aching of hammering hearts.

But then, it all fades away as if it were just a bad dream, no longer to be remembered, as a final bullet is sent piercing through the air and strikes the woven fabric of the yellow badge resting upon his chest and his final battle comes to a close.

And the days after the badge have begun.

~ ~
.

"ANDREW!"

I open my eyes with a jolt, panting for breath as my heart pounds in my ribcage.

I glance down at my own heaving chest, but no yellow badge waits there.

The badge is gone.

It has been ten months since Andrew went to Ghent to release imprisoned Jews with the Resistance, an assignment that would lead to a hard-fought battle, and ultimately, his death.

I still cannot believe it. Or, rather, *accept* it.

I glance at my surroundings swiftly, half-expecting to find myself in the midst of a battleground near the waterways of Ghent.

But my bedroom is dark and still as rain falls in sheets outside my window and thunder growls with a fierce urgency upon the window pane.

No Germans lurk in the shadows, and no bombs threaten to implode and carry me into the depths of their fiery folds of destruction and embers. Thunder has taken the place of the bombs and drumming boots of my imagination, clapping simultaneously with the beats of my hammering heart.

I am in Brussels; I am safe.

Aren't I?

It was only a dream, I tell myself.

I am shaking something awful, my heart rate rising with the billowing tide of emotion that swells in my chest. My entire body trembles with the weight of the dream, my chest heaving as silent tears dampen my cheeks.

It was only a dream, I repeat, though I know that it wasn't only a dream.

They are the memories that I never made. They are the memories of my brother's last battle that my imagination has formed of its own accord as if for consolation.

I close my eyes, but I only see his familiar face; and when I open them, I see the cold stare of the Germans from the Dossin Barracks.

Every day I relive the broken and fragmented memories of my past— memories of my brother and my time imprisoned in the Nazi camps; even a year and a half after I was captured, the memories still lurk in the recess of my conscious only to escape once the folds of sleep have encompassed me and the nightmares begin.

Every morning when I wake, I remember.

I am broken.

I hold your heart in my hand—you will not remain broken, My child, the still small voice whispers assuredly to my heart.

I glance up at the ceiling above me, the familiar delft blue flowers gazing back at me in the dimly lit room.

The words are hard to believe at this moment as the current of bitterness and grief rises in my chest, but I clutch onto them with every fiber of my soul.

Throwing the sheets away from my body, I step from the bed and onto unsteady legs, wading blindly through the darkness of my room.

Thunder groans once more, bringing with it many more flashbacks.

Shivering slightly, I stumble to the window, where the lacey white curtain flutters in the pale light of the coming day. I gaze down at the rolling hills and vast fields of the Brussels countryside that forms Ezra's farm beyond my window pane.

Beyond the curtain of pelting rain, rolling fog, and angry sky, the sun is chasing away the dark and unveiling an orange sunrise, blazing with vibrant rays of color in the midst of the storm.

The darkness has rolled away, and the light has come forth.

I close my eyes and press my forehead to the cool glass, breathing in the fresh scent of rain and grass that blows in from outside.

Somewhere, I know, beyond the boundaries of this land where the war still rages, allied men have crossed over Belgian lines.

They march onward, through the storm and through the night, into Belgium's towns and cities, liberating its people one by one from Nazi Germany's control.

Yes, the allied forces are advancing, and *Belgique* will soon be free.

CHAPTER TWO

NOUVELLE SÉRIE DE GUERRE

The burden that is left to be carried after the badge is heavy, and its price is costly.

But so is our freedom.

And it is men like my brother who have paid the cost.

The assuring sounds of allied planes journey through the air above the rooftops of Brussels as my heels click methodically across the cobblestone streets.

The streets are nearly empty despite the sunny skies and singing birds that have at last returned after the three days of incessant rain that we have endured.

I scan the streets and alleys carefully, but only vacant army jeeps line the opposite sidewalk as the remaining storefronts open for the day.

I wave a friendly hand toward the butcher as he flips his sign to say *open,* and he nods cordially back at me.

Good man, I think to myself. The old butcher has been a large asset to the Resistance for months, smuggling intelligence notes into cuts of meat and sending them home with known resistance members to pass the information on.

I continue down the street.

I hold myself upright and nonchalant, my steps purposeful and my manner determined.

I am dressed in the usual clothing of a professional working female, my skirts bunching modestly around my knees as my heels carry me a good three inches above my true height.

I glance down at the false identity card hidden in the crook of my palm.

Florence Archambeau stares back at me.

I bite my lip.

Florence, or simply "Flo," is my code name; it is the name Ezra had picked for me when he and our colleagues from the Resistance forged the false ID card for me shortly after returning home after the ambush.

According to the little card, I am a young French woman, a refugee born and bred in Paris.

I come to Rue Thomas Vincotte street, and pause.

My legs stiffen and my heart hammers as my gaze falls on the tall, daunting figure of a German soldier who holds the empty position guarding the street. He bears an uncanny resemblance to Lieutenant Wolfgang.

My blood turns icy as old memories rush to my mind, and I grit my teeth to force them into the hidden recesses of my heart.

I cannot let the memories taunt me now.

I have a job to do, I tell myself, then I pray, *Lord, help me go on. Our victory is nigh, Father. Let it be so.*

Taking in a raspy and ragged breath, I gather my bearings and step forward.

My spine stiffens as gooseflesh rises across my arms and legs as the German's cold stare follows me down the street, my heart pounding as I struggle to breathe.

I step unhindered up the few stairs of number 82 Thomas Vincotte, laying a gentle hand upon the gilded doorknob of the building. I press the door open swiftly with my hip and rush over the threshold.

The room I enter is the small and vacant lobby of a lawyer's office, thick carpet and wood paneling surrounding me.

I lock the door behind me, gasping for breath.

A thick-set young woman enters the room, her face pale as she looks at me with concern.

"Miss DeVos..." She catches herself, glancing at me apologetically. "I mean, Miss Archambeau, are you alright?"

"Yes, Rosa, I'm fine," I say, straightening my skirt and slipping the little card into my pocket.

Rose Hardouin, a formatter who works with *La Libre Belgique,* stares at me skeptically. She is slightly older than me, closer to Eline's age, and has been with the paper since its founding in early 1940.

"Do you have the document?" she asks.

I brandish my purse in front of her.

"Certainly," I say.

I would never come empty-handed.

She nods, motioning for me to follow her down the stairwell.

"Quickly, Miss. We must get the news out swiftly, else *they* will beat us to it."

I fall into step behind her.

"*They?* Who is 'they'?"

"The allies," Rosa states, meeting ground level and unlocking a second door with a key she pulls from her pocket.

She ushers me inside, and we enter the cellar of the office; painted brick walls surround me, covered in white to give the illusion of space, though only feeling all the smaller to me.

The stale stench of the dirt floor beneath me meets my nose.

It reminds me faintly of Avenue Louise.

I shudder as she locks the door behind us, the only light that illuminates the cellar being several oil-lamps arranged meticulously around the damp room.

In the corner of the room rests the large and rather frightening mound of metal, wheels, and ink that makes up the illegal mimeograph machine that belongs to the paper.

Genevieve Peutchin is bent over the printer, her fingers covered in the vestige of many weeks of ink as she fiddles with the large roller.

She smiles at me.

"Good, you're here, Ruth," she says, using my true name. "Where is the copying piece?"

I smile.

On the streets, I am Florence.

In the safety of home and the resistance, I am Ruth DeVos once more.

"I've got it right here, Genny," I say, slipping a hand into my purse and carefully pulling from it a piece of carbon paper that took me nearly three hours to properly copy.

I offer it to Rosa, and she immediately begins to scan the words.

"So, what's the news?" I ask, my voice echoing softly as I run a finger lightly over the roller of the large printing machine.

Genevieves's face brightens.

"The British allies are hand in hand with the Resistance; working together, they have crossed Belgian lines and are currently working to gain ground in Belgium's outskirts. Their first obvious choice of capture will be Brussels. Rumor has it that they will begin liberating us tomorrow."

My eyes widen. Hope rises in my chest.

"Is the Secret Army involved as well?" I ask, trying to mask the hopefulness in my voice.

Ezra's coming home, my brain tells me, which results in the familiar fluttering of my heart.

Ezra had written to me in November telling me of my brother's passing and later returned home in January on a brief leave to take me home to Vlissengen to visit Andrew's grave; he has returned to Brussels on several occasions since, though none of his visits lasted more than a few days. His last letter came in the early days of June, when allied troops stormed the beaches of Normandy, France.

In the letter, he told me that he had received a short letter telling of the account of his father's time spent under Nazi interrogation, where he was deemed mentally unstable and insane, and was later executed by the hands of the Germans.

Ezra's wounds were deep and his grief great, but still he continued on with the Resistance.

And I haven't heard from him since.

Worry churns in my stomach.

Our courtship has been prolonged longer than either of us has planned and hoped, though it has evolved into a silent engagement of sorts; the war has delayed any thoughts of marriage.

I turn to gaze at my hand, where on the fourth finger is a small ring.

It is petite and dainty, a yellow gold ring with a small, faceted diamond in a square setting and flanked by two stones on either side.

I smile softly, recalling the day he had given it to me on his last visit in May.

"I wanted to give this to you a long time ago, but I didn't have it then." He smiled up at me, the boyish look of spry joy overtaking his eyes. "I hope you like it."

I had blushed furiously, and my voice had abandoned me, but of course I readily accepted.

And so, we have worked and waited, prayed and hoped for the past year now.

Genevieve nods her head, pulling me from my distant thoughts.

"I'm almost certain all branches of the Resistance are involved; I know the White Brigade is."

She glances over at Rosa.

"How did she do? Is it ready?"

Rosa is silent for a moment, absently pulling an old typewriter across the table to her left.

"You did well, Miss. Now, sit and write furiously," she says, checking the time on her dainty wristwatch. "We must be swift."

Smiling, I sit down before the typewriter; I pull a crisp white sheet of carbon paper into its roll and lift my fingers to the metal keys once again.

It is not my old typewriter; that one was lost some time ago when I was captured early last year.

But it is still an old friend, and I begin writing furiously and rapidly, the French words I had copied and nearly memorized falling in neat columns upon the sheet as the final issue of *La Libre Belgique* comes to life before my very eyes.

"This is it, girls. Liberty has arrived, and the newspaper must come to an end," Geneive murmurs wistfully from the corner, where she is actively loading the latter end of the machine with a tall stack of blank pages.

"It's hard to believe, isn't it?" Rosa replies, a smile in her voice.

By the time I am finished typing, my hands are covered in black ink and my fingers are weary from exertion, but I smile with satisfaction as Rosa carefully hands the newly copied issue of the paper to Genevieve, who swiftly places it in the copying roll of the mimeograph.

She begins cranking the small limb of the roller, and the press immediately begins churning out pristine copies of the paper.

After the ink is soaked into the paper and they have air dried for a brief moment, Rosa and I take the newspapers and assemble the few short pages before tucking them safely inside my purse.

I pick one up from the pile, squinting down at it in the dimly lit room.

Le dernier adieu des brutes!

I smile, my boldness rising.

The final farewell to the bullies! Is the opening line written under the masthead of the paper.

I stare at my own words in disbelief.

The war is ending; it is finally over.

My heart refuses to believe it.

After all these years, after so much loss and devastation, it is at last coming to a close. I don't know whether to cry, laugh, or shout.

Perhaps all three.

For so long, our world, lives, and our very fate have been uncertain; it seems like the world's last breath is waiting, poised on the hinge of the war, as if the defining moment will only be met once the war comes to a close.

But, all along, God has been in control.

It is later on that morning, as I travel alone through the streets of Brussels distributing the illegal newspaper to civilians, tucking them into post-boxes, mixing them in the newsstands and all while avoiding the prying eyes of the soon-defeated Germans, that I watch the glorious truth dawn on my fellow citizens as they too read my words.

They are the words we have all longed to read and hear, but most especially, to live.

They are the words of freedom.

~ . ~

HONEST CITIZENS!

It is not cowardice to unmask and denounce the enemy's collaborators;

it is a duty of loyalty.

On the contrary, it would be half-complicit to encourage their impunity.

The blood of our martyrs, the suffering of our prisoners, the deprivations of the population seek revenge.

Someone will come who will pay for everything, they said!

The time has come!

Le dernier adieu des brutes!

The final farewell to the bullies!

The story of the clandestine press tells of the obscure heroism of those who worked to maintain the Belgian ideal and the morale of the people.

May they be honored and thanked on this day! To them, as to the workers of the first hour, goes a share of our glory, which marks this hour of deliverance.

Belgique is free.

Three words that ring like a song of bells. We would like to write them in gold—they resonate in our hearts like Heavenly music.

Belgique is free.

We wonder if we can believe it, and if we won't suddenly wake as if from a dream.

Belgique is free, and so is the ardent nature of its people; free from the bounds of heavy constraints and intolerable slavery.

Yes, praise be to God! For he has led us to victory, and we are free at last, free unto abundant and exuberant joy!

A.A.

CHAPTER THREE

NOUVELLE SÉRIE DE GUERRE
EZRA

Port of Antwerp

Ezra pulls the final box from the inner parts of his redbelly cargo plane, lifting it and carrying it stiffly to the open door of the port's warehouse.

The scent of the sea weighs heavily upon the crisp air surrounding the harbor, the faint cry of seagulls coasting above him seeming eerily calm and almost familiar.

He sighs, turning and walking aimlessly down the docks, gazing down into the depths of the waters below his boots.

He feels as if he has aged twenty years in the few short months that have passed, his reflection growing more and more foreign to even himself. He has seen things he wishes to forget and felt things he wished he'd never experienced, like the deep-rooted and malicious hatred for the Germans and the sorrow of his father's silent execution that drives him to such fits of rage he falls to his knees and prays that God will somehow keep him from the anger's hold.

Since Andrew's death late last year, he has been sent on countless missions for the Secret Army, witnessing unimaginable horrors and fighting fierce battles both on land and by air.

But all of this had carried him far from home, and he was unable to be with Ruth when she needed him the most, and he was unable to get to her when he needed comfort and consolation of his own.

He turns his gaze upward, to the cloudy, though clearing, sky above him; the storm clouds he had fought in coming to Antwerp from Liege have nearly all dispersed, now falling away to reveal a pale blue autumn world above.

It is nearly tranquil, save for the faraway groans and jolts of army jeeps that barricade the port behind him.

Something tells him that this is the calm before the storm.

The familiar longing and sensation of flying blooms as his foot begins to tap anxiously, as if pulsing the pedal of his beloved piano; the feeling builds in his chest, spreading through his limbs.

"Aviator," a muffled and grainy voice utters from his pocket. "Aviator Pik."

He reaches a large palm into the trouser pocket of his coveralls, pulling from its depths a small radio, static eluding from it. He slides a button with his thumb and the static clears.

He holds it closer to his lips.

"I'm here, Commander," he says into it.

"Good," comes the response a moment later. "Listen, the allies are on their way *now*. Lieutenant General Brian Horrocks of the British corps has just given his men the command to capture Brussels from Germany. Have you completed the mission and carried the necessary supplies to the men at the port?"

"Yes, sir, I have. I am at the port now, in fact," he replies, his mind reeling with the news.

"Excellent. Now, Pik, I need you to report back to Brussels and join the allies. They are working actively in Hainaut and gaining ground swiftly. The Prion Brigade has already joined them, and I have already sent several troops to aid them; I need you to command them for a short period until I can send a more suitable replacement."

He falls silent for a moment.

"Can I trust you, Aviator?"

Ezra sighs, his spine stiffening.

"Yes, Commander. You can trust me," he says.

"Do *not* do anything other than what I have just told you, Pik. We don't want a repeat of your last *assignment*, or else you may not come out of it alive. Do you understand?"

The commander pauses briefly, as if allowing Ezra a moment to understand.

Heat crawls into his cheeks, memories of the German whom he had fought coming into his mind.

Your last assignment, he repeats the words in his head.

Ezra nods, though he is alone.

"Yes, sir. I understand," he says stiffly.

"I knew I could count on you, Pik. Now, you must hurry, else we have a troop of aimless soldiers floundering and wandering like sheep without a shepherd. Fly, Pik. I will see you soon."

The airways fall and static takes the place of the commander's voice.

Like sheep without a shepherd.

Sighing heavily, he turns and walks with purpose down the dock and back the way he'd come.

He slips swiftly back inside the *Fokker,* slipping the face mask and thick glasses of an aviator over his face as the engine simultaneously roars to life and the propeller awakens.

Liberty is coming, Son. Be ready.

I am ready, Father, Ezra says in his heart.

Despite the heavy weight of the task before him and the burden of his actions behind him, he smiles to himself.

This is it, he thinks, *at last the end is in sight. Liberty is on its way.*

And he turns his face toward new horizons as his plane lifts from the safety of the ground, and he leaves the darkness of the past three months there; in the past.

Or so he hopes.

CHAPTER FOUR

NOUVELLE SÉRIE DE GUERRE

The final war issue of *La Libre Belgique* arrived in the days of our deliverance from the grueling clutches of the Germans as it came at last in the young hours of the first few days of September, 1944, when the allied forces advanced over Belgian lines and began swiftly capturing the cities that formed the country.

I stand in the midst of the crowded and triumphant streets of Brussels with Mr. and Mrs. Shepherd, Eline and Maya beside me as joy overflows in the city, where just days before I was tasked with the risky assignment of passing out the young news of our freedom.

These are the days of celebration, joy, and liberation as German jeeps are set ablaze along the roadsides and Nazi personnel are led away by allied forces and Belgium's own men from the Resistance.

Civilians flock to the streets of Brussels to witness their newfound liberty as the allied tanks, motorcycles, automobiles, and soldiers on foot form a vast caravan that only adds to the delight and joy of the people.

All tokens of Nazi occupation have been thrown into the streets and burned as women dance circles around the embers of the ash and soot that had once been gray Nazi uniforms and wooden notices that had been hung upon the shop windows declaring Nazi authority, and even a portrait of Adolf Hitler himself after the people had shot a hole clean through his cold and vacant painted blue eyes.

Miniature Belgian flags and tear-stained hankies are flown from the hands of the citizens as their cheers shatter through the morning air, and the heavy shuddering of the tanks rolling through the streets causes the ground to tremble beneath our feet.

The pale and tranquil faces of the soldiers of the allied British army smile and wave down at us from the tanks and trucks they ride upon as many others walk freely on foot around them, some even venturing into the thronging mob of people to greet them.

My heart pounds with every groan of the tanks and grind of the automobiles as I shift to peer over the heads of the pressing crowd around me, humming to the drilling tune that is being played by a passing army band.

We have been delivered, I think to myself, my heart still refusing to believe it.

This is the day we have been waiting for, fighting for, and dreaming about for four years now; and now that it is finally here, I cannot seem to convince my own heart of the freedom that is now offered to us.

A young woman riding upon the hood of a bedraggled jeep clamps a soldier's cap upon her curly head of hair and is now calling and cheering louder than the crowd as her voice is carried further down the streets.

Maya cheers from her vantage point upon Mr. Shepherd's shoulders, though I am nearly certain that the little girl doesn't quite understand what she is celebrating.

"Are you enjoying yourself, little goose?" I ask her, smiling softly.

She nods her head, her hands clasped tightly around Mr. Shepherd's throat as if she were strangling him.

Planes hum across the sky, and I glance upward, just as I do every time I hear a plane these days.

Welcome to the liberators! proclaims the white banner above my head, the joyous declaration echoing in the hearts of every person present as The Secret Army leads the newly captured and defeated Nazi troops into the streets.

"Here come the defeated *Mofs* now," a man calls from beside me, his voice exuberant though lined with disgust at the sight of our enemies. "The captured Nazi troops that shall never serve Hitler or his regime ever again."

He points a slender finger over the crowd in the direction the tanks have just come from.

Mr. and Mrs. Shepherd look to where the man points, and Eline stands on her dainty tiptoes to see over the heads of people.

"I don't want to see," I murmur softly, though no one hears me over the chorus of chanting civilians, and I find myself looking anyway.

The defeated Germans are just that; defeated.

They gaze helplessly at the allied forces who have captured them and so forth put an end to their fatal schemes, a few of them shedding bitter tears at their swift and sudden misfortune.

But their tears will not help them.

My mouth dries as my stomach churns, my gaze following their cold stares as they advance farther into the city.

My blood runs cold at the sight of them, and I am forced to look away as year-old memories of the German's cruelty rush to my mind once again, just as it did in the young hours of dawn as I awoke from the dream of Andrew, and then again when I saw the haughty German soldier in the street.

I shudder.

Mr. Shepherd looks away, and so do I.

He smiles gently down at me, and I know that he is thinking of Hugo and Andrew—the two boys he had loved as his own, one he lost and the other lost his way.

With his amicable manner and droll ways, my brother had been swiftly accepted into the heart of the clan in the few short months before his death, and Mr. and Mrs. Shepherd took him under their wing as their own, just as they had for all of us earlier in the days of war.

The cool breath of autumn has been ushered in with September, and I pull my green coat tighter over my shoulders, my palm brushing the bare six-pronged patch where the yellow badge had been sewn just months ago, before I had torn it from the garment after receiving the news of my brother's death.

In my anger and confusion just after his passing, I had torn the stitches loose that bound the putrid yellow cloth to the pale green garment as if it would somehow ease the pain.

It didn't.

Andrew.

I look around the streets and sigh.

This is the day that Andrew had fought for and had labored toward since the very beginning—and now he isn't here to see it.

And neither is Ezra.

The fractures in my heart split just a little bit more at the reminder of my brother's absence and Ezra's silence, and despite the tumultuous joy and enthusiasm of the people around me, I want to cry.

The bombs shatter through my memory and I can almost hear Andrew calling out to me with the cold grasp of the German officer on my shoulder.

I clamp my hands over my ears, but the noise remains and the weight on my shoulders only grows.

"Ruth, are you alright?" Eline's voice asks gently, her soft hand clasped firmly on my shoulder.

I don't answer.

"Ruth?" This time, it is Mrs. Shepherd.

I open my eyes, but the visions remain.

I let out a breath. "I'm alright."

Eline gives me a skeptical look. She knows that I am lying.

She and Mrs. Shepherd share a knowing glance.

"I heard you calling out in your sleep again this morning, Ruth. Do you need to go home?" Eline asks softly.

I swallow.

This morning I awoke from the fierce grasp of a nightmare once more, much like the one before.

"No, we need to stay. I'll be fine," I say assuredly.

I am saved from any further questioning as a wave of exhilarated and triumphant cheers and whistles erupt through the civilian crowds as Belgian soldiers with the armed Resistance enter the streets, all dressed in the uniform and customary beige coveralls of the Secret Army.

The men are obviously worn, their rifles hanging limply from their victorious arms, though their faces are contorted in such looks and smiles of happiness that they hardly seem to mind their injured and depleted bodily states.

"Ruth!"

My heart hammers in my chest at the familiar sound of the baritone voice, and I turn to find Ezra's face smiling at me through the crowd, his brown eyes eagerly scanning the thronging mob for the familiar faces of the Still Waters clan.

A rush of joy, love, and fear seep into my heart and I rush into the streets to meet him.

He is clothed in the beige jumpsuit of a fighter pilot, the red, yellow and black stripes of a Belgian flag peeking from the folds of his breast pocket; his face is worn and weary, covered with so much dirt that he is hardly recognizable as he smiles at me in the streets.

Our eyes meet, pale hazel into deep brown.

I don't hesitate.

I throw my arms around his neck as I embrace him, and he folds his arms around me as he picks me up and swings me in a circular motion in the middle of the street as the tanks roll and moan past us, but we don't even pay them any mind.

I breathe in the stark scent of gunpowder and sulfur that cleaves to his jumpsuit and the earthy smell that lingers on his skin.

He kisses me for a long moment, and all the uncertainty of the last few months fades away. He sets me gently on my feet, his arms still around me.

"I was so worried," I murmur, my voice filled with relief.

He lets out a slow breath and pulls away to look at me.

"Why? You had to know that I would come home if I was able," he says softly.

"You never wrote or called. I was beginning to think you had disappeared and were never coming home. I was so worried you'd done something foolish after you heard the news." *Of your father's death,* I add silently.

I try to keep the concern and frustration of the past few months from seeping into my voice.

His gaze softens, and he searches my eyes, the dirt and grime of war settling into the lines and crevices that have forever aged his young face; the shadows that dance in his eyes are darker than before, but the same familiar light still remains in their midst and in the depths of his irises, I see the reflection of rising pain and uncertain hope that inhabit my own.

"God kept me from revenge, Ruth. I didn't do anything foolish, not like I wanted to," he whispers.

I know that he saw and felt things in this war that will forever haunt him; and I know in my heart that he is forever changed since his father's death.

"I'm sorry, love," he murmurs close to my ear.

"Me too," I whisper.

Upon his cheek is a pink scar, just below his left eye; I wonder vaguely what put it there.

I reach up and stroke it gently, wiping the dirt away to reveal the white skin beneath.

"What kept you away so long?" I whisper.

He sighs, laying a dirty hand over my own.

"Yesterday is in the past, Ruth. Let's leave it there for today," he murmurs softly.

His smile is haunted.

I nod.

He doesn't want to talk about it. I swallow the bile that rises in my throat, and blink back salty tears.

"Is it over? Are we free?" I whisper, my voice merely more than a whisper.

He smiles earnestly down at me, his countenance brightening.

"Not yet, Ruth. But soon; we need only be brave." He caresses my chin lightly with his thumb. "We are headed to Antwerp next, and the northern districts have yet to be liberated. But soon, Lord willing, we shall be truly free of this war."

We share a soft smile.

"When are you coming home?" I ask, my voice hopeful.

"Soon, I hope."

I smile up at him, shaking my head.

"That isn't an answer."

He laughs lightly, stepping closer to the people and pulling me from the path of a passing army jeep.

"I know, but it will have to do for now," he says, his eyes brightening, "but I hear the Gilberts are having a little Resistance gathering this Saturday, if all goes well in the coming days. Lars tells me it is a gala of sorts. He called it an *Overwinningsgala.* Will you be attending, Miss DeVos?"

A Victory gala.

I smile.

Mrs. Gilbert, Lars' mother, had already asked Mrs. Shepherd and Eline to aid with the food, for money has grown scarce and food is now a rationed rarity, and so it was already planned that I will indeed attend the dance, even if only to help serve the guests.

"Yes, I believe I will, Mr. Pik."

He smiles. "Good. Promise me the first and last dance, won't you?"

A strong blush spreads across my cheeks, and I nod. "Of course."

I glance around at the smiling faces and cheering voices that rise together as one to Heaven and echo back all around us.

Ezra follows my gaze.

"This is it, Ruth. I know it," he whispers almost excitedly. "A new beginning for all of us."

I smile softly.

Why is it that all new beginnings are always so inextricably tied with endings? Why must they carry with them the marks and painful reminders of the loss and hurt of the past, along with the hope and gain of the future?

I suppose it is because to have a new beginning, an ending had to come first. Whether the ending is a sad one or a happy one depends on the story. But all beginnings are formed from either the wreckage or beauty of a prior ending.

I meet his hopeful gaze once more.

"It feels like the whole of Belgium has awoken from a dark and terrible dream," I murmur wistfully, almost sorrowfully, remembering my words from the farewell issue of the newspaper. "Only it wasn't a dream at all."

Ezra's smile turns rueful and thoughtful at my words, and I stand on tiptoes to kiss him, my lips leaving the vestige of lipstick upon his dirty cheek.

"I think you can wake up now," he says softly.

"I wish I could," I murmur.

His eyes flash with understanding.

"It will get better," he says with certainty.

I loop my arm through his, and we are joined in the streets by Mr. and Mrs. Shepherd, Maya, and Eline, who swiftly welcome Ezra home.

And somehow, as we walk hand in hand in the newly liberated streets among our victorious allies, defeated enemies, and joyous fellow citizens, I feel the slightest weight lift from my chest and for a moment, I forget the memories that torment me.

I smile.

Belgique is free.

This is freedom.

But in the depths of my heart, I know it isn't true.

I know better than to believe that a war such as this one could ever be dissolved in a matter of moments; no, it will take a lifetime before the war is over in the hearts and minds of its survivors.

Yes, the days of fighting are far from over.

CHAPTER FIVE

"Celebrations continue in the streets all across Belgium today as the final Germans are ushered away and their footing is pulled from beneath them. The Port of Antwerp has been held by the force of the Secret Army since August and remains under the Resistance control. As the words of the journalist proclaimed, *Belgique is free.* Oh, what joyous liberation!"

The Antwerpen broadcaster's voice eludes from the speakers of the small radio perched on my desk, his voice rising excitedly as he makes the evening announcements.

Two days after Brussels was liberated, Antwerp followed; the celebrations that had begun in Brussels on Saturday were carried on in the streets of Antwerp on Monday as the British troops filed through the streets just as I had witnessed them before.

I smile at the memory.

It has been several days since both Brussels and Antwerp were liberated, and since then we have all held our breath as we listen for the news coming forth from the radios each night and every morning, waiting for the dream of freedom to come to an end.

But still, it marches on with every drum and beat of the allies' boots.

Reaching across the desk chair to silence the radio, I turn and gaze at my reflection in the mirror that hangs on the wall behind the door.

The girl that stares back at me is familiar, though altered.

With the same pale complexion, defined cheekbones, and dark brunette hair that I have possessed since birth, I still bear the striking resemblance to my mother.

Not much has changed since my days at Still Waters, but the one thing that I notice each morning when I look at the girl in the mirror is the change in my own eyes.

While they are still the pale hazel color that I inherited from my mother, they now hold the familiar patient stare that had once belonged to my papa.

They are softer now, more thoughtful and tranquil than they once had been.

Perhaps it is the German's cruel touch and the war's harsh demands that weigh heavily upon my shoulders and have at last sobered my gaze.

I chew my lip.

Sighing, my gaze falls to my dress.

It is a stiff shirtwaist dress made of a deep mauve fabric with brass buttons lining the torso and falling down the pleated skirt, capped sleeves, and dainty lace trim lining its hem.

I comb through my hair one final time, raking the face-framing strands from my face and pinning them at the back of my head with a whalebone barrette, letting the rest fall loosely down my back.

I pull the gilded handle on the top drawer of my desk and take from its depths a small fountain pen, slipping it into the right pocket of my skirt; in the other, I slid a small reporter's notebook.

Now, I am ready for the *Overwinningsgala.*

The Victory gala.

And glancing up, I give the girl in the mirror one last look.

I smile, my pink-stained lips pulling into a soft curl, attempting to disguise the shadows in my eyes.

"Good enough," I say to my reflection.

I turn to face the wardrobe before leaving, the large doors waiting open from where I had pulled my dress from its inner chambers a moment ago.

Something below the last drawer in the empty cavity below, tucked beside a small wooden box, catches my eye.

It is Andrew's rucksack, still hidden within the wardrobe since the day it was returned to me by the Resistance several months ago.

I stare down at the green canvas of the rucksack, my trembling fingertips grazing the rough exterior as I struggle with the idea of opening it.

I cannot, I tell myself, *not yet.*

My fingers itch to open it and look within it at all the memories it holds, and every fiber and cell of my being longs to see what's inside; but I cannot bring myself to do it.

The drawstring is drawn tightly at the bag's mouth, the flap held shut by the metal buckles that jingle as I finger the small tag that has been attached to it, my thumb running across the smeared ink that bears his name.

A. DeVos

Andrew, my heart thuds.

It is heavy, filled with my brother's few remaining belongings that he had carried with him through all his days of toil and fighting.

I squeeze my eyes closed as memories of Andrew drift through my mind, each memory a time he had this very bag in his possession.

I swallow back the rising tears and open my eyes once more.

By its side, sits a pair of old work boots that had once belonged to my papa when I was younger, though Andrew had claimed them as his own when he left to join the Secret Army, the former Belgian Legion.

Upon their heels had been painted in faded red paint Andrew's blood type—O positive.

The boots still hold the vestige of life lived in the wilderness during the horrors of war, the dirt that is still dried to the bottom of their soles falling to the floor of the wardrobe as I brush my hand across them.

My gaze lingers upon both items for a long moment.

"Oh, Andrew," I whisper. I gingerly press the doors closed, and turning on my heel, I slip through the door and into the hallway, pulling the door of my room closed gently behind me.

My heels thud softly across the floor as the loose floorboards groan and complain beneath my shifting weight.

Passing the final door in the hall, my gaze lands onto the familiar black-and-white photograph that hangs in the hallway.

I wipe the gathering dust from its face, smiling at the small family of smiling faces that stare back at me from the glass.

The man, Jozef Pik, stands with a large meaty hand on the dainty shoulder of his wife, Valerie, who sits with their young son, Ezra, on her lap.

In the picture, Jozef is thick and broad with a heavy mustache over his smiling lips as his eyes flicker merrily at the camera as the picture is taken.

Valerie is a small dainty woman, the opposite of her husband, with light flaxen hair pulled into an elegant chignon as she smiles happily at her small three-year-old son.

I see in each of their faces the faint whispers and hints of their son, the physical attributes that Ezra had inherited from them both.

I smile softly.

Ezra had spoken very little of his parents on his few brief visits, but I could always tell by the wistful gaze he gives the house and even this photograph that their memory preys heavily upon his mind often.

But now, they are both gone.

It is this fact that has darkened the shadows in his eyes.

"I don't know about these shoes," a familiar voice says from behind me. "What do you think, Ruth?"

I turn.

Eline faces me from the open doorway of her room, her soft coral pink dress hanging in a becoming fashion around her thin frame.

She stares down at the white heels on her feet.

She looks up at me, her eyes pained.

"Oma had given them to me for the wedding, and I haven't worn them since. I've been saving them for a special occasion." She offers me a small smile. "I suppose today is the day, isn't it?"

I smile.

"Well, we *are* celebrating victory. I do not believe there is any other special occasion more worthy." I give her ensemble a once-over. "I think they go very well with the dress as well."

She smiles brightly, her cheeks coloring.

"It's settled then. The heels will do." She runs a hand through her curly flaxen hair. "Dear me, I've forgotten earrings."

She turns in a flustered manner and disappears back into her room.

I laugh softly, shaking my head as I continue my journey onward.

I enter the quaint little living room, where a varying assortment of chairs and stools wait to seat the frequent guests that filter in and out the door, most of them Resistance members and colleagues.

In the year that has passed, the little farmhouse has become familiar and welcoming, though we all agree that it is not our beloved Still Waters.

For several months, the house has aided in the hiding of several more persecuted Jews and allied airmen who have come to us for false identities and documents that would allow them to safely travel to neutral territory.

In the midst of the sofa, chairs, and coffee table, stands Valerie Pik's vintage piano; but no beautiful melodies rise from the redwood chest to greet me as I enter the room, and neither does the absent pianist.

I smile softly as I brush the collecting dust from the ivory keys with my palm. I gingerly close the lid with a gentle snap, and tread silently across the room and into the kitchen.

A second compact radio sits murmuring gently on the counter where Mrs. Shepherd is pulling sweet potato and Belgian pies from the oven.

Dressed in a dark purple day dress and apron that brilliantly contrasts the vibrancy of her red hair, little has changed with our dear Mrs. Shepherd.

Still her same motherly and hospitable self, she and Mr. Shepherd remain the center of our threadbare and somewhat ramshackle family.

"Don't you look lovely this evening, Ruth," she says to me, glancing up at me from the line of sugary goods on the counter. She smiles as our gaze meets. "That dress is perfect for you, dear; it somehow brings out the gold flecks in your eyes."

I smile, laughing softly at the strange sincerity of her comment.

Since the moment she first came home from Brussels where she'd been held under German questioning, Mrs. Shepherd has continued on in her normal fashion, becoming even more to me like my own mother.

"Thank you, Mrs. Shepherd," I say softly, stepping out of her way as she pulls yet more hot pies from the oven.

I reach over them to pour myself a cup of tea, stirring in the usual necessary two spoonfuls of sugar after it.

"My, it smells good in here," Mr. Shepherd says as he enters the house from the front porch, Maya in tow. He gazes at the pies.

"Don't you dare touch them, Dirk. These are for the Gilberts. Not you," Mrs. Shepherd says quickly, eyeing her husband with a warning, though she smiles.

"But, my dear wife," Mr. Shepherd says with a teasing smile, undaunted, "should they not be sampled before we go?"

"No, they indeed should not," comes the reply.

He sits Maya down in an empty chair with a forced sigh before brandishing her shoes from his trouser pocket.

"Maud, dear, please tell this rebellious child that she indeed *does* need shoes for a dance, regardless of her own opinion." His voice is tired, but he smiles at Maya in his usual fatherly fashion.

I stifle a laugh as Maya slumps in her chair, refusing to put the new shoes Mrs. Shepherd and I bought for her in Brussels last week onto her bare feet.

Mr. Shepherd leaves the little girl in Mrs. Shepherd's motherly care, pours himself a cup of black coffee from the pot near the radio, and sinks into the chair beside her.

His gaze lands on me and he smiles wistfully.

"I must say, Ruth. You are the spitting image of Judith DeVos," he says, speaking of my own mama, whom he and Mrs. Shepherd both knew in the past.

I smile over the rim of my cup as I take a sip of tea.

"So I've been told," I say with a soft sigh.

I am a walking, talking, breathing reminder of my mother's absence and unanswered imprisonment.

He smiles. "She would be proud of you, Ruth. I know you miss her. And Nathaniel."

Nathaniel.

Papa.

It feels like a lifetime has passed since I last saw them; I was eighteen then, and it feels like I have aged twenty years and am no longer their little girl.

I sigh, slipping into a third empty chair.

"I certainly do."

I watch as he slips a hand into his pocket, drawing it back with a small silver pocket watch in his palm. Clicking his tongue as he checks the time, he snaps it closed and returns it to his breast pocket.

He turns to face me, and I study him.

Like his wife, Mr. Shepherd remains the same. Though, upon closer inspection, I can see a few lines and creases on his face that weren't present before, and age has grazed the hair at his temples with white that has crawled all the way down to his cropped beard.

He walks slower these days than he had before, the harm of his many days under Nazi interrogation weighing upon him heavily.

I run a hand absently over the pink scar on the back of my neck— I cannot see it, but I know it is there.

A soft shudder runs down my spine at the gentle sensation of my own fingertips grazing the mark.

We are all this way; we forever carry upon our bodies the evidence and proof of the war's wages, never to be forgotten.

"Why the long face, my dear girl?" Mr. Shepherd asks, pulling me from my brief trance. He is still watching me.

I shake my head, and the memories disperse for another time.

"Just thinking, Mr. Shepherd. That's all."

He smiles slightly.

"I'd worry if you weren't, Ruth," he says. "Just try not to let those thoughts of yours steal this moment from you."

I meet his gaze, understanding the hidden message behind his words.

Don't dwell on the past so much that you lose sight of the hopeful future God has given you, he means. *Enjoy this freedom.*

The problem with my thoughts is that they have free will. They wander aimlessly down through the years of my life, and I cannot fight the strength of their churning current.

I smile at him softly. "I will try my best, Mr. Shepherd. I promise."

He smiles and sips his coffee.

A swift knock at the front door raises gooseflesh across my shoulder blades.

"I'll get it," I say, starting for the door.

"It's probably some of the boys from the Resistance asking for aid," Mrs. Shepherd says to my back.

I nod.

She is most likely right.

Random strangers show up on the stoop on a daily basis, soldiers and Jews alike, all of them asking us for the same thing: shelter, refuge, hiding, false IDs and food.

But as I lay a hand on the doorknob and pull it open, it is not a stranger who peers back at me from the other side of the screen door.

It is the bald head and large nose of Abram Fletcher.

His clothes are worn, and I am fairly certain that there is a hole in the toe of his left shoe as he smiles at me, returning home from his long travels. His limp is still present as he steps closer to the door, his own reminder of the war.

I smile.

"Fletcher?"

He nods his head, his brown eyes shining brightly as he steps over the threshold and into the house, where he has not been in nearly a month.

Since his and Eline's wedding, the two of them had moved into Oma Edward's vacant residency that Eline had inherited; a large stately mansion set upon a hill that can be seen in the distance from the porch.

But when Fletcher, who had long been deemed unfit for battle, was offered a job as courier working for the Comet Line, he and Eline decided it would be best for her to stay with us in Ezra's childhood home.

"That's me," he says with a droll smile, giving me a swift once-over, "How is the *Auteur?*"

"Alright, I suppose," I say with a short laugh at the familiar nickname. "Where have you been this time?"

"Paris," he says casually as we walk into the kitchen. "I was given a rather weighty packet of documents that the allied airmen located there needed. They informed me of the allies' plan to liberate Belgium next, so I thought it best to return home as swiftly as I could."

Mr. Shepherd stands from the table clasping hands with him. "Fletcher, my dear friend, how is courier life treating you?"

"Not bad, Dirk. Not bad at all." He smiles, giving Mrs. Shepherd a swift embrace and patting Maya on the head. He glances around the room, as if searching for something. "Say, where is my wife?"

Before he can say another word, Eline emerges from the hall and the two embrace.

"There she is." Fletcher laughs into Eline's curly hair, bending to kiss her. "How are you, my dear?"

Eline mumbles something that I cannot hear, and I look at my feet as the two share a moment. After the moment ends, they part and Eline brushes tears of relief from her pink cheeks.

"What are you doing here? I thought you were meeting us at Lars Gilbert's house later tonight?" she asks Fletcher.

He nods. "I was, but I thought I'd come home and be your escort. I am your husband, after all."

Eline laughs softly, lacing her fingers with his as she smiles contentedly at him.

Fletcher is silent for a moment.

"Have you heard anything from the *Pilot* lately, Ruth?" he asks.

The Pilot. It was the name Andrew had given Ezra, and it had stuck.

I smile softly, shaking my head.

"No, not since Saturday," I say. "He has promised to meet us at the Gilberts at seven o'clock sharp, though."

Fletcher gives me a pointed look, a look that suggests he knows more than he lets on.

I ignore him and reach for my coat by the door, shrugging it swiftly over my shoulders.

"Where has he been all this time? I thought he'd be home by now," he asks, helping Eline into her coat.

"I did too," I say with a soft tinge of regret in my voice, "but the supply chain has been held up and with Antwerp's Port under lockdown, supplies cannot be brought to and from Antwerp any other way than a plane. So he's been back and forth between Brussels, Liege, and Antwerp for the past few months."

I pause for a moment, thinking.

"Or, so I heard. He didn't want to talk about it when I asked, so I left it alone. I worry about him. Something is preying upon his mind but he won't talk to me about it. I suppose it's about his father."

The familiar thread of worry ties itself in knots in my stomach, reminding me of all the reasons I have to worry about him.

Mr. Shepherd meets my gaze.

"Perhaps he doesn't know *how* to talk about it, Ruth. Give him time, he'll come around," he says.

I glance around at the faces of the Still Waters clan, and I can see the change in each of us. We are fewer now than when we began two years ago, and the absence of Oma, Hugo, Andrew, and Ezra is felt in the room.

My stomach churns with anger at the thought of the malicious traitor, Hugo.

He had openly and voluntarily betrayed us; he had used us as an instrument to win back the favor of the Germans when he betrayed our hiding place at Still Waters.

He is the reason we all carry with us the memories and wounds of war.

Fletcher shakes his head, glancing at Eline.

"Well, I'm glad this blasted war is nearly over and those *Mofs* have been paid back; I'm tired of fighting another man's war."

Mrs. Shepherd smiles plaintively.

"I think we all are, dear," she murmurs softly, laying a gentle hand upon Maya's shoulder to still the little girl's incessant fidgeting.

Mr. Shepherd nods his head in agreement, taking a sip from his coffee as his eyes flash with memories.

"We best be off, else we're all late and they think we aren't coming," he says, absently gathering the pies from the counter.

And so with this final word, we are ushered out the door and into the cool breeze of autumn, vowing that nothing will deprive us of this fine evening ahead.

CHAPTER SIX

The sky has darkened into a soft lavender color by the time we reach the Gilbert's home; a large house set on the border of the heart of Brussels near the center of town, with slight nods to traditional Nouveau architecture in both its interior and exterior features.

The house's beautiful rock face welcomes us as we walk briskly up the walkway, enchanting vines crawling up its sides and to the many dainty windows that grace its front with a small brook running behind it.

"My," I muse softly to Eline, "I never knew the Gilberts were so well off."

Eline smiles, her cheeks coloring with a rosy glow as she gazes down at her simple, coral shirtwaist dress.

"Neither had I. I wish I would have worn something a little more elegant and suitable," she says.

Fletcher pats her hand consolingly.

"You look wonderful, Eline. Look at me, I'm the unsuitable one," he says, his voice droll as he waves a hand at himself.

Eline and I share a laugh.

Fletcher hadn't bothered to change from his travelers clothes—a thick and heavy threadbare overcoat, pressed trousers, ruined shoes, and slim cane that had served as a disguise for his Resistance work.

Maya slips her hand into mine as we approach the door, which is jarred and flanked by a waiting soldier, and I smile down at her.

At nearly six, Maya is tall for her age, though still just as skinny and delicate as before; her brown eyes are wide with wonder at the sight of the large house before us.

Music drifts through the door to greet us as Mr. Shepherd enters the house with Mrs. Shepherd on his arm, the joyous sounds of laughter, vivacious chatter, and colliding china falling upon my ears.

The soldier by the door nods at me as I step over the threshold, but I do not recognize him from the Resistance.

"May I take your coat, miss? And yours as well, young miss?" he asks Maya and I, a faint clip in his voice that tells me Dutch is not his native tongue.

"Yes, thank you," I say, and after abandoning our thin coats with the man we join Mr. and Mrs. Shepherd in the living room, where they have entered the company of the kind widowed hostess, Mrs. Gilbert.

Mrs. Gilbert is a tall and rather thin little creature, with placid white hair and pale cheeks, sullen green eyes, and a friendly smile.

"Miss DeVos," she says as I introduce myself, taking my left hand into her cool, thin ones, "Lars told me about dear Andrew. I am terribly sorry; your brother was a good man and gallant soldier from what my boy says. Please know that I am here if you ever need anything."

I smile, though my cheeks flush at such a swift and naked remark regarding my brother's passing.

"Thank you, Mrs. Gilbert, you're truly too kind," I say softly. "My brother is greatly missed."

She nods. "I'm sure he is."

She turns to Maya.

"And how are you, my dear little girl?" the old woman asks, reminding me vaguely of a thinner, more amicable version of our own late Oma Edwards.

Maya mumbles something in an inaudible voice, her fist tightening around my fingers.

Mrs. Gilbert laughs good-naturedly at the child, and continues on to greet Eline and Fletcher, who have entered the house behind me.

Billowing voices rise to the vaulted ceiling overhead, swelling with the rise of the beautiful music that is being played by a small band in the next room.

The soft notes of a piano greets my ear, mingling with many other instruments that form the small orchestra and stirring a familiar chord in my chest.

I smile.

The living room is large and spacious, with every chair and corner harboring a guest; upon my own observations, I conclude there must be over a hundred men with the Resistance, some of them still wearing their beige coveralls while others have changed into casual social clothing. There are men and women from the Secret Army, the White Brigade, the Comet Line, and I even recognize a few colleagues from *La Libre Belgique.*

Some men appear foreign, wearing navy uniforms and charming smiles, and speak with strange accents and the occasional, "Blasted Jerrys!"

British allies, I think to myself with a smile of gratitude.

My stomach tightens as my gaze lands on a group of men from Andrew's troop near the punch bowl.

Some of them I do not recognize, but others are familiar, like Lars Gilbert and Boris van Berg, along with their commanding officer, Berend van Branteghem whom I had met at Bram Hendrik's funeral last year.

All of them, however, were present for the ambush on the twentieth convoy headed for Auschwitz.

The men do not look up from their swift conversation, and I look away before they recognize me, memories of Andrew rushing through my mind.

These men were there the day he died, my heart whispers, my pulse quickening as silent dread seeps into my veins. *They watched him fight and die for our freedom and for victory, the very same victory that we are celebrating tonight.*

I swallow the bile that is rising in my throat.

I turn to Mr. Shepherd.

"I suppose I should go say hello to Andrew's troop," I say in a low voice before turning to Maya. "You stay with Mr. Shepherd, little goose. I'll be back in a moment."

Maya obeys, releasing my hand and latching herself immediately to Mr. Shepherd's side, her usual wild and confident nature now docile and behaved as she gazes at the glass chandeliers hanging from above her and at the grand floral portraits painted on the rafters of the ceiling in a Swedish fashion.

Mr. Shepherd nods sadly, his gaze soft as he hears the note of hesitation and hurt in my voice. He lays an assuring hand on my shoulder.

"Give them my regards, Ruth. Maya and I will wait for you in the dining room," he says with a glance over his shoulder. "Maud has already been carried off to help in the kitchen, it appears."

"I will only be a moment. Let me know if you find Ezra. I've promised him a couple of dances," I reply, stepping away.

Mr. Shepherd smiles, his eyes brightening.

"Certainly."

I smile softly. I slip through the crowd, the guests striding past me, all of them laughing and happy.

Fletcher leads Eline to the open floor of the dining room, where a dozen other couples have already paired off and are dancing as elderly gentlemen sit in circles at small tables throughout the room, conversing amongst themselves as their wives have gathered in the kitchen.

Lars Gilbert stands tallest of the men in his troop, his blond head rising nearly to the light fixture that hangs low from the ceiling.

In the early days after Andrew's death, the troop had come to visit me personally at Ezra's residence; I have not seen them since.

The memory of when I first received the news of his passing shatters through my memory; I remember clutching Ezra's letter to me that was unusually long, his writing uneven and nearly illegible due to the trembling of his hand as he wrote the very words I'd always been afraid of reading; I remember with clarity the day he took me home to Vlissengen where I saw Andrew's grave for the first time, and finally, I recall when the troop came to Brussels, and knocked on the door of the little farmhouse.

The memories result in such a rise of emotion in my chest that my breathing is nearly constricted. What is it that comes upon me in such sudden spats of sadness and sorrow, only to leave me depleted and discouraged moments later?

Grief, my heart tells me.

No one ever told me that grief could feel so much like fear or could come upon me under the cloak of a memory.

"Good evening, Commander Branteghem," I say with a curt nod to the boisterous man wearing a beige army uniform, much like Ezra's, but decorated.

The commander turns, his blue eyes clearing with recognition as he smiles at me.

"Good evening to you as well, Miss DeVos. I am happy to at last be meeting you on a joyous occasion such as tonight," he says with a robust laugh, shaking my hand cordially. "I offer my regards to you, once more, concerning your brother."

I nod. "Thank you, sir."

"It has not been the same without Andrew fighting beside us, Miss. The troop suffered greatly the day he died, but at last we have victory. And so does Andrew," Boris van Berg adds, his voice filled with the genuine enthusiasm of the evening. He waves a hand toward the fountain of punch on the table to my right. "Punch?"

I smile. "Yes, please."

Nodding, Boris pours a second glass of punch and offers it out to me. Lars Gilbert is silent beside him, sincere sorrow written across his face.

He leans closer to me.

"I was honored to call him my friend, we worked beside one another daily." He shakes his head sadly, sipping from his own cup of punch, before turning back to me. "He was a true hero, Miss, and a prime example of courage and valor. We respect his bravery and honor his sacrifice."

Boris smiles.

"Well said, Gilbert," he says, though I cannot tell if he is truthful or teasing his friend. He turns to me, pulling a wisp of paper from his pocket and offering it to me. "We found this, Miss DeVos, not long after we visited you. I guess we must have missed it when we were gathering his other things."

I eye it hesitantly, my heart pounding as my finger reaches forward without permission of my brain.

It is long and white, though covered with obvious traces of dirt and abuse from the travels of the men who had possessed it for so long.

My mouth dries.

A letter?

All this time, I thought I would never read a particle or paragraph more of my brother's written words, but here it is.

A letter addressed to me, with the address of Ezra's farm in Brussels written in neat Dutch upon the top left corner. He had used my codename, Florence, to ensure my safety from prying German censoring that all letters had gone through in those days.

The postage date claims it's nearly a year old, written to me in early October 1943.

Just a month before his passing.

Hope rises in my chest as my throat threatens to close, and I open my mouth to reply, but Lars speaks first.

"We are terribly sorry it has taken so long for this letter to be returned to you, Miss. We knew that you would want it desperately, but with the postal service like it is, and with all the foolish Nazi censoring all packages had to undergo, it was too dangerous to send it back. We would have sent it to you by way of Ezra, but we were never able to meet him at a time when he could take it to you. So we held onto it until we saw you in person."

I plaster a smile to my face, forcing my eyes to remain steady and clear as I look up at him.

"I'm quite speechless, truly. Thank you," I say, slipping the letter into my pocket before the sense of both hope and dread can choke me as I stare at it. "I haven't seen Ezra yet this evening. Do either of you know where I could find him?"

Boris shakes his head.

Lars smiles, laughing softly.

"My mother needed a piano player for the music, and Ezra was swiftly volunteered to fill the role. He obliged," he says with a teasing glance into the dining room. "I'd say that is where you'll find him, Miss DeVos, so long as the music keeps up. I'm rather impressed with the pilot, I never knew he was such a savant *maestro.*"

I smile, this time letting a genuine laugh fall from my lips.

Of course! I think to myself. *The piano. I knew the music sounded familiar. Almost like an old friend.*

"I should have known that is where he would be," I say, dipping into a soft curtsy. "It was good to see you all again. If you'll excuse me, I must go find him."

Lars straightens, nodding his head graciously as if he only just now remembered that he is the young host, alongside his mother.

"I hope you enjoy your evening, Miss," he says.

"Thank you." I smile, and with a final parting nod to the commander and his men, I retrace my steps back the way I came.

Two large mahogany doors have been thrown open, allowing ample room for the various foot traffic of the gala's guests to dance from the dining room and drift into the quieter chambers of the parlor.

The hum of a hundred exhilarated voices meets my ear as I am met with the scenes of dancing couples and laughing bystander's in the dining room.

Banners decorate the walls, some bearing messages such as *Long live Liberty and those who are bringing it back to us!* While another simply lists those who have lost their life for our liberty, paying homage to them by listing their first and last name along with what branch of the Resistance they served under.

I quickly pick out my brother's name near the top of the list, under category D.

Andrew DeVos, the Secret Army.

Sisterly pride swells in my chest as I gaze upon the name that I have known all my life, knowing in my heart that this moment as we celebrate victory is what Andrew died for.

His death was not in vain.

I turn away from it before the tears can arise, continuing on with my silent observations.

The scents of Mrs. Shepherd's pies and Mrs. Gilbert's contribution of *Stoemp,* a traditional Belgian dish of mashed potatoes and other vegetables, along with a large pot of *Stoverij,* beef stew.

This is where the unattached men, aimless soldiers, and elderly men have gathered to either discuss our victory or appear uninterested in dancing.

Through the swinging door to my left, I can hear the croonings of the old maids and married women who have gathered in the kitchen, their laughter rising like that of a cackling hen.

A small stage has been fashioned and set in the far-left corner of the room, where several soldiers are positioned, some blowing expertly into trumpets and trombones while a woman plays the flute and another the violin.

My gaze travels through the assortment of instruments and their composers, only stopping when I find a familiar head of mussed brown waves, bent contentedly over the ivory keys of a finely tuned piano.

I smile, my heart fluttering in my chest.

His fingers run along the distance of two octaves at once, playing both major and minor scores just as elegantly as he always has.

I step into his line of sight, waving a gentle hand in the air to gain his attention.

He glances up, and for a moment appears startled as his fingers incessantly press the keys that produce a slower refrain, but his taut features soon fall into a familiar charismatic grin and his brown eyes brighten as his gaze falls upon me.

He slides over on the bench, making enough room for a second person to sit beside him. His fingers never leave the keys, and the music never once falters.

"Do you care to join me?" he calls softly over the music.

Smiling, I nod.

I slip unnoticed and unhindered through the churning sea of dancing couples and conversing colleagues as I mount the platform swiftly, acknowledging the few puzzled musicians I pass with a soft nod, my cheeks blazing with a deep blush as I maneuver around the piano's side, and slip silently into the empty portion of bench beside him.

"What song is this?" I whisper softly.

The music swells one moment only to fall the next; it is slow and intimate, vivacious and spunky all at once with the swift and simultaneous groans and sputters of the trombones to the pianist's left, perfectly timed with the softer accompanying notes of the piano.

"*A string of pearls,*" he says, his gaze resting on the keys beneath his fingertips.

He gives me a fleeting glance, and I catch a glimpse into his eyes.

They are bright and clear, shining happily for the first time in many long months. Along with the happiness, I can see the age in his eyes, and in the softened features of his face.

He has both shaven and bathed since I last saw him, now appearing more of an average young man rather than a war-beaten aviator. He is now dressed in classic black trousers and pinstripe shirt tucked in at his waist with a becoming tie at his neck, his hair combed and cropped at his ears.

Glancing down, I catch a glimpse of a holster at his hip, still harboring the pistol he has carried for two years now.

He smiles at me, his gaze traveling from my face to my dress, and I feel myself begin to blush. He studies me for a moment before turning back to the sheet of music in front of him, which he methodically turns.

"You look..." he searches for a word worthy enough.

"Captivating?" I offer, meaning it in a teasing manner.

Ezra smiles, nodding. "That's it. Yes, *captivating.*"

I laugh softly.

"I was only teasing," I say, recalling the word he had described me as so long ago at Christmas. I smile fondly at the memory.

"I'm not," he says. His voice is serious.

I blush furthermore.

I haven't seen him in so long that I'm uncertain as to what to do. For weeks, three months to be exact, I didn't even know if he was alive; but now he is safe and home, and we have been given the victory.

I smile.

He glances at me, his eyes narrowing.

"What is that look for? What are you smiling for?" he asks.

I shake my head gently.

"I'm glad you're home, Ezra."

He smiles softly, a shy boyish grin creeping across his lips.

His gaze shifts away from me.

"Me too, Ruth," he says, his voice thick.

His gaze softens, and I can see wistful shadows dance across the irises of his eyes; there is something there that is bothering him, but I do not know what it is.

There is a darkness swirling in the serene depths of his familiar brown irises behind the facade of joy, and it worries me.

Something *is* troubling him.

He catches my worried gaze, and swallows. His eyes brighten as if an idea occurs to him.

"Give me just a moment to finish this song, and I'll take you for a dance," he says, his face turning a slight shade of red. "If you still want to, that is."

"Of course," I say, "but I thought you had to keep playing?"

"Surely I can find someone to play a song for me long enough for one dance, although you *did* promise me two."

I smile despite the pit of worry growing in my stomach, smirking at his words.

"I think this dance will be my first *and* last of the evening," I say.

He laughs lightly.

I fall into a wistful silence for a moment, watching as his fingers swiftly pick out the tune of the song.

There are so many things I want to say, but I do not know where to begin. I want to ask about the shadows that dance in his eyes, but

I know that they will only remind him of what he is obviously trying to forget.

I press my head to his shoulder, sighing gently.

He lets out a slow breath and smiles softly, the both of us falling into silence for the remainder of the song.

I gaze out across the wide dance floor as I sit contentedly by his side, my eyes picking out Fletcher and Eline, who have danced every dance since our arrival, walking hand in hand to the table Mr. Shepherd has reserved for us.

Maya trots around the room with Henri and Cleo Gilbert, Lars' nephew and niece, her courage growing as the house and guests begin to feel familiar to her.

At last, the song comes to a close and the trumpets quieten down as the melody dies away in the chest of the grand piano, and the dancers part, clapping for the wonderful performance of the little orchestra.

Ezra pushes himself from the bench, giving a curt bow to the people as the other musicians do the same.

He gallantly offers me his hand.

I glance up to meet his gaze as I take it, lacing my fingers through his.

His eyes are soft and knowing as he smiles at me, the familiar warmth coursing through me as his hand folds around my own.

He glances over his shoulder.

"Johannes, my friend, come play a song for us," he calls softly to a young man, whom I vaguely recognize from the Resistance.

Johannes steps lightly onto the platform, wiping sweaty palms on the leg of his trousers. He replaces Ezra at the bench.

"What song do you want me to play, Pik?" he asks.

Ezra smiles.

"Do you know '*A nightingale sang in Berkeley square*'?"

Johannes nods slightly.

"Yes, sir, I do. But who will sing the refrain?"

Ezra nods toward the trumpeters in the corner. "Ole Eddie over there could certainly do it."

With the song choice settled, Ezra and I walk arm in arm from the platform and to the hardwood floor below, joining a half-dozen or so other couples who wait for the song to begin, Mr. and Mrs. Shepherd being among them.

Ezra and I face one another, my right hand clasped in his left as his right arm folds across my shoulder blades and I drape my left arm over his broad shoulder. I lean into his familiar arms, feeling the strength of his protective embrace around me.

"Don't step on my toes, please," I say winsomely, teasing.

He smiles brightly, his brown eyes glancing swiftly around the room as if to ensure no Germans lurk in our midst before returning back to me.

"No promises," he murmurs.

We share a soft laugh as the music begins, drifting from the collection of instruments around the room and to the rafters above our heads as our feet move in perfect unison, as if the steps were rehearsed and well-known.

I gaze up into his face as we dance, together once more as the nightmare of our past fades away, and it is just the two of us as our own Ray Eberle replacement begins softly crooning the elegant and heartfelt verses.

> *"That certain night, the night we met*
> *There was magic abroad in the air*
> *There were angels dining at the Ritz*
> *And a nightingale sang in Berkeley Square...."*

CHAPTER SEVEN

HUGO

Ghent, Belgium

The German soldier slinks through the streets of Ghent in a haggard and elderly fashion, his stark head of white-blond hair preventing all opportunities at hiding from the occasional enemy ally or Belgian citizen that crosses his path.

His lip is busted, along with his nose, and he is fairly certain that the throbbing in his left eye will eventually turn black.

He had barely escaped their clutches alive.

When the British allies of Belgium were advancing, and had crossed over the Belgian lines, battle ensued; but the German troops were taken by surprise, and the allies were paired with the strength of the Resistance, and the Nazi's surrendered.

And like the other defeated Nazi soldiers under Hitler's command, Hugo was taken into the victorious clutches of his enemies, where he was spat upon, beaten, and ruthlessly mocked at the hands of the angry and oppressed civilians who for so long had been victims under Nazi authority.

He growls in anger and pain.

He spits bloody saliva on the cobblestones below his weary feet.

The soldier stops.

Something has caught his eye.

It is only a faint gleam, in fact only a hint, of something gold in the otherwise black and gray color palette of the deserted streets around him.

Stiffly, he bends upon his left knee, as he grasps at the soft golden hue of the object that had been so recklessly thrown about and forgotten in the rubble of Ghent's streets.

Once it is safe in his small, childlike palm, he wipes its face with his shirt sleeve, the yellow gold plating of its dented face shining in the late evening light.

It is a book, perhaps a small hand-held journal.

"May this keep you safe from harm," he reads the words etched upon it aloud, in a soft whisper.

It almost looks familiar.

Why would someone have left this here, discarded as if trash? he thinks silently to himself.

So that you would find it, that you may believe.

The voice is faint, and he takes it to be the distant call of an allied soldier.

His pulse quickens.

He needs to find somewhere to hide.

Soon.

But he only turns the little book over in his palm, inspecting it. It appears to be a little book, made partly of gold-plated metal and partly of black leather. He opens it, expecting to find the few final lines written in it by its last owner. But instead, printed words in red stare back at him.

He grimaces and almost returns the little Bible back to the street floor where he'd found it.

But something bids him to look into it further.

Open it, Hugo.

He jolts upward, pouncing painfully to his feet, his heart pounding in his chest as he glances swiftly over his shoulder.

Hugo.

"Who said my name?" he whispers, his voice muffled with fear.

But no one is there. The streets are empty.

He is utterly alone.

His heart rate rises further as a strange heat crawls into his face.

He wants to flee, to leave the Bible where it was and hide. He wants to forget everything that has happened. He wants to no longer remember what a fear-driven fool he'd been.

But no amount of wishing or drinking himself into oblivion will remove the guilt from his heart or the stain from his soul.

He rakes a trembling hand through his hair, gazing down at the Bible in his hand.

The desire to abandon it overwhelms him.

But he doesn't.

Instead, he opens it.

And a loose piece of paper falls from its inner pages and flutters to the ground.

He picks it up and squints at the hastily written words.

Bergen-Belson, Germany

Edwin van Beek

His breath catches.

What does it all mean?

He doesn't know, but with a hammering heart, he slips the Bible into the breast pocket of his shirt as the strange sense of being followed washes over him.

And glancing one last time over his thin shoulder to make certain he is alone, he enters the darkened alleyways, the faint sounds of his own raspy breathing chasing him.

CHAPTER EIGHT

Letters

Later that night, when all have returned home from our evening of celebrations, Eline and Fletcher having returned to their own home together, and everyone has drifted off into the keeping of sleep in their own rooms, I sit rigidly at my desk, alone.

The oil-lamp that still burns in front of me illuminates the delicate flowers painted across the ceiling and casts shadows across the room and out the window, but I pay them no mind.

Instead, my gaze rests on Andrew's letter that is poised between my thumb and forefinger.

My heart throbs.

If I open this letter, that will be it.

I will never receive another note or particle from my brother as long as I live. There will be no other parcels or letters from Andrew, no more notes filled with his accounts and descriptions of his life with the Resistance, nor any words telling me when he is coming home. No, this will be the final time that I hear from my brother.

Do I open it?

Yes, my daughter. You may open it, the familiar voice whispers to my heart.

I take a shaky breath.

"Okay," I whisper, pulling the silver letter opener from the desk, lifting it to the lip of the letter, and slicing it open.

Inside is a crisp white piece of rationed paper, covered on both sides with my brother's familiar handwriting.

My breath catches and it takes a moment to regain my composure before I begin to read.

Dearest Ruthie,

I am sorry that I have not written in so long.

I know I will have to listen to your remarks concerning my delayed and few letters, but I cannot help it.

As you know, we have been working near Ghent for a while now, trying daily to gain territory as we prepare to follow through with the rescue assignment that we have been sent on.

There are three Jewish families and five allied airmen who have been captured by the Germans and are now being held somewhere in the depths of Ghent.

We are struggling to find them and designate their exact location. Our intelligence notes are not aligning well enough to be trusted; there are far too many lives at stake for error.

We pray for guidance, and hope to have a breakthrough in the coming days. We plan to begin advancing closer first of next week.

Pray fervently and incessantly for this mission, Zus.

I trust that you will.

I saw the pilot a few days ago, in Antwerp, as I was heading out to join the troop before leaving for Ghent. He was of good spirits, and was working with other fighter pilots as they plotted a strategic assignment of attack upon the German intelligence lines, especially after last month's raids on Belgian Jews such as ourselves; if they can gain control of these lines, the Resistance will have a tremendous footing in conquering them.

Pray for your pilot as well, Ruth.

I believe that I am at last growing closer to finding Mama and Papa.

Papa, at least.

According to trusted sources with the Resistance, I believe he was released from Germany earlier this year, but I cannot be certain.

If he was in fact released, he must be traveling under a False ID or pseudonym of sorts to protect himself against any remaining charges and accusations, which may prove difficult to identify and track him down; I already have a few leads, though the accuracy levels of each seem bleak.

Do you know if Papa had a colleague by the name of Edwin van Beek?

I have written to Mr. van Beek for details concerning Papa but have yet to gain a reply.

I know that after Mama was captured, the Nazi's took her to a camp in Holland, but what happened after, I do not know for certain.

I have a hunch, however, that she is in the Bergen-Belson camp.

I have written to my intelligence friends for definite answers.

All will work out for good—as Paul writes in Romans—for those who love Him.

I find myself clinging to those verses more and more with every day that passes; they have become a lifeline of sorts, along with the reminder found in Matthew to not be afraid of those who have the power to kill the body, but can do nothing more.

Send my love to the clan, and send my appreciation to Mrs. Shepherd for the care package that was sent to me, along with the notes of well-wishes, and greetings, from the others.

I love you, Zus.

Until we next meet,

Your brother,
Andrew

This is it.

These are my brother's final words to me.

I will never hear from him again for as long as the Lord lets me live on this Earth.

I stare at the signature with sorrow, my eyes burning with unshed tears as I fight the urge to sob.

I let the letter fall to the desk, turning my gaze away from it and training it on the familiar floral ceiling above my head, thinking.

The mission he had described in the letter was the very mission that would claim his life. For nearly two months, the Resistance worked toward the goal of rescuing the group of nearly two dozen prisoners in Ghent. They advanced into Ghent late in October, but they would not execute their assignment until November the second, when they stormed the streets of Ghent and pulled the prisoners from Nazi authority, but not without a fight; they were met on the streets by an approaching German troop and were tailed by the defeated and enraged officers from whom they had stolen the prisoners.

In total, seven lives were lost that day; three of the prisoners, and four Resistance fighters.

I run a hand across my face, the familiar current of grief and anguish washing over me with such ferocity it is frightening. I bury my face in my hands, trembling all over as memories rush with a turbulent force through my mind.

I tuck my legs to my chest, curling my body so tight that I can hardly breathe as the tears run down my face unhindered.

Why Andrew?

Why my brother?

Why did he have to be the one to leave?

I clinch my fist and grit my teeth against the current of physical pain that blooms in my chest.

"God, I am so angry," I whisper, my voice broken and defeated.

It is more of a yell than a thought.

I know, my child.

I have not crumbled like this over Andrew's death since receiving his Rucksack. I have tucked the grief in the depths of my heart, buried them beneath the weight of the work to be done, and tried my hardest to just *forget* it; but the events of the past few days and the weight of the burden I've carried for so long now has finally caught up with me.

I can no longer ignore it.

The pain we feel after someone is taken from us is the happiness that we felt when we still had them.

I guess that is the deal.

I want to tear the letter in a million pieces and tell myself that it isn't true, but I don't.

Because I know it's true.

It always has been.

"God, how can *this* be used for good?" I whisper indignantly, my voice breaking.

Even in laughter the heart may ache, and rejoicing may end in grief, my child. But you have been called according to my good purpose, and I will not fail you.

I close my eyes.

I just do not understand, Lord. Why Andrew? He was obedient and faithful, I don't see why you had to call him home so early.

You don't have to understand, Ruth. Just believe.

I do believe, my heart whispers back. *I just don't want it to be true.*

I have a purpose for you, my daughter. I will carry you through, not without pain, but without stain.

I blink as tears fall softly down my cheeks, the familiar tendrils of hope and assurance washing over me.

I fold the letter and return it to its envelope.

I force myself to stand upon shaky legs, and creep softly to my bedside, where the small black Bible from my childhood rests on my nightstand.

I leaf through the familiar whisper-thin pages, turning swiftly to the very back of the New Testament, where an old letter awaits the new one.

I pick up the old letter, reading my nickname *Ruthie* upon its face, along with the Antwerpen address of Still Waters Inn.

It is the first letter Andrew had sent me after he joined the Resistance over two years ago, the letter that Bram Hendrik had brought with him when he arrived at Still Waters for the first time.

The memories bring a rush of comfort and consolation to my heart, like salve to the aching wound that is on the mend.

Smiling softly through the pain in my chest, I slip both letters, the first and last, into the safekeeping of the Bible.

And climbing into the warm folds of bed, I extinguish the lamp and succumb to the weighty hand of sleep and dreams.

CHAPTER NINE

The remaining days of September drift by swiftly after the liberation, the inhabitants of Belgium eager to move on with their lives and forget the dark hours of war as October dawns anew with hopes of the declaration of the war's end as Nazi Germany's hold on the occupied West weakens day by day.

For weeks after the liberation we live in the glorious freedom of liberty as we all struggle to return to normal life; but our memories simply will not let us.

Sometimes I feel as if I am two different people, like I am split into a before and an after, but both at war within my heart and mind.

I had hoped that life would be able to return to normal after the liberation.

But it seems like the shadows haunt the very halls of the house, reminding us each at every turn what we've lost, and that life will never be "normal" again.

No one had thought that adjusting to daily life after the war would be so difficult.

But the hard truth that many of the people we lost aren't coming home after the war is a heavy burden that weighs upon all of our shoulders.

"Can you believe the restrictions on these ration cards?" Mrs. Shepherd asks as she sets a large pot of *boulets,* more commonly known to most as meatballs, onto the table alongside a dish of *frites.* "I can't even get a five-pound sack of flour for a household with as many people as ours, let alone the eggs and sugar. I had hoped they would let up after the liberation."

The boulets that we will soon enjoy for our meal were given to me by the kind butcher for half price, along with cold cuts of meat, all of which no longer harbor intelligence notes.

The ration cards Mrs. Shepherd speaks of are piled on the china cabinet in the corner, the gathered remains of all of our ration books totaling to an assorted mere dozen coupons left.

Like I said, money is scarce, and food is a rationed rarity.

Around me ensues the usual happenings of our clan under such a small roof as we gather for Sunday lunch.

Since our first Sunday gathering at Still Waters, Sunday remains the one day where work is left behind as we begin the morning with scripture reading, accompanied by a song—just the way we have done it since the beginning of the war when churches were closed and both Jewish and Christians were persecuted.

The radio murmurs lightly to itself in the corner as the tea kettle whistles on the stove where I had forgotten it and Maya strides around the house, disappearing and reappearing at will, as Eline bustles about helping Mrs. Shepherd prepare the food as Fletcher sits leisurely observing from the table.

"I hear that the supply chain isn't improving; they say the rations could continue on for months more, maybe even close to years," Fletcher replies from his seat at the table. "But with a war so fierce as this one, it wouldn't surprise me if it took a decade to fully recover from its damage and destruction."

"I fear you are right, Abram," Mr. Shepherd says from gazing down at the newspaper in his lap.

"It will take a lifetime to regain our composure after all the war has done," I murmur softly, lifting Valerie Pik's tea tray from the counter, balancing the seven jars filled to their mouths with semi-sweet tea lined up in neat rows.

Mr. Shepherd sits at the table's helm, as usual, sitting calmly reading in the midst of the incessant happenings ensuing around him.

I stride to the table swiftly before Maya can upset the tray in my hand as she runs through the kitchen like a banshee, laying my burden down on the table with a soft thud.

"Here you are, Mr. Shepherd," I say, offering him a glass.

He glances up at me.

"Thank you, Ruth," he says, pulling his thin spectacles from the bridge of his nose as he turns from the newspaper in his hand to gaze at the scene in front of him. He taps the newspaper in his hand. Its headmast reads *De Peter Pan.* "Have you heard any news for the paper?"

I shake my head, taking a glass from the tray for myself.

"Not a word, Mr. Shepherd. My friend, Rosa, promised to let me know what the future of the paper was, but I haven't heard from her." I sigh softly. "I hope they have a job for me; I cannot stand being idle."

I slip to the backside of the table, where I take my usual seat near Mr. Shepherd, though leaving an empty chair waiting between us to my left.

The table has been extended with a second slightly longer table attached to one end and covered in an old table cloth to accommodate the growing number of guests the house serves on a daily basis, covered now with a rationed feast as we gather together.

Eline takes the seat to my right, Fletcher occupying the one beside her as the radio is silenced, and Mrs. Shepherd removes the kettle from the stove.

"Maya, sit down, please. Lunch is nearly ready," Mrs. Shepherd says, ushering the wispy and energetic little girl into her seat. "You may play outside when we are through."

Maya slips into her chair with little complaint, though she groans audibly as a small serving of the boulets are placed upon her plate.

The screen door opens and slaps closed once more unnoticed by all save for me as my gaze follows Ezra across the room.

"There is the *Piloot,*" Fletcher says as he fills his plate with the steaming boulets and a handful of *frites.*

"Where have you been all this time?" I ask Ezra, though I already know the answer.

I can tell by the scent of hay and grass that covers him and the particles of dust and dirt upon his knees that he had been in the barn. Underneath his fingernails, I can see red dirt and black grease, which also stains both the front and back of his once-white shirt.

"Working in the barn. The *Fokker* needed some repairs, and the horses needed hay," he replies, striding to the sink where he pumps water into a basin and begins washing the grime from his calloused hands.

He smiles at me from across the room as he dries his hands on a towel that Mrs. Shepherd offers him. I watch patiently as he slips into his chair beside me, his brown eyes clear and bright.

I return his smile.

Mrs. Shepherd at last joins us at the table, bearing the final contribution to our meal; leftover pie.

She smiles as she sinks into the chair beside Mr. Shepherd.

"I believe we are ready to begin now," she says with a nod to her husband.

"Yes, dear." Mr. Shepherd smiles, shifting in his seat. He glances across the table at the many familiar faces that he has been gazing at for two years now.

He smiles, his Dutch blue eyes crinkling.

"Let us pray," he says with a solemn air, his voice thick and strong as he bows his head, eyes closed.

I feel Ezra take my hand beneath the table, lacing our fingers together. I peer at him, noticing a slight sag in his shoulders, as if bearing a burden I cannot see.

His eyes are closed, his face placid and his cheeks taut as he bows his head.

Leaning closer to him, I bow my head as Mr. Shepherd begins.

"Dear Father, we are gathered here together on this fine Sunday, your day, to commune together and celebrate these days of freedom. Moment by moment, you have guided us through the darkest days of our lives, you have led us through the valley of loss and grief and to this day of gain and triumph. I pray that you will continue to do so in the days to come.

"Lord, bless this meal laid before us and bless this day. Protect us, dear Father. Keep us from wrath and harm." He pauses for a brief moment, and I imagine he takes a swift glance around the table, taking a slow breath before whispering, "In Jesus name, Amen."

"Amen," Ezra says beside me, lifting his head.

And thus, the meal begins in its usual ramshackle fashion as silverware collides with the old china plates that Ezra had pulled from the basement, where he had packed all the valuables to protect them from the looting Germans before he left for Antwerp long ago, as the incessant chatter rises and questions circulate around the table swiftly and methodically.

"May someone pass the butter?"

"Fletcher, dear, the butter is to your left. Beneath your hand."

"Oh, I see it now, thank you."

"Where are the forks?"

But our voices are silenced abruptly as the telephone rings in the living room.

We gaze at one another.

"Who could that be?" Eline says.

No one knows.

"We never get phone calls, let alone on Sunday," I murmur softly.

Ezra shakes his head, wiping his lips with a napkin as he stands.

"I'll go see," he says, his heavy boots treading across the moaning floor as he disappears into the living room.

"Eat your food, Maya. It's alright," Mr. Shepherd croons softly to the little girl as he takes a meatball onto his fork.

I reach across my plate for my glass, lifting it to my lips as I take a sip.

"Have you heard from Alice lately, Mrs. Shepherd?" Eline asks.

Mrs. Shepherd shakes her head.

"Not since she and her mother left for London last fall. Perhaps I should try and write to her some time."

The phone rings again, sending a violent shudder down my spine.

My heart thuds in my chest.

The phone's jingle brings me back home to Vlissengen as a child; many times I had been awoken in the middle of the night to the crying of the Bell telephone in my papa's study as my papa scurried through the darkened house, floundering for his doctor's bag and coat as he headed for the door.

"I'll be back before you wake, *Dochter.* Go back to sleep," he'd say to me, planting a swift kiss on my forehead before disappearing through the door.

Sometimes he would be home when I woke early the next morning. Other times he wouldn't be home until noon; but one day, he never came home.

That is when he left for Germany over two years ago, and it was there that he was captured.

I close my eyes, pushing the memories away.

I can hear Ezra in the next room as he picks the phone up off the hook and lifts it to his ear.

"Hello?"

Silence.

"Yes, who is this?" he asks.

A moment passes.

"Yes, certainly. Hold one moment, please."

Heavy footfalls pull my gaze back to the living room entryway, where Ezra's face soon appears.

"It's for you, Ruth," he says.

I raise my brows.

"Who is it?"

"A Paul Struye? He claims to be with the Resistance, namely, *La Libre Belgique,"* he says with a slight smile pulling at his lips. "He asks to speak with you."

"*The* Paul Struye? The lawyer and journalist?" I ask, turning in my chair.

He shrugs, laughing lightly.

"That's what he said."

I stand from my chair and follow him into the living room, where he offers me the small cherry-red telephone that sits on the piano.

I gaze at the funny-looking device, my gaze meeting Ezra's as I take it from his grasp.

His brown eyes are soft as he watches me. He nods his head assuringly, giving my hand a gentle squeeze.

"I'll be in the dining room."

I nod and he disappears through the doorway once more.

I swallow as I lift the mouthpiece to my lips.

"Hello?"

"Yes, is this Miss Ruth DeVos?" asks the grainy voice of the telephone operator.

"Yes, sir. It is."

"Good, I hope you are well, Miss DeVos. This is Paul Struye, from the clandestine newspaper *La Libre Belgique.*" He pauses a moment. "I apologize, Miss, for calling on a Sunday. But I have some rather important matters that I would like to discuss with you today. I hope I did not interrupt any family gatherings?"

"Only lunch, and that's quite alright, sir," I say, smiling.

"I'm glad to hear it, Miss. Do you have a moment to spare?"

"Of course, Mr. Struye."

"Alright. As you know, Miss DeVos, the newspaper here in Brussels was once a very prestigious and beloved symbol of Resistance throughout the great war early this century. It dissolved, however, until the invasion of Nazi Germany early in 1940." He pauses for a moment.

"It has been said that the people love the paper for its frankness and relatable qualities; our writers, as you well know, do not wish to pull the wool over the readers eyes, but simply inform them and relate to them. For that is what the people want; they are tired of the old worn tried-and-true writings of the past. They want something that ties to their own experiences and solidifies the allegiance of our free Belgium."

He clears his throat.

I raise my brows, listening to his speech.

"Of course," I murmur, unsure of what else to say.

"They want to relate with the words on the page and *feel* the truth behind what they read about. I believe that the people want their own stories to be told to them from the pages of the next best-selling novel, or in our case, the newspaper. They want their past experiences to be echoed by an author much like themselves. Would you agree, Miss DeVos?"

"Yes, I suppose I would," I say softly.

What does he mean?

"To be frank, Miss, I would like to formally offer you a job in journalism with us working for the reformed newspaper. Up until now, you have been writing voluntarily with the illegal underground version titled under the masthead *De Peter Pan—*"

My heart rate quickens.

"This position I am offering you is a paid position, and you will work alongside many other journalists and formatters like you have been in the past, only you are no longer confined to the dark depths of the basement of my office." He chuckles lightly. "What do you say, Miss DeVos?"

I smile.

...You will work alongside many other journalists...

I twist the telephone cord around my fingers.

"That would be wonderful, Mr. Struye. Thank you," I say.

"Of course," Paul Struye says to me, and I can hear the notes of a smile in his middle-aged voice, "you may take a few days to consider before you answer assuredly. Meet me at my office on Monday morning and we will discuss and consider payroll and job hours; then you will receive your first assignment, if you should consent to the offer."

"Thank you for your consideration, sir. But as for the offer, I feel that I need no time for considering; I readily accept."

I can hear him smile as he laughs.

"Excellent! I have seen your work, Miss, and I trust that you have the talent and the brains for this industry. You have proven your loyalty all through the war; you will be a trusted ally with *La Libre Belgique,*" he says. "Well, I have taken enough of your Sunday afternoon, Miss DeVos. Thank you for your time. Be at my office on Monday, one week from tomorrow, at nine o'clock sharp and we shall further discuss this business. If you can, Miss, bring with you a portfolio of your work. Just so I can see your skills outside of the assignments you were given."

"I will be there, Mr. Struye, most certainly. Thank you."

"Certainly, Miss. Goodbye now."

"Goodbye," I repeat softly.

He hangs up the phone, and the line falls into dead static.

I return the earpiece back to the receiver.

I let out a breath.

My mind is spinning and my chest swelling with hope, pride, and fear.

Thank you, Lord, my heart whispers.

This is my first step toward moving on after the war, to life afterward; now if only I had my parents, and Ezra and I were happily married.

I smile to myself, wandering absently back into the kitchen.

Mrs. Shepherd looks up at me as I enter the room.

"What did he say, Ruth?" she smiles, her eyes knowing.

My cheeks blush scarlet as I catch the whole lot of them staring at me.

"Well, he offered me a job," I say shyly.

Mr. Shepherd smiles.

"That's wonderful, Ruth," Eline says cheerfully.

Fletcher smiles, sipping his tea.

"Congratulations, *Auteur,*" he sputters with a sarcastic, if not proud, smile.

Author. I smile at him.

"Thank you, Fletcher."

Ezra smiles up at me from his chair. He stands and steps toward me.

"I knew he would," he says, kissing my cheek. "I'm happy for you, love."

I smile, blushing all the more.

"Thank you," I say, my lips pulling into a grin.

Mr. Shepherd smiles at me, lifting his glass from the table.

"This, I think, calls for a toast."

He smiles, his eyes flickering merrily across the room.

"To Ruth, and *La Libre Belgique!*" he says.

Everyone follows suit, even Maya, as they lift their glasses from the table and repeat Mr. Shepherd's toast.

Smiling, I lift my glass as well.

"Long live liberty," I say, the other's joining me to finish the motto we have repeated for so long, "and those who are bringing it back to us!"

~ ~
.

I OPEN THE WARDROBE silently, reaching inside and feeling blindly for the small wooden box that I know awaits inside.

Grasping it between my palms, I pull it out into the evening sunlight that illuminates my small room.

I gaze down at it.

It is small, about the size of a loaf of bread, with four bare oblong sides and a brass lock that keeps it securely closed. Upon the lid has been carved in intricate detail small flowers and birds; it was once a gift from Mr. Shepherd to Mrs. Shepherd but has since been repurposed into a hiding place for my oldest and most painful memories that have forever been preserved on paper.

It is the box that Ezra had carried across Belgium with him on his various missions after he had discovered Still Waters had been betrayed, and he had meticulously collected the most precious belongings of each member of the clan.

With nimble fingers, I unlock the latch, and the lid falls open to reveal the hidden treasure within.

My breath catches.

Laying upon a bed of yellowing parchment and carbon paper, in the midst of ink pots and pens, is the green journal that Ezra had given me for my birthday nearly two years ago.

I smile as memories rush to my mind; good and pure memories before the war took us captive and forced us all to very nearly succumb to its darkness.

A gentle knock at the door claims my attention.

I pull my gaze away from the box and to the doorway.

"What are you doing?" Eline asks, her coat in hand. "Preparing for your interview?"

I smile, motioning down at the box on the bed.

"Just looking through my old odds and ends. Old memories, you know. Paul Struye asked for a portfolio of my other work, and this is all that survived Still Waters." My gaze falls on the black coat in her hand. "Are you leaving?"

"Yes, Abram and I must be heading home." She nods, stepping over the threshold and to my side where she gazes down at the small box, smiling. "I remember that journal."

She sits on the foot of my bed, setting her coat aside as I gingerly pull the journal from the box, clutching it to my chest.

My fingers run eagerly over its clothbound and embroidered cover as I remember all the secrets and memories that it holds.

I remember all the nights I spent documenting my life in hiding before the Germans came. I remember the early days after the ambush when I returned home and painstakingly poured every memory and bad dream from the Dossin Barracks into its pages, so that maybe I may not carry the burden of them with me wherever I go.

But I still do.

Tears sting my eyes as I am forced to relive each moment, and with trembling fingers, I open the journal. The memories, words, and pages greet me like an old friend.

I flip incessantly through the many pages, glancing swiftly over my words as I recall the memories they are tied to.

Old photographs and newspaper clippings among letter remnants are scattered through the entries of the journal.

Some moments, I want to laugh and smile, and other times I want to cry as the pain rushes through my chest like a rip current. It is at the moment when I turn to the final entry that the pain only worsens and I feel as if I may break, truly, for the last time.

The last few pages describe the day Ezra had taken me to visit my brother's grave.

I had written the entry soon after, when we returned to Brussels, but I could write no more.

The journal, I felt, was complete, and I could no longer bear to relive the memories it held.

So, I hid it inside this box, and it lay forgotten about in the depths of my wardrobe until this very day.

Eline glances at the journal over my shoulder.

"It isn't finished," she observes gently, pointing to the blank pages in the back.

I offer her a sad smile.

"I couldn't finish it. Not after Andrew."

She smiles, nodding.

She reaches across the footboard and lays a gentle hand on my hand.

"I'm sorry," she says, her gaze sincere.

I brush the moisture from my eyes.

Keep going, I tell myself.

Laying the book aside on the foot of my bed, I turn back to the papers below.

These are papers and documents that the Germans had missed in their hurried and reckless search of Still Waters after I was taken captive; they are odds and ends of my writing career that Ezra had reduced from the grueling clutches of the enemy.

I find random poems and half-written stories and early newspaper articles.

I find a multitude of letters, mostly from Andrew, a few from Ezra, all describing to me the horrors of war and the hope that God had instilled in each man's heart.

Eline flips through the various papers, smiling at a few while shaking her head at others.

She picks up what appears to be an old picture, its edges worn and tattered as she gazes down at the black and white scene it holds.

She smiles, her blue eyes brightening.

She holds it in front of me.

"Is that Vlissengen?"

I squint at the photograph.

It shows a serene beach landscape with low dunes flanked by sea oats and calm waters with seagulls flapping overhead.

I smile.

"It is. It's the beach right in front of my family's cottage. Mama must have taken that picture on one of her walks; she liked to walk alone early in the morning before Andrew and I woke up. It was the only moment of peace in her day."

Eline laughs softly.

Once the box is nearly empty, my bed is covered in papers with my own cursive handwriting covering them from front to back; only one last document remains tucked in the depths of the box.

"What's this?" Eline asks, reaching with dainty fingers and pulling it from the bottom of the box.

She offers it to me.

I take it, shaking my head.

"I don't know," I murmur.

My trembling fingers unfold the many folds in the papers, and I soon realize that it is several pages folded on top of each other to form a story of sorts.

I gasp, clamping a hand over my mouth as I stare down at the earliest draft of my first newspaper column for the paper.

Eline gazes at it, her brow furrowing.

"Is that... a newspaper?"

I nod.

"It's the rough draft of the first article I wrote for *La Libre Belgique,*" I say.

Its title gazes hauntingly back at me, almost daring me to relive the most harrowing moments of my past as I nearly choke on tears.

The Yellow Badge.

It's the story of mine and Andrew's childhood in Vlissengen.

Eline smiles, pushing herself from the bed and returning to my side, wrapping an arm around my shoulders.

"You've come so far since then, Ruth," she says.

I smile wistfully, leaning my head on her shoulder.

"We all have," I say.

She laughs softly, nodding. "Yes, we have."

We stand for a moment side by side, the sisterly connection that has bound us for so long only growing stronger.

She pulls away, pulling her coat over her shoulders.

"Well, I must go now. Abram is waiting for me. I have a blue suit you can borrow for your interview on Monday, I'll bring it by tomorrow."

I look away from the papers fluttering in my hand. I smile.

"Thank you, Eline."

She nods, her curly hair bouncing with the swift motion as she steps to the door.

"Sure, Ruth." She smiles. "I'll see you tomorrow."

And with that, she disappears down the hall.

Smiling softly, I turn back to the paper in my hand.

This paper is where it all began two years ago.

You were my instrument then, and you will be again. I have chosen you to speak, Ruth. So do not fear, for I am with you.

I glance out the window, setting my jaw as the familiar current of boldness courses through my chest.

I smile.

"Yes, Lord," I whisper.

CHAPTER TEN

It is a few days later when a faint melody rings through the house as the grandfather clock by the hearth in the living room announces the hour.

I count the many rings of the melody.

Eight.

It is eight o'clock.

I sit at the kitchen table, writing by the faint light cast across the old table by the warm flame dancing in the globe of the oil lamp sitting to the right of my journal that rests open upon the table.

The kitchen is still and quiet around me, the air thick with the scent of fresh rain and roses drifting in through the many open windows, the comforting sound of persistent raindrops pelting the tin roof above me almost enough to drive me to sleep.

I retrieve my pen from where it had rolled halfway across the table a moment ago, gripping it firmly between my thumb and forefinger as I bring it to the surface of the paper, and I begin to write.

Ezra paces in front of the door, as if anxious for the rain to end and allow him to get back to work, despite the late hour. His boots cast a rhythmic and incessant drill upon the hardwood floor that resounds through the quiet house.

I stare down at the page, frowning at the words I have just written and gazing at the ink that covers my hands.

I sigh softly.

"It's getting late, Ruth. Why don't you join everyone in the living room?" Ezra asks, absently gazing outside, his dark eyes swirling with thoughts.

I let the pen fall from my hand, turning to face him.

He is looking out the door, upward toward the swiftly darkening sky.

I smile gently.

No matter where he is or what battle he is fighting, he will always be anxious to fly again.

"I think I may. I'm nearly done anyway," I murmur, admitting defeat. "Is something bothering you, Ezra?"

Ezra pauses mid-step.

He turns to me, stepping closer to the table.

"Just thinking, love. That's all."

He bends to gaze over my shoulder at the paper in my hand, his dark eyes sweeping quickly over my neat cursive lines.

He glances at me, motioning toward the page. "May I?"

I nod, and he picks it up from the table.

Woven through the tapestry,
I see the familiar loving thread
Cascading through my every memory,
The never-ending strand of red.
Lord, all along it was thee,
The scarlet weaving in sins stead.
Moment by moment, you guided me,
Along the narrow path seldom tread.

R.M.D.

He smiles brightly at the poem as the paper flutters in his large hand.

"That's really good, Ruth," he murmurs.

His gaze rests a moment longer over the uneven stanzas before he offers it back to me.

I smile and return the loose page to my journal.

"Thank you," I say, standing from my seat. "I suppose I'll go catch the radio broadcast. Are you coming?"

"Just a moment, yes," he says.

And he continues on pacing before the door, or as he puts it, *thinking.*

The living room is small and homey, filled with the nostalgic scents of humid rain and smoke and embers from the hearth as the few of us gather around it.

Mr. Shepherd sits in the rocking chair, his Bible open in his lap with his fingers laced together upon its pages as he dozes by the cold hearth. Mrs. Shepherd sits absently sewing Maya's torn stockings as Maya herself sits gazing dreamily out the window at the pale evening sky as it darkens with rain.

Eline and Fletcher had already returned to their own home earlier, before the storm had come upon us, leaving the house quiet and lacking in its usual lively nature.

I step softly across the room and to the tall radio in the corner beside the piano.

With a swift flick of my wrist, static fills the speakers and I quickly turn the little black knob until the static clears, and I meet the BBC's channel.

Mr. Shepherd jerks awake, cracking his Dutch blue eyes and peeking around the room.

"I'm sorry, Mr. Shepherd. I didn't mean to wake you," I say, apologetically.

He yawns, his joints popping as he straightens in his chair.

"That's quite alright, Ruth," he says, with a smile, turning to the radio.

A familiar voice eludes its speakers; a sharp and cultured English voice that I have listened to over the radio many times now throughout the days of war.

C.S. Lewis.

I lean closer to listen.

"Our life comes to us moment by moment," the voice states. *"One moment disappears before the next comes along, and there's room for precious little in each. That's what time is like. And, of course, you and I tend to take it for granted that this time series—this arrangement of past, present and future— isn't simply the way life comes to us but is the way all things really exist. We tend to assume*

that the whole universe and God Himself are always moving on from the past to the future just as we are..."

Ezra stops pacing.

Moment by moment.

The voice breaks as static overtakes it for a moment.

Maya sits on the floor by my feet, listening to the program with all the interest a six-year-old could give it.

I smile.

"Just a moment, Maya, and I will turn it to one of your programs," I tell her in a soft voice. "Just let me listen to this one."

I recognize this particular broadcast from early this year, when it was aired live on the airways.

I suppose this must be a recording of the same broadcast.

Ezra steps closer, listening as the static clears and the voice continues.

Mrs. Shepherd pauses in her sewing, letting it fall to her lap as she, too, bends to listen to the man on the radio.

"...Almost certainly God is not in time. His life doesn't consist of moments following one another. If a million people are praying to Him at ten-thirty tonight, He hasn't got to listen to them all in that one little snippet which we call 'ten thirty.' Ten thirty, and every other moment from the beginning to the end of the world, is always the present for Him." He pauses for a single moment. *"If you like to put it that way, He has infinity in which to listen to the split second of prayer put up by a pilot as his plane crashes into flames."*

My mouth dries at his words as a vivid and blazing scene of a downed airman plays on in my mind.

I swallow, glancing at Ezra, who has at last stopped pacing.

His dark eyes rest on me, blazing with the memories of his past. A current of shadows dance across his eyes, and I can see the pain that is haunting him. He still hasn't spoken to me about what happened while he was gone.

Wordlessly, he strides to seat himself onto the empty sofa, crossing his legs as his foot bounces in an anxious twitch.

He nods softly as if he understands my thoughts.

Soon, his gaze seems to say.

I think of all the prayers I prayed over the past several years. God has heard them all, even if at times it seemed he was silent.

He alone had brought Ezra safely home again.

I offer Ezra a gentle smile as I lean my head back against the side of the radio, Maya propping herself against me as we listen. I spread the bare leaflet of paper across my lap and pull the pencil from the knot of hair upon my head, letting my dark hair fall down my shoulders.

Lewis continues on and I raise my pencil to the surface of the paper as his sharp English accent escapes the radio speaker and captures the attention of every person in the room.

"The point I want to drive home is that God has infinite attention, infinite leisure to spare for each one of us. He doesn't have to take us in the line. You're as much alone with Him as if you were the only thing He'd ever created. When Christ died, He died for you individually just as much as if you'd been the only man in the world."

~ . ~

A FAINT AND FAR-away *boom!* shatters through the night.

I wake with a start, glancing around the room.

Germans had been chasing me in my sleep, haunting the halls of my sleepless mind and dancing through the shadows of my dreams.

I glance out the window, the cold air raising gooseflesh across my bare arms.

Shadows dance outside with every gentle sway of the white oak trees and gardenia bushes in the yard, shifting from one moment to the next.

But all is tranquil and serene.

What, then, woke me?

A bomb?

I shake my head.

No. There were no air raids.

I close my eyes and return my weary head to my pillow.

I try to sleep, but sleep doesn't return to me. I toss and turn in the lonely solitude of my room.

I soon give up as the morning dawns cloudless and bright, the early sun casting light rays of pastel purple hues peeking in through the windows as I stumble sleepily through the still and quiet house full of slumbering inhabitants, just as I always do when forced awake by the dreams that haunt the night.

I slip quietly into the kitchen as if drawn by force to the tea kettle that is already simmering on the stove.

Someone must already be awake, I think to myself absently, pouring the warm water into an empty cup sitting on the counter waiting for me.

I reach into the jar beside the cookstove where the last few remaining tea bags wait, drawing one from inside it and plunging it into the depths of the water with my forefinger.

Turning on my heel, I trudge to the front door, which is already standing open to allow the pale wisps of morning sunlight to filter in the small house. I smile, gathering the hem of my nightgown into one hand as I step over the threshold and through the screen door, praying that I do not wake the others with its audacious racket.

The sun is nearly above the horizon and the faint sounds of autumn wind rustling in the treetops greet me as I step onto the porch, where I find Ezra swinging lazily in the porch swing to my left, already dressed in his work clothes, with his Bible resting open in his lap.

"What are you doing up?" he asks me softly. "Was it the dream again?"

True concern lines the raw edge in his voice as he recalls the way the dreams and memories have haunted me so terribly in the past. He motions for me to sit in the empty seat beside him as he forces its incessant motion to stop long enough for me to sit.

I smile, shaking my head.

"No, not entirely. I heard something that woke me, but I am not sure what it was. Did you hear it?"

I step closer to the swing.

He nods.

"That awful screeching noise? It sounded nearly like a bomb," he says softly, his eyes wistful and pained. "Reminded me of June."

June.

June was when we experienced the most bloodshed and bombing at the hands of the Germans as the allies invaded the beaches of Normandy; it was also during the fighting that Ezra received the news of his father's death.

"I was afraid of that," I say softly, slipping into the swing beside him. "Have you been awake all this time?"

He smiles softly, his face tired.

His gaze travels to the land surrounding the house, to the green pastures that are swiftly turning to an ugly shade of brown as the air grows increasingly cooler, and autumn stretches its wings upon us.

"No, I woke up about an hour ago. I went to feed the horses. It's nice to see the old birds again." He smiles softly, his gaze returning to my face. "They remind me of times before the war."

He drapes his arm across my shoulders and pulls me to himself.

Once the swing is in motion once more, propelled by his feet which remain firmly planted on the floorboards of the porch, he turns back to the good book in his lap.

"What are you reading?" I ask.

He smiles up at me, memories dancing in his eyes.

"I thought I'd visit our old friend, Job."

I smile, bending closer to read his page. "Really?"

"Truly. I have been reading over the first chapter all morning," he murmurs softly, his brown eyes running swiftly over the small black text. "Shall I read it to you?"

I smile, stifling a laugh.

"Please."

He smiles warmly, and I lean my head on his shoulder contentedly, gazing into the depths of my tea as his thick and rough voice begins to read aloud.

"Naked I came from my mother's womb,
and naked I will depart.

The Lord gave, and the Lord has taken away;
May the name of the Lord be praised."

His voice conjures old memories to my mind, though good ones that are not haunted by darkness.

"There is more truth in that passage now than there was before." I smile wistfully.

Ezra nods.

"There certainly is," he murmurs thickly, his voice distant and wistful.

He reads on, reading through chapter two and three; I sit beside him, my mind wandering around the words he reads as the sunrise wraps its golden tendrils around us and the day dawns once more.

Ezra's voice trails off, and he stops reading.

I glance up.

"Why did you stop?"

He is quiet for a moment.

He looks down at me.

"Ruth, I've been thinking a lot about what that British man said on the radio last night. About our lives being lived moment by moment and that we often take time for granted, thinking that our past, present, and future is all there really is."

I can tell by the wistful and forlorn notes hidden in his words that he is thinking of his father.

He fingers the delicate pages of the Bible with his anything but delicate hands, thinking.

My mind wanders to the picture in the hall. As I shut my door last night, I saw Ezra in the hall, and he had gazed at it with so much pain and longing in his eyes that it nearly broke my heart. But yet he doesn't speak of his parents.

Perhaps he doesn't know how, Mr. Shepherd's voice says in my ear.

I think of C.S. Lewis' words from last night's broadcast.

"Our life comes to us moment by moment. One moment disappears before the next comes along, and there's room for precious little in each..."

Ezra looks away as he speaks again.

"This war has taught me, among other things, that a moment is all it takes. A moment too soon, and you'll make a mistake. A moment too late, and you have to pay the consequence. A moment can give life, and it only takes a moment for that life to come to an end." His voice is steady and gentle, his eyes distant and dark.

I meet his gaze.

"Ezra," I whisper his name softly. "Are you talking about your father?"

He nods, smiling softly.

"Yes, I am. And Andrew, and every other person who paid the price of this war." He shakes his head, his smile somehow brightening. "Our lives are not *ours*. They are God's. They always have been, and they always will be. God alone has the ability to take, but he alone has the ability to give again."

I hold his brown eyes steady, the darkness finally fading into light.

To give again.

I return his smile.

"Tell me about your father."

He meets my gaze.

"He was a good man, Ruth. He worked all his life and lived by the work of his hands and the sweat of his brow. That was his way. He had his sights set on me becoming a lawyer or preacher, anything but a lowly horse farmer."

He shakes his head, looking down at his hands with a smile.

"But that's all I'll ever be." He thinks for a moment, adding, "That and a pilot."

I smile, taking his hand.

"There is more to you than that, Ezra. You know that. And I am sure your father knew that; and he would be proud of the service you have done for our country during the war."

I gaze down at his hand, my keen eyes catching sight of the scars on his knuckles, the dirt beneath his fingernails, and the red dirt that is still evident on his palm.

Dirt must run deep through his veins.

He takes a slow breath.

"I was so angry when I heard about his execution," he murmurs.

His eyes hold the same grief that I have carried with me for a year now.

Grief is a curious thing. It is the price that we pay for love.

But, in my experience, it seems that if we do not have the one, we have most likely got the other.

"I'm sorry, Ezra," I say, knowing well the threads of grief that must swell in his chest.

"I did not know how to face the truth of it, so I turned to my work. I worked all hours of the day, fulfilling as many assignments as I could. I went on dangerous rescue and sabotage missions. I flew to France and over Poland beneath the Germans noses." He shakes his head softly. "All this time I was running, and I didn't stop until my last mission, when I was sent to Amsterdam to carry forged IDs and ration cards to Dutch refugees."

I raise my brows.

Dangerous. Sabotage. Germans.

He sees the question on my lips and holds out his hand to silence me. He points to the scar below his eye.

"I was discovered soon after completing the task but fortunately was able to escape the German's grasp. He put up quite the fight, but in the end, this scar is all he left me with." He smiles gently, as if his memories do not truly bother him.

But I can tell by the naked and undisguised emotion in his eyes that they do.

I brush the scar gently with my fingertip.

"Why didn't you tell me all of this before?" I whisper.

"I was angry. I still am, I suppose. I saw so much darkness in the world and so much evil, that I guess I didn't know how to tell you. It was pure shadowlands. You have no idea how I longed to come home to you, Ruth. But I didn't want you to worry." He lowers his gaze, smiling. "I guess you did anyway."

I smile, laughing lightly as I nod my head.

"Yes, I did. Very much."

He folds both his hands over mine.

"I'm sorry, Ruth."

"You don't have to apologize, Ezra. I understand," I say softly. "But we cannot face the 'shadowlands' alone. We need God to carry us through, as well as company to help bear the burden."

Ezra smiles at me, and for a moment, I see the familiar gaze of the youthful and brown-eyed boy he had been when we first met at Still Waters, his gaze holding mine fiercely.

Understanding passes silently between us, and it is almost as if we understand one another's grief and sorrow; and slowly, we begin to shoulder one another's burden.

"I can think of no better companion than you, love." He smiles.

I smile, leaning my head on his shoulder as I turn to face the golden rays of the rising sun.

"I'm glad."

The warm scent of fresh coffee drifts through the windows to greet us out on the porch swing as Mr. Shepherd shuffles through the kitchen, quite awake, murmuring to himself as he goes about his morning routine.

A moment goes by before I hear the soft hiss of static as he turns on the small compact radio on the kitchen counter, followed by the faint clicking and grinding of the knob as he turns to find the right channel.

Listening to the rustle of the wind and the faint song of the last few remaining birds as Ezra and I sit contentedly in each other's silence, I can hear the vague and grainy report from the Antwerpen radio broadcaster.

"...we have just received the news from witnesses and victims. In the early hours of dawn, a V-2 rocket was dropped on Antwerp, in Schildersstraat, near the museum of fine arts. Many fatalities and injuries are the result, among tremendous devastation. The Germans have retaliated, fighting back with their final desperate attempt to gain control of the port..."

CHAPTER ELEVEN

HUGO

Antwerp, Belgium

Hugo stumbles from the wreckage of an abandoned general store where he had spent the night.

While just the night before the store had been in operating condition, though empty and void of produce and inventory, now it stands in utter shambles.

The roof is caved in, and the north-facing wall is no longer present, revealing the devastation of naked brick walls, splintered wood rafters, and dirt ground beneath the old floor that had been pushed up.

I shouldn't be alive, he thinks to himself as he kicks a tin can across the street. *Why am I alive?*

He runs a hand over his forearm, where he had received a bloody gash as the ceiling caved in over his head.

The ground had shook, and the sky had been torn apart by the screech of a bomb as it fell not two streets away, and now the vestige of the attack lay right before his very own eyes.

The museum had been utterly devastated, with the remains of buildings and stores that had once lined the streets falling all around it as people herded in the streets, distressed and dumbfounded by the ruthless attack on their recently liberated city.

Their faces are ashen and covered in dirt and soot with trails upon their cheeks, as if trodden by tears, as weeping mothers clutched their frightened children to their chests.

Townsmen work through the rubble in a feeble attempt to rescue any surviving victims as army vehicles pull into the streets, both allied soldiers and local Resistance men disembark and swiftly begin aiding in the search.

Hugo's heart sinks to the pit of his stomach as the familiar urge to run awakens in his chest and travels to his limbs.

If for some reason these people didn't hate him before, they certainly had reason to now.

He is still a German in unoccupied territory, wandering from one city to the next with nowhere to go.

He may be clothed in the Dutch uniform of a fallen enemy soldier, his face may be covered in rubble and marked by scars and cuts, and his stark white hair may be hidden beneath the layer of ash and smoke, but his heart still beats with the pure cold German passion just as it had in the days of old.

Doesn't it?

He sighs.

He has been questioning his own heart for months now. He no longer knows who he is, what he is doing, or where he is going.

He gazes at the gathering crowd, his pale blue eyes growing pained and distant, blazing with the hunger for truth that he can no longer deny himself.

A Resistance man turns, and seeing Hugo's bedraggled state, calls out to him.

"*Gaat het, Broer?*"

Hugo stills, his heart pounding.

The man thinks he is a fellow Resistance-worker.

And he had called him *brother.*

Broer.

He cannot speak, or else they will hear the distinguished German tone to his Dutch words. So, he simply waves back, nodding his head as he turns and walks away.

Breathing heavily, he doesn't stop.

He keeps going, farther into the heart of the city, avoiding the eye of any individual he passes as his feet absently carry him to a familiar street near the Cathedral.

He reaches a thin, stained hand to his chest, patting the breast pocket of his uniform.

Beneath the beige cloth, he can feel the hard edges and familiar form of the Bible.

Absently, he pulls it out.

It falls open to a passage, and his eyes travel to a verse that had been underlined in blue ink, the vestige of dirty fingerprints still marking the thin page.

He squints down at the small print.

Whoever loves his brother abides in the light, and in him there is no cause for stumbling. But whoever hates his brother is in darkness and walks in darkness, and does not know where he is going, because the darkness has blinded him.

Hugo swallows, shaking his head violently as the words conjure old memories.

But no matter how much he tries to forget the words from his past, they come circling right back to his memory.

Brother will betray brother to death.

"Broers?"

"...you are still unable to see the light and are totally blind as you walk in the path of darkness laid ever before you."

The words spoken to him so long ago have resounded through his mind often, and they bring an unavoidable heat crawling to his cheeks as the familiar grasp of guilt and shame wraps its dark tendrils around his heart.

Suddenly, he stops walking.

He glances up.

He is standing in front of an old three-story brick building, with green awnings covering the few windows that dot its face, many of them broken and boarded up from the raid he himself had led.

He had never returned after what had happened that day, after what he had done.

He swallows.

Over the door hangs a sign, swinging absently in the wind, the soft gleam of the golden words still visible through the layers of dirt and grime.

Still Waters Inn.

And a sign on the door, reading:

Guests welcome!

The house stands empty now, no guests grace the front door or inhabit the many halls and stairways, nor do the hospitable host and hostess lurk behind the walls, waiting with a warm welcome and kind word for him.

He looks away from the building, his mouth turning bitter and his stomach churning as memories rush to his mind.

"I cannot do this," he murmurs, his jaw tightening.

Yes, you can. Step into the light, Hugo.

He turns back to the Bible clutched in his hand.

He wants to yell at it and throw it down the alleyway.

But he doesn't have the strength.

The wind blows the cover open in his palm, and he sees handwriting on the inner page.

Andrew Nathaniel DeVos

And beneath that, he can clearly see something else.

With love, Zus.

Recognition dawns on him as a wave of remorse nearly takes his breath away.

DeVos.

He rakes a hand through his hair, the heat of shame crawling into his cheeks.

"Why?" he growls to the empty streets around him.

No response comes, save for the faint whistling of the wind and the heavy scent of smoke hanging on the air around him as Still Waters stares bleakly back at him.

He sinks to his knees, his hands gripping at the sidewalk.

His voice echoes as he speaks, traveling through the barrier that has at last been broken in his heart.

"Oh, God, I am a sinful man!"

CHAPTER TWELVE

My fingers drill incessantly on the arm of my seat; the nauseous churning of my stomach tells me I'm about to be sick.

I do not move or blink, or barely even breathe.

I sit stiffly beside Mrs. Shepherd on the sofa, my foot tapping a rhythmic tune as we wait.

I can hear Mr. Shepherd and Ezra murmuring in low voices in the kitchen.

"I had truly hoped that it would be over," I murmur softly.

Mrs. Shepherd is silent. She lays a gentle hand on my knee, stilling my foot.

"We all did, dear," she says.

A low rumble can be heard, growing louder as the origin of the noise approaches the house.

I sigh softly.

"That will be Fletcher and Eline."

I stand from the couch and stride to the window, peering out the dirty glass pane as the thin drapes flutter in the draft.

I watch as the black shiny 1928 Minerva auto rolls into the yard, pulling to an abrupt stop in front of the porch stoop. The automobile had once belonged to Oma Edwards, but since her death has been passed down to her only granddaughter, Eline.

With its slim body and extended snout that ends in a sharp grill and strange headlights, it had once been deemed the car of the century and the pride of Belgium.

Maya sprints across the front yard, her bare toes digging into the dirt and grass beneath her as she greets the newcomers.

Fletcher exits the car first, his bald head reflecting the midday sun as he strides to the passenger door and opens it, pulling from within his wife's small bag of belongings as Eline herself steps lightly from the passenger seat and to the ground.

I open the front door, pushing through the screen door and out onto the porch.

Fletcher smiles as Maya plows into him, wrapping her arms around his waist.

He waves at me.

"I suppose you heard the news?" he calls, taking Eline's hand as they approach the porch stoop.

"I believe the whole country heard by nine o'clock this morning, Fletcher," I say, teasing.

Eline smiles softly at her husband, her knuckles flashing white as she clutches his arm, fear evident in her eyes.

I take her free hand into my own and squeeze it gently, knowing that the same fear courses through my veins as well.

"Is the *commanding officer* ready to go?" Fletcher says dramatically, smiling as he teases Ezra's rise in rank.

Eline and I share a knowing smile.

Since he did so well temporarily leading the troops during the liberation and due to his devoted work after his father's death, Ezra has been promoted for this mission as commanding officer.

Ezra is honored by the position, but undoubtedly disappointed that he will not be flying for this mission since the bombs that pelt the city prove far too dangerous a risk for the aviators and pilots.

I smile wryly.

"Unfortunately, he is. He and Mr. Shepherd were talking a moment ago," I say ushering Maya inside. "What is your assignment, Fletcher?"

Fletcher groans as we step over the threshold and inside the house, the screen door slapping closed behind us.

"Due to my hip, as you know, I have been deemed unfit for combat," he says, motioning toward his limping leg. "So I will be working with the field medics. Aiding with wound care and bathing, that sort of thing."

Mr. Shepherd is taking both Ezra and Fletcher to the train station, where they will take the hour-long ride to Antwerp by train. Upon arrival, Ezra will immediately begin various rescue missions with his troops, along with defensive maneuvers to protect the Port of Antwerp.

I smile, closing the door gently as he, Eline, and Maya join Mrs. Shepherd in the living room.

I steal a glance over my shoulder into the kitchen.

Mr. Shepherd sits at the table talking softly as Ezra paces in front of him.

My gaze lingers on the two of them for a moment, watching as Mr. Shepherd stands and clasps hands with Ezra as I catch a brief moment of their conversation.

"—worry about her. She has already lost Andrew, and now she is afraid that if I leave today, I won't come back either," Ezra says softly, shaking his head gently. "And I am worried that she is right."

My heart hammers softly as his words fall on my ears, and I watch as Mr. Shepherd shakes his head thoughtfully.

"Don't say that Ezra," he says, his voice raspy.

"You know what I mean, Mr. Shepherd," Ezra says, lowering his voice.

Mr. Shepherd sighs softly, holding Ezra's gaze as he runs a weary hand over his face.

"I do," he says.

They fall into a solemn silence as they gaze at one another, and Ezra turns suddenly to glance over his shoulder, gooseflesh racing up my limbs as his eyes meet mine.

He holds my gaze for a moment before turning back to Mr. Shepherd.

"So you'll do it?" he asks softly.

Mr. Shepherd smiles gently, nodding.

"Of course I will," he says.

Ezra nods, his spine stiffening as he smiles softly.

"That's all I needed to know. Thank you, Mr. Shepherd. For everything."

"I'm proud of you, *zoon,*" Mr. Shepherd says, his eyes shining with the fatherly affection I have grown used to catching in his gaze.

Son.

Ezra had in fact lost his father, whom he loved greatly, but all along God provided him with Mr. Shepherd in his own papa's stead.

I swallow the bile that is rising in my throat, and I smile softly as they part with a final whispered word, and turn to join the rest of us in the living room.

Ezra smiles softly at me as I wait for him by the door.

I give him a questioning look.

He nods softly, as if to assure me that all is well, though I am not sure it is.

I slip my hand into his.

"Are you ready, Abram?" Mr. Shepherd asks Fletcher, a smile plastered to his lips.

"As I'll ever be, Dirk," he says, turning to give Eline a charismatic smile as she leans her head on his shoulder, her face worried as he weaves his fingers through her own.

We all stand together with solemn faces and silent lips for a brief moment, gazing at one another as we all know that we will soon be split up once more.

Ezra turns to me.

"I must go now, love," he whispers.

I smile softly.

"I know."

He nods his chin toward the others. "I have asked Mr. Shepherd to escort you to Brussels. He said he would."

I scoff.

"He doesn't have to do that. I'll be fine."

Ezra gives me a wry look.

"I know you can take care of yourself," he says with a smile. "But the Germans are still out there, regardless of the progress of war. It is far too dangerous for you to go alone, and I need to ensure that you are safe."

His voice is soft, though firm.

I sigh softly, recognizing his words to be forms of the same worry that inhabits my heart about *him.*

He is right.

"Alright."

I pull a small, folded piece of carbon paper from my skirt pocket. My gaze lingers on it for a moment, catching sight of the neat cursive that spans the paper in lines, and then I tuck it into the breast pocket of his beige uniform.

He raises his brows.

"What was that?"

"The poem I wrote the other day. *Moment by Moment.*" I meet his gaze, my voice lowering. "When you are surrounded by shadowlands and you are discouraged, I want you to read it and remember that all along God has been faithful."

He smiles brightly at me.

"That I will most certainly do, Ruth. Thank you."

He takes my left hand into his large calloused one glancing wistfully down at the ring he had given me so many months ago when we first became engaged.

He sighs.

"One day we will be married, Ruth. We may just have to wait a little longer for God's timing." He smiles wryly, a look of longing filling his steady gaze.

"You'll come back?" I say, watching as he pulls his old leather bomber jacket over his shoulders. I try not to notice the way it matches the color of his caramel hair.

He nods, smiling.

He catches the look of fear rising in my eyes.

Silent panic swirls in my chest as I remember the last time Andrew had left me. He said he would come back, but he never did.

Ezra nods, understanding my silent fears.

"Of course, love," he whispers.

He gives my hand a gentle squeeze before he, Fletcher, and Mr. Shepherd stride single-file out the door.

I join Eline at the window, where we watch in silence as the Minerva rumbles to life and slowly pulls out of the driveway, carrying them far from home and from us once again.

I would have thought that after all this time of war, during all the various times I have watched various loved ones leave, I would grow used to the dread churning in my gut. That I would have grown used to being left behind.

But I haven't.

Eline sighs beside me.

"Well, girls, come along," Mrs. Shepherd says with a worried glance out the window pane. "I have a whole pile of laundry to be done."

I glance at Eline, and we share a sad smile.

~ . ~

THE TWIN MAHOGANY doors stand tall and daunting, daring me to come inside like I have so many times before as Mr. Shepherd and I walk briskly down the sidewalk three days after Ezra and Fletcher left for Antwerp.

My heart pounds in my chest, both from nerves and fear of meeting a German, but the Germans that had once been positioned at the post near number 82 Thomas Vincotte street are no longer there.

Sighing in relief, I slow my brisk pace to match that of Mr. Shepherd's.

Dressed in his customary wool-rayon suit, worn Oxford loafers and weathered fedora, he looks every bit the true hospitable gentleman he is.

I glance down at myself.

I feel overdressed in the office clothing Eline lent me, wearing a pale blue blazer jacket with shoulder pads adding figure to my shoulders, a white blouse beneath, and a matching pale-blue pencil skirt cinched at my waist and falling at my knees.

I brush a hand self-consciously over my hair as we stop short before the doors.

"Are you ready, Ruth?" Mr. Shepherd smiles.

I nod.

"Yes, only nervous."

"You'll do fine, I'm certain."

I offer him a bright smile as we make our way up the stairs and to the door.

"Thank you for escorting me here today, Mr. Shepherd. Especially when you didn't have to."

Mr. Shepherd laughs softly, holding the door open for me in a gentlemanly fashion.

"It was my pleasure, Ruth. The streets are no place for a young woman to be traveling alone, especially with these blasted bombs," he says, glancing around at the lavish lounge-like lobby we step into upon entering the office. "Besides, Ezra made me promise to escort you. He practically forbade me to allow you to go alone."

I smile, shaking my head as I straighten my skirt.

"He worries too much."

Mr. Shepherd raises his brows.

"Like you worry about him?"

I narrow my eyes at him, catching his drift.

He knows how the worry churns in my stomach and troubles my heart; between nightmares and worry, I can no longer sleep at night.

"That's different," I say softly.

He shakes his head, glancing up at me with keen eyes from the potted plant he is examining in the corner.

"No, it's not, dear girl. In my own experience, where love abounds, so does worry. And separation and distance only enlarges that worry."

I smile softly.

His eyes brighten as the plump little secretary, Rosa Hardouin, waves at me from the front desk.

"I'll wait for you here." Mr. Shepherd smiles, seating himself in one of the many lounge chairs.

Nodding, I turn and stride to the front desk with all the courage I can muster.

"Good morning, Rosa. I hope you are well today?" I ask my old friend.

Rosa smiles at me with red lips.

"I'm fine, Miss DeVos. I hope you are as well." She lowers her voice. "I am *so* glad that Struye decided to hire you. I did, after all, put in a good word for you, dear," she says.

I smile.

"Well, thank you very much, Rosa. I am thrilled to be working for the paper."

She stands from her seat at the desk, cradling a stack of papers to her chest as she walks around to join me.

Dressed in a classic and feminine black blazer suit, with a polka dotted blouse beneath her coat and pearls hanging from both her ears and neck, Rosa looks classy and well-suited for an office job such as this one.

"Struye is not quite finished with his other clients yet, Miss. So I will show you to an empty office where he will join you shortly. Once you have both gone over payroll, assignments, and work hours, I will introduce you to the rest of the staff," she says, her red heels echoing upon the marble floor beneath our feet as she struts across the room.

I nod. "Certainly."

Throwing my purse over my shoulder, I follow her.

We walk farther into the little building than I have ever been before, passing many small offices harboring small desks and other elegant furniture, each room complete with a low-hanging chandelier.

Rosa turns left, and we enter yet another hallway, though this one appears longer than the others, where we stop at the door at the end of it.

The door is mahogany, as are all the wood features of the office, polished and elegant with a gold plaque on its forehead reading, *Attorney Paul Struye.*

My stomach churns as Rosa opens the door without hesitation, stepping over the threshold.

I follow, gazing about the room.

The office is undoubtedly the largest of all of the smaller ones we passed on our way, with the marble floors continuing beneath my feet, and four walls made entirely of dark mahogany bookcases, every shelf of them being filled with glorious titles, both old and new spines.

Only a single window that faces the streets below allows the faintest glimpse of natural light into the room.

In the center of the room sits a large desk, a chair on either side of it; my stomach churns silently as I wander around the room aimlessly.

"You may have a seat, Miss DeVos. Struye will be with you shortly," Rosa says, pulling me from my thoughts.

I turn to face her.

"Oh, um, thank you, Rosa," I say, hurriedly seating myself in the seat she motions toward.

She smiles, laying the large stack of papers she carries onto the desk in front of the empty seat opposite me.

"Of course." She bows her head slightly, and disappears out of the room, shutting the door softly behind her.

I glance around the dimly lit room with keen eyes, scanning the room for anything to distract me as my heart hammers in my chest.

I take a breath to calm my nerves.

The door handle grinds as it is pushed open, and I sit straighter in my chair as sharp footsteps echo from the marble floor and around the room.

"Ruth DeVos," says a familiar voice.

I turn to find a middle-aged man with graying hair and thick black-framed glasses striding into the room.

I stand from my seat, extending my hand to him.

"It's nice to finally meet you in person, Mr. Struye," I say winsomely, smiling.

He nods.

"You as well, Miss DeVos. Please, sit," he says with a charismatic smile as he waves his hand toward my empty chair.

I do so, and I watch as he pulls a large black box from beneath the desk, setting it heavily upon the desktop.

"My secretary, Rosa, informed me that you no longer had access to a typewriter, and so on behalf of the newspaper, I took the liberty to replace it, Miss."

He opens the case, revealing a new black typewriter with smooth keys arranged in order, a clean roll, and chrome levers and accents along its face and within its inner-workings.

"Oh, how lovely! You're too kind, sir," I say, my fingertips eagerly grazing the cold keys as excitement rushes through me. Memories of my old typewriter from long ago filter through my mind, ending with the last time I laid eyes on it in Lieutenant Wolfgang's interrogation office in Avenue Louise.

He sits down across from me in the large straight-back chair at the desk.

He smiles, flashing white teeth.

"It is my pleasure, Miss DeVos," he says. "Were you able to bring a portfolio with you?"

I pull a thick green folder from my bag, brandishing it upon the desk.

"I did. It is mainly odds and ends. You know, the occasional poems, news articles, half-written stories, and unfinished thoughts."

He nods, taking the portfolio from my grasp.

"That is fine, Miss. Thank you."

He opens it, plucking the first sheet of carbon paper from within.

His quick eyes scan the words written so carefully upon the pages.

I stare at my hands, my cheeks blazing scarlet as my foot begins tapping against the floor incessantly.

Several moments go by with the occasional fluttering of the paper as he moves from one page to the next until he lays the pages aside and clears his throat.

I look up.

I study him, judging the features of his face to see what he thinks.

His gaze is hard and distant, though perhaps thoughtful. His jaw is set, and he blinks down at the pages below his laced fingers.

"That first story, Miss, was published in the late October issue of *La Libre Belgique* in 1942, wasn't it?"

I nod.

"Yes, sir, it was. That was when I first began working with the Resistance."

He points down to a small collection of observations that I had written during my time in hiding.

"And these?"

"Some of them were published, yes. Some were used in pamphlets to pass on to the men with the Resistance, others I just kept for myself."

He nods. "I see."

He turns to a sheet of carbon paper beneath his left hand. He picks it up and holds it out to me to examine.

"And what about this one?"

I glance up at him. His face is steel and hard, but his voice has softened.

I take the page and begin to quickly read my familiar handwriting. My mouth dries.

> *Then this last summer, sadder now,*
> *Did see him 'ere he died;*
> *His right to live, to prove, then how*
> *His head to fate reside.*
> *There's many men who pledge their hearts*
> *To answer freedom's call,*
> *But few are they who freedom asks*
> *To glorify their all.*
>
> *And so when summer comes again*
> *To warm our peaceful land,*
> *The hills and fields and marshy glen,*
> *The willows where they stand*
> *Beside the stream and share our tears*
> *For him who died to give*

Fresh life to summer through the years;
He gladly died—and we live.

R.M.D

My cheeks burn.

I sweep my hair from my face, tucking it behind my ear.

I lay the paper down in my lap, my hand beginning to tremble as I grip it tightly.

I had written that poem nearly a year ago, in the dark days of winter in 1943.

"I apologize, Mr. Struye, but this particular poem was never meant to be included in the portfolio. It is rather... personal."

He smiles softly.

"I can see that, Miss." He leans back in his chair, peering at me through the thick glasses perched upon his nose, his fingers forming an arch as he thinks. "I have heard a vague account of your past encounters with both the Germans and the horrors that the war brought with it. I know that you were arrested early last year, and you narrowly escaped your own execution when the Resistance attacked the train you were on that was headed for Auschwitz."

He is silent for a moment.

I swallow the bile that is rising in my throat.

I nod my head, bidding him to go on.

"It is evident by this personal poem and other documents that you have shared with me today that those encounters have dramatically shaped your writing, Miss DeVos. I can see the marks of loss and gain, of both joy and pain in your writing. . And it is this raw vulnerability and relatability in your words that I feel may just cut right to the core of our readers." He smiles. "That is good. That is what we want."

I smile.

He collects the papers and returns them to the security of the portfolio and offers it back to me.

"I need to see no more," he says. "I am rather convinced of your ability, Miss."

"Thank you," I say graciously, retrieving my portfolio and gingerly returning the tear-stained poem back within its folds.

He folds his hand in on the desk.

"Tell me, Miss DeVos, what you would like to do for this newspaper."

I open my mouth to speak but then shut it again.

I gaze down at my hands, thinking. My foot continues to tap the floor.

"I am not quite certain where to begin, sir," I say with a soft smile. Clearing my throat, I let my words fall from my lips unrehearsed into the air around me.

"My papa was a trained physician. A very fine physician, I might add. He trained in Holland. All my life I worked under him, unknowingly training myself in the ways of a nurse as he taught me to care for other people's pain. Not only this, but he also instilled in me a desire to spread the truth, in the form of writing." I take a breath, my courage rising with every word I speak.

"Mr. Struye, I have seen so much evil and darkness through the duration of this war, I felt firsthand what it's like to lose the ones you love and to worry about those you still have, and what it is like to nearly lose your own life. But I have also witnessed on a personal level, the strength of the human spirit and the power of faith in the face of unimaginable horror." I smile softly, my voice cracking from the weight of my memories. "And I am a living testimony to the fact that light *can* conquer all darkness, if only we have the courage to spread it."

I lift my chin to meet his gaze.

"*That* is what I hope to do for this newspaper, sir. To spread not only truth and hope, but light as well. I have faced the darkness of this war, and felt its grasp upon me and my family, but God has carried me through. And I hope to offer this same assurance to others who are facing such darkness."

He stares at me, a new look of blazing ferocity in his gaze.

He is silent, drilling his fingers against the desk to the rhythm of the clock in the corner of the room as it counts the seconds as they pass.

My heart pounds harder with every second that his silence spans into minutes.

He watches me closely.

Suddenly, he smiles.

"That is just the thing I was hoping to hear, Miss. What a wonderful speech!" he says.

I smile hesitantly.

"Now, on to your assignment," he says, his fingers searching through the multitude of pages in the stack sitting before him. "I have this particular story in mind for you, Miss. It is our biggest story at this time."

He sighs with satisfaction as he pulls the desired page from the stack and offers it to me.

My eyes sweep eagerly over the paragraph.

Last Friday, October the thirteenth, only five weeks after our liberation at the hands of the allied troops, Bombs fell on Antwerp.

Antwerp lies in ruins, and her people have been devastated. Wounded, defeated, and homeless, the citizens need medical attention.

The heart of this assignment is to aid in the reconstruction and reformation of our beloved Antwerp by caring for her people, as well as to boost morale, encourage our soldiers, and inform our citizens with the messages of endearing truth and hope that we all need in so dark an hour.

We must meet the needs of the people, care for their wounds, and therefore must learn to listen to their stories as well as write them so that they are never forgotten.

My heart flutters.

This is the assignment for me?

Paul Struye stares at me as I look at the document.

He must see the surprised look on my face, because he quickly picks up his hand in defense.

"You mentioned briefly that your father was a trained physician, yes?" he asks.

I nod tentatively.

"That's right."

"And you trained beneath him?"

"Yes, my brother and I both did as we were growing up. But I have no official qualifications, I am afraid." I smile meekly, my hands beginning to shake with the heavy weight of Papa and Andrew.

Mr. Struye nods.

"Certain qualifications aren't always necessary, Miss DeVos," he says absently. "It is important that we remember this is not a mere story but breathing human beings in the midst of dark turmoil who need medical attention. I have spoken with my Resistance colleagues. They are in dire need of help. Do you think you can do this?"

I chew my lip.

Growing up, Andrew and I spent many long hours with Papa on various medical trips when we weren't at home in Vlissengen with Mama; Papa ensured that we had the proper education to communicate and treat his patients.

But I never had to do it alone.

I always had Andrew with me or Papa and Mama to guide me.

Now they are all gone.

But you are not alone, Daughter.

After a moment of silence, I find myself nodding despite my thoughts.

"I suppose so, yes," I say softly.

He smiles.

"I know it is risky, and it is absurd for me to send you, my new hire and a young woman, to Antwerp where it is currently being pelted with bombs four times the speed of sound, but this felt *right*. You are just the person for the job, Miss. I am convinced of it. Your writings, your testimony, they all proved that to me just now."

My cheeks burn with a strong blush at his remarks.

Silent dread seeps into my bones at the thought of leaving the others behind in Brussels and my stomach churns at having to face the horrors of the bombs and their violent destruction—not to mention having to face the people left in the bomb's wake. But also, amidst the dread, is rising hope and peace that this is what I am meant to do.

"I am flattered, sir. Truly," I say.

But how am I supposed to help people when I cannot even face my own past? When I am still so damaged and broken and still fight my own memories? I ask myself silently.

But the truth of the matter is, *I don't know.*

Therefore, I must rely simply on faith.

I do my best to ignore the inner doubts.

Slowly, a soft smile pulls at my lips.

Paul Struye smiles. "So you'll do it?"

I nod, swallowing as I try to mask the uncertainty in my voice as I speak.

"Of course."

He leans back his chair, pulling open a drawer to his left.

"Of course, transportation is provided by the newspaper," he says, sliding two crisp new train tickets down across the desk in my direction, followed by four five-franc banknotes. "I have you booked for the noon train bound for Antwerp the day after tomorrow. And if you wish, you may take a companion with you."

I brighten, taking the train ticket he offers and slipping it into my purse.

"Wonderful. I have just the person in mind."

I smile.

"Also, I have given you some currency to supply you with any paper and ink, etcetera hat you may need while there," he says, offering me the francs, which I quickly stow away in my purse.

"Where will I stay?" I wonder aloud.

"For your board I have spoken with the Resistance, and you may stay with the Secret Army at the *Koloniale Hogeschool.* That is where they have gathered the sick and wounded. I will inform them immediately that I have help on the way."

He smiles, his eyes almost questioning.

"Are you certain that you can handle this assignment, Miss DeVos?" he asks.

No, my heart whispers.

But I nod with confidence.

"Quite certain indeed, sir," I say with a certainty I do not feel.

I watch as he stands from his chair, extending his hand out to me.

"I suppose, then, that you are going to Antwerp, Miss DeVos," he says with a smile.

I push myself from my seat, taking his hand and shaking it firmly.

"Thank you so very much, Mr. Struye," I say, smiling. "I will do my job dutifully, and I will try my best to please you."

He smiles, laughing softly.

"I have no doubt that you will, Miss. But you must be careful. I do not wish to receive any calls or letters telling me that my newest journalist has gone and gotten herself killed over an assignment that *I* sent her on."

I smile, knowing that despite my quiet fear, this is *exactly* what I am meant to do.

CHAPTER THIRTEEN

"They are sending you to Antwerp?" Eline asks, audible disbelief and wonder in her voice as she pulls her unruly hair from her face and pins it at the nape of her neck with a silver barrette, several corkscrew curls escaping its confines and returning to her face as she sits bent over her sewing basket. "Are you sure you are up to that?"

I shake my head, glancing up from the short stack of mail I had received in this morning's post.

"Truly? Not really. But it is my duty, I feel, to pursue this story. Paul Struye was convinced that this was just the story for me, and I can aid the efforts far more there than I can by simply sitting here at home," I say softly. "Besides, Papa made sure that I knew basic medical drills, so I will be able to help with the sick and wounded in between my assignments."

Eline smiles at me, her dark blue eyes sparkling as she absently twists the wedding band on her left hand.

Mrs. Shepherd gazes down at the assignment document in her hand, her brow furrowed in concentration as she reads.

She glances at me with concern building in her soft eyes.

"Good Heavens," she murmurs. "Antwerp. I understand that you want to aid the war efforts, dear. And I admire your courage. But are you sure about this? Isn't this a bit dangerous?"

I smile softly.

"The Bible never spoke of avoiding danger, Mrs. Shepherd," I say.

Mrs. Shepherd laughs.

"I suppose you are right, Ruth." She cackles, her eyes dancing with memories as she reaches across the coffee table between us and lays a thick hand over my own, smiling. "I am immensely proud of you, dear."

I smile, laying my free hand over hers.

"So you approve of my going?"

"Well, I don't see that I have much of a say, but yes I do. So long as you are careful and write often. Although, you will have to discuss this with Maya. She is fond of you, and she will miss you the most."

I nod, glancing over my shoulder out the window, where Maya sits cross-legged in the yard in the midst of a multitude of chickens as they peck at the ground.

She laughs with delight as one pecks at her bare foot.

"I know," I say, smiling softly. "She wasn't very happy when she heard earlier."

I return my gaze back to the half-open letter in my lap. The return address claims to be from Paul Struye.

"When do you leave?" Eline asks.

"Tomorrow at noon," I say.

I gaze down at the letter in my lap. It is small, with familiar handwriting on its face.

Miss Ruth DeVos.

My heart flutters.

It's from Ezra.

Smiling to myself, I slip the note into my skirt pocket to read in my room later.

"I believe we could use some tea," Mrs. Shepherd says, standing and bustling swiftly into the kitchen.

The cellar door opens and shuts, followed by the soft shuffling of Mr. Shepherd's dress shoes as he strides across the kitchen, appearing in the doorway of the living room, a small hand-held trunk clasped in his left hand.

"I found this in the cellar, Ruth," he says, brandishing the trunk to those of us seated in the living room. "Do you think it will work for your trip?"

I nod.

"It should. Thank you."

He nods, setting it down at my feet. He clears his throat.

"Listen, Ruth," he says, sitting down lightly in his chair by the hearth, "I know that you are an adult, and fully capable of taking care of yourself. But I feel that I owe it to both Judith and Nathaniel to do everything in my power to keep you safe. Especially after Andrew's passing."

He smiles softly as my brother's memory comes to his mind, and he continues.

"Not to mention that Ezra made me promise to keep you safe while he was away. He is *not* going to approve of this, Ruth."

I smile softly, shaking my head.

"I know, Mr. Shepherd. He isn't," I say wryly, my hand brushing over my pocket where the letter is pressed against my leg. "But Paul Struye said I could take a companion with me, if I wanted to."

Eline smiles, laying her sewing down in her lap.

"I will go with you, Ruth," she offers.

"Really?"

She shrugs.

"Of course. I can help care for the wounded and sick, as well as all the poor children who have lost their homes to the bombs. Besides, Fletcher is already there," she says, her cheeks turning a soft shade of pink.

We share a smile.

"It's settled then. We leave tomorrow."

~.~

"WHAT ARE YOU BRINGING, Ruth? What do you think of this dress?"

Eline holds a pale pink day dress to her chest, its soft skirt falling at her legs.

I smile, softly as I stand in the doorway of her temporary room, shaking my head.

"Only the necessities; Ink, paper, a shirtwaist dress or two," I say, gazing at the dress in her hand. "I think it's a bit too pretty for a ramshackle hospital in the middle of a bomb field."

Eline sighs, dropping the dress into her bag.

"Perhaps you're right, Ruth," she says, twisting her wedding band around her finger once again as she stands for a moment thinking. "I wonder if dear Abram will need anything."

She rambles on quickly about Antwerp and Fletcher, murmuring to herself as she goes through the various belongings she carried with her.

I stand in the doorway as my mind turns over the prospect of my assignment, the weight heavy upon my heart and shoulders.

Shaking my head with a soft smile, I step from her doorway and cross the hall, pulling the letter from my skirt pocket and begin to read Ezra's neat Dutch lettering.

My dearest Ruth,

Fletcher and I arrived in Antwerp safe and sound last Saturday.

Immediately upon arrival, I was given command over a troop of twenty-three men. I have led them through countless rescue missions on the mere three days we have been here, searching through the rubble for survivors and pulling citizens from buildings where they had been barricaded.

The Resistance is at its peak, with numerous persons making up its vast body as each man fills his own role in defending the port as British allies along with Dutch soldiers are positioned along the coast.

You wouldn't believe what destruction our beloved Antwerp lies in today, love.

It is disheartening and discouraging to look upon so many distraught citizens who have lost both loved ones and dwelling places as the cost for Hitler's bombs.

Vile man!

Perhaps one day we will be free of him.

Until then, I suppose we must keep fighting.

I pray for the day when this will be over for good and we will all be truly free of this war and everything that has happened. Ruth, I am sorry that we cannot be together; I know you are growing tired of waiting, and so am I. But God will bring us together in his own timing and according to his will.

That is His promise to us.

How did your meeting with Paul Struye go?

I hope you are well and safe. Send my love to the others, won't you?

With all my love,
Ezra

I smile softly at the letter in my palm as I walk down the hall, the small trunk hanging limply from my hand.

"'It is disheartening and discouraging to look upon so many distraught citizens who have lost both loved ones and dwelling places as the cost for Hitler's bombs,'" I whisper to myself, re-reading bits of Ezra's letter.

I swallow, his words painting vividly heartbreaking scenes of the devastated streets of Antwerp in my mind.

We had thought that we were free, or nearly to freedom; how could we have been so wrong?

I shake my head sadly, stepping through the doorway of the spare bedroom I call my own. I lay the trunk on the foot of the bed, sidestepping the footboard to reach my desk, where I lay Ezra's letter down.

I turn back to the small trunk, opening its worn brass latch with nimble fingers; I open the lid and peer inside.

The vintage yellow daisy lining of the interior had been torn long ago, and it smells of dirt inside.

Oh, well, I think, *it will have to do. I have nothing else to carry with me.*

In the bottom of the trunk, I lay my green portfolio, a new package of carbon paper, an ink pot and fountain pen, along with random pencils and pen nibs I found in my desk drawer.

I open the wardrobe to my left, gazing in at the few meager clothing options I have within.

I pull from the wardrobe two simple shirtwaist dresses, an old shawl, an extra pair of stockings and a green gingham housedress.

All of these I gingerly place upon the paper in the bottom of the trunk, along with the Bible from my nightstand.

Kneeling down, I retrieve the wooden box once again and pull from inside it my small teal journal.

I straighten and am about to stand when Andrew's rucksack catches my eye.

Slowly, an idea takes form in my mind and my breath catches as the familiar emotions stir in my heart.

I watch as my hands pull the bag heavily from its hiding spot, and my fingers quickly open the mouth.

Taking a breath, I reach my hand gently inside.

I close my eyes as my fingertips brush against a soft cloth, and I pull it out. I open my eyes, looking down at the garment in my hands.

It is the shirt Mama had given Andrew for his last birthday at home, when we were all still together. It is a plaid pattern in a soft yellow color that accents with pale blue, made of thick wool cotton that is soft to the touch.

A million memories rush to my mind as I sit there on the floor, smiling at the old shirt in my hands.

Slowly, I push myself from the floor and return the rucksack to the wardrobe once more. With shaky hands I gingerly add the shirt to the pile of clothes already in the trunk.

My belongings complete, I close the lid.

"Do you *have* to go?" a sharp, young voice says.

I smile as Maya walks through the open doorway of my room, her face sullen and her voice dramatic.

"Yes, little goose, I do," I say, sitting lightly on the bed and motioning for her to join me. "It is my job, Maya. I have to go help these people and share the burden of their hearts in order to effectively translate their stories for the paper. Do you understand?"

She looks at me, the faint evening light shining on her young face as she thinks over my words. She shakes her head.

"No, I don't," she says.

I laugh, wrapping an arm around her small shoulder as she leans closer to me.

"You will one day," I say softly, my grip tightening on her as I recall the hard memories of the day I found her at the Dossin Barracks.

A soft shudder runs down my spine, but I force the memories away.

"I will be home before you know it, Maya. We *all* will," I say, praying that my words are truthful and prophetic.

She turns her face to me again, her brown eyes wide and doe-like.

"Do you promise?"

I smile, turning my gaze to the window.

I promised, didn't I? Ezra had said once to me before. I wonder where he is right now, and what type of danger he is facing.

That is His promise to us, I think, recalling Ezra's words from his letter.

God will bring Ezra and I together in marriage in his own time and will restore all of us once more as a family.

I smile, my gaze still lingering on the evening sky outside my window as Maya awaits my reply.

"I promise."

And as the cold wind begins to blow, rustling through the oak and willow trees, I can almost hear the words spoken back to me.

I promise.

CHAPTER FOURTEEN

EZRA

Koloniale Hogeschool, Antwerp

When Ezra arrives in Antwerp an hour after boarding the morning train, he is not prepared for what is waiting for him in the streets.

Burning buildings and walls of smoke encompass the city as rubble lays scattered across the cobblestone streets where men call to one another as they pull survivors and victims alike from the ruins and women stand gazing helplessly at the scene before them with their children clinging to them for comfort.

Ezra shakes his head in disbelief.

"Lord, have mercy," he whispers softly, gazing sadly around him as he stands on the steps of the *Koloniale Hogeschool,* a handkerchief pressed over his mouth and nose.

In the month and a half since his last assignment to carry supplies to Antwerp, the city has been destroyed.

Demolished, he thinks to himself.

Ezra squints through the veil above his head at the cloudy, gray sky. No birds fly, and neither do planes, or bombs; all is still and quiet for a brief time.

Uneasiness washes over him.

"We must go," he says, turning to gaze at the ragged group of men under his command.

"Dietrich, Bakker, and Groban, take with each of you four men. Scan the dwelling places surrounding the cathedral. We must ensure that all civilians are evacuated and taken to safety immediately," he orders. "I will take the remaining men with me and do the same on the western streets."

He scans the faces of the thin and weary men, his gaze landing on the youngest face in the group. Eighteen-year-old Niclas Faibber is young and excitable, with a deep-rooted hatred for Germans that drives him to passionate rages whenever the need arises.

"Faibber, you're coming with me," Ezra says.

Something about the young man makes him uneasy; perhaps it is the wild burning look in his young eyes or the quick word of malice that falls from his lips from time to time that irks Ezra, but he doesn't know.

Either way, Ezra knows that he is responsible for the young man, though he is only a mere five years older than Faibber.

"Yes, sir," Faibber says, his voice rising above the quiet murmurings of the others around him. He steps to Ezra's side as the others split up into four small troops.

A tall blond-headed man steps forward.

"I am with you, Pik," he says.

Ezra smiles.

"Good, Lars. I could use a man like you." Ezra smiles.

Since the day Lars had saved his life, Ezra has felt a deep respect for him, and the two had truly become brothers in the midst of battle.

The two men share a knowing glance.

"Remember, this is a rescue mission. We must save all who are willing; but we cannot waste our time. We do not know when the next bomb will strike, or where it will strike," Ezra says over the faint whistling of the wind.

He swallows.

One moment too swift, and one moment too late. They all count for something, he thinks in his heart. *Lord, let them count for good today.*

And with that, the men set out on their various rescue missions, spreading from the western streets to the eastern coastlines.

Ezra leads his men deep into the heart of Antwerp, the streets familiar to his memory though now altered and partially destroyed as he sidesteps the rubble at his feet.

Onward they march, their footsteps echoing in the midst of downed buildings and smoky piles of burned rubble as they venture down alleyways.

The first house they enter is empty and abandoned, the entire north-facing portion destroyed by the bombs. The next one harbors no survivors.

For hours, Ezra commands his troop onward, searching through every last residence and through the rubble that they had once called Antwerp.

By the time they are nearly finished with the western streets and alleyways, they have rescued three different families, an elderly woman and her cat, and a rebellious teenager.

Weary and tired from physical exertion and saddened by the devastation surrounding them, they retrace their steps back toward the university.

Lars pauses by the door of a vacant residence.

"Pik," he says, his gaze penetrating the boarded windows of the brick building to his left.

Ezra stops, glancing over his shoulder.

"There is someone in there," Lars says, his voice low as he peers through the boards nailed across the broken windows.

Instinctively, Ezra raises his pistol at the door, his heart rate quickening.

"I'll lead. You follow closely, alright?" he says, glancing at the tall man at his side before turning to the many other faces behind him. "Faibber, you and Hans scan the streets. The rest of you, follow Lars and I."

The men obey swiftly, and Ezra lays a large hand upon the door handle, twisting it softly and prying it open. It opens without complaint.

The house is dark and still when Ezra steps over the threshold, the floor moaning beneath the weight of the men who follow him.

They rush in swiftly, keen eyes searching the dim light for any movement or sign of life within the seemingly vacant residence.

The kitchen is empty, the drawers pulled and hanging from their cabinets as silverware and random belongings lie scattered across the floor as if the former inhabitants had left in a hurry.

"*Is hier iemand?*" Ezra calls softly, his thick Dutch voice echoing around him, the toe of his left boot sending a fork sliding across the floor.

Is anyone here?

No answer comes, save for the soft thudding of boots across the floor and the quick breaths of the men around him. He stops short at the bottom of the staircase, listening for any sound that might hint at what lies ahead.

"The first floor is empty, sir," Janssen calls.

Ezra nods, his gaze lingering on the stairs.

"Let's go upstairs," he says.

His heart pounds in his chest with every step he takes climbing further up the stairs, his heartbeat drumming in his ears and drowning out any other noise.

The staircase falls into an open hallway consisting of only two doors, one standing wide open while the other swings on old hinges, jarred.

"I'll take the left, you take the right?" Lars murmurs softly from beside him.

Ezra nods silently, stepping toward the jarred door on their right as his pistol is poised for action.

He pushes the door open slowly, peering through into a small bedroom; a small iron-framed bed sits in front of a window overlooking the streets, the walls covered in a dainty floral wallpaper and a dresser stands in the corner, harboring various knickknacks and personal belongings upon it. Small toys lie abandoned upon the small bed, along with wooden blocks and teacups.

Ezra's heart sinks.

Once, children lived here. But where are they now?

He combs through the room swiftly, searching for anyone or anything in need of saving. But still, no sign of life.

He faces the small closet door.

Lord, give me the strength to go on. I cannot do this alone, he prays silently, laying a hand on the closet doorknob. And with a hammering heart, he opens it.

And staring back at him, frightened and trembling, are two children, one girl and one boy.

The girl appears older, perhaps twelve or thirteen, with dark hair and piercing blue eyes. Her face is dirty and her hands tremble as she clutches tightly to the boy, who appears to be several years younger.

Brother and sister, Ezra thinks to himself.

"*Ben je gewond?*" he asks softly, returning the pistol to his hip and raising his hands as if to prove he doesn't wish to harm them.

Are you hurt?

The boy gazes at him with hungry eyes as his sister shrinks further into the darkness of the closet, wrapping her arms protectively around her brother.

She shakes her head furiously.

"It's alright, *kinderen,*" he says softly, stepping closer, bending on one knee to look the children in the eye. "I am going to help you."

The girl stares at him questioningly.

"Are you a *Mof?*" she asks.

Ezra smiles, shaking his head.

"No, I am not a German," he says. "I am with the Resistance. I mean you no harm, but I must get you two to safety before the bombs arrive. I need you to go with me; you will be safe at the university. Where are your parents?"

The boy stares at him, silently, still kept a safe distance away by his sister. The girl's eyes blaze fiercely.

"We do not know where mama is. I think the *Mofs* took her," she says, her voice hushed and bitter.

Ezra swallows, catching sight of the pain in the young child's stare.

"And your father?"

"Our father is dead," she says softly.

He nods slightly.

"Mine is too," he says, his voice soft and strained.

The voices of the men downstairs below him reach his ear, and he can hear Lars hurrying his search in the next room.

We have to get out of here, he thinks to himself, *or else we'll be too late and get trapped here with the bombs.*

He offers the children his hand, calluses lining his palm as pink scars form a trail across his knuckles.

"I need you to come with me, children. Trust me."

The girl stares at him for a moment longer, her eager eyes searching his face for any signs of deception. Finally, she steps forward.

Her brother follows her obediently.

And scooping the small boy up into his arms and taking the girl by the hand, he leads them away, to safety.

CHAPTER FIFTEEN

The central railway station in Brussels is lively and bustling, the platform being filled with many soldiers and volunteers on their way to aid the efforts in Antwerp as the gray sky churns with rainclouds overhead, Eline and I being the only women present.

We stand side by side on the platform as passengers board the large locomotive waiting for us nearby, the stench of burning coal hanging thick in the air around us and bringing bitter memories to my mind.

I close my eyes against the current of memories of my past spent on rambling, steaming locomotives such as this one that waits for me to climb aboard today.

"Are you alright, Ruth?" Eline asks, her gaze resting eagerly upon the slowly diminishing line of passengers ahead of us.

I nod, opening my eyes as I clutch my small trunk tightly in my hands.

"I do not like trains very much, that's all."

My foot taps anxiously against the pavement beneath my feet as the ground trembles from the groaning and grinding of the train's inner workings and gears. I glance over my shoulder at the clock face on the lamp post.

It's a quarter till noon now.

The train will be leaving in a mere fifteen minutes.

"Well, ladies, you two best climb aboard. It's a quarter till," Mr. Shepherd says, nodding at the open train car entryway in front of us. "Please be careful. Antwerp is no place for two women such as yourselves to be traveling alone right now."

Eline and I share a smile.

"We will be alright, Mr. Shepherd," Eline says. "You needn't worry."

Mr. Shepherd smiles, his blue eyes dancing behind his glasses.

"I hope so," he says, clasping Eline's dainty hand in both of his own. "Say hello to Abram for me, Eline."

She nods, smiling.

"I certainly will," she says.

Mr. Shepherd nods, turning to me.

"Remain faithful to your job, dear Ruth, and remember why you are there. Never stray from your duty," he says, laying a gentle hand upon my shoulder. He smiles at me, his eyes meeting mine, and I understand the hidden message in his words.

Remain faithful to the one who has sent you. Remember your calling.

A smile pulls at my lips, and I nod, telling him that I understand.

"I will, Mr. Shepherd. I promise," I say, my shoulders straightening under his grasp.

He smiles, fatherly affection dancing in his eyes.

"I know you will, Ruth," he says, his hand falling away as he reaches into his pocket, pulling from it a small envelope. His gaze softens as he looks down at it. "When you see Ezra, would you give this to him?"

I take it from his hand, fingering it lightly between my fingers. It is only a small note folded over thrice, the large loops of Mr. Shepherd's neat handwriting visible through the backside.

I nod.

"Of course. May I ask what it is?" I ask, glancing up at him, concern lining my voice.

Mr. Shepherd smiles softly.

"He spoke to me about something before we left for the train station the other day. He had asked me something that I have been pondering, and I wanted to write to him regarding it."

I tuck the note carefully into the inner pocket of my green coat, my mind wandering to the broken fragments of their conversation that I had heard before the boys left.

"I will give it to him as soon as I can find him."

He smiles, glancing up as the train whistle blows, warning any remaining passengers of its approaching departure.

"Thank you, Ruth. Now, you two must go. Else you miss the train, and it leaves without you," he says.

I pick up the small black briefcase sitting at my feet, the heavy typewriter it holds weighing me down like a troublesome burden.

Eline waves, smiling as we step away and to the entrance door, where I produce the tickets from my purse and offer them to the conductor by the door.

"Goodbye, Mr. Shepherd."

"Goodbye and well wishes, my dears," he calls from the platform. "My prayers are with you always."

And with one final glance over my shoulder at the kind man, we step aboard the train that will soon carry us to Antwerp.

~ ~
.

EVERY JOLT, BOUNCE, and grind of the train is familiar, bringing a multitude of unpleasant memories to my mind and heart as I grip the bottom of my seat, raindrops beginning to pelt the window pane to my right.

Eline grips my hand tightly, our shoulders nearly touching as we sit beside one another in the cramped little train car, the tumult of clamoring voices rising around us from the other passengers that inhabit the remaining seats behind, beside, and before us.

Trunks and random articles of belongings lie scattered in the storage cubicles above my head and in the aisle between our seats as weary-eyed soldiers gaze hopelessly out the window across from us.

The roar of the train grinding down the tracks results in an incessant and familiar hum in my ears, and chills run down my limbs.

I sigh.

"I had forgotten how much I truly despise trains," I say softly.

Eline smiles gently at me, as if understanding the memories that filter through my mind as my knuckle flashes white where I grip the edge of my seat. The hours spent in the dark prison of the train wagon reckon through my memory with a vengeance.

It'll be alright, Fletcher had told me as we arrived at the Dossin Barracks, though neither of us had believed his words at that moment.

Memories rush vibrantly to my mind, and I fail to fight their strength.

Panic rises in my chest as the stench of sulfur, straw, and dirt comes to me once more, and I can almost see the darkness of the wagon that I was placed in so long ago.

"I know, but it's only for an hour, Ruth. We will be in Antwerp in no time at all," she says consolingly.

We travel through Mechelen, crossing the Mechelen-Leuven railway, a journey for which I mostly keep my eyes closed until we arrive in the open fields of Flanders, where we go through wide and expanding fields of cattle on either side of the train tracks.

The hour ride passes swiftly as the rain persists in falling from the angry clouds swirling in the sky above, and we are soon entering the familiar cobblestone streets and gothic architecture of our beloved Antwerp.

I lean eagerly from my seat as I peer out my window at the streets we pass, the locomotive slowing rapidly in speed as we approach the Antwerp central train station.

My heart sinks.

The streets lie in ruins, mere remnants and memories of what it once had been.

Shadows. They are only shadows of the once vibrant and friendly city of Antwerp that I had grown up in, the very heart of Belgium.

Bits and pieces of former buildings lay scattered upon the ground, the funnels of smoke rising in the air from the smoldering piles of rubble so thick that it hangs like a veil over the city. Men work swiftly to rescue any survivors, their faces weary and ashen, covered in a thick layer of ash as they continue for hours searching through the remains of the city even though the burden weighs heavily upon their shoulders.

A few women usher a gang of uncertain and shaken children along the streets, and even from my viewpoint from my train car window, I can see the terror of the last week written upon each of their small faces as they cling to their mothers and sisters for all they are worth.

I frown at the scene before me, my heart refusing to believe the state of my broken, shattered, and war-torn homeland.

Ezra was right, I think to myself *I cannot believe what destruction Antwerp lies in. And it is both disheartening and discouraging to behold.*

"Oh, Ruth, look!" Eline breathes sadly, gazing out the window of our train car beside me. "What have they done to this place?"

I shake my head gently, as the same displeased and disbelieving murmurings erupt from the soldiers and other volunteers in the car with us.

I meet Eline's gaze, her eyes harboring the same sorrow and fear that I know are in my own. Sorrow for our country, and fear for our men.

The train whistle blows sharply as the train pulls to an abrupt halt at the train station platform at exactly one o'clock sharp.

The train car is small and equipped to hold three dozen passengers, with its padded seats and trolley of rationed goods at the door; but no one seems to pay this any mind as the volunteers and soldiers bustle swiftly out the door, murmuring amongst themselves all the way to the platform.

I stand shakily from my seat, clutching my small trunk in one hand and the typewriter in the other as Eline stands to follow me into the aisle.

A young soldier stops to let us pass.

"Ladies first," he says, waving his hand in front of his chest as he smiles at the two of us.

I smile, nodding my gratitude.

"Thank you, sir," I say, meeting the man's gaze.

Eline smiles her greeting. "Thank you kindly."

He nods curtly.

He appears calm and unaffected by what he sees around him, his face pulled into a smile as he gazes with fervent burning in his eyes as he tips his hat to Eline and I.

He reminds me faintly of Andrew.

I push the thoughts and memories that arise out of my mind, stepping into the aisle and lightly down the few steps, where the elderly train attendant offers his hand to help me to the ground.

"Did you enjoy the short trip, Miss?" he asks, his raspy voice nearly lost in the churning voices around us.

"Yes, sir," I lie with a soft smile. "It was quite satisfactory."

He smiles, as if genuinely pleased by my words. His face is wrinkled, and his short-cropped hair is white while his shoulders are bowed and withered. He looks from me to Eline, then back at me.

"Say, are you ladies here to volunteer?"

"Yes, we are," Eline says, straightening the small hat perched upon her head as she smiles sweetly at the elderly man.

"We are on our way to the Koloniale Hogeschool now, where I have been told they are in need of nurses," I say, nodding my chin ahead of us, where I can already see the few Belgian flags flying above the university's head.

The attendant looks almost relieved.

"Are you nurses?"

I shake my head, laughing softly.

"Not officially, no. But we are willing to help in any way we can. I am a journalist from the newspaper," I say, glancing at Eline, "and Eline is an English teacher."

He smiles as if impressed and nods, turning from us for a moment to help an elderly lady from the train car as the same young soldier from a moment ago disembarks the train.

"What newspaper do you work for, Miss?" he asks.

"*La Libre Belgique.*"

He raises his snowy eyebrows. "The free Belgium."

I nod.

"Yes, that's the one."

He offers me his wrinkled hand. "I am Bart Alders, by the way."

"Ruth Devos," I say, shaking his hand.

"And I am Eline Fletcher," Eline says as he offers her his hand in a gentlemanly manner.

"Well, it is nice to meet you, Mrs. Fletcher. And you, Miss DeVos," he says. "If you two ladies need anything, give me a shout. You know where to find me."

"Thank you, Mr. Alders. We will be sure to do that," Eline says.

"Bart, please," he corrects her. "Now you two ladies best get going. The university will be glad to have your help. Good day."

"Good day, Bart," I say with one final smile in the old man's direction, lifting my load off the ground and turning to face the university.

The Koloniale Hogeschool.

"Charming old man," Eline muses as she falls in step beside me, gazing at the varying destruction that lay between us and our destination. "I just cannot believe what has happened to Antwerp. It hardly appears to be the same city anymore."

"I know," I agree softly, nodding to a man in uniform who brushes past me. "Ezra told me that it was in shambles; I guess I just didn't believe him until I saw it for myself."

Eline smiles gently, and we fall into comfortable silence as we make our way through the desolate streets, our footsteps echoing upon the cobblestone beneath our feet.

We are soon climbing the many stairs of the stately and elegant school, the white pillars and intricate molding surrounding the brick exterior telling of the school's wealthy and beloved history, though now turned into a hospital for the sick and wounded in battle.

We are greeted by yet another soldier who stands waiting at the grand double doors leading into the building.

"Good afternoon, ladies," he says with a cordial nod toward each of us. "What is your business here at the Koloniale Hogeschool?"

We tell him, and he swiftly lets us enter, sending us to a squat little woman called Margaret who meets us in the foyer of the grand school.

The foyer is elegant and high-class, with a grand staircase leading to an unknown upper floor with a large chandelier suspended twenty feet up from the ceiling, casting glittering fragments of light down to greet us where we stand.

"Ah, more volunteers! Thank you, Lord! We are in dire need of someone to look after the children in our ward," Margaret exclaims, the worry lines etched into her face relaxing slightly at the sight of Eline and I.

"I am Ruth DeVos. I was sent here on assignment for the newspaper, *La Libre Belgique.*"

Margaret smiles at me, embracing me in a friendly manner.

"Yes, of course. Paul told me that you'd be coming. We have a place for you and your friend here in the nurses' quarters where you can write when you aren't on duty. Do either of you have a preference on where you will serve?"

Eline smiles softly.

"I would be happy to help with the children, if you need me."

Margaret smiles.

"Certainly, Mrs. Fletcher. The children's ward is growing fuller and fuller by the minute as our men are rescuing more and more from the wreckage; most of them have lost their families and homes."

Eline and I share a knowing glance.

Margaret turns pointedly to me.

"And you, Miss DeVos?"

"Oh, I can help wherever I am needed," I say softly, "so long as I can write."

"Of course," she says, smiling as we follow her down the hallway and she nods to a door with a brass number seven upon it. "You may interview as many of your patients as you wish, but I suggest speaking with Mrs. Cornelia Levy. She is an old soul and has seen a great many things in this war. The poor thing lost both her husband and all three of her boys to the war."

I swallow, shaking my head.

"Poor woman," I say softly, knowing that Mrs. Levy's grief must be four times the weight of my own. "I don't want to bother her; she must be terribly bereaved."

Margaret smiles at me, shaking her head gently.

"You can't bother her, Miss Devos. I assure you. She is a strong character with an even stronger will; her loss has not daunted her in the slightest, though I feel she is lonely. You may do her some good just talking with her."

I smile, nodding.

"Perhaps I will, then," I say, resolving to speak with this poor woman first thing in the morning.

Margaret leads us onward, deeper into the school. We pass several classrooms that now sit dark and empty, each one still harboring the elegant appearance and staunch scent of aging literature of the glory days past.

But it is only when Margaret leads us to the lower floors that the scenery changes, and I stumble upon the beginnings of a ramshackle hospital room.

I clamp a hand over my mouth, my heart beating violently in my chest as memories rush to my mind anew.

They are memories of Papa, bent lovingly over his newest patient, murmuring to them as they tell him of their pains and fears; memories of Andrew and I, working side by side with Papa as we tend to the abundance of people after the snowstorm in 1936.

I shake the memories from my head softly, gazing at the scene before me with clear eyes.

Men lie scattered across the floor, some on cots, other's on blankets. Some of them groan while others simply try to sleep a shallow sleep haunted by dreams of what got them here. A few meager nurses and attendants filter around the room, aiding whomever may need them.

"Oh, Lord, have mercy on them. Please," I breathe softly, remembering the threads of Papa's prayer he would whisper as he prepared for service.

"Almighty God, you have created the human body with infinite wisdom. In your eternal providence, you have chosen me to watch over the life and health of your creatures..."

His voice fades in my mind, replaced by the soft whispering of my Heavenly Father.

I have chosen you, Ruth. You will speak to my creatures, and care for their wounds.

The compassion that my papa must have felt for his patients so long ago stirs in my own chest right now, compelled by the familiar boldness that I received from Mama.

Margaret leads us on, and I am pulled from my memories.

"How many physicians and attendants do you have on staff?" Eline asks, no doubt searching for her beloved Fletcher.

I give her a soft smile, but she doesn't notice.

"At this moment, two trained physicians, three nurses, and four attendants, myself included. So you two ladies will be a great aid to the efforts being made here with the Resistance," she says, coming to a small set of ebony doors and pushing the right one open with her hip and stepping over the threshold of another room.

"The boys have been working tirelessly for days on end, each day bringing in more surviving victims. The poor lads and lasses have nowhere else to go."

Eline and I follow her inside, our belongings still in hand.

A near two dozen pairs of little eyes are trained on us as we step through the door, the children silent as they gaze upon the newcomers with undaunting curiosity.

On one side of the room a small row of cots has been placed, while on the other a few makeshift cribs have been put up for the youngest of the children, while a few small tea tables wait in the center of the room for playtime.

"Oh my," Eline murmurs in surprise. She smiles wistfully at the room full of dirty and tired-eyed children, and I notice a faint look of remorse and longing in her clear blue eyes.

Since their wedding, she and Fletcher had prayed for a child of their own, but the answer to their tender prayers hasn't been answered.

I squeeze her hand gently, letting her know that I am here.

"Children," Margaret calls, her voice rising to gain their attention, "this is Miss DeVos and Mrs. Fletcher. They are going to take care of you for the next few days, alright?"

Their soft voices rise into one chorus of excited mumbles in reply.

A small, courageous young girl steps forward, slipping her tiny hand into mine almost immediately.

"You can come play with me. If you want to," she says, softly, her large, doe-like blue eyes shining up at me bravely.

I laugh at her naked courage.

I am a stranger, yet she is not afraid of me.

I nod.

"I would be happy to, dear." I smile down at her as she pulls me across the room to one of the tables as Eline crosses the room to gaze at the sleeping faces in the cribs lining the wall, her face soft and solemn.

"What is your name?" I ask the girl holding my hand.

"Heidi," she says quietly, pulling a pad of paper and colored pencils across the table in my direction as I take a seat. "What is your favorite color?"

I have to stifle a laugh at the strange sincerity and simplicity of the little girl's question.

Even though she is far from her family, her home has been destroyed, and our world lies in ruins, she is still spry and happy.

I wish I could be like you, Heidi, I think to myself.

"Green," I say.

She scrunches her nose, offering me the green pencil from her arsenal. I roll it between my fingers, gold stamping on its side stating the color.

532- Emerald Green.

"Pink is prettier," she states.

"Maybe so." I laugh softly, turning to the other children who wait nearby, gazing at me as if I were a rare exotic new animal just introduced in the *zoo Antwerpen.* "Would you like to join us, children?"

Their eyes widen at my acknowledgment of them.

Compelled by my offer and inspired by Heidi's bravery, they swiftly join us at the table. Soon, every last seat is taken and I have a small boy called Jorge on my knee as we color with the green pencil together.

And so, Eline and I spend our first day in Antwerp like this, in the light-hearted company of these innocent children and sleeping babies.

And for the rest of the evening, I forget the responsibility weighing heavily upon my shoulders and the memories that have followed me here.

CHAPTER SIXTEEN

Letters

*M*y *dearest Ezra,*

I am sorry it has taken so long for me to respond to your last letter, but I hope my letter finds you safe.

Paul Struye has sent me to Antwerp on assignment.

I have been assigned the story of following the bombardment through the citizens' eyes as I serve the wounded.

I know that you will oppose the thought of me in Antwerp, because it is such a dangerous and absurd idea.

But, as I am sure you know, I readily accepted.

I couldn't turn down an offer like this, one where I can truly help people instead of just sitting at home sick with worry.

Eline and I arrived this afternoon, and we are staying at the Koloniale Hogeschool, where Eline has been placed in charge of the children's ward.

Eline has already found Fletcher, and the two haven't left one another's side since.

The children here are a wonder, Ezra.

They have been taken from their homes and most of them do not know where their parents are, and yet they keep going. They still laugh and play, though the darkness only grows around them.

I wish I could be like that. Don't you?

Unaffected and innocent of the war's wages upon the world?

I have spent the day interviewing a wide assortment of victims as I treat their wounds, and you would not believe some of their stories.

The school has been transformed into an efficient and operating hospital, though I hear the supplies are low and we must continue to ration them. It brings me back to the days when Andrew and I helped Papa with his patients, and I trained beneath him.

I miss them both so much.

I know now that God trained me all those years ago as a child for this reason, to serve his war-torn people in such a way. I do not know everything, and I certainly do not have the proper training, but I know that this is what I must do, alongside my writing for the paper.

I wish you were here with me. But at least we are in the same city again, though separated by our duties and the fear of bombs.

I am proud of you, Ezra.

You have proven your loyalty to both our country and the Resistance, and so you have won the trust of your commanders, who have entrusted you with your own troop and the rescue missions that are saving lives daily.

I know that it is dangerous work; but it is also work worthy of your time and effort.

I only pray that you are careful and return to me safe and sound.

If you ever have a moment to spare, come to the Koloniale Hogeschool; that is where I will remain working.

I keep holding onto God's promises, Ezra. I know that He does not forget his promises to us. And we mustn't either.

Stay safe, dear.

I pray for you daily.

With love,
Ruth

P.S.

I have sent with this letter a note Mr. Shepherd asked me to give to you.

CHAPTER SEVENTEEN

The next morning, I rise early. I slip quietly though the school, unnoticed by everyone as the various nurses, attendants, physicians, maids and cooks rush about in an orderly fashion like a well-oiled machine.

I had left Eline with the children as I embarked on my first endeavor, striding briskly down the long hallway as I passed the many tall windows that offered me a view at the once beautiful landscape of Antwerp that now lies in ruins.

In my hand is a small bag of medical supplies, along with a notebook, and a pen poised above my right ear.

I stop suddenly to let a breakfast cart pass me, nodding cordially at the young woman at its helm before glancing over my shoulder at a group of Resistance men.

They are dressed in identical brown jumpsuits with small Belgian flags stitched onto their sleeves, but as I study their tired faces, they are not familiar to me.

I run my hand absently over the edge of the letter in my pocket.

Setting my jaw, I return my gaze to the many doors to my left as I step toward room number seven. I raise my clenched fist to the door's face, gathering my courage before knocking.

Once, and then twice.

A moment of silence.

"Come in!" comes the shrill reply.

I let out a soft breath, laying hold of the knob and pushing the door open with my hip.

"Hello, Mrs. Levy?" I say, my voice soft and winsome as I step over the threshold. "I am Ruth DeVos. I have come to check on you, and I wanted to ask you a few questions regarding the war for the newspaper. Do you have a moment to spare?"

The room I step into would more accurately be defined as a mop closet rather than a capacious room, for there is hardly enough floor space to hold the small bed and washstand that sits on either side of the small elderly woman that greets me as she rocks gently in her chair.

With soft blonde hair that has slowly faded into white and large dark brown eyes set on a thin face accented by high cheekbones, Cornelia Levy gazes back at me with the keen and knowing gaze of a woman who has lived a hard and enduring life.

"Life is made up of moments, dear girl. I suppose I could spare you just one," she says, her voice high and brittle as she smiles in a perplexing manner. Her gaze travels from my dress and up my torso, and finally to my face, where her crow-like eyes scan my face studiously. "Who are you again?"

I smile gently as I sweep loose strands of dark brunette hair behind my ear.

I offer her my hand.

"I am Ruth DeVos. I am a nurse with the Resistance, and I also work with the newspaper," I say, to which she raises her brows.

"Ah, I've heard of you," she muses, taking my hand and shaking it gingerly, as if my palm were a flower that could be crushed.

I raise my brows softly.

"You have?"

She nods.

"Of course. I know everything that goes on with the Resistance. I may not leave this room much, but believe me, you can learn a lot from simple observations," she says, her eyes twinkling with a spry youthfulness to them. "It is at times when the enemy thinks you are sleeping that you must watch for his attack."

I smile softly at her, something about her striking me as familiar.

"You speak in riddles," I say softly.

"So I have been told." She cackles, turning her ear to my voice. "You have a slight accent in your voice, Miss. What is it?"

"Netherlandish," I say simply.

"Amsterdam or Holland?"

"Neither. I grew up in Vlissengin."

Mrs. Levy smiles as if satisfied. "Ah, the coast."

I nod.

"Yes, ma'am."

"Have a seat, dear." Mrs. Levy sits straighter on her chair, adjusting the quilt in her lap as she motions toward the bed. "Let us begin the interview."

Setting my bag down at the door, I position myself on the foot of the bed, facing the single tiny window that is behind her as I perch my notebook open in my lap.

"Alright. Can I have your full name for the paper?" I ask, poising my pen over the page.

"Cornelia Jane Murry Levy," she says, her thin lips pulling into a soft smile as she gazes at me.

I return her smile, studying her wrinkled face.

"Wonderful," I say, copying the name at the head of my page, "and how long have you been working with the Resistance, Mrs. Levy?"

"Please, call me Cor," she says.

I smile, nodding.

"Of course," I say gently.

She clears her throat before proceeding to answer my question.

"I have been with the Dutch Resistance since the Great War, I suppose. My husband, Frank, joined to fight the Germans in 1914 when they crossed Belgian lines to reach France, and I signed up for the nurse corps soon after," she says softly, her gaze falling to her wrinkled hands folded peacefully in her lap, her eyes distant. "And our boys joined the Resistance early in , as soon as Nazi Germany invaded Belgium; they were such brave and passionate lads. They were never afraid of much as they were growing up, but I suppose most boys aren't. But when faced with the cruelty of the German's, their courage only rose to the occasion."

She laughs gently as her voice fades.

I smile softly, her words reminding me of something from my own childhood as I copy her words down.

She smiles fondly at the memories that I can see dancing in her gaze as she clutches the arms of her chair with trembling hands.

I notice the red scars along her knuckles and the old abrasions that left their marks in the midst of brown freckles that line her forearms.

"How did you get these scars, Cor?" I ask softly, running a gentle fingertip across the older woman's arm.

She swallows, smacking her lips audibly as she gives me a questioning look.

"I was serving in a hospital in Waterloo when a bomb made landfall; I happened to be tending to some young, wounded men near a large window when it happened, and the glass shattered from the blunt force of the bombs, and all over me. Everyone thought I would die from blood loss, but I survived." She smiles wistfully, as if the terror she must have felt then is only a vague memory now. "Things like that happen all the time in a bomb field, Miss."

I nod.

I know, I think to myself.

She gives me a soft look, her brows raised.

"You said you were a nurse, yes?"

"Sort of, yes."

She nods, as if satisfied with something.

"Let me tell you something I learned in all my years of work, Miss DeVos," she says, her voice stern and her eyes wide as she takes my hand to ensure that I am listening. "You *never* show the boys your fear. Even if they are grotesquely wounded and near dying, do not let them see your fear, or even your tears. You must be strong for them; for in their dying moments, you are their only comfort."

We must meet their needs, Ruth...

Papa's voice comes vibrantly into my mind as I gaze at Mrs. Levy in wonder.

Do you understand? he had asked me while preparing me for his work.

"Do you understand?" Cor asks me now, echoing Papa's words from my memory.

I smile at the sweet irony of the moment.

I do understand.

"Yes, ma'am. I do," I say.

"Good. Now, on to your next question," she says, lacing her fingers together in her lap as she gazes expectantly at me.

"How did you end up here, at the Koloniale Hogeschool?" I ask. She smiles softly.

"I came here to be with my eldest son. He had been caught in the bombing, and was dying when I got here," she whispers softly. "His younger brother, his wife, and their child were all killed during a German raid earlier in the war. My husband was so furious that he joined the troops not long after, even in his old age."

Cor shakes her head softly, her gaze falling to the two withered hands in her lap.

"And as for my youngest son, I haven't heard from him in two months. I fear he met the same fate as his brothers," she says, her voice gentle as she falls silent.

My heart jolts.

"Oh, Mrs. Levy, I am so sorry," I say softly, my voice gentle as I lean toward her and lay a hand over her wrinkled one.

When she looks back up at me, she is smiling.

"Don't be, dear," she says, her face brightening as if a brief cloud has passed over her face and now lets the sun shine once more. She pats my hand in a consoling manner. "My husband and my sons are together, and I will soon join them. I am no spring chicken, after all."

She laughs softly, waving a hand at her brittle and war-trodden body.

I smile softly, reaching for the small bag I left by the door.

"You must be very proud of them," I say gently. "I am certain that they were very valiant men."

Cor nods.

"They *were* indeed, Miss DeVos," she says.

We sit in silence for a moment as I gaze down at my notebook, my hands trembling as my pen nib leaves a trail of damp blue ink across my page.

Cor watches me.

"All my life, I have witnessed and felt the valor and courage of freedom fighters. My husband and I fought side by side, and so it is no surprise to me that our boys followed behind us." She meets my gaze, her dark brown eyes swirling with pride, and surprisingly, joy. "And it pleases me immensely to know that their sacrifice was a worthy one, even if it pains me greatly."

I hold her gaze, her eyes challenging me.

I swallow.

And it pleases me immensely to know that their sacrifice was a worthy one, even if it pains me greatly.

How can this woman, who has lost everything and everyone she holds dear to this war, still be so accepting and joyous?

She is not bitter or even grieved, nor has she cursed the Germans for what they have done.

So how can I be bitter when in light of her sufferings, I have suffered so little?

"You have lost someone to this war, haven't you, Miss DeVos?" she asks bluntly, pulling me from my thoughts.

I nod, clearing my throat.

"Yes," I say, smiling softly up at her, my pen still poised over the paper. "I suppose we all have."

She nods.

"Yes, we have. But no matter the magnitude of the loss, whether considerably small or great, we still have a right to grieve. God allows us that." She smiles winsomely, her keen eyes filtering over my face swiftly.

I smile softly, my heart hammering under her gaze.

"You have done a great thing for our country, ma'am. You have given back to God what he gave you, and your story will be an inspiration to our men and women still fighting," I say with sincere admiration, "and I admire your strength and courage."

Cor cackles softly.

"Oh, pish posh, Miss. I haven't done all that much; I have just lived my life," she says, her gaze falling to my hand as I pull it away to begin writing on another page.

Her gaze softens.

"You remind me of myself at your age, Miss DeVos. I was in your shoes once. Forced from home and thrust into a world divided against itself as if *I* could somehow change the course of the war. I pray for the day it is over at last, but I suppose that there will always be some reason to fight."

I sigh softly.

"As long as there's light in this dark world, the darkness will never stop trying to extinguish it; but we mustn't give up hope," I say softly.

Cor smiles, her eyes blazing.

"Right you are, Miss," she says, shifting in her chair as she reaches for a stack of newspapers on the nightstand to her left. "I have read some articles of yours, and I am rather glad you came to see me today. It's nice to know that not everyone has forgotten the value of faith and freedom in our world."

I smile, glancing up at the charming old woman.

"I think I am still learning their value myself, Mrs. Levy," I say, smiling softly at her.

"Cor," she corrects me once again with a wry smile over the newspaper clutched in her fist. "Read this, dear. I feel you know more than you let on."

She offers me the paper, and I take it, my eyes scanning the masthead of last month's issue of *La Libre Belgique*.

"Freedom is a fragile thing.

It is hard won and yet lost in a moment.

For years we have fought our enemy, and still we fight.

But what do we fight for?

The answer is quite simple.

Freedom.

It is the one thing that we long to gain, and to hear, like the joyous cry of the trumpet when the battle is at last over. But even then, freedom still must be fought for.

It is not given to us by inheritance, nor is it free.

The price of our freedom is great, but not as great a cost as the loss of liberty.

Freedom must be fought for from generation to generation, and it must be protected at all costs.

For if we do not protect it, we are certain to pay the price once more."

R.M.D

CHAPTER EIGHTEEN

EZRA

Port of Antwerp

Ezra stumbles through the darkened streets of Antwerp as evening settles over the port, the gentle ebb and flow of the murky water of the river Scheldt tiring him further.

His body aches and his legs are weary from his long day of pulling victims from the rubble and searching the remains of the city for missing persons; his heart is heavy, burdened with the load of broken families and distraught individuals who have lost their homes and loved ones to Hitler's bombs.

The bombs have held off for four days now, though the wreckage of the last one still lies across the city. Barricades have been established along the narrow sandy shores of the coastline as various soldiers stand positioned at their posts in defense of the port.

The supplies coming into Antwerp have stalled entirely, and the soldiers as well as citizens are growing low on rations and other necessities as Hitlers bombardment grows dangerously close to threatening the port—the Resistance and Allies one advantage point.

The bell-tower clock strikes seven, the familiar and haunting chanting of its melody crying throughout the city.

He closes his eyes, and for a moment, he is back at Still Waters with the clan; everyone is together and safe, waking to the faint cry of the clock tower as it warns them of the hour.

"Commander Pik!"

He opens his eyes and stops abruptly, his hand flying instinctively to the holster at his hip.

He glances over his shoulder, his shoulder's sagging in relief at the sight of a young Dutch soldier approaching him.

"What's wrong, Faibber?" he calls to the younger man as he approaches him, waving a paper in the air.

"I was told to give these to you," Faibber says, holding two small letters out to Ezra.

Ezra takes them, gazing down at the delicate words written across the first letter's face.

Mr. Ezra Pik.

He smiles.

The first is from Ruth; the second appears to be from Mr. Shepherd.

He glances up at Faibber.

"How did you get these?"

"A young woman heard that I belonged to your troop, and asked if I would personally deliver them to you, Commander," Faibber replies, his young eyes gazing up at Ezra with silent respect.

Ezra nods, worry gnawing at his stomach.

"Well, thank you, Faibber," he says. "You go on down to the bunker and get some rest. I will be there shortly."

Faibber nods, turning and walking a few paces away before stopping.

"Commander?"

"Yes?"

Faibber turns to gaze at him.

"I have been meaning to ask you something," he says, his eyes swirling with either fear or anger, Ezra cannot tell which.

"And what is that, Faibber?" he asks softly, the letters fluttering in his hand as his heart yearns to open them.

Faibber clears his throat.

"What are we doing, Commander?"

Ezra raises his brows. "What do you mean?"

"What are we fighting for? What is it that the Germans want so badly that they are willing to kill every last one of us for it?"

Ezra can hear the obvious note of hatred and remorse in the young man's voice.

It is the same hatred that lurks in Faibber's heart tonight that had overwhelmed Ezra when he first learned that Hugo had been the one to betray the Still Water's clan.

And his questions are the same ones Ezra had asked himself three years ago when he joined the Resistance.

Ezra swallows, thinking over his response carefully.

"The Germans want control, Faibber. They want power and dominion over us," he says softly. "But we are fighting for freedom, and we do not fight alone. God is on our side. He has been since the beginning, and he will be in the end too. He will give us the victory."

Ezra gazes at Faibber steadily, praying that his feeble attempt at witnessing will not be lost on this rebellious and zealous young man.

Lord, let him understand.

"Do you understand, Faibber?" he asks gently.

Slowly, Faibber nods.

"I think I do, Commander," he says. "Thank you. Goodnight."

"Goodnight," Ezra says softly, watching as he walks away.

Uneasiness churns in his stomach.

No matter what he does, he cannot rid himself of the incessant worry that Faibber is going to do something foolish with his anger and rage against the Germans.

One wrong decision or one swift mishap could cost the young man everything.

Shaking his head, he turns to the letters in his hand.

He opens Ruth's first.

He scans her words swiftly, his eyes running eagerly over her neat and familiar cursive writing.

"Paul Struye has sent me to Antwerp on assignment.

I have been assigned the story of following the bombardment through the citizens' eyes as I serve the wounded. I know that you will oppose the thought of me in Antwerp, because it is such a dangerous and absurd idea.

But, as I am sure you know, I readily accepted."

Ruth was right.

He most certainly *does* oppose the thought of her risking her neck to come to Antwerp for the sake of the newspaper. But he also knows why she agreed to come, and he cannot say that he blames her.

She is tired of hiding out in Brussels, worrying about him and mourning over Andrew when there is work to be done here, in Antwerp.

She is like Andrew in that way.

He smiles softly to himself.

He cannot deny the small stirring in his chest as he learns that she is in town, nor can he rid his face of the smile that is pulling at his lips now, as the letter flutters in his hand.

Stay safe, dear. I pray for you daily, Ruth says in the closing of her letter.

He turns his face to the darkening evening sky above, starless and smoky. He smiles to himself.

"What am I going to do with you, Ruth?" he whispers softly, but no one is there to hear him.

CHAPTER NINETEEN

For days, Eline and I work in the children's ward, waking at various hours of the night to check on them and running around tirelessly as we go through bomb drills and false air raids.

"We must get ready for the new physician this morning," I hear Eline murmuring to a little boy who is tugging on her skirt tail.

I stand in the doorway of the children's ward, gazing wistfully at the little faces that inhabit the room. I watch as they pick at the toast and rationed jelly we had fixed for the older children for breakfast, none of them enjoying it very much but knowing better than to complain.

"Sad sight, isn't it?" a sharp voice says from behind me.

I glance over my shoulder, startled.

A middle-aged man standing in the hallway proves to be the owner of the crisp voice, with a balding head, extended chin and warm eyes. He stands in a heavy overcoat and polished dress loafers, a small book clasped in his hands.

"The little lads and lasses, I mean. It is a sad state to be in when even our own children have nowhere to go." He offers me a friendly smile. He catches me staring at the book in his hand.

It appears to be small and thin, with a hardbound leather cover protecting yellowing pages within.

"I have come to read to the children before the new physician comes in. I thought it may cheer them and bring some joy to their morning," he says, as if in need of explanation.

I return his smile.

"That is very kind of you, sir. I am certain that they will thoroughly enjoy that. What will you be reading to them?" I ask the stranger.

There are familiar clips and notes in his voice that almost sound familiar to my ear, though foreign. I cannot place it.

Perhaps it is simply the English accent.

He smiles down at the little book in his hands.

"Oh, it's just a little fairytale that I wrote for my goddaughter, Lucy. She's quite old for them now, but one day I hope that she will enjoy them again," he says meekly, his warm eyes growing distant and wistful.

I smile brightly at him.

"So you are a writer, are you?"

"Sort of, I suppose," he says, offering me his hand. "I am Jack Lewis, but my friends call me Jack."

I accept his friendly extended hand swiftly, something about the older man intriguing to me. It feels almost like I have met him before, but I have never seen his face before in my life.

"I am Ruth DeVos," I say, motioning for him to join Eline and I in the room with the children. "May I call you Jack?"

He searches my eyes for a moment, his gaze lingering upon me for a span of silence. He smiles as if he has found something in my face that is satisfactory.

He nods decidedly, his coat tails brushing against the floor as he strides into the room.

"You may indeed call me 'Jack.'"

I nod, smiling at the strange man.

"Jack it is, then."

Eline smiles graciously up at the newcomer from where she sits perched in a rocker by the hearth with a small baby clutched to her chest as Jack introduces himself to her.

"It's lovely to meet you, Jack," she says.

I stride across the room and pull a second rocker into the center of the room before the fireplace so that he can sit down in front of the children.

"Here you are. Let me gather the children around, and then you may begin," I say as I twist the ring around my finger as we speak, my mind struggling to place him in my past memories.

"Thank you, Miss," he says, seating himself stiffly into the chair and cracking open the spine of the book in his hands.

I brush past him on my way to herd the children to their seats, and he gazes at me over the pages of his book.

"You are a writer as well, aren't you?" he asks after a moment of silent observation.

I gape at him, my feet stilling.

"How did you know that?" I ask.

He smiles, pointing at the ink stains on my hands.

"I can always tell, Miss. By the wistful stares and ink-stained fingertips," he says, his face softening. "But there is something else about you that I have noticed. There is a pained look in your eyes, Miss DeVos; a look that hints at dark memories and a haunted past. I noticed it when I stood in the hall just a moment ago."

I smile softly at the accuracy of his friendly and genuine words, nodding for him to continue.

"You have a history with this war, yes?" he asks, eyebrows raised.

"To say the least, yes I do."

"A rather painful one?"

I nod, confirming his words.

He smiles softly.

"I thought so, Miss," he says kindly as he crosses his legs and his foot begins tapping the floor. "I have seen, and heard of, a lot of pain during this war. And I have learned that God whispers to us in our pleasures and speaks in our consciences; but he shouts in our pains. It is his megaphone to rouse a deaf world."

I hold his gaze steadily.

"Yes, I suppose it is," I say softly, uncertain as to what to say.

His words conjure old memories and new alike to my mind; memories of the agony of Andrew's loss, the confusion after Papa's disappearance and Mama's arrest; along with the paralyzing worry for Ezra and the solemn sorrow that has cloaked our world like a wool blanket.

He smiles softly at me, a look passing his face that suggests to me that he knows more than he lets on.

There is something *so* undeniably familiar about him.

What is it?

My lips part as I begin to ask if we have met before, when Heidi marches up to the kind stranger and boldly introduces herself.

"Hello, my dear. My, how very brave you are!" Jack smiles at the audacious little child as he lifts her to his lap, perching her on his knee.

Heidi smiles brightly, whispering something in Jack's ear that I cannot hear.

Julia and James, a set of twins who Eline has grown particularly fond of, sit cowering in the farthest seat from the strange man as possible.

Once the children have been herded into their seats at the table and an almost eerie silence has fallen over the room, Jack begins to read.

"*Once there were four children whose names were...*"

They are engrossed with the story, some of them growing sleepy-eyed while others go wide-eyed with wonder at Jack's sharp and inquisitive voice as I circle around the room.

I finally settle in my usual position gazing out the single window pane overlooking the city, my eyes drifting to the streets below at the many soldiers marching up and down the alleyways and canalways, both Resistance and allies.

There are a million shadows dancing in a million ways across the rooftops and smoking chimneys that dot the Antwerp skyline; they are the shadows of war and penetrating darkness falling on a deaf world.

I twist the chain around my neck absently between my thumb and forefinger as my mind begins to wander over Jack's strange, yet truth-filled, words.

Through the mountains and valleys of my life thus far, especially these last four years, I have experienced more pain than I ever thought possible.

But I have also experienced God's grace and guidance through it all; through the persecution, betrayal, arrest, interrogation and imprisonment, God was there, orchestrating a story of conquering grace.

God has not been trying an experiment on my faith and love in order to find their strength and quality.

He already knew it, I think silently in my heart.

It was I who didn't.

And slowly, he is restoring to me what has been lost.

A small smile pulls at my lips as I gaze at the smoky gray sky of my beloved Antwerp just as I had so many times before at Still Waters.

The room around me fades as I drift through memories, and I do not even hear Jack finish reading the story to the children, nor do I hear the soft knock at the door.

"I'll get it," Eline says, stepping lightly around the children and to the door, little Henk on her hip.

"Oh, my," Eline says, and I can hear the startled notes of shock and surprise in her voice, "you must be the new physician."

"I am."

My heart nearly stops beating at the familiar aged tenor of the voice, the thick Netherlandish accent almost too much for me to bear.

"I am Doctor Edwin van Beek," comes the soft and kind reply from the door.

Edwin van Beek.

My heart pounds.

Lord, can it be? My heart whispers in disbelief.

Look, my daughter.

I obey and turn just as the newcomer enters the room.

Our eyes meet, and his widen in surprised joy.

His face is long and worn, a short graying brown beard falling from his chin and covering the thin features of his aged face and the defined dimples on either cheek, with familiar brown eyes that gleam with a soft and kind patience to them.

I notice the gray of his hair and the wrinkles that have formed upon his thin face that were not present before, and I realize that he has aged very much in the nearly three years since his disappearance. I notice, also, the old worn doctor's bag clutched in his hand.

"Ruth?" he whispers my name, his voice thicker with both emotion and age than it had been before.

I open my mouth to speak, but my voice has abandoned me.

My heart pounds as relief washes over me.

The physician has returned.

CHAPTER TWENTY

"**P**apa!"

I finally breathe his name as my father wraps his familiar arms around me in an embrace, tears running down my cheeks and onto his shoulder.

"My *Dochter*," he says, pulling away and looking at me, his eyes shining with love and relief as he searches my face.

Daughter.

It has been so long since I heard him say that.

"I cannot believe you are really here, after all this time," I say softly, blushing as he gazes at me, his warm and familiar hands brushing against my cheek.

"Neither can I." He smiles, shaking his head. "You look just like your mother, Ruth."

I laugh lightly, brushing the tears from my eyes as I lean into his hold.

"That is what Andrew had told me," I say before I can think of what my words mean.

Andrew.

Papa's eyes sadden.

Sorrow churns in my stomach as bile rises up my throat.

"Oh, Papa, Andrew is—"

Papa holds up his hand, his face pained, and his voice gentle.

"I know, Ruth," he says hoarsely, swallowing as his hands fall to my shoulders. "I know."

I shake my head.

I do not understand.

"How do you know?" I whisper.

He smiles softly, tears brimming his eyes.

"I went home to Vlissengin. I saw *it,*" he whispers, his voice growing softer and more brittle with each word as his grip on my shoulders grows tighter.

Andrew's grave, my heart whispers as it beats violently in my chest.

I blink back the tears in my eyes.

"Oh," I murmur.

He nods, glancing around the room as if just now realizing we aren't alone.

"Ruth, may we talk privately? Perhaps in the hall?" he asks with a soft smile in Eline and Jack's direction.

"Of course." I nod, glancing at Eline.

Eline smiles at me, tears glistening upon her own cheeks.

She nods, and I offer her a broken smile.

Papa and I step quietly back out into the hall where he had just come, shutting the door silently behind us.

"Oh, Papa, I am so sorry. Everything fell to pieces after you left; Andrew left to join the Resistance and Mama was captured. I was on my own when the Shepherd's offered to take me in ..."

My voice trails off as I gasp for breath, the memories rushing through my mind so swiftly it takes my breath away.

Papa smiles softly at me.

"Quiet, *Dochter.* I already know. Andrew told me what happened." He must see the dumbfounded look on my face, for he smiles gently and leads me to a small bench at the end of the hall. "Sit, and I will explain."

I do as I am told, sitting and folding my hands calmly in my lap as he pulls a letter from the inner breast pocket of his coat.

He flattens it upon his knee.

"I was released from a Nazi camp in Germany late last year; I was traveling under the false pseudonym of *Edwin van Beek* when Andrew tracked me down and wrote to me, asking if I was indeed Nathaniel DeVos." He pauses, smiling wistfully down at the letter. "I was overjoyed that he had found me, and so we quickly began writing to one another."

I shake my head in wonder at my dear brother.

He had indeed found Papa, but he never got to see him again.

Papa continues.

"He told me he had joined the Resistance, and about your mother, and how Dirk Shepherd took you in. He even mentioned a certain Ezra Pik."

He gives me a pointed look.

I blush, smiling softly at Ezra's name despite my confusion.

Papa smiles softly at me, patting my knee gently with his thin hand.

"Andrew told me that you and the Shepherd's household had been betrayed, and that you were on your way to a death camp in Poland when he, Ezra, and the Resistance devised an ambush on the train that you were on." His eyes darken as emotion stirs in his chest. "He told me how near death you were when they found you."

We are both quiet for a minute.

"But, Papa," I whisper, "it's been over a year since Andrew's passing; where have you been all this time?"

He sighs.

"Well, I was held up in Germany as they released several of us inmates whom they had deemed innocent. And I was lying low when I was given my false ID documents from the German Resistance and I was able to travel. I looked everywhere for you all. I went to Vlissengen, but I found the house empty. I sought the Resistance's aid, and that is when they notified Andrew. That is when he first wrote."

He swallows, his eyes distant and wistful.

"He told me everything in that first letter, his second arriving with the news that he had nearly located your mother in Germany and promised that you were then safe in Brussels. He gave me the information concerning your mother's whereabouts, and I have since been in contact with her."

My heart stops.

Mama.

"Mama's alive?" I ask, grabbing his hand.

He smiles, nodding.

"Yes; she is terribly ill, but alive," he says with a soft smile, a look of longing filling his eyes. "She is in the Bergen-Belson concentration camp in Germany."

He pauses for a moment, thinking as he gazes down at the letter once more.

"I wrote back to Andrew several times, but I never heard back from him after his third letter to me, and I never discovered your true location. I suppose he had already been called home before then. That is when I decided to return home to Vlissengen, praying that I would find you there."

I bit my lip, sighing at the memories in my head.

"I found him instead," Papa says heavily.

The grave.

I nod softly as tears threaten to choke me.

Papa glances up at me.

"Ruth, how did it happen?" he asks, his voice tentative and flat.

I swallow the bile in my throat, taking a shaky breath before speaking.

"He was on a mission with his troop in Ghent, where there were several Jewish families and allied airmen being held captive by the Nazis. Andrew and his troop had plotted and planned the mission for weeks in advance before they were finally ready to execute it." My voice trembles and I take a steadying breath before continuing.

"They were able to rescue the prisoners and get them into the streets before the German troops caught up with them and trapped them in the city. The Germans began firing at the prisoners, and Andrew was shot defending them."

I stop talking, my fingers trembling so badly I am forced to slip them under my thighs to stop their shaking.

"He was shot in the chest, and he passed immediately," I say softly, almost choking on the words.

Papa is silent, a hand clasped over his mouth as he takes in my words. Tears fall silently down his face.

It is the first time I have ever seen him cry.

"His comrades tell me that he was a hero," I say, my lips trembling as they pull into a soft smile, "but I already knew that. He has been a hero since we were children."

Papa smiles at me softly, a broken sort of smile that I am well-acquainted with by now.

He wraps his arm around my shoulder, and we sit there in silence, tears falling down both of our cheeks as our pasts collide once more with the future.

And as we sit side by side, father and daughter, it is like no time has passed at all.

For a moment, everything is as it was before the war tore us all apart.

~ . ~

"DO YOU THINK YOUR father will like me?" Ezra whispers in my ear as he escorts me into the dining hall the next afternoon.

We have only just now been reunited, Ezra only arriving at the Hogeschool a mere fifteen minutes ago to see me when I told him about Papa.

Voices rise and join as one in the end of the dining hall, where a long table has been set up for the nurses, medical attendants, physicians, Resistance workers and such to gather for dinner.

"Of course he will," I say, flattening the cowlick at the back of his head with my palm. "Why wouldn't he?"

He shrugs as we sidestep the long row of cots along the wall, most of them inhabiting soldiers as they eat their meager suppers of chicken broth and dry bread.

The dining hall is long and wide, with thick brown carpet beneath our feet and cream walls with thick molding at the floor and ceiling.

"I'm not sure, but with the way you're grooming me, I am led to believe that you are anxious," he says with a swift glance at a soldier we pass before he looks at me. "You are, aren't you?"

I nod.

"A little," I tease, moving out of the way of a passing nurse as she is pushing a rolling cot down the hall.

Ezra smiles, running a hand across the stubble on his face.

"I'm glad you're confident in me, love," he whispers playfully.

I swat him lightly on the arm, smiling.

"If Andrew accepted you, I am certain Papa will too," I say, catching sight of the bearded man as he bends over his last patient of the evening.

His face is calm and worn as he works, and as I stand here now, I can clearly see the age of his countenance and the slowness of his limbs.

Papa wraps the soldier's wounds with one final skilled and gentle flourish straightening his spine as he murmurs kindly to the man.

Turning, his gaze falls on Ezra and me.

Ezra's hand tightens over my own.

Papa smiles softly, meeting my gaze.

His eyes fill with love and fatherly affection, as well as the same anxious wandering gleam that had been in Andrew's.

I smile softly.

Like father, like son, I think to myself.

"Papa, this is Ezra Pik," I say softly.

Papa steps forward, wiping his hands on a towel absently before extending his right hand to Ezra.

"So it is," he says, his eyes brightening as he searches Ezra's face. "I have heard much about you, Ezra. I am Nathaniel."

Ezra laughs softly.

He releases my hand as he steps forward to take Papa's hand, his grip firm and steady.

"I hope it was all good, sir?" he asks good-naturedly, brows raised in my direction.

I smile, nodding my head encouragingly.

Papa smiles.

"Yes, very good indeed. Andrew gave me his report." He smiles sadly, his gaze between Ezra and I. "I hear the three of you faced a lot together in the past."

Ezra nods, swallowing as I slip my hand back into his.

"Yes, sir, we certainly did. Those were some dark and hopeless days that still haunt us even now; and it is only by God's grace that Ruth and I are still here today, along with the surviving Still Waters clan. I just wish Andrew could be here as well." His words are soft-spoken and sincere.

I smile softly up at him.

"As do I," I murmur thickly, and Ezra steals a glance at me. His eyes are calm and thoughtful.

Papa smiles, laying a hand on Ezra's shoulder.

His eyes are soft, and I can tell by the way he is looking at him that Ezra's few, though heartfelt, words have touched him deeply.

"God takes, but he gives again, Ezra," he murmurs, smiling.

I almost laugh at my papa's sentimental words, for they are the very same words Ezra had read to me many days ago on the front porch swing at his home.

The Lord gave, and the Lord has taken away;
may the name of the Lord be praised.

Ezra smiles, his eyes brightening.

"So I have learned, sir," he says.

Papa smiles in return, nodding in approval at Ezra.

He turns to me, taking my free hand.

"I am proud of you, Ruth; you have grown very much since I left you all that time ago. You have faced more than I ever knew you would, but I can see that God has used it for good." He gives my hand a gentle squeeze, pushing his glasses up his nose as he smiles at the two of us.

"It is plain to me that I have missed far too much, and we have lots of talking left to do," he says wryly, "but for tonight, let us go join the others for the rationed meal."

I laugh softly.

And smiling at one another, Ezra and I fall into step behind him as we approach the table at the end of the hall.

Eline waves her hand to gain my attention, smiling at me as she motions toward the empty chairs beside her and Fletcher.

"How did it go?" she whispers, nodding toward the two men behind me.

"Very well, I believe," I whisper with a smile of satisfaction, slipping into the seat beside her.

The men take the two chairs beside me, where Papa begins interrogating Ezra further.

"So, Andrew told me that you are a pilot with the Resistance?"

Ezra nods beside me, lifting his fork to his lips.

"Yes, sir; I was given the position of Commanding Fighter Pilot not long after Andrew's death. Though, since the bombardment I am simply commanding officer." His words are soft and nonchalant, but I can see his cheeks deepening to a shade of pink as he speaks of his rank.

"Very good," Papa says approvingly. "So you have your own troop?"

Again, Ezra nods.

He slips his hand into mine, smiling sheepishly at me as he talks with the others.

Fletcher soon joins their conversation, adding embellished stories about our dark and hopeless pasts as he shares them with Papa.

"Did you truly combat two armed Nazis on your own?" Papa asks, eyebrows raised doubtfully at Fletcher.

Fletcher nods gallantly, his bald head reflecting the rays of the dim light in the room.

"Sure did," he says.

Eline laughs.

"Fletcher, dear, you did nothing of the sort." She smiles at her husband.

"Why, I certainly did, my dear wife," he says, a droll smile pulling at his lips as his ears turn a dark shade of red.

Our end of the table laughs unanimously at his words.

Eline and I share a smile as they continue with their questions and storytelling as we share the rationed meal with the thirty-something strangers around us.

And looking around me tonight, I see all that is missing from our company, wishing that Mr. and Mrs. Shepherd and Maya were here with us.

And the familiar fracture of pain opens up on my heart as I long for Mama and Andrew.

But as I listen to the thronging voices around me and see all the men and women who have come together to combat and defeat our foe, I know that no matter what happens, no matter who returns home from this war and who loses their life fighting it, God will carry us through once again.

Just as he has in the past.

And as I gaze at Papa and Ezra talking together side by side, I know that God has restored one thing to me that I thought I had lost forever.

PART TWO

Antwerp, Belgium

Do not be afraid of those who can kill the body, but cannot kill the soul.

MATTHEW 10:28

CHAPTER TWENTY-ONE

Three months later

The days pass in a strange blur of bombs, wounds, and darkness; November brought heavy rainfall and light snow and soon drifted into December, and still the bombs pelted the city.

Christmas of 1944 proved to be the darkest and bloodiest of all the Christmases during the occupation as soldiers fought, and succeeded, to free Antwerp's Port, along with the Americans and other allies facing a cruel battle with invading Germans in the Ardennes forest between Belgium and Luxembourg.

For over a month they have fought, and the battle rages on through the cold snowy month of January as the new year dawns upon us.

"It's alright, dear," I murmur to the frightened little boy, wiping the soot and grime from his little face with a damp cloth. "You are safe now, I promise."

His lip trembles, but he doesn't reply.

Last night, bombs fell on Antwerp once again.

There were many of them falling through the sky in a blazing trail of fire and destruction.

The whole school has been sent into a flustered scramble as we attempt to take in and care for the many wounded civilians and soldiers as Resistance men and allied troops work to extinguish the fires that dot the housetops and rooflines of our beloved Antwerp.

"What is your name, honey?" I ask the next small girl in the long line of newcomers.

Her arm bears the marks of the wreckage she was pulled from, her little face nearly black with soot that has settled into the small abrasions on her cheeks.

"Tess," she whispers.

"That's a lovely name, Tess." I smile at her.

I take the cloth and dip it into my basin of water before wringing it out and setting to work on her arm.

A few grueling moments pass and the children surrounding me grow restless, each of their young eyes wide and fearful.

I glance over my shoulder.

"James, get away from the window, please," I call to the small blond-headed boy peering through the blackout curtain. "There is nothing out there that you need to see."

The door opens and shuts again as Eline and Fletcher enter the room.

"Ruth, dear," Eline says, stepping into the room and picking up the small baby, Henk, from his crib, "your father has asked for you to join him upstairs. The wounded are still coming in and they need help."

I drop the cloth, wiping my hand dry on my skirt.

"There are *that* many wounded?"

Fletcher nods, his face grave, though he offers the children a smile.

"The men will enjoy waking up to your face much more than they would mine, Ruth," he says.

I smile softly, wishing the situation weren't so dire or I would laugh at his feeble joke.

I turn to Tess.

"I will be back in a little while. Fletcher and Eline are here to help you, alright?"

The little girl nods.

I smile at her and stand from the floor, turning to face Fletcher.

"Have you seen Ezra yet, Fletcher?"

He shakes his head, his brown eyes meeting mine.

"No, I haven't," he says, his voice soft. "It has been madness up there all morning. But I am certain that he is fine, Ruth; he has most likely taken his troop on another rescue mission."

I nod, offering him a small smile.

"I'm sure you are right," I say, though worry churns in my stomach as I step toward the door, where I pull my coat over my dress.

I haven't seen Ezra in many days, nor have I received a letter or note telling me of his whereabouts.

"Be careful," Eline calls as I step through the door and into the darkened stairwell.

My footsteps echo as I climb the stairs, the light of day greeting me as I step into the large dining hall that has now been converted into a lobby and burn care center.

I turn on my heel to my right, striding briskly through the many soldiers and civilians, nurses, and random individuals that stand between me and the foyer.

"Ruth!"

I glance over my shoulder.

It's Papa, his eyes calm and patient even though his step is rushed and he is breathless as he travels from one new patient to another.

"Yes, Papa? What do I need to do?" I ask.

"Can you help guide the men into the dining hall, and get them comfortable?" he asks, his eyes worried.

I nod.

"I certainly can."

Papa nods, smiling softly at me.

"And Ruth?"

"Yes?"

"Prepare yourself, dear girl. Some of them are not pretty."

His face is sorrowful and solemn, his stern voice holding a warning.

I nod my chin, standing straighter under his watchful and loving gaze.

"Of course, Papa."

He smiles, his eyes brightening.

"I am proud of you, *Dochter,*" he says, "Now, get to work. I will get to these men as soon as I can."

And with that, we get to work, and I face the task at hand.

The foyer is crowded with Resistance men in beige jumpsuits as they usher in large groups of children and families, while others simply carry the wounded on their shoulders through the front door.

I lead several of the wounded into the dining hall, where I take their pulse and get their names as they wait for one of the three physicians to see their wounds.

I catch sight of a familiar tousled caramel-headed soldier, grimacing under the weight of a wounded comrade he carries through the room upon his shoulder.

"Ezra!" I say, rushing forward to help him.

Relief floods his eyes as he sees me.

My heart flutters at the sight of him, but my head is in control, and I focus on the comrade he carries.

Working together, Ezra and I lay the wounded man down on his back upon an empty cot.

"He belongs to my troop; he was caught in the middle of the bombing last night. Lars and I found him and were able to free him from the rubble, but not without pain," Ezra tells me, his own face covered in soot and ash in his hair.

I place my thumb on the inside of the man's wrist, quickly calculating the beats of his heart just as Papa had taught me.

Elevated, but steady, I think to myself.

"It's alright now, Bakker," Ezra tells the young man, gazing sorrowfully down at his sad physical state. He steals a glance up at me, a small smile pulling at his lips. "You have a very fine nurse watching over you."

I smile softly at Ezra.

The soldier looks absolutely terrible, with burns covering his body and a pale pasty complexion, and his right leg has been broken and damaged to the point where I fear amputation; but what concerns me the most is the large knot on the back of his head, along with swelling and bruising.

Head trauma.

"Can you tell me your name, sir?" I ask the soldier gently, assessing his bodily state as Ezra waits patiently by my side.

Broken leg.

Possible infection in the bloodstream.

Second-degree burns along the torso and arms.

"Lucas Bakker," the soldier says, his voice raspy.

I glance up at Ezra to confirm.

Ezra nods, his eyes meeting mine for a fleeting moment.

"Yes, that's right," he says, his eyes sad as the truth that we both know is reflected in each other's eyes.

I know, his eyes seem to say to me, *it isn't good.*

I shake my head sadly.

No, it isn't.

I turn back to Bakker.

"Do you know where you are right now, Lucas?" I ask, my voice gentle as I straighten the pillow beneath his head.

Bakker grimaces, as if thinking causes him pain.

"Somewhere in Antwerp, I guess?" he asks, though it's not really a question.

"That's right, my friend," Ezra tells him with an encouraging smile. "We are at the Koloniale Hogeschool right now."

Bakker doesn't reply but only groans as I check the feeling in his legs.

I sigh, knowing that Bakker needs the attention of a trained physician.

Namely, Papa.

"Alright, Lucas. I am going to go get one of our physicians to come look at you," I tell him, waving my hand to a female attendant waiting nearby.

"Johanna, please ask for Doctor van Beek; I have a soldier over here with burns and slight head trauma."

Johanna does as I say, turning on her heel, scurrying down the hallway, and knocking swiftly upon the door of a classroom that has been transformed into an examination room.

Ezra moves to my side as we wait for Johanna to arrive with Papa, and I can see an obvious weight resting upon his broad shoulders, bowing them in a way that physical work alone could never achieve.

He sighs, shaking his head sadly at his fallen comrade.

I run my fingers through his hair, brushing the ash from the waves that fall into his eyes before wrapping my arm through his.

"I am sorry, Ezra," I murmur softly.

"Me too," he says, pressing his lips to my forehead in a swift and affectionate kiss. "I love you."

Despite the turmoil around us, I smile.

"I love you, too," I whisper.

I wish we could continue on talking about whom we love, but we cannot.

We both have work to do.

His work is searching through the rubble of our city for survivors and protecting the port, while mine is here, nursing wounded patients and writing.

Then Papa arrives, immediately beginning to assess Bakker's wounds as I obediently join him at his side.

"I need penicillin and sulfa drugs. Powder—no, tablets," Papa murmurs softly, his eyes never leaving the patient as he begins conversing with him.

Ezra clears his throat softly as I begin to retrieve a large amount of the drugs as requested to administer to the patient.

"I must go back; there are still dozens of people who are lost and unaccounted for," Ezra says with a grave look passing his face. "I will be back after a while to check on Bakker."

I reach for his arm.

"Be safe," I say softly.

I fear that he, too, will eventually be carried in here like Bakker has just been, and I believe that would kill me.

He nods, smiling softly.

"I will most certainly try," he says, and with one last word to both Papa and Bakker, he rushes back through the multitude of soldiers and passing individuals, and through the door he'd come in.

"Ruth," Papa says to me, pulling me back to reality, "I need your assistance. I am afraid this man is going to lose his leg."

~.~

WE WORK ALL DAY and practically all that night too; Eline works tirelessly with the new children and Papa and I work silently by the bedsides of the various and countless wounded soldiers as Fletcher flitters around offering his aid anywhere he can.

Ezra does return during the late evening, he and his troop remaining near Bakker as they help distribute and pass our rationed vittles to the wounded men, homeless women, and uncertain children.

And so the lot of us work restlessly, and it is only late the next day that we are able to truly rest as the victims at last slow in their coming and we are given a brief moment of peace.

It is then that I pull from beneath my coat the black typewriter from Paul Struye, and I begin to write.

~.~

THEY SAY THAT THE heart of man is a reflection of the man itself. They say that the heart is formed and built around those it holds dearest, the people to whom we voluntarily lend the largest and deepest portions of our hearts.

And it is when these people are either taken from us or leave us that the heart begins to fracture, for its very foundation is being threatened.

If this is the case, then the reflection of Antwerp has been shattered in a million pieces beyond recognition.

The heart of Antwerp has been broken and damaged by the burning destruction of the bombs; her foundation has been threatened as have the homes and lives of her citizens.

But, my dear people of Antwerp, do not despair.

Do not lose faith.

God is still in control now just as he was in the early hours and beginning moments that this war began nearly five years ago.

And we will not be overcome.

R.M.D.

CHAPTER TWENTY-TWO

I stare into the cold depths of the German's vacant gaze, my heart pounding in my chest as my stomach sours with dread and my body begins trembling all over.

"We meet again, *Jude,*" he sneers at me.

His breath smells like smoke and sulfur.

Jew.

It is Lieutenant Wolfgang.

I swallow.

His gaze travels to the yellow badge on my chest, his eyes flashing with malice as his lips curl into a haunting grin.

No, it cannot be, my heart whispers in disbelief as my fingers instinctively reach to cover the putrid cloth.

I want to scream at him and rip the badge from my chest, but what good will it do?

Do not be afraid of those who can kill the body, but cannot kill the soul, Andrew's voice says softly in my ear, but when I glance around me, I do not find him.

Lieutenant Wolfgang reaches for me swiftly with a large hand stained with an unknown substance, and I recoil in disgust and fear.

"Do not touch me," I say sharply, my fear colliding with courage as boldness surges through my veins.

Hatred gleams in his eyes as my open defiance only angers him further.

He lifts his palm and strikes me across the face before I even have time to blink. My cheeks burn scarlet from pain, shame, and anger.

He jerks me to his side, hissing lowly into my ear.

"You are coming with me, *Fraulein.*"

~ ~
.

I WAKE UP SCREAMING.

I open my eyes, the searing heat of the German's strike still burning on my cheek.

The air smells thick of smoke and sulfur.

Bombs.

I am in Antwerp, panting on my small cot in the corner of the nurses quarters where I had at last fallen asleep from exhaustion.

The small room is dark and cramped, with several other cots lining the opposite wall, each harboring a sleeping nurse. The furnishings are few and meager, with only a few oil lamps perched by the door for each nurse as we wake to do our rounds throughout the night; a single window rests between my cot and the next to my right, a thick black cloth covering it.

Blackout, I think to myself.

The whole city has been in blackout for days now. No lights, no candles, and no head beams of an automobile can be seen; else we usher the bombs directly in upon us.

You are coming with me, Fraulein, Wolfgang's sinister voice still echoes in my mind.

I swallow.

"Ruth, what is it?" Eline rushes to my cot, perhaps returning from her night check on the young little patients, her blue eyes shining with fear and worry. She is dressed in the simple red shirtwaist she was wearing yesterday, her wild hair pulled back into a twist at the back of her neck.

"Are you alright?" she whispers.

Am I?

I truly no longer know.

I glance down at my chest before answering her.

My nightgown is bare; no yellow star gazes back at me, gleaming in the dark of the night.

I sigh. It was all a dream.

"Ruth?" Eline presses, glancing at the few sleeping nurses in the room with us.

"It was only a dream," I say, a shudder running down my spine and raising gooseflesh up and down my limbs as the draft greets me.

Eline sighs, her gaze softening as she sits down on my cot beside me.

She wraps her arm around me.

"Oh, Ruth. You're shaking! What was the dream about this time?" she asks softly.

I brush a hand gently across my cheek, where Wolfgang had struck me in my memory-haunted dream.

"It was a German, who just so happened to be the very one who interrogated me at Avenue Louise. He struck my cheek and told me that I was going with him." My voice quivers as I speak, my fingers trembling beneath Eline's firm hold. "I do not know where he was taking me, only that it wasn't anywhere good."

"Ruth, I am sorry," she whispers, true and genuine concern and horror written across her face.

I brush a hand across my face and through my hair, my body trembling as silent tears fall down my cheeks.

"I can't do this, Eline," I say softly.

She pulls me to her side in a sisterly embrace. I lean my head on her shoulder.

"It was only a dream, though. That is all over now," she says gently. "You are safe, regardless of what the dreams tell you. The Germans are gone, even if they have sent bombs to us in their stead."

I shake my head.

"I know that, but I still cannot shake the memories. They pursue me until I no longer have the strength to combat their force." I swallow, glancing out the small window above my cot that has been covered in a black sheet.

"Every time I begin to believe that it is all truly over, the nightmares return, reminding me that the war will *never* be truly over, so long as I carry the memories of my past with me."

"How am I supposed to help these wounded men when I haven't even gotten over my own wounds?" I ask softly.

Eline is quiet for a moment.

"We all have wounds. They are all different, I suppose, and they do not always heal like we want them to," she says gently, her voice soft and low so as to not wake the other nurses around us. "But it's not about your wounds, Ruth. It's about helping them with their own; and, perhaps, in the process, yours may begin to heal as well."

Truth runs strong in her words, and I grasp onto them tightly with my heartstrings.

I smile softly, giving her hand a gentle squeeze as I lean my head on her shoulder.

We sit like this for a long moment, side by side in the dark as the silence grows into a void and I begin to nod off again.

I jerk upright.

"What time is it?" I wonder aloud softly.

Eline glances down at the watch on her wrist.

"A quarter till four," she murmurs, yawning at my reminder of the early time of dawn. "Why?"

"Papa asked me to do the early morning check-ins on the soldiers upstairs while he and the other physicians get some rest," I say, yawning.

I stand stiffly, forcing my limbs to work as I wade blindly in the dark room.

"You best be off then, Ruth," Eline says, standing beside me and stepping back to her own cot. "But I believe I'm going to try and get a little more sleep before the clock strikes again."

She smiles wryly, and returns to her cot, fully dressed.

I turn to pull my trunk out from beneath my cot, propping it open on my bed covers.

I step behind the small dressing screen and change from my nightgown swiftly, my body trembling as I pull my green gingham house dress over my head, and stockings up my legs.

I step out a moment later, and Eline is already asleep again.

I pull the small oil lamp from the night table, a flash of vibrant yellow catching my gaze.

My breath catches.

The yellow badge.

But it isn't the badge at all.

It is Andrew's yellow plaid shirt.

Setting the lamp down for a moment, I pick up the shirt, gingerly pull my arms through the sleeves, and drape the collar over my neck.

I smell the sleeve. It smells like gun smoke, dirt, and salt air.

It smells like Andrew, my heart whispers.

The shirt hangs off of my frame in a boyish manner, and it looks quite horrid with the feminine green of my dress, but it is somehow comforting and protects me from the draft of the large stone walls of the school around me.

I retrieve the lamp and slip my hand in the right pocket.

My fingers meet something small and thin; paper-like.

I pull it out, squinting down at a small envelope with my brother's name printed across the front in a familiar hand.

Mr. Andrew N. DeVos

My heart pounds harder as my breath catches in my throat.

I glance up at the return address.

Edwin van Beek

Frankfurt, Germany

Edwin van Beek?

Papa.

Hadn't Andrew mentioned him in the letter the Resistance gave me?

I smile softly.

All along, Andrew had known the truth about our parents. But he had died before he could tell me.

I flip the letter over in my palm. It has been opened.

Andrew must have read it.

I am about to slip my fingers inside to pull the mysterious letter from the envelopes grasp when the clock upstairs in the old dining hall strikes four, four rings echoing throughout the slumbering school.

I jerk in surprise, as if I had been caught defying someone's orders.

I sigh.

I may read the letter later on today, but right now, I have work to do.

And picking up the lamp and slipping the letter safely into my pocket, I scurry off into the night, up the old stairwell, and to the upper floors where the sleeping soldiers lie waiting.

~ . ~

FOR HOURS I GO from one soldier to the next, wrapping bandages and cleaning wounds while administering medicine.

One poor man saw hallucinations and asked if I was his wife, which resulted in me having to gently tell him I was indeed *not*, and he soon fell back into a fever-driven sleep.

Some men are well enough to return to service and would be leaving by dawn's light to rejoin their troops.

A few soldiers guard the doors and the exterior premises of the property all night, marching to and fro, keen eyes searching for anything out of order.

I mop my brow with the back of my hand, sighing as I pull Andrew's shirt tighter around my shoulders to combat the cold January night air.

My footsteps ring rhythmically upon the old hardwood and carpeted floors of the school echoing in an almost frightening manner as I glance across the room one last time at the slumbering patients lying on cots and upon the floor, some children curled up asleep next to their wounded fathers and frightened mothers.

I wander absently through the school, too restless and anxious to return to bed and yet too tired to do anything truly productive.

I step into the elegant foyer of the school, where a small group of able-bodied Resistance men have gathered to rest for the night.

I search their faces, my gaze landing on a familiar pair of deep brown irises that stare back at me, awake while the others sleep.

"I was wondering where you had disappeared to again," I whisper as Ezra silently stands from the bed that he had made from his jacket and rucksack upon the floor. "I have been doing my rounds."

Ezra nods, a faint smile pulling at his lips.

"I know. I have been watching you," he whispers, his gaze wistful and genuine. "I am proud of you, love. I admire what you are doing for these men. I admire all of you medics; I know that it isn't easy work."

I smile, shaking my head.

"I will never know how Papa does it every day of his life; I suppose he has just had a calling, and he pursued it," I murmur, glancing up at him with raised brows. "Does that mean you aren't mad that I came to Antwerp?"

He smiles.

"Of course I would rather you were somewhere a bit safer, but I understand why you came; *you* had a calling, and you pursued it," he says. He tugs at the sleeve of my shirt. "Nice shirt by the way."

I smile down at the vibrant yellow fabric.

"It was Andrew's," I say.

He smiles sadly, nodding his head good-naturedly.

"It reminds me of him," he murmurs, wrapping an arm over my shoulder.

We stand like this for a long moment, neither of us having the words to say but just enjoying the silence of the dark as old memories are conjured up in each of our minds.

The exhaustion of the past two days has finally hit me when I hear a faint voice call out.

"Nurse?" a faint voice calls from somewhere to my left.

Pulling from Ezra's grasp, I glance over my shoulder, my keen eyes catching sight of a pale hand motioning for me.

It's Bakker.

I cross the room and step swiftly to him, bending down by his side with Ezra following me.

"Yes, I am here," I whisper with a soft smile on my face.

"What is it, Bakker?" Ezra whispers softly to the man, bending gently over him.

The soldier is pale and ghostly in appearance, his lips parted as he gasps for breath, his chest rising and falling rapidly, though only shallow breaths are produced.

Bakker gazes up at Ezra, his eyes glassy as he acknowledges him.

"Commander," he breathes softly.

I press my fingertips to the inside of his wrist, counting mentally as I gaze at the watch on my own wrist.

I frown, counting far too few beats of his heart.

"How do I look, Miss?" he asks, his voice raspy as a small smile creeps across his face, though I know that it is forced.

My heart sinks to the depths of my stomach as I am faced with the truth.

He is dying. He isn't long for this world, I know in my heart.

The truth of it is written in his face.

I glance up at Ezra. His dark eyes shine in the dim darkness around us, sad and knowing.

He shakes his head sadly, his lips beginning to move in a silent whisper.

I plaster a smile to my face as I turn to face Lucas Bakker, patting his hand gently in a consoling manner.

"You look just fine, Lucas," I say, busying myself with re-positioning his pillow and adjusting the bandages wrapped around his amputated leg.

I learned a long time ago to never let your fear show in the face of those you care for. Even if you do not know them.

It's just like Cor told me when I first arrived in Antwerp.

Fearful soldiers spread fear and discouragement to those they protect, Ezra's voice says in my mind from a memory from nearly two years ago.

"You do not have to lie, Miss," the soldier says, his blue eyes knowing and soft. "I know I am going home. It won't be long now."

Home.

He smiles softly up at me, and this time, I know that it is real.

Chills race up my arm, and I find myself returning his smile.

Even in the face of death, he is not afraid.

Because he knows where he is bound.

I nod, tears welling in my eyes.

"No, it won't," I say gently as Ezra and I share a glance. "We will stay right here with you."

He smiles plaintively.

"Thank you."

Ezra smiles solemnly, his hand resting firmly upon Bakker's shoulder.

I nod and busy myself with silently adjusting his bandages and the blanket that covers his trembling body in a desperate attempt to ensure he is comfortable, beginning to absently hum a tune as the darkness lightens rapidly and the sun begins to rise and drift in through the curtains over the windows.

"My mother used to sing that song to me," the soldier murmurs.

I glance up.

"I'm sorry?"

His face is wistful, and for a moment I am afraid he has already gone when he turns to look at me.

"That song you were just humming. It brings me back to my childhood," he says, his eyes brightening. "Would you mind singing the first or second verse for me, Nurse?"

I open my mouth and then shut it, surprised by his strange and sentimental request.

I steal a glance at Ezra, who smiles softly at me.

You can do it, his gaze seems to say.

Sing, child, the inner voice bids me.

Slowly, I nod my head.

"Certainly."

And clearing my throat, I begin to sing the words to the song I have loved so long, the same song that has carried me through so much hardship in the past three years.

> *"When peace like a river, attendeth my way,*
> *When sorrows like sea billows roll;*
> *Whatever my lot, Thou hast taught me to say,*

It is well, it is well, with my soul.

I pause for breath before entering the chorus, and a rush of warmth rushes through me as Ezra's baritone voice joins my own, his voice raw and crisp while mine is soft and thick and our voices collide to perform the beautiful verse that he had played on the piano on the young Christmas morning when he first kissed me.

It is well,
With my soul,
It is well, it is well, with my soul.

Though Satan should buffet, though trials should come,
Let this blest assurance control,
That Christ hath regarded my helpless estate,
And hath shed His own blood for my soul."

Our voices fade softly as dawn arrives, the fragile refrain echoing across the room and greeting each and every soldier in the room as they wake, and their comrade is called home.

Several moments go by as the melody still rings in my ears and the morning dawns fresh and new.

I slip a gentle hand on the inside of his wrist, nodding gently as I find no pulse in his veins.

"He is gone," I whisper softly, swallowing.

Ezra brushes the moisture from his eyes as he gazes at me.

"In His hand is the life of every creature and the breath of all mankind," he murmurs, the familiar words bringing me back to the friendly pages of the book of Job. "Farewell, Lucas Bakker."

I nod silently as I drape the woolen blanket gingerly over Lucas Bakker's peaceful face in respect for the fallen man.

Ezra wraps his arms around me as I bury my face into his neck, the words to the beloved hymn still ringing in our hearts.

And somehow, in the very depths of my broken heart, I can feel that the stranger I had just sung back home had offered a bit of healing to my heart.

I still do not know why Andrew was taken from me, nor do I understand why this man was called home, or why I still fight with the memories of my past each night.

But I am reminded that whatever my lot, God has taught me to say,

"It is well, it is well, with my soul."

CHAPTER TWENTY-THREE

Air raids screech.

Children murmur in alarm.

Swift footsteps echo down the halls.

These are the sounds that I hear around me.

I stride briskly through the dark, feeling my way almost blindly through the dining hall as I search for the door leading to the stairwell to the children's ward.

The school is dark, the thick drapes, sheets, and cloth that covered the windows during the night still hang even in the late morning as nurses and Resistance members alike rush to and fro in a hurried and desperate attempt to shield the wounded inhabitants of the school from incoming bombs.

"Hurry now, hurry!" I hear a female voice call somewhere behind me.

"Get everyone in the center of the building, away from the windows!" another voice calls.

"Ruth!"

I glance behind me, finding only darkness.

The blackout surrounds me, threatening my mind with memories of the dark cells of Avenue Louise and the Dossin Barracks; my breathing is constricted as I struggle to force the flashbacks away.

"Papa?"

"Where are you, *Dochter?*" he asks, his voice low and urgent.

"I am over here," I say.

I can hear swift footsteps echoing on the carpeted floor as he follows the sound of my voice, and a moment later, I can faintly see his pale face.

"Quickly, Ruth; go downstairs. It will be safer down there," he says, his hand ushering me along the dark hall.

"Where is Ezra?" I ask, my voice fragile and desperate.

I can hear him swallow.

The air raids grow louder, ringing violently in our ears.

"I don't know," he says as the siren's wail grows softer, his voice gentle, adding urgently, "Go down *now*."

My hand brushes against the cool metal of a door knob, and I push the door open and gingerly step down the stairwell, the hurried rasps of my own breathing echoing against the stone walls around me.

I stumble down the first few stairs, my feet stiff and uncertain as my heart hammers in my chest.

The bombs are coming! my mind screams at me.

I reach out to steady myself by placing my hands on the cold stone walls on either side of me, gooseflesh running down my limbs at the rough and cold sensation that runs up my fingertips.

Carefully, I feel my way down the stairs and am nearly to the bottom when the floor begins trembling so violently I fear the whole school may collapse upon us; a deafening screech reckons through the morning as the trembling only grows worse, and my foot slips.

I fall down the remaining stairs, landing with a hard jolt on my hands and knees at the bottom.

I can feel the impact of the bomb as it collides with the city somewhere outside the school as I lie upon my stomach on the floor; the school's very foundation moans and rocks with the blunt force, dirt and dust falling from the ceiling above me.

"Lord, please carry us through this. I fear these bombs," I pray softly, my voice a mere whisper so that the bombs overcome my words as my face is pressed against the cold floor. "Do not let this darkness overcome us."

Do not fear, the voice whispers in the darkness, ***those who can kill the body but cannot kill the soul.***

Andrew.

The agonizing rush of sound fades as the bomb's destination is met, and everything succumbs to an eerie and frightening silence.

I breathe heavily, my heart pounding so terribly my chest begins to ache. The dust slips down my throat as I breathe, rousing the familiar rattle in my lungs.

I push myself from the floor, coughs sputtering from my lips as I press my palm to my right temple, where I can feel the numb pain of the gash that I must have received when I fell.

"Ruth!" comes Papa's voice, echoing strangely, "are you alright?"

"Yes, I'm fine; are you?"

I can hear the hard rasp of his breath.

"Quite," he breathes.

I stand unsteadily to my feet, laying my hands on the wall for support. I can hear Papa's shuffling footsteps as he gingerly follows me down the stairs.

"Ruth, you're bleeding," Papa says, his keen eyes catching sight of the wound on my head even in the pitch-black stairwell.

I press my palm to the wound, grimacing.

"I'll be alright, Papa," I say softly.

He sighs in a breathy way, and I can hear the faint turning and grinding of the door knob as Papa opens the door to the children's ward, a sliver of light greeting us.

I step hesitantly over the threshold, almost afraid of what I will find inside.

The room is dark just as every last one before it, though light filters in through the shattered window as it lands upon the dozens of huddled individuals that huddle along the opposite wall.

"Nathaniel! Ruth! Oh, thank goodness!" Eline exclaims, her head of blonde curls visible as she separates herself from the group of mangled children that have clung to her for comfort and support.

She rushes across the disheveled room, stepping over toppled chairs and abandoned toys as she embraces me, nearly knocking the air from my lungs as I struggle to breathe through the veil of dust and smoke that enters in through the window.

"Are the children alright?" I ask her, my voice muffled in her shoulder.

She nods.

"Yes; shaken and frightened, but alright otherwise. Are you two alright?" she asks, pulling away and looking us both over.

"As well as we can be, Eline," Papa says to her, gazing at the others in the corner and swiftly beginning to assess them. "Is everyone here?"

I follow his gaze, mentally counting the several dozen children under our care, along with Fletcher and Mrs. Kipling, Hiedi's mother.

My heart hammers and my head throbs.

I meet Fletcher's gaze, his face long and worn as his brown eyes shine in the darkness.

"Where is Ezra?" I repeat my question from before.

He shakes his head, holding my gaze steady.

"He and his men left earlier this morning on a rescue mission near the Cathedral." he says, his voice soft and carrying a note of fragility that I have heard from him before. "They were evacuating the streets."

My mouth dries.

I shake my head, and Eline pulls me to her side.

"No," I say, my voice merely more than a whisper.

"Quiet, Ruth," Eline says to me, her grip on me tightening. "Everything is going to be alright."

But neither of us truly believe her words.

I bite my lip.

Oh, Father, do not let it be so, I pray silently.

We stand gazing at one another in fearful silence as the hollow quietness of the world outside and billowing smoke encompass us and the calm after the storm gives way to the utter devastation the bomb left us in.

The upstairs door is jerked open, its hinges squeaking loudly.

"Is everyone alright down there?"

I jump at the sudden voice.

The voice is familiar, but it is not Ezra's.

Fletcher steps back out into the hall and to the stairwell where Papa and I had just come from, gazing up at whomever owns the voice.

"Yes, I believe we are all well enough; is that you, Boris? How are things up there?" he calls.

"Yes, Fletcher, it's me. It is pure fire and brimstone. The city has been pelted with V1 bombs and the V2 rockets; the boys are already setting out to assess the damage," Boris calls back.

I shake my head sadly.

Papa gazes at me with a soft burning look in his eyes; the same look I saw many times when he was saddened by the state of his patients that could not be helped. He steps over the threshold and joins Fletcher in the hall.

"Has anyone been injured?" Papa calls up to Boris.

"The school has suffered serious damage, but I do not believe anyone inside it has been seriously injured. Though I fear what the streets look like, and what we have lost to the fires this time; we will need you on hand, Mr. DeVos."

Papa nods, glancing over his shoulder at me.

"Of course," he says, his voice strained as he reaches for his bag where he had dropped it moments ago. "I am coming right now."

I step forward after him.

"I am coming too," I say voluntarily, my voice low.

Eline squeezes my hand gently as I leave her with the children, and we both begin to take action.

I take a shaky breath and step over the rubble between myself and the doorway, where I join Papa and Fletcher at the foot of the stairwell I had just fallen down.

"Do not fear those who can kill the body, but cannot kill the soul," I murmur softly, and the bravery that I had known to be my brother's courses through my veins.

And with heavy hearts and prayers on our lips, we begin the descent up the stairs to behold what damage awaits us.

~ ~
.

"Bombs rain, a thunderous sound
Shouts arise where fears abound
Yet in despair, courage found
Amidst the turmoil, hope is crowned."

R.M.D.

CHAPTER TWENTY-FOUR

EZRA

Streets of Antwerp

zra works swiftly as he searches through residences for any lingering inhabitants, every moment that passes carrying him and his men closer to the brink of the bombs as the air raids scream through the city.

They could fall at any moment.

A moment is all it takes.

"Pik!"

Ezra glances over his shoulder, his heart beginning to pound as he catches sight of Lars lunging through the rubble of the streets toward him.

He jumps into action immediately.

"Lars, what is it?"

Nazis?

Bombs?

Lars shakes his head, his eyes wide with a desperate terror.

"It's Faibber," he says, breathlessly. "He has found a man in the streets—a fellow Resistance member. He is about to kill him, Ezra. He wouldn't listen to me, perhaps he will listen to you."

Ezra mutters something under his breath,

"We must hurry; the bombs may fall soon," Ezra says. "Take me to him."

And so the two men rush to the streets recklessly, and down a long alleyway somewhere near the Cathedral of our Lady beside the river Scheldt.

It is there that they find Faibber, unauthorized and alone, staring down the barrel of his rifle that is pointed directly at a heaving figure lying on the street floor, blood smeared across the man's cheek.

Beneath the dirt and blood across his pale features, cold blue eyes gaze piercingly back at Ezra.

His heart jolts.

It can't be, he thinks to himself.

Love your enemies.

"Faibber, stop it," Ezra orders, his baritone voice thick and authoritative as he calls over the screeching air raids that still shatter through the morning air.

Ezra steps closer to Faibber, and the man on the ground watches him intently, his cold eyes following Ezra's every move.

"Faibber. Listen to me." he says to the young man, "Put the gun down. He is not worth it, I promise you."

Faibber steals a glance at Ezra.

"But he is a German," he states, as if this is reason enough to justify his acts. "He is no fellow soldier of mine."

"I don't care if he is German, Polish, Dutch, Russian, or Japanese. Faibber, give me the gun."

He shakes his head.

Ezra lays a hand on the rifle's barrel just as Faibber pulls the trigger. Ezra lifts the gun just in time, and the bullet is sent ricocheting through the many rooftops and chimneys of Antwerp—missing the desired destination entirely.

Faibber breathes softly, his shoulders slumping as the weight of the sin he has wished to commit falls bare upon his young back.

Ezra pulls the rifle from his trembling hands, emptying it of the empty brass shell and slinging it over his own shoulder.

"Report back to the Port, Faibber," he commands him, gazing into the young and fearful brown eyes of the younger man. "I will have a discussion with you later. I hope you understand what danger you have placed us all in at this moment."

Faibber nods meekly, speechless.

Ezra turns to Lars.

"Lars, accompany him and inform Commander van Branteghem of this incident. You must be swift and get both yourself and Faibber to safety before the bombs arrive. I will follow you shortly, after I speak with Faibber's friend over here."

Ezra nods his chin toward the stunned and silent victim.

Lars meets his gaze, his eyes burning with respect and camaraderie as he nods, laying a firm hand on Faibber's shoulder.

"Yes, Commander Pik," he says with a slight and grave smile, and Ezra knows that there is no amount of teasing in his voice.

Lars leads Faibber away like a shunned child, leaving Ezra alone with the stranger on the ground.

Ezra's heart pounds in his ears as he gazes down at the thin man, his pale skin and stark white hair obviously not belonging to the beige jumpsuit that he wears.

Ezra knows that he does not belong to the Secret Army. And he knows that Faibber had been right about one thing; the man *is* German.

His leg has been wounded, a deep gash visible through the blood soaking into the right pant's leg of his jumpsuit.

The German stares back at Ezra, the icy blue eyes still harboring the same passionate and cold glare they did when Ezra last gazed in them over two years ago.

Hugo.

But as he steps closer, he can see a hunger in his gaze that wasn't present before; a softer, aged look that he has often seen in his own reflection.

Hugo has not had an easy past either, Ezra can tell.

Whatever he has faced has changed him; but what he *did* has changed them all, not just him.

Broers? Hugo's voice echoes through his mind.

Broers, Ezra had answered, truthfully and sincerely.

Ezra had trusted Hugo.

A broken growl crawls up his throat, but he forces it back down.

The familiar hot rush of anger for Hugo rises in his chest, built upon the foundation of fierce protectiveness for his family and enlarged by two years of pent-up anger.

Ezra wants to scream at him, beat him until he's purple and tell him just how much grief and pain he has caused him and the Still Waters clan.

He wants to tell him just what he took away from him when he took Ruth away, and the way it felt to find Still Waters utterly deserted and empty; he wants Hugo to know *that* kind of hollow pain.

He wants him to know what he took from him the day he betrayed the clan, his own family; and he wants Hugo to know how much it cost to get them back home again.

And he wants to let him know how much his cowardice had damaged them all, and how they are still carrying the weight of the consequences even today.

But he doesn't do any of this.

Instead, he bends down and extends his large, tanned and calloused hand out to Hugo.

He is mine now, Ezra. He has changed, the still small voice whispers to his heart. **Seventy times seven, my son. Remember this.**

I know, Father. Give me the strength to obey, his heart whispers.

Hugo glances doubtfully at him, searching his face.

"Ezra?" he whispers, his voice faint, though the chilling tones of German leak into his Dutch-speaking voice.

Ezra nods, grimacing as his voice hits him like a knife in his heart.

This man is a traitor, a coward! he thinks to himself.

"Yes. It's me," he says through clenched teeth.

Hugo swallows, his thin cheeks taunt and ghostly white.

"Why did you do that?" he asks.

"Do what?"

Hugo's eyes cloud.

"Stop that boy from shooting me; I certainly wouldn't have blamed you had you let him or even done it yourself," Hugo says with a broken laugh.

Ezra shakes his head softly.

"I don't want your blood on my hands, Hugo. And I didn't want it on Faibber's either," he says, his voice growing urgent. "We must go now; the bombs are coming."

Hugo nods, his gaze softening as he understands.

Slowly, he takes Ezra's extended hand and Ezra helps him to his feet, grimacing as his wounded leg straightens.

He stands in front of Ezra, not knowing what to do as they both stare at each other with blazing eyes, deep brown into cold blue.

Once they had been innocent boys who shook hands as brothers.

Now they stand on opposite ends of the war, facing one another for the first time as damaged men the war had formed into soldiers.

"It's been a while, Ezra," Hugo murmurs thickly, wiping the blood from his cheek with the back of his hand.

Ezra nods, his voice like steel as he speaks.

"It certainly has, Hugo."

But his voice is drowned out by the shattering caterwauls of a bomb as it falls through the morning air, ripping through the city in a blazing trail of damage and destruction as the ground beneath their feet begins to tremble from the force of the bomb.

"Go!" Ezra screams, but Hugo cannot; the wound Faibber had given him leaves him nearly lame.

Love your enemies, the voice repeats softly, whispering to his hammering heart above the deafening sound shattering his ear drums, **And do not be afraid of those who can kill the body, but cannot kill the soul.**

Without thinking, without even knowing a bit of what he is doing, Ezra listens to the voice.

And as the bomb collides with the old charismatic buildings and cobblestone streets, Ezra lunges toward Hugo, and shields his foe with himself, protecting Hugo from the rising smoke and flames as the blunt force of the bomb knocks Ezra to the ground and his body collides with the snow beneath and the fire above.

And the world around him fades into darkness.

A moment is all it takes. A moment too soon, and you'll make a mistake. A moment too late, and you have to pay the consequences...

CHAPTER TWENTY-FIVE

*N*o, not again.

I cannot do this again.

I cannot face losing someone else.

Not Ezra.

Ezra is pale, his eyes closed as his face is cloaked in a veil of shadows, abrasions, and burns as his lips are pulled into a thin grimace.

The four of us work in grave silence, praying for the moment when he wakes up.

We have taken up residence in classroom number five, chairs and desks stacked up in the corners of the room where opposite from it the teacher's desk has been pushed back along the wall beneath the large black chalkboard.

Eline and I stand together at the head of the cot that Ezra is lying upon, watching quietly as Papa dresses the various wounds along Ezra's body, Fletcher obediently assisting him.

From where I wait, I can clearly see the burns that are crawling up his left leg, where Fletcher had skillfully cut the leg of his beige jumpsuit off, and Papa has peeled the brown cloth from the burns beneath with the trained gentleness of a veteran physician.

The burns are red and angry, and in a few places, dangerously white.

Third-degree burns.

Nerve damage.

Slight concussion.

This, I know, is only a part of the diagnosis.

I grimace, my fingers trembling as I bend over him to wipe his face with a damp cloth, wiping the dirt and ash gently away from the small burns from the fire and the tiny cuts along the left side of his face from the flying debris that had been unearthed by the bomb.

The scar beneath his left eye still tells the story of how he had fought the German last June, and the scars on his left shoulder and upon his knuckles are the remaining vestige of the ambush in April 1943.

I absently reach a hand over my neck, where the scar still remains from the Nazi's lashing.

We all have scars, I think to myself, *some seen, and some unseen. But all are deep and prove what God has brought us through.*

I step closer to his side silently, slipping my trembling fingers into his large hand, feeling the comforting and steady beating of his heart beneath my fingertips as I press them to his wrist.

I push a shaky breath through my lips.

Ezra's eyes flicker open at the sound, the brown depths of his irises brightening as he sees me.

I smile softly, relief flooding my soul.

"Thank you, Lord," I breathe, my voice soft and fragile as the prayer of gratitude falls from my lips, smiling at Ezra. "I thought you were leaving me."

A groan issues from his throat as he is greeted with the pain of his wounds and the vague memories of what has happened.

"Now you ought to know better than that, love," he says as he attempts a small smile, but grimaces as Papa wraps his burnt legs gingerly in a damp cloth.

A small growl escapes his lips as Papa works first with his right leg, and Ezra tries to pull away, and it is up to Eline and I to hold him still.

I grip his forearm, holding him gently down on the cot he is lying on as Eline does the same across from me.

"You must hold still, and it won't hurt so bad," Eline murmurs in her gentle way as she glances worriedly at me.

Papa smiles at Ezra, an odd sight really, in the midst of such a dark and tender setting.

"Pain. That's good, Ezra. Real good," Papa says, his gaze softening. "It proves to me that not all has been lost; there is some feeling left."

He finishes treating the wounds with a flourish as Ezra grits his teeth through the pain, and Eline and I struggle to keep him still.

I observe Papa's movements intently, watching closely as he treats first the right leg, and then the left.

I notice that Ezra doesn't even flinch as Papa touches the white portion of the burn on his left leg; he doesn't complain, groan, or even grimace.

Papa and I share a glance, my heart sinking with the truth.

Nerve damage.

Loss of feeling.

I swallow, giving Papa a look of questioning.

He simply shakes his head.

"Now you had a pretty hard fall, Ezra, and your head took a good beating; do you remember anything that happened before the bomb struck?" Papa asks, obviously avoiding any alarm with our silent discovery.

Ezra swallows as his chest rises and falls in a rapid motion, his brown eyes darkening as the shadows of his memories dance across his irises, his grip tightening around my hand.

"Lars was there before it happened, and Faibber," he says tentatively, closing his eyes against the current of memories.

Fletcher nods.

"Yes, Lars is the one who found you, Ezra," he says softly.

"Faibber had been unauthorized, and Lars and I found him in the streets near the Cathedral. He was raging mad when we got to him, and had his gun raised at a... at a—"

Suddenly, Ezra opens his eyes with a jolt, attempting to sit up.

I lay a hand on his shoulder, gently forcing him to lay back down.

"It's alright, Ezra. Lie back down," I say softly, sitting lightly on the edge of the cot at his side, our hands still intertwined as I try in vain to calm him. "What was Faibber aiming at?"

Again, Ezra swallows, a breath falling from his lips as his chest heaves.

Our eyes meet, deep brown into hazel, and the familiar course of warmth spreads through my veins.

His eyes are filled with equal parts of pain, anger, and longing, the shadows that dance in them telling me of what he has seen.

"Hugo," he whispers.

My heart stills for a fleeting moment, the name of the traitor sending a stunned silence across the room as a familiar wave of pain and grief washes over my chest.

Eline's eyes widen at the familiar name, and she presses her palm to her mouth in shocked silence.

"What?" I ask gently, searching Ezra's worn face for any hint of truth in his eyes. "Please don't tell me that Hugo did this to you."

Hugo.

Ezra shakes his head as he holds my gaze steadily, the familiar calm and tranquil look building in them as he remembers more clearly what has happened.

"No, love. He didn't. Not really," he whispers softly. "Faibber was going to kill Hugo."

Fletcher gaps at him, confusion and anger written upon his face as the name serves as a reminder of all that we went through because of Hugo's cowardice when he betrayed us.

"And you stopped him," Eline breathes, though it is not a question. She looks at me, laying a gentle hand on my shoulder as I sit trembling.

Ezra nods, confirming the accuracy of Eline's words to the stunned silence of us all in the room.

Silent rage flickers in Fletcher's eyes.

"Why?" he asks, exasperation and confusion in his voice.

"Faibber was about to shoot him when I lifted the rifle from his hands and the bullet missed Hugo; Faibber had beat him something awful, and his leg was badly wounded to the point that he was lame." Ezra shakes his head, his eyes flitting across each face in the room.

Eline, Fletcher, and I share a three-way glance, the memories and darkness of our past resurfacing in each of our eyes as we are reminded of Hugo.

Papa meets my gaze, his eyes knowing as they flash with protective anger.

He has heard plenty of Hugo; he knows well what he did to us.

He purses his lips and remains silent as he continues examining the small abrasions along Ezra's opposite forearm.

I swallow.

I am silent as I gaze steadily back at Ezra, the inner war of anger raging in my chest as I recall everything that Hugo has done to us; I never trusted him, and the feelings were mutual.

But the others had.

Mr. and Mrs. Shepherd welcomed him into their home and loved him as their own son as they offered him the refuge that he had been seeking for so long.

But, he had squandered their kindness when he betrayed us all ruthlessly, mercilessly tying us up and leading us out on the streets to load us up on trucks like sheep being sent to the slaughter.

Tears sting my eyes, burning in the back of my throat as Ezra searches my eyes.

"I don't understand, Ezra," I murmur, shaking my head as I stand abruptly, anger boiling in my veins. "That man is a traitor, you know that. He was never our *broer*. He betrayed us and led us to the Germans to die."

I am shaking, memories ripping through my mind as Eline wraps her arm around me.

Fletcher sighs heavily.

"I am with Ruth on this, Ezra," he says, his hands clenched into tight fists at his side as he paces at the foot of Ezra's cot, frowning. He glances swiftly to Eline. "Hugo handed us mercilessly over to the Germans, as if we were nothing but mere trash to be discarded and rid of."

We can all hear the anger in his voice.

"Ezra, I love you like my own brother, and it pains me to see you like this," he continues as he stops abruptly to gaze ruefully at Ezra, his voice pained and oddly thick. "Especially because of a man like Hugo. He isn't worth it. Not *this*. Not your life."

Tears fall down my cheeks and threaten to choke me as the truth of Fletcher's words collide with my heart, ripping through me just as they had the day I heard that Andrew was dead.

Eline pulls me to her chest, knowing by the stricken look on my face what I am thinking.

Ezra could have easily lost his life defending Hugo today, and the wounds along his body and the memories in his eyes tell me that he has lost something today, but not his life.

He has lost the feeling in his left leg, though he has not expressed it openly.

I can tell by the way he is gazing down at it now that he doesn't feel the pain from the burns that he should.

We gaze in solemn silence at the burns that line his body, covered in damp clothes to bring the temperature down and prevent infection from settling into the open pink flesh.

"I know, Fletcher," Ezra says softly, his voice stiff as he grimaces from the burns on his legs and Papa rushes to adjust the cloth over his torso.

My heart jolts.

He is in pain.

"I know that you are all angry with me for this," he begins again, giving Papa a grateful glance. "It was reckless and stupid; and I am fully aware that Hugo did not deserve it."

He looks around at us, his eyes landing on me where I stand with Eline.

I know you are angry. But listen to me, love, his gaze seems to plead.

I nod gently.

I am angry, I am confused, and I am grieved.

I am all these things and more.

But I *am* listening.

"So why did you do it?" Fletcher asks, breaking the moment between Ezra and me.

He continues to pace across the room, to and fro at the foot of the cot, thinking.

"Abram, dear," Eline says, laying a firm, but dainty, hand on her husband's shoulder.

Fletcher stills at her touch, leaning closer to her and murmuring a hurried word in her ear that the rest of us cannot hear. His face is wistful as he stares down at Eline, pain obvious in his eyes.

Ezra glances down at the scars along his arms, absently picking at the threads of the cloths covering his body. He pushes a soft breath through his lips, the steady heaving of his chest falling into a rhythmic motion as he begins to speak.

"There was something about him that was different; somehow, he has changed. Not much, but a little. There was pain in his eyes and weight on his shoulders that told me as much," he says softly, "and I couldn't bring myself to beat him or leave him lying there, despite how much I wanted to. And I could tell by the fearful and guilty look in his eyes that that was just what he had expected me to do. But I couldn't."

He glances up to ensure we are all listening.

"So I went to help him. I offered him my hand, and I helped him to his weary feet. I held my tongue for fear of what I might say, and so neither of us spoke much. We stood in a tense silence for a moment before the air raids began, and I knew we had to go, else we would be too late, and the bombs fall on us." He pauses for a moment to catch his breath.

"But Hugo couldn't run; he could barely even walk. There was no way for him to escape the bombs in time, not in his condition. So I just took action and did the one thing I thought to do; I threw myself at Hugo in a desperate attempt to shield him. The last thing I remember clearly is the screech of the explosion and the heat of the flames, and the taste of smoke on my lips as I fell to the snow."

The room is quiet.

His words raise gooseflesh across my skin as I understand what he has done, and tears sting my eyes once more.

Despite everything that Hugo has done, all the grief and pain that we have dealt with and endured because of him, Ezra still chose to risk everything in order to save him.

Not because Hugo deserved such an act of sacrifice, and not because we owe him that sort of love and forgiveness, but because Ezra knew and believed in his heart that was what he needed to do.

"You tried to save him, despite what he truly deserved," Eline says beside me, understanding in her voice as she breaks the silence in the room.

He nods, smiling softly up at us.

"I guess so," he says, his voice thin and weary.

He is tired, the exhaustion of the bombs toil on his body and the emotional and mental accounts of what happened to him draining him of his strength.

He reaches for my hand.

I take it, feeling the strange coolness of his skin as our fingers intertwine and love courses through my veins. We share a soft smile, knowing that whatever happens, we will face these shadowlands together.

"I am sorry, Ruth," he whispers. "I know this hurts you."

I shake my head softly.

"Hugo hurt everyone, Ezra," I say, "Not just me."

He nods, his gaze soft.

"Are you mad?"

"Yes, but not at you, Ezra," I say truthfully, brushing the tears from my cheeks. "I am proud of you. I know that I could never have forgiven Hugo enough to do what you just have."

He smiles, though his eyes cloud with pain.

Many waters cannot quench love, my heart whispers silently.

Neither of us say anything more.

Fletcher sighs.

"What do you say, Fletcher?" Ezra asks softly.

Fletcher is bent over the foot of the cot, his gaze meeting Ezra's and a solemn look of respect and admiration passes between the two of them as Fletcher begins to speak.

"The true heart of a man is proven in the heat of battle, when he can either save his own skin, or that of his comrade. And perhaps the most courageous act a man can do, is to return to the battlefield to save the wounded," he whispers wistfully. He smiles brokenly down at Ezra. "But when the wounded is your own enemy and you *still* choose to save him, well that's a sacrifice few are willing to make. It isn't pretty, and it isn't for valor. It's simply a choice."

The room is silent.

No one speaks.

The four of us gaze at Fletcher in silence, his words falling on our ears and soaking into our skin like light spreading over a darkened alley as they enter the deep cavities of our hearts. Words that reach our hearts and touch our wounds the most are not shouted but whispered.

It's simply a choice, his words ring through my ears.

Ezra smiles softly at Fletcher, his grasp tightening around my hand.

Eline and I share a glance, a look of knowing and pride passing between as our eyes grow glassy from tears.

Papa smiles softly from where he stands gazing at us younger people, his eyes shining.

"Well said, Fletcher," Papa murmurs.

Silence grows into a shallow void when a knock comes from the door.

We all jolt awake as if from a dream as Papa rushes to the door, finding Lars Gilbert on the other side.

"How is he?" Lars asks, glancing over Papa's shoulder at the lot of us in the room.

"Breathing." Papa smiles wryly, stepping aside to let him in. "He is awake and alert, but terribly burnt."

Lars glances over his shoulder at something in the hall before he steps through the door swiftly, his blond head nearly touching the ceiling as his heavy footfalls echo loudly around the small classroom that we have transformed into a hospital room, his gaze nervous as he glances at us each.

"Hello, Lars." I smile softly, my voice still thick from tears as I step away to let him bend at Ezra's side.

He nods graciously, slipping his hat from his head, his eyes scanning my face almost nervously.

"Hello, Miss DeVos," he says in greeting, smiling good-naturedly at Ezra. "I hope *Commander* hasn't frightened you too much with his courageous act today."

Ezra laughs softly from his cot.

A small smile pulls at my lips, and I shake my head in a teasing manner at the two men.

"Not at all," I tease with a soft glance over my shoulder at Ezra.

Lars bends to Ezra's side, and the two clasp hands.

"How are you, my friend?" Ezra asks him, his voice growing softer as the effort of it all tires him.

"I was alright until you were struck by that bomb. I thought for certain that you were gone when I found you, Ezra." He shakes his head. "What were you thinking, throwing yourself at that man like you did?"

Ezra shakes his head, closing his eyes as weariness washes over him.

"I wasn't thinking; I was just acting," he says simply.

Lars shakes his head, breathing heavily.

"Where did the bomb hit exactly?" Ezra asks softly, his voice tentative.

Lars sighs.

"The destruction is so bad and what is left is in so much ruins that it is hard to tell exactly where the bomb made landfall, but we believe somewhere between the Cathedral of our Lady, and the *Zoo Antwerpen*," he says.

Fletcher straightens at his words, his face paling.

"You mean near Still Waters," he says, his voice flat.

Lars nods.

I notice the pained and soft look on his face, telling us all the truth that we already know.

Still Waters is gone.

Our beloved refuge where God had led us all together during the darkest hour of this war, where so many fond memories were made, and where we spent that last Christmas together before the war finally wrapped its cruel tendrils around us, is *gone.*

My heart drops as we gaze at one another in silence.

Memories or our time spent at Still Waters dances through each of our minds, flashing wistfully in our eyes.

"What will Mr. and Mrs. Shepherd do?" Eline asks softly, concern written across her face.

Ezra sighs heavily, his eyes sad.

"That is what I was afraid of," he whispers, running a tired hand over his face.

Lars nods.

"I am sorry, I know how much that place meant to you all," he says apologetically, turning back to gaze at his fallen comrade. "Don't worry yourself about it right now, Ezra; you cannot change it, I am afraid."

Ezra nods ruefully, whispering something I cannot quite hear.

We stand for a moment longer in silence, mourning over Still Waters Inn as if for a fallen friend, because it had been one for all of us for a time.

A friend and a refuge.

I step to where Papa stands at the door, absently listening to the conversation between Ezra and Lars as I lean my head tiredly on his arm, trying to forget this news by focusing on Ezra.

"How bad do you think the damage is?" I murmur absently to him, my voice merely more than a whisper.

Papa shakes his head, his gaze resting upon Ezra as he speaks to his friend.

"Physically or emotionally?"

I bit my lip.

"Both, I suppose," I say softly.

"Well, I am afraid of his left leg, Ruth," he says, his voice serious. "I know you saw it. I tried everything to get some sort of reaction from him, but to no avail. It will possibly take grafts and weeks of therapy to properly heal and recover what I fear has been lost. But only time will tell."

I sigh, weariness washing over me like a punch in the gut.

"I wish this all weren't so hard," I say.

Papa smiles softly.

"We were never told it would be easy, *Dochter.* But we were told where to go if the burden ever got too heavy for us to bear," he says.

I smile softly, his words true and clear despite the inner confusion and turmoil of my soul.

The burden that is left to be carried after the badge is heavy, and its price is costly.

But so is our freedom.

"How is Faibber?" Ezra asks Lars, pulling me back to their conversation.

Lars's grimaces, a worried look flickering across his face.

"We both got out of range of the bomb unscathed, but when I went back to look for you, Faibber fled. I don't know what he was running from or where he was headed, but I was more concerned about you at that moment. So I let him go."

Ezra shakes his head, swallowing as he sighs heavily.

"I knew from the moment I met that man that he was troubled, Lars. I should never have kept him in the troop so long, but I felt responsible for him. I still do," he murmurs.

Lars looks sadly down at the floor.

"Well, that man you saved is waiting outside in the hall; he has asked to see you, if you are feeling up to it."

My heart pounds as my spine stiffens.

Hugo is out there? my mind says frantically, before I begin to pray. *Lord, please, I cannot face Hugo. Not today. Far too much has happened, and I am afraid I may break with anything more.*

The room is silent around me, save for a small whisper spoken softly to my heart.

Come to me, my daughter. I know the anger and the burden you carry.

I swallow, tears stinging my eyes.

Yes, Father, my heart says in return.

"He is a strange one, he is. He won't look at me, nor will he speak. He won't give his name, age, or anything. I assume he is in some sort of shock," Lars says, glancing around at the sudden and strange tensity in the room as he mentions Hugo.

He turns back to Ezra.

"He was very insistent that he see you *now*. Shall I tell him to come in?"

The lot of us share a dark look, a look of which Lars knows nothing about as we all share mutual dread over the reunion with the traitor we haven't seen in over two years.

"Yes." Ezra nods with a tentative glance at me. "You may tell him to come."

CHAPTER TWENTY-SIX

HUGO

He doesn't know, Hugo thinks to himself, tapping the wooden crutch against the floor in a rhythmic manner, *else he wouldn't have done this. He would have killed me for certain, had he known the truth.*

He doesn't know all that I have done.

How does he not know?

Hugo had seen plainly the weight upon Ezra's shoulder that had bowed his back and aged his body much more than any physical labor could have done. And the age that he saw in his brown eyes told Hugo that he was somehow different.

But while time had changed them both in various ways, and the war had them on opposite ends of the field, Ezra still possessed the same tranquil demeanor and thoughtful gaze he always had; even when in the midst of a bombardment so fierce as this one.

He is not different, only aged.

But no matter how far his mind travels over the recent events of the day, Hugo's weary mind returns once more to the same question it had before:

How does he not know?

The swift rush and clamor of the various Resistance men, nurses, and wounded civilians rushing around him where he sits on a small bench waiting out in the hall of the school is the only answer to his silent question.

He doesn't observe those around him or study the elegant features of the large and prestigious school. Instead, he only gazes at the floor, and at the long, angry wound along his leg that prevents him from standing and fleeing before Ezra or anyone else can find him again.

He pushes a breath through his lips.

Why would he risk it all to save me?

Because I told him to.

The quaint whisper had once frightened him with its frequent stirrings and murmurings to his heart, but he has long grown used to it.

Why?

Because you were lost and have been found.

Hugo doesn't understand the meaning of the words but knows that they are true; he has been lost for so long now, seeking desperately for something to fill the void in his heart.

He had found it for a brief time while he was with the Shepherd's. But he had denied the truth of their kindness and the hope they offered him, and he instead fled back to the Germans.

Lord, I am a sinner; I do not deserve to be found by you. I do not deserve this kindness. Ezra is a fool for saving me.

I know, Child. But Ezra did not save you. He simply did what I asked him to; and he obeyed. It was I who saved you when you called upon my name.

The little Bible weighs heavily in the breast pocket of his uniform.

"You may come in, but do not be long; he needs to rest," the large Dutchman says, stepping from classroom five, his face pale as he holds the door ajar for Hugo to limp through.

Hugo nods, pushing a shaky breath through his chapped lips as he pushes himself to his feet, grimacing from the pain that racks his body from the wound on his calf.

"Thank you," he mumbles to the Resistance man, avoiding his gaze as he limps up to the door.

The Dutchman nods in return.

"Certainly."

Hugo brushes past him without another word, his breath growing raspy as he steps over the threshold of the darkened room before him, not knowing what waits for him within.

CHAPTER TWENTY-SEVEN

A few painful and awkward moments of silence go by, and Hugo only stands in the doorway, his shoulders squared, and his chin held high like the German soldier he is, though I notice quickly the beige jumpsuit of the Secret Army that covers his pale skin—nearly identical to the one Ezra wears.

I notice, too, the crutch under his arm and the leg that he holds tenderly hovering above the floor, as the pain travels from his leg to his entire body, causing a slight grimace to cross his face.

Wormwood has returned, I think to myself.

He doesn't speak, and neither do we.

He doesn't even acknowledge that Eline, Fletcher, and I are here, alive.

I want to spit in his face.

I want to scream at him and tell him just how I detest and despise him, and how much his cowardice has damaged us all.

Bitterness and grief stirs in my chest, the current so strong that I am forced to look away from Hugo as the emotions and memories rise up my throat and threaten to choke me.

Papa stands protectively beside me, his face grave as he gazes steadily at Hugo, knowing within his heart what this man has done to all of us.

Fletcher's normally smiling eyes now flash angrily as his gaze penetrates through Hugo's cold blue eyes, memories of their last meeting stirring in his mind.

Eline stands near me, her face pale and taut as she avoids Hugo's stare all together. I can feel her wrap her hand gently around my right wrist, and I open my eyes to find Hugo limping steadily to Ezra's cotside.

My throat closes up as he extends a small, bony, white hand out to Ezra.

The same hand that had struck me mercilessly and had given me a bloody lip. The hand that had taken hold of me and dragged me down the street and ordered his men to beat the others while he muttered hateful words to me, and I spat them back; and the hand that had forced me into the back of a cargo truck and carried us all to a place we did not want to go.

The memories come to my mind with such violence and vibrancy that I begin to physically tremble, and the rising notion to vomit stirs in my gut.

Ezra's face is soft and veiled with a look of emotionless steel, though I can plainly see anger and compassion colliding in his brown eyes.

He shakes Hugo's hand.

I'll find him next, Hugo's voice hisses in my ear, the words he had spoken to me concerning Ezra the day he betrayed us.

My heart pounds, and the trembling only increases.

No! my heart cries out.

I gasp for breath, the memories weighing heavily on my chest and nearly suffocating me as I want to run and claw and scream to get away from Hugo.

Without thinking, and without knowing what I am doing, I step forward.

Ezra watches me, his eyes sad and pained.

Slowly, he nods.

He knows that I cannot stand this.

"I am going to go phone Mr. Shepherd," I say, excusing myself as I silently cross the room and slip out the door.

"I will go with you," Eline says behind me, swiftly accompanying me out the door and into the crowded hallway.

I plunge absently into the sea of people around me, some I can recognize as my own patients, while others are newcomers with new wounds and injuries to be tended to.

The hallway is still intact, and so is the foyer, along with the entire entryway of the school; it appears that only the east end has suffered damages from the bombing.

But the people are another story entirely.

Some of them lie barely breathing on cots, blankets, and stretchers, while others hobble aimlessly through the school, badly burned and half delirious; some of them are even calling out to one another, their ears still filled with the incessant ringing and damage of the bomb's explosion that leaves them nearly deaf.

My heart sinks as I look around me at the bombs' destruction.

When will this blasted war ever end?

I shake my head sadly as I stumble through, my heart pounding in my ears and drowning out the incessant echoing chatter of the people as my feet carry me farther down the hall—and away from Hugo.

Eline catches up with me, her heels pumping against the floor as she falls into pace beside me, breathless.

"So, you are just going to ignore the fact that he is back?" she asks, glancing nervously over her shoulder.

I nod, pushing a shaky breath through my lips as I train my gaze ahead of us, staring at the small telephone booth in the foyer.

"That's my intention, yes," I say.

Eline sighs, grabbing my forearm.

I stop walking.

"You cannot keep running from the past," she says, forcing me to look at her.

"I cannot face it today, Eline. I am far too shaken from today's events to be worried further by Hugo and all the unpleasant memories that he brings with him. I must focus on Ezra," I say, shaking my head as tears sting my eyes. "I don't know what I would have done if I had lost him like I did Andrew."

Andrew.

They say that the heart of man is a reflection of the man itself. They say that the heart is formed and built around those it holds dearest, the people to whom we voluntarily lend the largest and deepest portions of our hearts.

And it is when these people are either taken from us or leave us that the heart begins to fracture, for its very foundation is being threatened.

If this is the case, then my reflection is shattered in a million pieces beyond recognition.

With each memory and reminder of my haunted past and Andrew's loss, I feel the fractures in my heart begin to break into a gaping chasm within my chest.

Eline purses her lips, her knowing blue eyes searching my face as we stand arm in arm in the midst of the thronging and crowded hallway.

"I know," she says, her voice soft and thick as we share a look of passing understanding and grief.

She holds my gaze, her grip on my arm tightening as she speaks.

"I know that what Hugo did was terrible, unforgivable even," she says slowly.

I nod gently.

"It was," I murmur softly, the memories rushing through my mind so terribly now that I begin to tremble once again.

The memory of the day comes with a raging and violent vibrancy.

The cold hiss of the wind.

The silence of the snow-blanketed morning.

The growl of an automobile just outside Still Waters.

The rush of sharp, swift footsteps.

The rise of German voices.

The sudden clamor of the door being thrown open and gunshots firing through the floorboards as their footsteps rose up the stairwell and fell on our ears as we turned to each other in dread as the pale faces entered our refuge and their ruthless hands began beating us mercilessly as they seized each and every last one of us...

Gooseflesh runs up my limbs, and I can feel all color drain from my face as I relive the moments of our betrayal, and it is as if it were happening all over again.

I run a shaky hand over my face as I shake my head.

"No, I cannot remember it. I *won't,*" I say, my voice trembling as I speak.

Eline gazes at me, her eyes worried.

But then, all at once, the memories prove too much for my weary and trodden heart, and I succumb to the weight of my memories.

In that moment, it feels as if every pressing weight of all my anger, grief, bitterness, fear, anguish, and sorrow of these past three years collide and fall upon my shoulders, and I buckle beneath the weight.

And I can feel the fracture in my heart split for the final time.

Eline reaches for me, wordlessly wrapping her arms around me and pulling me to her chest as I crumble into her hold, knowing full well what has happened.

"You must face it. I know it hurts, but you cannot keep burying it. The wounds will never heal unless you face this," she murmurs into my hair.

I press my head onto her shoulder, closing my eyes against the memories and rising anger.

"I can't do it, Eline. Hugo nearly killed all of us," I murmur into her shoulder, my heart hammering and my mind reeling from the bewildering events of the day. "I *loathe* him. The very sight of him sends me right back to that day it all happened."

I take a breath.

My body trembles as a broken sob erupts from my mouth, but no tears accompany it.

I am not sad, or sorrowful. I am not really one single emotion or stirring, but rather, a colliding force of them all.

I am *angry.*

"I have been so angry for so long. Angry with Hugo for betraying us, angry that Andrew left me and now he isn't coming back. And now Ezra has nearly been killed by the bombing today and it's all because of Hugo," I say softly, the words falling from my lips and into the open air for the first time. "What is it all for? Why have we been made to endure all of this? I have pleaded with God, but I do not get an answer as to *why.*"

Eline pulls away slightly, looking at me.

"Sometimes we aren't meant to know why, Ruth," she whispers, her blue eyes glassy as she somehow manages to hold me together. "In the middle of our anguish, we are blinded by the pain. And it is often only on the other side of the valley when the pain and anger subsides that we can fully understand and see God's purposes behind it all."

"But why did he lead us here? Why has he called me to such places of darkness?" I ask.

Should we flee from dark places simply because we are afraid of them?

Or should we be a light in them?

The voice whispers to my heart, cutting through the turmoil that surges within me and rising above the clamor of questions and doubts rushing through my mind, the question thundering in my heart with the truth I knew all along.

Eline sighs.

"Sometimes, God calls us to places that frighten us so that we will fully trust *Him,*" she whispers in return, her voice soft and thick as she lifts her eyes above us as she pulls me back into a sisterly embrace.

We stand like this for several long moments, and to the bomb-ridden and destroyed passersby around us, we are only two broken women holding onto to another as we mourn the loss of a loved one to the bombs.

I suppose that in some ways, we are.

When several minutes pass and my lungs are receiving adequate air once again, I pull away.

"I guess we better go call Mr. Shepherd now," I say, my voice shaky as I take a deep breath.

I loop my arm though hers, swallowing the bile in my throat.

"Let me call him, Ruth," she says, her voice stern as her gaze travels worriedly over me. "You do not need to try and explain everything that has happened to him. Not right now."

I shake my head.

"I need to talk to Mr. Shepherd."

She sighs again as we begin walking to the phone booth.

I reach for the glass door of the phone booth as the man holds it open for me to step inside, giving me a concerned look as I pass.

I step over the booth's threshold with trembling legs as the glass door closed behind me.

I grip the black earpiece tightly as I pull it from the wall and swiftly dial Ezra's home telephone number into the rotating disk, turning to gaze at Eline through the glass.

Static comes from the other end of the phone.

For a few painstaking moments, the static echoes in my ear.

Eline watches me worriedly through the glass.

Please, answer.

The static clears.

"Hello?" says a familiar and tentative voice.

Relief floods my soul as pictures and memories of the kind man come to my mind. It's been over three months since I have seen him and Mrs. Shepherd and Maya, and after what has happened today, I long to see them even more.

"Yes, hello? Mr. Shepherd?" I say into the telephone.

"Ruth!" Mr. Shepherd says, his voice relieved and happy. "My dear girl, it's so good to hear your voice. I pray everything is alright in Antwerp?"

My heart sinks as I am reminded of my endeavor—of the reason I am calling him.

What do I say?

I take a breath.

"Well, no. It isn't," I say, my voice pained as I try to think of the best way to speak the truth.

A moment of silence passes.

I can hear Mr. Shepherd's quick breathing from the other end of the line.

"What is it, Ruth?" he asks, his voice serious and harboring a worried and fearful note.

I lean my head against the cool glass of the booth, sighing as I fight the urge to fall apart once again.

"It's Ezra. He's been injured," I hear myself say.

CHAPTER TWENTY-EIGHT

Later that night, after we have all prayed over Ezra and toiled through the remaining hours of the day by aiding those injured and missing while meticulously avoiding Hugo, we gather once again into classroom five.

Eline and Fletcher sleep soundlessly side by side upon a blanket spread across the floor in the corner beneath the chalkboard, their hands intertwined even in sleep.

Hugo sits in an old wooden student's chair in the corner, his head tilted back, and his eyes closed as his leg is propped up in a chair opposite the one he sits on.

I know he isn't asleep.

I can tell by the twitch of his fingers and slits in his eyes as he peers at the night around him.

I sit in a wooden chair facing the only window in the room, where I had pulled the blackout curtains back, and the faint moonlight now shines on the carbon paper in my lap.

The nib on my pen scratches across the paper with every flick and flourish of my wrist, leaving behind it a trail of black ink that is weaving the draft of my newspaper article.

My dear people of Antwerp...

I sigh, grimacing down at the paper.

I cannot write, my weary and worn mind unable to focus on the task tonight.

The room around me is silent, save for Fletcher's faint snoring and Ezra's groans breaking the quietness of the night.

I turn to gaze out the window.

The night sky is dotted with millions of dainty stars that gaze back at me blankly, the same as they had the night before.

For as long as I can remember, I have gazed upon these stars; when I was young, Andrew and I gazed upon them while on the beach at home in Vlissengen, and later Ezra and I had read beneath them on the rooftop of Still Waters.

And it was the night sky and these stars that had gazed down on me in the Dossin Barracks each night that I couldn't sleep and lay awake praying that God would carry us all together again.

I sigh softly, leaning my head back on my chair.

February snow clouds swirl in the sky, soon encompassing and covering the stars, and slowly, the moon as well.

I close my eyes, taking a deep breath as a prayer is whispered silently from my heart, falling on the ears of my Heavenly Father above.

Father, help us through this.

These are the days where our pasts collide with the present, and determines our future. Lord, you are a refuge, for both the free and the oppressed.

Father, by your grace I have gazed in the face of the Germans, Nazi Lieutenants, and officers who persecuted me.

But this is something I do not know how to face.

You called Andrew home with you, and now my dear brother is gone; I still cannot accept it.

Ezra risked his life for the man who betrayed us, and I nearly lost him too.

And now Hugo has returned, reminding me of all things that I have fought so hard this past year to forget.

How do I face this?

The words echo around my mind for a moment as my head begins to nod, and the murky scene of Germans advancing toward me dances across my mind like a motion picture reel, accompanied by the recurrent dreams of Andrew calling out to me.

No. I nearly succumb to the weariness and exhaustion of the day as the desire for rest weighs heavily over me.

I jolt upright, my eyelids flying up as a slight startled breath falls from my lips. I gently brush the sleep from my eyes with the back of my hand.

"Go to sleep, Ruth," a soft voice murmurs as light footsteps tread against the floor behind me, and I sit up swiftly, my heart rate quickening as I glance over my shoulder.

Papa steps away from Ezra's cot, his shoes echoing across the room as he lays a hand on the back of my chair.

"How is he?" I ask, my voice soft and wispy as I gaze behind him at Ezra.

Papa sighs softly, running a hand through the graying beard that falls from his face.

"He hasn't been able to rest; he moans and jerks awake just as sleep comes to him. I have just given him some strong medication that the American troops have given to the Secret Army. It should allow him to sleep through the pain of the burns and any flashbacks that keep waking him." He follows my gaze to Ezra, his gaze lingering on his lame patient for a moment before he turns back to me, his eyes somber.

He glances down at the watch on his wrist, the faint light of the oil lamp resting beside Ezra's cot casting an odd reflection across the watch face.

"Well, I must go do my rounds," he says. "I will be back shortly, Ruth. The medicine should begin to take effect soon and Ezra should sleep until this time tomorrow. Perhaps longer."

I nod, smiling softly.

"What did you give him?"

"The Americans call it *Blue 88.* It is a sodium Amytal tablet that induces sleep," he says, grimacing down at a small bottle he brandishes from his pocket.

I push myself from my chair, tucking the nearly blank paper beneath my arm as I yawn.

"Get some rest, *Dochter,*" he says softly, smiling as he kisses my forehead. "Else I will have to medicate you as well."

I smile.

"I wish it were that easy," I whisper, gazing at him as he crosses the room to the door, where he picks up his bag and slips quietly into the darkened hall.

The door shuts softly behind him, and I am left to my own thoughts as I stand in the dim darkness.

Softly, I sigh.

Silently, I step around my chair and to the window, standing on my tiptoes to reach for the pin that is holding the heavy blackout away from the glass pane.

I gaze down at the disheveled streets that wait in their desolate states, gazing back at me through the glass.

Antwerp had once been beautiful and lively.

Now it is dark and desolate.

"Oh, Antwerp. Where have you gone?" I whisper softly, my breath fogging up the glass. "Where is your *faith?*"

Silence.

I glance down at the failed attempt of a newspaper article, sighing.

A few moments pass, and the only answer to my question is Ezra's soft moans behind me.

I turn swiftly, gooseflesh rising across my arms as I let the curtain fall from my grasp against the glass window pane.

I step lightly across the room and to Ezra's side, gazing down at him as he stirs once more from a restless and shallow sleep.

"Ezra," I whisper softly as I swiftly place another layer of damp cloth over his legs.

Nearly his entire body is covered in the same damp cloths wrapped around his legs and torso, his chest rising and falling gently beneath his white undershirt.

It is only now as I gaze at him that I see the age in his face and how thin he has gotten.

His checks aren't quite so full, with his cheekbones more defined than before, and his shirt fits loosely around his broad Dutch shoulders.

I close my eyes against the current of sorrow and bitterness that wells up in my chest.

Why Ezra?

A small groan escapes his lips as he opens his eyes, his lips drawn once more into a tight grimace as the anguish of the burns reminds him of what has happened.

"Oh, Ruth," he whispers, his eyes adjusting to the vibrancy of the lamp at my side.

"Are you alright?" I murmur gently as I dry my hands on my skirt tail, seating myself gently in the chair by his bedside, where Papa has been watching over him all night.

He nods stiffly.

"I'm fine," he says, though we both know that he isn't. "I hope I didn't wake you, did I?"

I shake my head, helping him as he repositions himself.

"No, you didn't. I never went to sleep. Too much on my mind, I suppose," I say softly, smiling.

He smiles wryly in return as he leans back against the pillow behind his head, gazing at his legs.

"You can't feel it, can you?" I ask softly, my voice gentle.

He stills, our eyes meeting once more as the current of our day washes over us once again, and with it, weariness.

Slowly, he shakes his head.

"No, I can't. Not a thing," he murmurs, sighing as if frustrated. "I knew from the moment I woke up that something wasn't right. It was numb, and for a moment, I thought I had lost my leg entirely in the bombing."

"For a moment, I thought I had lost *you,*" I say softly, though I know that it will only be moments before he is asleep.

He shakes his head softly.

"I know," he says, his eyes darkening as he gazes at me. "Are you alright?"

He motions toward the door, and I know that he is referring to my swift exit earlier.

I smile softly, a gentle blush creeping across my face as I nod.

"I will be," I say.

He nods.

He is silent for a moment, thinking.

I watch as his gaze travels to the corner of the room, where the German lies sleeping.

Ezra clears his throat softly, turning back to face me.

"I was so angry with Hugo, Ruth. I have been for a long time. The wrath and the rage that has stirred in my chest over these past two, nearly three, years is almost frightening, and there were countless times when I committed murder in my heart, wishing to take revenge on him myself." He shakes his head as he holds my gaze steadily. "The day I found out it was him that betrayed you all, I wanted to kill him."

There are notes of passion and anger in his voice, and I know that he has battled the same anger I have for so long—but has never spoken of it.

He has kept it hidden inside after all this time.

He is allowing me to shoulder his burden, I think in silent wonder.

"And when I saw him today for the first time, it all came back to me just as raw and violent as it was two years ago," he says thickly.

I gaze into his blazing brown eyes, taking his hand into mine.

"Why didn't you tell me?" I ask softly.

His gaze softens and his hold on my hand strengthens.

"Because I was ashamed. Because I knew that I could never trust the temptation of the revenge that I craved. Because God tells us to forgive. Seventy-times-seven." His voice is firm, and his words are earnest.

Seventy-times-seven.

Tears sting my eyes as I understand his words.

"And that is why you chose to save him, isn't it?"

He sighs, nodding as his eyes gaze at me with sincerity.

"'How many times will my brother sin against me, and I forgive him?'" he whispers softly, his voice damp and hoarse.

"*Have* you forgiven him?" I ask, my voice soft and tentative.

He swallows softly, shifting gingerly beneath his blankets.

"I am trying, love," he says softly.

I nod gently, a small smile pulling at my lips as I hold his gaze.

"Me too," I say.

We fall into silence for a moment as Ezra's gaze falls back to his numb legs.

He sighs once more, shaking his head.

"I know this isn't fair. I know that he nearly killed you all, and it may seem like I betrayed you by saving him. Not to mention that you and I are pledged to one another, and now I have gone off and made a decision that affects us both and left me like *this*."

"Ezra," I whisper softly, smiling, "I am trying to make sense of all this. But I think I understand why you did it, and it wasn't to hurt me, though I am afraid it does. But you need not worry."

I motion my hand toward our surroundings, from his condition, to the sleeping persons around us and even out to the demolished and darkened streets of Antwerp.

"*This* will not hinder us in the slightest, if God chooses to bring us together." I whisper softly, my voice almost fragile. "I just don't want to lose you."

His hand tightens over mine as his eyes flash gently.

"I have learned that God lets us feel the fragility of human love so that we will fully appreciate the strength of His," he says gently, the familiar and customary rasp of wisdom filling his voice.

There is my Ezra, I think with a soft smile.

Ezra has lost not only his mother, but now his father as well.

He knows well the fragility of human life and love.

His brown eyes are tired as we begin shouldering one another's burdens, and he holds my gaze, his eyes growing heavier as the medication settles throughout his body and he fights to stay awake.

I smile softly, leaning closer to kiss his rough cheek.

"Get some rest, Ezra," I whisper softly as he closes his eyes. "Just don't leave me, okay?"

His brown eyes open slightly, and he smiles softly at me, his hand tightening around mine.

"I'm not going anywhere, Ruth," he murmurs softly, love shining in his eyes as he smiles. "Not until the Lord bids me home."

Home.

I smile softly.

CHAPTER TWENTY-NINE

"**W**ho are you?" a heavy-set Frenchman asks me, peering up at me through a permanent grimace as I examine the abrasions along his arms from falling debris left over from the bombing.

I stand in a large classroom once used for biology in the school's glory days, where Papa and I now work side by side with the various patients that come through the door.

It has been three days since the bombing, and the city is still reeling from the most recent attack, the death total rising by the hour as the Resistance men continue to plunge into the rubble and ruin of the streets.

"*Je suis la fille du médecin,*" I tell the man in his native tongue of French, the words falling from my lips crisp and rehearsed.

I am the physician's daughter.

Papa stills, glancing up at me from across the room where he stands tending to a woman and her young daughter.

He smiles brightly at me, his eyes shining with wistful pride.

Yes, you are, his gaze seems to say.

I return his smile before turning back to the Frenchman.

I clean the abrasions with a cloth soaked in alcohol, the man sucking air through his teeth as it burns. I wrap the largest portion of the thin wounds on his forearm with gauze, pulling his sleeve down over the top of it.

I straighten, smiling at the Frenchman.

"How does that feel now, sir?"

He twists his wrist and straightens his elbow, grimacing only slightly as he tests out the wrapping on his arm.

"Better. *Merci, Mademoiselle,*" he says, standing from his chair.

I nod.

"My pleasure," I say, turning to my next patient, a little girl of five with a deep throaty cough and a gash cut along her forehead.

For the next two hours, I follow the same routine.

I help a young woman dress a wound on her mother's cat, I tend to a soldier who has lost his left arm, I assist Papa in performing a small miracle by sewing a man's ring finger back onto his hand, and I effectively calm a man battling violent flashbacks as he thrashes in his cot.

By the time the afternoon dawns, Papa and I have attended the majority of the injured and wounded, with all of them being treated for their wounds with careful hands and a dose of medicine, and only a few being so difficult and complex that they too, get a dose of *Blue 88.*

And it is while Papa and I are rushing back and forth between patients in the classroom and down the hall for the final time before we must leave, and when I am about to go check once more on Ezra, that I am given a letter that has just arrived in the post.

Miss Ruth DeVos

The return address claims to be Thomas Vincotte, Brussels.

It is from Paul Struye.

I had written to him two days ago, informing him of the recent events that have befallen the Still Waters clan, and telling him that this Friday's article will be delayed.

Stepping away from the mass of patients around me, I tuck myself in the crook of the hall and read the letter.

Miss DeVos,

I am saddened to hear of your finance's incident, and the destruction and desolation that the bomb has left Antwerp in.

In your brief letter, you apologized for not being able to complete this week's article on time.

Do not apologize, Miss. You must take this time to focus on your family. I understand, and I will gladly send another journalist to cover the remainder of the assignment for you.

But I am not firing you, Miss. I still need someone like you in my arsenal, and you proved to be a wonderful asset not only to La Libre Belgique, *but to the people of Antwerp. I can tell by the depth in your early and late articles that you care deeply for the people, and over time, have developed a kinship with those that you are helping.*

It is important to remember that while you are a journalist sent to write about a story, the people you are working beside are not just a story.

They are breathing the same air you are and facing the same turmoil as you.

I am glad to see that you already know this.

Keep writing, Miss DeVos.

I pray for you and your family, and that you all return home safely in the coming day.,

Paul Struye

P.S.

I have included your pay and some currency for your trip home.

In the depths of the envelope, he has tucked a five-franc bank note, along with my meager paycheck for this month's work.

"Kind soul," I murmur to myself.

I sigh softly, observing the scene around me as I gaze upon the familiar and unfamiliar faces of those striding up and down the hall.

The bombing has taken its toll and Antwerp has suffered greatly because of it, but the courage of the Resistance has only risen each time Hitler has tried to defeat and conquer us with his bombs.

Dozens of women now make up the Secret Army's nurse corps that I have been a part of for so long now, complete with five trained physicians and several attendants.

In the nearly five months I have spent here in the stronghold of the Resistance, I have met so many people and helped so many wounded, that I hate to leave now, when there is yet so much work to be done.

"Miss DeVos!"

I jolt upright, turning to glance over my shoulder as I tuck the letter in my pocket.

A tall, thin man dressed in beige coveralls marches toward me, followed by a beastly man in decorated uniform, their boots echoing across the floor as they near me.

It is Lars, and no other than Commander van Branteghem.

My heart pounds, fear seeping into my heart as memories of Andrew resurface in my mind.

Papa stands from where he was kneeling beside an injured man lying on a blanket on the floor. He glances at me questioningly.

I give him an assuring glance.

"Good afternoon, Lars," I say, smiling softly at Ezra's comrade, nodding cordially to the commander behind him. "To you as well, Commander."

Commander smiles and nods his head.

"It's a pleasure as always, Miss," he says, nodding his head graciously.

"What can I do for you gentleman today?" I ask, glancing between the two of them.

Lars nods.

"Yes, we were hoping to speak with Ezra, if he is up to it. You are all still planning to go home, yes?"

I nod.

"Yes we are, just as soon as Mr. Shepherd comes in from the train station."

"We were hoping to discuss a matter of rank and discharge with Ezra before he leaves. Is he in any condition to speak with us?"

Rank and discharge?

"Well, I am not sure. But I was just about to go check on him. You are welcome to join me, if you like," I offer kindly.

Lars nods. "Certainly."

Papa steps behind me, joining our conversation.

"Is everything alright?" he asks, glancing from me to Lars.

I nod, remembering my manners.

"Um, Papa, you have already met Lars, but this is Andrew and Ezra's commanding officer, Berend van Branteghem," I say to Papa, motioning toward the broad man beside Lars. "Commander, this is mine and Andrew's father, Nathaniel DeVos."

Papa offers the commander a friendly smile as they clasp hands.

"It's good to meet you, Commander," he says, sadness thickening his voice at the mention of my brother.

The commander nods.

"Likewise, Mr. DeVos," he says, his blue eyes crinkling around the corners as he smiles. "I want you to know, sir, that you should be very proud of your son. Andrew was an obedient soldier and a valiant man. A true hero to say the least. He was the heart of our troop for a time, and he is greatly missed."

Papa nods gently.

"Thank you, Commander. You are kind in saying that," he says with a prideful, if not wistful, smile. "I am glad to hear that my boy did his job well and fought bravely to the end."

Lars nods.

"That he most certainly did."

We fall in a moment of silence as Andrew weighs heavily upon our minds.

I sigh softly, offering Papa a soft smile, which he returns.

Laying a hand on my shoulder, he nods gently.

"Well, shall we go see Ezra then?" he says after a moment.

I nod.

"Yes, of course."

~ ~
.

"LARS, YOU ARE THE commanding officer now," Ezra says, his voice stern and authoritative as he gazes up at his comrade.

I can tell by the softness in his eyes as he glances at me that his own words pain him.

He has worked so hard during the war with the Resistance, and he has faced more shadowlands for the sake of liberty than I will ever know.

But now he is being forced to return home before Liberty has been won, and before Hitler has been defeated.

I fold Ezra's few clothes and meager belongings and return them to his rucksack while silently listening to their conversation, adding his bag to the pile of our other belongings at the door where mine and Eline's two bags sit beside my typewriter.

"What? Me?" Lars asks, gazing from Ezra to the commander. "But, Ezra, the troop doesn't trust me. Not like they do you."

"I know, Lars. But what kind of commander am I if I cannot even be with them?" he asks, motioning meekly down at his painful and idle legs. He shakes his head softly. "Commander and I have already discussed this, Lars. Besides, with what happened with Faibber, you are the only one I trust to command these men."

Lars shakes his head, a breathy laugh escaping his lips as he squares his shoulders and stands to his full height.

"Then I would be honored, Ezra," he says.

Ezra smiles, clasping hands with Lars.

"It's settled then, my friend," he says good-naturedly.

They talk for a moment longer before they both prepare to leave.

"Goodbye, Miss DeVos," the commander says to me, shaking my hand in a friendly manner. "Keep me informed on Pik's condition, won't you?"

I nod, smiling.

"Of course, Commander."

He smiles. "Good. And if you ever need a thing, you know where to find us."

I smile as he steps through the door, followed by Papa as the two of them step outside to discuss Ezra's condition and discharge matters.

"Please say hello to my mother for me, if you see her, Miss DeVos," Lars says, nodding at me as he steps to follow Commander van Branteghem. His gaze travels to Ezra for a moment. "I pray he will be alright."

I smile softly.

"Me too."

He nods gently, his eyes still anxious as he bends his head to step out the door.

"Goodbye, Miss DeVos."

"Goodbye, Lars," I say as he turns and steps out the door. "You take care."

Ezra sighs softly behind me, and I turn to face him.

"Are you alright? I know that was difficult for you," I say, nodding toward the door where Lars and the commander had just left.

He nods, his eyes blazing.

"It was, but I am alright. It needed to be done. I am no good to my men like this anyway," he says, grimacing down at his legs.

"Don't say that, Ezra," I murmur softly, tipping his chin up so that he will look at me.

He parts his lips to reply when the door opens and Eline steps in.

She appears flustered as she brushes moisture from her red eyes.

"Oh, Eline, what is it?" I ask gently as I step toward her, taking her hand.

She smiles at me softly, shaking her head at me.

"Don't look so worried, dear. Nothing is wrong," she says assuringly. "It's just the children. I went to visit them again, and I just hate leaving them all behind while we are going home. Most of them don't even have homes to go to."

My heart sinks at her words.

I nod. "I know, Eline."

She is right.

She has grown attached to the children placed in her care just as I have grown used to caring for the various patients that inhabit the school.

"I just hope that we may be able to come back. Perhaps when the war is over," she murmurs wistfully.

I nod, a small portion of my heart hoping that her words will turn out to be true.

She smiles at me, squeezing my hand gently.

"What about your assignment?" Ezra asks, eyebrows raised.

Eline nods.

"It is the reason you and I are here, after all," she says.

I smile, shaking my head sadly.

"Paul Struye is sending someone to replace me," I say.

Her shoulders fall, and Ezra sighs.

"I'm sorry, Ruth. I know how much this assignment meant to you," he says.

I shake my head.

"It's alright, truly. He didn't fire me, so with any luck I will have another assignment in the future. For now I must focus on you, Ezra."

The door opens once more, breaking our conversation as Fletcher enters the room.

"Look who I found," Fletcher calls to the room as he smiles at the lot of us, stepping lightly over the threshold, followed by Mr. Shepherd.

A unanimous murmuring of greeting is aroused across the room as the kind old host returns to us once more.

"Mr. Shepherd!" Eline says, greeting the dear man with a swift embrace.

"Hello, Eline," he says to her as she pulls away, smiling at us all as he gives Fletcher a pointed look. "I see you have at least kept Fletcher in line."

A soft laugh runs through the room.

He smiles at the four of us, relief washing over him as his shoulders straighten as if relieved of a burden.

"Thank the Lord you are all alright." He sighs, his gaze traveling over each of our faces, and landing on Ezra's.

I study him as he crosses the room and comes to Ezra's side, opposite from me.

He is thin and rather pale, dressed in a thick black trench coat and dress shoes still harboring wet traces of the snow from outside, and his pale cheeks are almost ruddy from the stink of the February wind he braved in coming here.

His beard has grown longer in the several months of our separation and possesses a few more strands of gray than it had before, along with a few more wrinkles etched in his face, but his Dutch blue eyes remain the same as he smiles brightly at the lot of us, the same fatherly affection shining unhindered in his face.

He bends down at Ezra's side, laying a gentle hand upon Ezra's shoulder.

"How are you, my boy?" he asks, his voice thick.

Ezra smiles, his gaze soft as he stares steadily back at Mr. Shepherd.

"I have been worse, Mr. Shepherd," he says, though I can see that he grimaces as he attempts to straighten himself. "But I have certainly been better."

Mr. Shepherd smiles gently, his eyes rueful.

"And he is too stubborn to complain," I say softly, teasing.

Ezra smiles at me, his eyes knowing.

Mr. Shepherd glances up at me.

"Ruth, my dear girl!" he says as he embraces me in a father-like fashion. I lean into his familiar and steady arms, feeling the warmth and nostalgia of Still Waters encompass me.

"I am glad you came." I laugh softly as the dear man pulls away.

"Of course I would, Ruth. Not even snow and bombs could keep me away from you all. You are my children," he says, his Dutch blue eyes flickering over my face, as if searching for something, though I know he only sees the bags beneath my eyes. "You still aren't sleeping are you?"

I shake my head, looking away.

"No. I can't."

He is about to speak when the door opens once again, and someone steps inside.

I glance over my shoulder to find Papa gazing at the scene the five of us make.

"Well, if it isn't Dirk Shepherd," Papa says, breaking the silence of the room, a broad smile spreading across his face.

Mr. Shepherd smiles brightly.

"Nathaniel DeVos, my old friend," he says, his eyes soft.

I watch as the two men meet, clasping hands.

"I never thought I would see the day when you are at last home; it has been far too long. You have a lot of catching up to do," Mr. Shepherd says.

Papa laughs, clapping Mr. Shepherd on the shoulder, nodding.

"So I have heard, Dirk," he says, his eyes sobering as he turns to look at me where I stand beside Ezra. "I cannot thank you enough for taking care of my *Dochter* all this time."

He smiles pointedly at me.

"Although you did let her fall in love, it appears."

A deep blush takes root in my cheeks as the room shares a laugh, and Ezra takes my hand, unaffected by their teasing as he smiles up at me.

I meet his gaze, and for the first time since the bombing, his eyes smile back, filled with the light they once had.

I smile, warmth spreading through my limbs.

"Well, Nathaniel, I tried my best to keep her out of harm's way, but I am afraid I have no control over matters of the heart," Mr. Shepherd says with a smile, his gaze traveling to Ezra and me. "That is something only the heart can do, and does of its own accord—"

Mr. Shepherd stops speaking abruptly as Hugo limps into the room.

The room stills as Hugo meets Mr. Shepherd's gaze, each of us holding our breaths as we sit in stiff silence.

My spine stiffens as my heart hardens toward him.

No one utters a word.

And slowly, Mr. Shepherd steps forward and embraces Hugo, wrapping his arms around Hugo's thin shoulders as a father would a lost son.

With tears shining in his kind eyes, Mr. Shepherd holds him close and kisses Hugo's forehead like a child.

Hugo tentatively leans into his embrace as he too, realizes that he has been forgiven.

"My son, welcome home," Mr. Shepherd murmurs softly as he gazes wordlessly into Hugo's face.

Under his gaze, I can see Hugo begin to soften, and in the afternoon light, tears glisten in trails down his pale cheeks.

This is true forgiveness, I think to myself, my heart beating steadily as I witness the tender moment as the prodigal son returns home once more.

CHAPTER THIRTY

The air is icy and still when I step onto the front steps of the snow-covered *Koloniale Hogeschhol,* my breath forming into a cloud as its warmth collides with the cold world around me.

I glance down at my dark green blouse that is tucked into the black pencil skirt at my waist in a feminine manner, pulling the pale green cloth of my overcoat closed at my torso.

My feet crunch beneath me as I shuffle through the snow that covers Antwerp in its usual blanket of ice that will remain draped across Belgium until early April, as Papa and Fletcher stand on either side of Ezra, gingerly supporting him as he limps through the snow. They labor toward an old army jeep, provided for us by the Resistance, that will take Ezra and Hugo to the train station, preventing further exertion for the wounded and weary travelers.

"Do *not* let the snow touch those burns," Papa says, his voice thick with warning.

"I think Ruth and Eline put enough cloth around his legs to ensure that won't be a problem," Fletcher says breathlessly, his cheeks growing pink from the effort of helping Ezra.

I smile at Fletcher's remarks.

Eline and I had carefully and meticulously wrapped the burns covering Ezra's legs with saturated sterile cloths, rolling his pants legs over the top of them loosely with a prayer that no bacteria would find its way to the delicate tissue left naked by the burns.

The third-degree burns on his left leg are dangerously susceptible to infection, and have left him with no feeling, even four days after the bombing.

Papa had refused to let Ezra return home at the first thought of it, for traveling in his condition is risky, but after four days of drugging him with *Blue 88,* Papa had agreed that home is probably the best place for him.

And so, here we are, beginning our short journey back to Brussels.

I had said goodbye to my new companions, Heidi, her mother Mrs. Kipling, Cor, and Margaret.

But I couldn't find Jack.

Hugo limps through the snow, aided by Mr. Shepherd, and Eline shuffles beside me as I ignore the German altogether, her cheeks pink and her eyes sad as she leaves behind the lot of children she has grown so fond of.

Dressed in a placid gray blouse cinched at her waist with a matching pencil skirt that is covered by her soft blue overcoat, Eline reflects the wintry scene around us.

I take her hand.

"We will come back, Eline. There is still work to be done," I say, my cheeks stinging from the cold breath of winter.

I loop my arm through hers, and we walk side by side down the many steps of the school, just as we had five months ago when we first arrived.

She smiles softly at me, her blue eyes shining brightly.

"I know, Ruth. And I hope you are right," she says.

On either side lies the destruction of our homeland; smoking buildings lie in the wreckage of their glory days that are now passed as the faint humming of automobiles and the call of the soldiers breaks the silence of the peaceful morning.

My gaze travels to the men walking ahead of us, watching as they journey through snowy streets of my beloved Antwerp.

We are going home, I think to myself.

Although, I am not sure that home is a place for me anymore.

Home is not in Antwerp, Still Waters, Brussels, or even Vlissengen.

Home is wherever *they* are.

My people.

My clan.

My family.

I smile softly to myself.

"Miss DeVos!"

Eline and I stop walking abruptly, and I glance swiftly over my shoulder.

A middle-aged man dressed in an old tattered brown trench coat waves his hands above his balding head to gain my attention, his voice foreign as his sharp and well-cultivated English voice falls on my ears.

"Jack?" I call, turning to face him.

He steps down the remaining stairs, his gait graceful and aged as he comes to where Eline and I stand in the midst of the snow.

"Is everything alright?" I ask the kind older gentleman, my throat straining to speak clear English.

"I apologize, Miss. But I heard that you were all leaving, and I was compelled to give this to you," he says, offering me a small brown parcel. He smiles as I glance curiously up at him. "It is not much, I fear. But I hope you enjoy it."

I steal a glance at Eline.

She smiles warmly at the older man.

I study his face, his warm eyes gazing soulfully at me, appearing as if he were a hundred years old instead of forty.

Slowly, I take the parcel from his grasp.

"Thank you," I say, smiling.

I reach to open the lip of the parcel, and Jack reaches out a long hand to stop me.

"Do not open it here in the snow, please Miss. Wait until you are on the train home," he says.

He smiles kindly, and I nod, raising my brows.

"Alright then." I smile.

"What's the matter?" Fletcher calls to us from where he and Papa successfully reach the two waiting jeeps and begin helping Ezra inside the first one.

Eline waves her dainty gloved hand at him.

"Nothing, dear. We will be right there," she calls back gently, the wind carrying her voice to them.

Jack smiles at us.

"Well, I suppose you ladies must go now." He pauses, looking up at me once more before departing. "Have you written anything more, Miss DeVos? Any new stories?"

I sigh, shaking my head as the February wind sends a chill down the collar of my coat; I pull the green fabric tighter around my torso.

"I am afraid not, Jack," I say softly.

"Why is that?" he asks.

I shrug softly.

"I haven't written any. I just... *can't.* There has been so much work to be done and so much darkness since the bombing that I cannot seem to write a word, let alone a story."

I pause for a moment, thinking as my own words settle unwelcoming in my own ears.

"And now that Ezra has been injured, I am nearly too worried to write," I say, motioning behind us at waiting men. "I haven't written anything more for the newspaper. My replacement should be here any hour."

Jack's gaze softens at my words, his eyes filling with understanding as his lips part.

"I am sorry to hear that," he says, thinking for a moment as he gazes at the snowy ground, his extended chin visible behind the collar of his coat. "May I offer you some advice?"

I nod once more, smiling at my friend.

"If you would, please," I say.

He meets my gaze once again, his eyes blazing with a winsome and wise glare as his lips pull into a soft smile.

"Do not write for the newspaper, or the people of Belgium. Do not even write for yourself, Miss DeVos," he says, pointing a long, slender finger at my chest. "But write for someone else. When *you* cannot do it, or you feel as if no one cares, write for the person who would."

Write for the person who would.

I muse over his words for a moment, a small smile pulling at my lips as the hidden truth in them is found by my heart.

I nod.

"I understand, Jack." I smile. "Thank you."

He smiles in return, offering me his hand in a friendly gesture.

"You are very welcome, Miss. Now, you two ladies must be off, else those gentlemen leave you to walk to the station yourselves," he says, nodding toward Papa, Fletcher, and Mr. Shepherd as they wait outside the two jeeps.

Eline and I laugh softly.

Eline offers him her hand, and he shakes it heartily.

"Goodbye, Jack." She smiles.

"Goodbye, Mrs. Fletcher. I hope you do indeed return to those children; they seem to love you dearly," he says.

Eline smiles, her cheeks blushing despite the cold.

"I do hope to return in the days to come," she says.

He smiles, turning one final time to me.

"Goodbye, Jack," I say, "and thank you for the parcel."

He nods, beginning to turn away.

"You are very welcome. I do hope you like it," he says, waving his hand to us as we part. "Goodbye, now."

And with that, Eline and I turn and trudge through the snow to join the men, where Fletcher sits waiting in the driver's seat of the first jeep that harbors Ezra, Hugo, and Papa.

Mr. Shepherd waits by the open door of the second jeep, ushering Eline and I inside.

"Abram, you head to the station; I'll take Ruth and Eline with me," he tells Fletcher, his voice thick and somber. "I must go check on Still Waters before we go."

My heart sinks.

Still Waters.

We gaze at one another in thick silence as we are reminded of just what the bombing has taken from us.

Fletcher nods, his eyes sad.

"Certainly, Dirk. Tell the Inn farewell for me, won't you?" he says softly, slipping the key into the ignition as the jeep stirs to life and he calls over the roar of the motor as it rolls into motion, "Be careful, and do not linger. Remember the bombs."

Remember the bombs.

How could we forget them?

I step into the back of the jeep with a heavy heart as Eline slips into the passenger seat and Mr. Shepherd into the drivers', and we begin the short journey through the streets of desolate Antwerp on our way to our beloved Still Waters Inn.

The jeep groans and whines in unearthly ways as its wheels grind across the shattered ground beneath us, bouncing roughly as it crawls through the streets.

The journey is quiet and heavy as I gaze out my window as Mr. Shepherd maneuvers the vehicle through the rubble, ruins, and remains of the street that used to surround the inn.

To our left is the remains of the quaint row of canal houses where many small shops and markets had once inhabited; and to our right, is the row of houses under the shadow of the Cathedral.

In all the many long months I spent at Still Waters, I only walked these streets openly twice.

The first time, when I first arrived at Still Waters alone in late June 1942 just weeks after Andrew's departure and Mama's arrest.

And of course, the second one was when we were betrayed, and Hugo led us out onto the sidewalk of the street and beat us all before loading us up into the truck that would carry us to Avenue Louise.

The cathedral rises above the demolished and smoldering rooftops, its gothic architecture casting a faint shadow over the streets below as its steeple rises high in the pale gray sky in all its stately glory.

For many days, I had gazed out across the city of Antwerp and this very cathedral, where now it still stands in timeless beauty in the midst of smoke and ash.

In fire and brimstone.

The street curves slightly, revealing the house I have longing to come back to for so long.

Except today is no happy homecoming.

Mr. Shepherd sighs audibly, and Eline gasps.

I am stunned into silence.

Once a large brick building with many windows dotting its face and quaint green awnings fluttered in the wind stood here; where rich and poor alike gathered for refuge every night under the kind and friendly roof of their host all those years ago, and where Jews, Dutch, and Germans gathered within its walls for a time even when all the rest of the world was fighting a bloodthirsty enemy in gray.

But the place no longer stands.

In its place is a mere pile of rubble, the fine building now reduced to bricks and ash.

The bomb had shaken the very foundation and what had not been burned in the flames had collapsed upon the lower levels, smoke still smoldering and rising in the air from the splintered rafters and floorboards that protrude from the ashes.

Lars had been right.

Still Waters is gone.

Along with the Hawkins home next door.

Mr. Shepherd steps out of the jeep in a silent daze, and I rush to follow him, opening my door with a loud screech and stepping out onto the smoky and ash-covered streets.

His footsteps echo eerily across the desolate streets as he stops in front of the ruins, his face ashen and pale as his eyes gaze at his beloved home with a sharp and defeated pain settling in his bright blue eyes that I have never seen before.

I stand silently behind him, giving him a moment alone as I study him.

The wind stirs his graying brown hair as he bends and takes a handful of the ash in his palm, gazing down at it absently.

Eline steps out of the jeep beside me silently, and we watch as Mr. Shepherd slowly lets the wind carry the ash from his palm back to the ground at his feet.

He straightens, slipping his hands back into depths of his trench coat pockets and returns his gaze to the ruins.

"Mr. Shepherd?" I ask gently, my voice so soft that it is nearly lost in the midst of the whistling February wind.

I step tentatively to his side, laying a gentle hand on his forearm as I follow his gaze to what remains of Still Waters.

And I want to sob from what I see.

Through the veil of smoke, I can see that the remains have been burned beyond recognition, everything the light touches being either black and charred or covered in white ash so thick I can no longer identify what it is.

Wordlessly, Mr. Shepherd lays a wrinkled hand over mine, holding me there at his side as Eline joins us.

"*He* led me beside the still waters for twenty-five years," he says softly, his voice gentle as a small smile crawls across his face despite the sorrow in his eyes as he glances at the two of us. "I suppose he led us all, didn't he?"

Eline and I share a sad glance.

"He certainly did," Eline murmurs softly, smiling fondly at the ash at our feet.

We stand there for a moment longer like this, as memories roll through our minds like a motion picture.

I brush silent tears from my cheek.

It is almost as if we are mourning for a fallen friend that we have known all our lives.

Because we are.

Goodbye, Still Waters, my heart whispers.

I take a sharp breath, the thick smoke in the air around me entering my lungs and arousing the old rattle in my chest from the Barracks as a violent cough shakes me.

Mr. Shepherd grips my hand.

"Come, let us go," he says gently, giving Still Waters one final glance.

And slowly, he smiles.

~.~

WE ARRIVE AT THE Antwerp Central train station several minutes later, just as the whistle is blowing at the platform.

Everyone can tell by our somber moods and crestfallen faces that Still Waters is indeed gone, but no one utters a word regarding it.

We do not have to.

The feelings in our chests are mutual.

"We must hurry," Papa says as he steps out from the Resistance jeep. "The train is about to leave."

"Hang on," Eline says, catching sight of a familiar white-haired and withered man standing beside the boarding entrance. "Bart!"

Old Bart straightens, his eyes brightening as he recognizes Eline, and his gaze travels to where I stand.

"Ah, Mrs. Fletcher. Miss DeVos!" He smiles, his voice thin and raspy. "What can I do for you two ladies today?"

Fletcher shakes his head at his wife as she converses with the old man about our situation.

He looks at me.

"How many friends do you two have here?" he asks, teasing.

I smile at him.

Ezra grimaces as he follows Papa from the jeep and reaches the ground, and my smile falls as Fletcher and I immediately rush to support him.

"Are you alright?" I ask him, gently gripping his right forearm as Mr. Shepherd helps Hugo join us at the platform.

Ezra nods, holding his left leg up tenderly from the ground.

"Yes, I'm fine, it's just strangely numb. That's all," he says softly to me, his eyes sorrowful. "It was gone?"

I bite my lip, nodding.

"Yes, it was," I whisper.

He sighs heavily, leaning on Fletcher's forearm.

"How is Mr. Shepherd?" Fletcher asks in a low voice, nodding his chin to the dear host of Still Waters.

"As well as he can be, I suppose," I say, following his gaze. "Still Waters was everything to him and Mrs. Shepherd. I do not know what they will ever do now that it's gone."

Ezra and Fletcher nod solemnly, a sorrowful look passing between them.

"I had always wished to go back to Still Waters after the war," Ezra says softly, shaking his head.

Fletcher smiles ruefully.

"At least you got to see it one last time, Ezra. Ruth and I haven't seen it since the day we were betrayed," he says, his voice low so as to not let Hugo hear us.

Ezra sighs.

"My last visit wasn't a happy homecoming though, Fletcher," he says, his eyes flashing darkly as the memories of the day he had found Still Water's empty flashes through his mind.

I part my lips to speak when Old Bart interrupts our conversation.

"Right this way, folks!" he calls to us.

And so the seven of us board the train, where we are greeted by a multitude of wounded civilians and soldiers alike as they too head home, leaving the destruction of Antwerp behind them. The rising voices of groaning soldiers fall on my ears as I am pressed between passing passengers, a nearby soldier muttering something about, "Going home with my tail between my legs."

"Out of the way, folks. Make room, I've got some wounded men here," Bart calls to the idling passengers in the aisle. "That's right, move along."

Old Bart helps us all to our seats as we struggle through the throng of passengers around us, ensuring that the wounded men in our company are given the necessary attention and respect.

"Thank you, Bart," I say to the kind old man as I settle into my own seat beside Ezra, Eline, and Fletcher taking the seats across the aisle from us as Hugo, Papa, and Mr. Shepherd inhabit the few remaining seats behind us.

He nods as he brushes through the narrow aisle of our train car.

"It is my pleasure, Miss DeVos. I wish you all safe travels and good health," he says kindly, with a nod toward Ezra. "And may I add, a swift recovery."

Ezra nods at the man, a smile playing on his lips.

"Thank you, sir," he says.

Bart shuffles off after that, and we are left in the midst of the groaning and conversing crowd around us.

Ezra wraps his arm around my shoulders.

"Who was that man?" he whispers close to my ear.

I smile, glancing up after Bart as he disappears into the next train car.

"His name is Old Bart, but that is all I know. Eline and I met him when we came to Antwerp a few months ago," I say, turning to smile up at Ezra.

He shakes his head, smiling.

"No, the other man. The English speaking one at the school," he says softly.

"Oh, that was Jack Lewis. He is a writer who came to read to the children on a few occasions. You never met him?"

Ezra shakes his head.

"No, I am afraid I didn't get the chance to," he says, his gaze turning to the small brown parcel in my lap. "What did he give you?"

I shake my head, picking it up and fingering the thick beige covering in my hands.

"I'm not sure," I say.

Ezra smiles, his gaze playful.

"Do you want to find out?" he offers.

A small laugh escapes my lips as I shake my head at him.

Smiling, I pinch the brass clasp that holds the parcel's lip closed and open the package to find a small sheaf of parchment.

A note has been attached to the top.

Sweeping the hair falling from my braid away from my face, I read the tight English words Jack has written.

Miss De Vos,

Included in this package is the early draft of the first few chapters of my newest manuscript. I would be honored if you read them.

It isn't much, and I am uncertain as to whether anyone truly cares what I have to say, but I trust that you do.

I hope you enjoy my work, and I hope you will take my advice to heart.

Yours, Jack

I smile at the note, turning to the manuscript below as Ezra bends over my shoulder to squint at the handwritten words sprawled across the first page, though I am fairly certain that the English words are foreign to his Dutch eyes.

I flip through the many leaflets of the sheaf, my eyes stealing bits of the carefully written paragraphs it holds.

"It's a manuscript," I breathe gently.

"Read it to me," he murmurs softly, leaning his head against the back of his chair. "I think we could all use a distraction."

I glance up at him.

"Aloud?" I ask, glancing at the multitude of individuals clamoring about us in the train car.

He cracks one eye, smiling brightly down at me.

"Yes, aloud," he says, his arm tightening around my shoulder as he pulls me closer to his side.

I smile softly, leaning into his arm.

And clearing my throat, I begin to read in a soft, clear voice the words to the book in my lap, only stopping at times when a passage is particularly moving.

And as we sit reading side by side, I do not even notice as the train jolts into motion, nor do my memories sear through my mind and leave me broken and defeated as the journey home begins.

No, for a moment it is just Ezra and I, side-by-side reading together once more, just as we used to on the rooftop of Still Waters.

For a time, as the words carry us into a world free of war, the hour slips by and so do our silent fears.

And it is only when I reach the last page that my lips stumble across the Authors name that completes the manuscript's excerpt.

"*...by C.S. Lewis.*"

CHAPTER THIRTY-ONE

"**R**uth!"

Maya plows into me, nearly knocking me back against the door as she embraces me, wrapping her thin arms around my waist as a breathy laugh escapes my lips.

"Goodness, Maya." I smile, wrapping my arms around her shoulders.

"You're home!" she exclaims, looking up at me with wide eyes.

"Of course, little goose," I say, regaining my footing as I step over the threshold and into the farmhouse, the welcoming scents of dinner in the kitchen greeting my nose and the warmth of the hearth draws me into the living room as the others follow me through the door.

"I told you we would all be home again, didn't I?" I ask, smiling as Fletcher and Papa help Ezra through the door, followed closely by Eline.

"It's certainly good to be home," Ezra says as he breathes deeply the scents of home, glancing around the living room of his childhood.

The room is still just as threadbare as before, its lively and most prominent fixtures being the people who inhabit it, with a warm fire casting a warm glow throughout the room despite the darkening sky outside as we congregate in the small room once more.

Maya smiles at everyone as they come through the door, running to greet Eline just as she had me.

"Oh, Ezra dear, look at you!" a familiar voice scolds from the kitchen as Mrs. Shepherd bustles through the thronging reunion to see Ezra while Papa and Fletcher lead him to Mr. Shepherd's chair before the hearth.

"I'm alright, Mrs. Shepherd. Don't worry." He smiles at the motherly woman as she plants a kiss on his forehead, sinking contentedly in the chair.

I laugh softly as she scoffs at him.

"Don't worry? Ruth sure worried Dirk and I on the telephone the other day. Scared me nearly to death!" Mrs. Shepherd says to him, her merry gaze landing on me as she wraps her arm around my shoulders. "How are you, dear?"

I lean into her embrace with a soft sigh, the red strands of her hair tickling my cheek as I sigh into her thick shoulder.

"I am worn and worried, but glad to be here," I say with a smile.

She smiles brightly at me, kissing my forehead just as a mother would a daughter.

"I am glad you're here, too, Ruth. It just wasn't right having the lot of you *children* gone. Especially through the hard, cold winter and lonesome Christmas we just had. We missed your twenty-third birthday," she says with a wry smile.

I laugh softly.

"It's alright, Mrs. Shepherd. Prayerfully, I will have many more to celebrate with you all."

She smiles, turning to see an old face beside Ezra.

"Goodness gracious," she exclaims. "Nathaniel DeVos!"

Papa smiles at Mrs. Shepherd's odd, though sincere, greeting.

"Hello, Maud," he says, standing at least a head taller than the sweet woman as she embraces him just as she had me a moment ago. "You haven't aged a day."

She smiles up at Papa.

"I honestly doubt that, Nathaniel. But you're kind to say it," she says. "I was beginning to believe that you were never coming home. Your daughter has been worried sick."

Papa laughs softly at the vivacious and hospitable woman.

"Well, I am here now. And that is what matters," he says gently. "Thank you for watching over Ruth, Maud. I'm not sure I'll ever be able to repay you and Dirk for your kindness to me and my family."

"We *are* family, Nathaniel. That is what we do; we watch out for one another. Besides, Ruth is like a daughter to me," Mrs. Shepherd says sweetly. "Now, I have fixed up a room for you, but it will be tight with the lot of us here. I am certain that we will manage."

Papa laughs softly, nodding.

"Yes, we will. But I will only be visiting for a short time, unfortunately."

He meets my gaze, his eyes soft and sad as he speaks of his all-too-soon departure.

"You will?" Mrs. Shepherd asks, brows raised.

Papa nods.

"Yes, only a few days. I wanted to make sure that Ruth was safe and settled back here, and also to ensure that Ezra's wounds are healing properly." His voice is thick with sadness, but his eyes harbor the familiar look of daring certainty that Andrew's once had as he lays a firm hand on my shoulder, "After then, though, I am afraid that I must return to my work in Antwerp. There are numerous individuals in need of a physician, and I cannot neglect them."

My heart sinks with his words even now.

Mrs. Shepherd nods, catching the sadness in her old acquaintance's voice.

"I understand, Dirk. But what about Judith?" she asks. "I haven't seen my dare friend in years. I pray she is alright."

Papa nods.

"She is being held in the Bergen-Belson concentration camp in Germany. I have been in contact with her, but it is nearly impossible for the Resistance to get within the camp to find her. It is far too dangerous."

I swallow.

"So what do we do?" I ask softly, almost afraid of his answer.

He sighs softly, stepping toward me.

"We wait and pray, *Dochter.* That is all we can do," he says, his eyes soft. Mrs. Shepherd nods softly at us, her face sad as a familiar voice speaks from behind her.

"Hello, Mrs. Shepherd," Hugo says thickly as he limps through the door, his gaze flickering quickly over the woman's face.

Her eyes flash with darkness, perhaps from the memories that we all recall so well and that rush to each of our minds with a raw vibrancy each time we see Hugo.

But she doesn't utter an unkind word or spit in his face, for the years of hardship through this war has trained her well, and she willingly, though somewhat rigidly, welcomes Hugo home.

"Welcome back, Hugo." She smiles warmly up at him, her eyes damp as she gazes at him.

I look at the floor, my bitterness nearly getting the best of me as I force my tongue to remain silent.

Mr. Shepherd smiles softly at me from where he stands near the door, his keen eyes penetrating my mind.

His sharp gaze meets mine for a brief moment, holding my gaze steady as a soft heat blooms across my cheeks.

His blue eyes are gentle, but I can see in them for a fleeting moment, a look of pleading.

He knows the anger toward Hugo in my heart. He knows the hidden pain and resentment that I have been struggling against all this time, not only against Hugo, but against what has happened to us and the loss of Andrew.

And he wants me to let it go.

I nod softly, understanding his gaze.

I will try.

He smiles brightly at me, nodding in return.

Slowly, Mrs. Shepherd recovers from the shock of seeing Hugo again as she greets Eline and Fletcher by the sofa, her and Eline whispering for a moment before Mrs. Shepherd's gaze travels to each face around the room.

"Well, I suppose now that we are all together again," she says, putting her hands on her hips as she joins Mr. Shepherd at the door, "shall we eat?"

Mr. Shepherd nods, smiling at us all.

"Let us eat," he says to the room.

"You do not have to tell me twice," Fletcher says with a smile, starting for the kitchen.

And with a soft laugh, we stride, stumble, and limp to the kitchen, where we gather around the extended dining room where a spread of meats, potatoes, and cheese wait for us, complete with tea, coffee, and glazed *appelflappen* for the final course.

Ezra and I walk into the dining room arm in arm as he limps by my side, leaning heavily against my grasp as he grimaces, each step causing him to take a sharp breath as if he were walking on knives.

He bears it gallantly, never once uttering a complaint as he holds my hand tightly in his own.

A soft smile pulls at my lips.

We find our normal places around the table, and I help Ezra into his chair as I slip into the empty one beside him, with Papa sitting to my right.

From the corner of my eye, Hugo catches my gaze.

He stands in the doorway alone, always at a distance, a look on his face that I have never witnessed before.

It is almost soft despite the chiseled features of his face, and joy and sorrow mingle in his pale blue eyes as he gazes at us all around the table, memories of our lives before the betrayal running through his mind.

He is fighting with his guilt; I can see it in his stare.

The German meets my gaze, and for a brief moment we are back at Still Waters once again on the night of Christmas Eve.

Listen here, Jew, he had said to me in the kitchen as the guests congregated elsewhere in the inn, *do not think for a moment that I cannot and will not hand you over to the Germans you speak of. Because I can.*

And he did.

But as he holds my gaze now, his stare is neither lifeless nor cold, but simply sorrowful; his shoulders are no longer square, but bowed with a burden that I cannot see as he still stands at a distance, as if kept back by an invisible barrier.

I swallow the feelings of deep hate that churn in my chest, and nudge Ezra's arm gently, gaining his attention.

"Look," I whisper softly, tipping my chin in Hugo's direction.

Ezra follows my gaze to the man in the doorway and sighs heavily, his eyes sad as he tries his best to smile.

His hand tightens over mine beneath the table.

"Have a seat, Hugo," he says, waving an inviting hand to the empty seat between Maya and Eline. "There is room at the table for you."

Mr. Shepherd smiles at him through his spectacles.

"There most certainly is," he says softly.

Hugo smiles hesitantly, and limps tentatively to his seat between Eline and Maya, and it seems in that moment that the barrier is broken, and he is restored to the family.

Well, mostly.

He gives me a questioning look from across the table, as if to test my courage.

My heart jolts, and I shake my head softly.

I look away from him, turning my gaze to Mr. Shepherd as the table prepares for a moment of prayer.

He rises from his seat at the table's head, clearing his throat.

He smiles at us each before bowing his head.

I close my eyes and bow my head, leaning on Ezra's arm as Mr. Shepherd's voice rises throughout the room and to Heaven above.

"Lord, we come to you tonight with hearts of gratitude as you have gathered us all together once more and returned us all to each other's company. Lord, the last few days have been hard and filled with all sorts of trials. The bombing nearly took our Ezra from us, and it left our home in desolation. But through it all, you have been gracious, and it was your will to spare Ezra as well as to lead Hugo back home to us again."

He pauses softly, and as I hold my eyes closed, I can feel the weight of Mr. Shepherd's gaze upon Ezra and I, and it lightens as I imagine him gazing at Hugo.

"Father, though Still Waters has been lost, it is not the building I loved, nor the loss of the material things that I mourn. It's the people that you brought together under its roof that I love and cherish in my heart, and it is the memories that we share that I mourn. But I learned a long time ago, Father, that home is not a place, but home is wherever these folks around me tonight are. For this is the family that you have so graciously given us."

He clears his throat as his voice falls thick, and I smile softly as his words find their place in my heart.

I sigh softly.

"So I want to thank you, O Lord, for bringing us all home again tonight. In Jesus name I pray, Amen."

"Amen," Papa says beside me, nodding his head as his eyes shine with approval.

"Amen," the table murmurs in soft agreeance.

And with that, the meal begins.

The dishes are passed around as the usual chatter soon grows to the ceiling and silverware begins grinding against the old plates that had once belonged to Valerie Pik, and we are a family once more.

"I would like potatoes, please."

"We need a knife."

"Have you forgotten your manners, Fletcher?"

"Do you remember that winter it was so cold?"

"Winters are always cold, my child."

"Has anyone heard news on Glenn Miller?"

"Will someone pass the gravy?"

"Have you heard of how I met C.S. Lewis"

Shielded from the snow that falls outside and laughing contently with one another by the warm glow of the hearth, we laugh and talk late into the evening, passing stories from one person to the next, Fletcher sharing his trademark tall-tales as Ezra provides us with both harrowing and heartbreaking scenes from his own journeys into the shadowlands, and Eline and I reminisce of our brief time in Antwerp with the children and wounded while we all somehow laugh over our days of boredom spent in our beloved Still Waters.

Yes, I think as I look at the many familiar faces around me, *it is certainly good to be home again.*

CHAPTER THIRTY-TWO

Later that evening as night settles over the farm and the others lie sleeping in various locations around the house, I lie awake in my room.

I toss and turn for what seems like hours, though only minutes and yet sleep doesn't come.

The moment my eyes begin to close, memories dance in my mind; memories of loathsome Germans and Andrew calling for me, but I cannot find him.

And finally, the dream will end with a curious scene of a star. A yellow star. With the word *Jude* inscribed into the fibers of its putrid cloth.

The yellow badge.

I wake with a jolt, fear, anger, and sorrow budding anew in my heart with a raw violence that leaves me breathless.

When will it end?

When will my past leave me alone to tread the unknown ways of my future, free from the heavy burden of the yellow badge that still haunts me even now?

Maya whimpers softly beside me, her small body tucked tightly beneath blankets as her wide eyes are closed in sleep.

Mrs. Shepherd had tried to convince her to sleep alone tonight and give me privacy, but in the many long months since I left, it seems that Maya has truly missed me, and so I insisted that she stay with me, just like old times in Still Waters.

I sigh, pushing myself from the warm depths of the bed and to the floor, pulling Andrew's yellow shirt from my trunk by the door and shrugging it over my nightgown as I shiver from the cold air around me.

I tuck the covers around Maya's shoulders, smiling to myself as she continues to sleep soundly.

At least one of us can rest.

Grabbing the small oil lamp from off my desk and lighting it, I step out into the darkened hallway as my bare feet step silently along the rough floorboards of the farmhouse.

I tread past the closed doors of the few spare rooms where I know the others rest. Mr. and Mrs. Shepherd sleep in the first door I pass, while Hugo sleeps in the spare room intended for Papa.

I pass the picture of Jozef and Valerie Pik as I come to the final door at the end of the hall, where Ezra's room door stands ajar.

While Ezra was gone for so long with the Resistance, we kept his bedroom door shut. On his few visits, he would always enter his room and close the door behind him, and there have been many nights when I pass his door to hear the hurried whispers of him praying.

But tonight, all is silent.

Through the open door, I can see that Ezra lies still in his own bed, his chest rising and falling rhythmically beneath the damp cloths that Papa has laid over the burns along his body.

He sleeps soundly for once, the security of home and family driving away the fears of the bombs that slip into his consciousness when sleep is aroused.

Papa sits stiffly in a chair in the corner of the room, his head pressed against the side as his mouth hangs open and soft snores elude from his nose.

I smile softly.

I had offered for him to take my room for the night since he selflessly gave his own to Hugo, but he had declined, telling me that I needed to get some rest.

I haven't yet.

Once I ensure that they are both sleeping peacefully and stoke the fire in the hearth to prevent it from going out, I make my way silently through the living room, where I am greeted with two more slumbering persons.

Fletcher sits upright on the sofa, his legs propped on the coffee table as his head is turned toward the ceiling, his mouth open as he snores drastically.

Eline rests by his side, her dainty feet tucked beneath her as she sleeps peacefully with her head pressed against Fletcher's shoulder, the two of them inseparable even in sleep.

I sigh softly.

A wave of loneliness washes over my chest despite the full house of people.

Turning away from them, I step silently into the dining room.

From the doorway, I can see a faint light casting a warm glow across the floor of the kitchen, and it is not the oil lamp balanced in my hand.

Someone must have left a light on, I think to myself, stepping over the threshold and into the kitchen.

Even with the faint glow of the single candle alight on the table and my oil lamp in one hand, the kitchen is still dark, heavily veiled with shadows that dance in the corners and taunt my memories.

The floorboards moan somewhere across the room, and I still, my heart hammering in my chest.

Thoughts run through my sleep-deprived and weary mind.

Germans! my heart screams at me.

I wave my lamp in front of me, swallowing the bile that rises in my throat as the lamp illuminates a thin figure sitting at the dining table, pale blue eyes gazing up at me.

My heart jolts as dread fills my veins.

Hugo.

I sigh audibly, a soft groan rising in my throat.

"There is coffee on the stove," he says, his eyes following me as I cross the room, fighting the urge to turn and recoil in disgust.

He sits rigidly in the dim darkness, his spine curved as he sits hunched over a mug of black coffee clenched in his hand, a both sour and thoughtful look inhabiting his face.

"No thank you," I say sharply, bitterness and anger welling up in my chest.

Hugo gazes at me dauntingly, his face pale and emotionless, though in his eyes I can see a soft glimpse of sorrow and guilt.

He has changed, Ezra had told me.

My mind wanders back to the moment at dinner; he had seemed different.

Perhaps almost sincere.

But my wits tell me not to believe it, and my heart refuses to.

"I know that you are angry with me. I understand that," Hugo says suddenly, his voice sharp as it slices through the tense air around us. His eyes are dark as he lowers his voice. "But why don't you say anything?"

I hold his gaze defiantly.

"I do not have anything to say, Hugo," I reply flatly.

He scoffs softly.

"I seriously doubt that," he says.

It takes all my strength to hold my tongue.

Set a guard, O Lord, over my mouth, my heart prays an old psalm silently. *Keep watch over the door of my lips!*

There is a time to speak, and a time to keep silent.

Silence grows into a gaping void as moments go by and neither of us say a word, memories of our last meeting rushing through my mind with such ferocity that it brings tears to my eyes as my lip trembles from the words I wish to speak at this moment.

We remain silent, glaring at one another across the room, his defeated blue eyes holding my tense hazel ones as one thought runs through my mind:

We are enemies.

No matter what has happened or how much Hugo may have changed, he is still a German.

And I am still a Jew.

And he still betrayed us all.

That is our past, and the past is not just a story of what has been, but a reflection of what will be.

I warned you, Jew, he had hissed in my ear the day he betrayed us. *And now that traitor of a broer is far away—and all of you are utterly hopeless. But don't worry.*

He had bent closer to me then, so close I could smell the stench of his breath and see the malice in his cold and vacant eyes.

I'll find him next.

My heart pounds in my chest, casting a thunderous drumming in my ears as I nearly drown in the rush of anger and hatred that the memories stir in my heart.

My mind wanders to Ezra, lying motionless in the next room, his body covered in burns that will take weeks to heal and his mind harboring wounds that will never fade.

Hugo had been right; he *did* find him next.

Hugo notices the look on my face, and sighs.

"Look, you have every right to be angry with me. And I do not expect your forgiveness," he says tensely, looking at his hands.

I face him.

Thin and wispy, he looks every bit the wounded and guilty man that he is; but as I look him in the eye, all I see is the taut German soldier dressed in the gray woolen coat and trousers of the Nazis, the silver buttons lining his coat reflecting the malicious grin pulling at his lips as he gazes at me.

I want to spit in his face.

"I am not angry because of what you did to me, Hugo. I am not that selfish," I say.

He glances up at the sudden fierceness in my voice.

"I am angry because of what you did to *them,*" I say, shaking my head as I take a daring step toward him.

Slowly, the familiar thread of mettle courses through my veins as my courage to face him rises.

The prowling lion of my temper within my chest has woken once more, and I cannot fight it any longer.

"I *never* trusted you. But they did. They loved you and welcomed you into Still Waters despite your being a German. Mr. and Mrs. Shepherd overlooked the blood on your hands and the hatred in your eyes and adopted you as their own, voluntarily risking their own lives to hide you."

I take a breath, my heart hammering in my chest as the words fall from my mouth and bitter tears fill my eyes.

"They didn't deserve betrayal. *We* didn't deserve to be handed over to the Germans on a silver platter, like sheep being led to the slaughter. But you willingly offered us to them, and you forced us into those trucks without guilt or remorse, knowing good and well where we were headed."

I stop, my lip trembling as I gaze at him.

He sighs, his cold eyes growing red and glassy.

"I know," he whispers so quietly his voice is nearly lost in silence.

I wrestle with my bitterness.

This man is the symbol of the cruelty and reproach that we have all endured, not just the Jews, but everyone affected by the German regime. More than that, he represents the worst of this war, the worst of the torture and dehumanization that we faced in the camps.

Mof, my heart whispers.

Vermin.

Traitor.

Coward.

I shake my head, my heart pounding.

"No, you do not," I whisper, my voice nearly breaking from the weight of my words.

I want to scream, but I cannot.

"You *don't* know what we went through after you betrayed us. You don't know what torture and cruelty we all had to suffer all those months in transit camps, being beaten and interrogated and starved half to death. Nor do you know what it took for us to be able to return home, how many lives it cost for us to be free, and what price we are still paying even now, two years later. And *you* are the reason we still carry with us every day of our lives the memories and wounds of our past."

I fall silent for a moment, breathing heavily as I stand still, holding his gaze steadily.

Hugo sits in his chair motionless and pale as a statue, his face void of all emotion as he cups his chin in his hand, gazing up at me.

Still, he is silent.

"I have tried and fought to forget everything that has happened these past two years. I wanted the pain and anger of the loss and grief to numb, so I buried it. Deep."

His eyes darken considerably at my words, and I continue.

"But then I was sent to Antwerp, and then Ezra was injured by the bombs, and I almost lost him. He nearly died just to save your skin, knowing good and well what you did."

I whisper the words softly, my voice growing faint and fragile as my anger boils.

I take a shaky breath.

"We have all worked so hard to move beyond what has happened, and by God's grace, we are still here together and alive today. Most of us. But here you are, reminding us of everything we've tried to forget."

I fall silent, my speech finished and my courage nearly spent, leaving me even more worn out and exhausted than before.

"I am well acquainted with my mistakes, Ruth," Hugo says, holding my gaze.

A chill runs through me as I hear the icy and sharp German's voice utter my name.

Since the day he met me, my name has been *Jude.*

Jew.

He motions toward the chair across from himself.

"Please sit. I am not going to strike you," he says flatly.

I eye him wearily, questioning his motives.

Slowly, I do as he asks, and I slip into the chair, folding my hands calmly in my lap as I meet his gaze.

His eyes are angry, though something tells me not at me. His shoulders sag beneath the heavy burden of my words, and his face is covered in a veil of pain.

Or perhaps remorse.

I cannot tell which.

He looks me in the eye and the overwhelming sensation of him striking my cheek blooms across my face from my memories, and I want to recoil, to put as much distance between us as possible.

But I do not.

I sit stock still as we gaze at one another in mutual silence and dislike as he begins to speak once more.

"I have carried the guilt of knowing what I did for so long now, it has become a part of me. It has weighed upon my heart and preyed upon my mind," Hugo hisses, shaking his head at himself.

"I was running long before I came to Still Waters. I have been running all my life. Running from my family, and even God. And when I came to Still Waters, it was no different. I was faced with the Shepherd's kindness and the faith that you all shared, and I knew that I couldn't remain there long. And so I ran again," he says, gazing down at his hands, which he now holds palm face up. "And I have been running ever since. I have fought with remorse and guilt for what I have done every day and every waking moment since it happened."

Squaring my shoulders, I push a shaky and fragile breath through my lips.

"And?"

He glances up at me from his pale, childlike hands.

"And *nothing* will take the blood from my hands. And I have found that no amount of drinking or wishing could remove the guilt from my soul."

I swallow, tears pricking my eyes.

"How can I trust that you are sincere? How can I know that you have truly repented?"

How can I know that you aren't lying to me?

Hugo sighs.

He rakes a hand across his face before reaching suddenly into the chest pocket of his shirt.

What is he doing?

My heart pounds as he draws his hand back out once again, gazing at whatever lies in his palm.

"I think this belonged to you, once," he says, his gaze flickering across my face.

And slowly, he slips it across the polished surface of the table toward me, a familiar flash of gold meeting my gaze as the pale sunlight reflects off its face.

May this keep you safe from harm.

My breath catches, and my hammering heart stills.

No, I think to myself as my anger vanishes, only to be replaced by raging sorrow, *it can't be.*

Tears burn my eyes as I reach with trembling fingers to retrieve the small Bible from the tabletop. My fingers are shaking so terribly when I open its cover that I can hardly turn the thin pages as my gaze lands on the name I had written in the inside cover before sending it to my brother for Christmas three years ago.

Andrew Nathaniel DeVos.

Tears fall down my cheeks now, and I am too shaken to care to wipe them away.

Andrew.

It has been so long since I laid eyes on this small golden Bible, and I had just assumed it had been buried with him.

My fingertips graze the dent in the Bible's left corner, where it had shielded him from the first bullet that had threatened to take his life earlier in the war.

But it failed to shield him from the final one.

I steal a glance at Hugo, my eyes blazing as I speak, my voice surprisingly steady and clear.

"Where did you get this?"

He searches my face for a moment before answering.

"I was running from the British soldiers when I found it in the streets of Ghent a few months ago," he says, his voice flat. "I recognized the name immediately when I opened it. It's your brother's, isn't it?"

I nod, biting my lip.

"It was, yes," I say softly, nearly choking on the words. "He passed away a year and a half ago."

His gaze falls from me to the desk as he shifts in his seat.

He clears his throat.

"Oh. I am truly sorry to hear that," he says, almost sounding sincere as he lays his hands flat on the desk in front of him. "How did it happen?"

"He was shot by a German," I say shortly, my voice on the edge of breaking as I gaze in wonder at the small Bible in my hands.

I look up again.

"What does Andrew's Bible have to do with your story?"

He drums his thin fingers against the tabletop, his cold blue eyes distant as he seems to be recalling memories from his own past.

"Because when I found that Bible and I saw Andrew's name written on the inside..." He shakes his head, the shadow of a smile pulling across his face. "That is when I stopped running. That is how I believe God got my attention after all this time. *DeVos.* That is how he at last sobered my rebellious heart and claimed my life as his own."

I chew my lip, remembering the words that had been spoken to me when I saw the cross at the Dossin Barracks.

I loved you enough to die for you...

"The guilt I had carried for so long had at last taken its toll on me, and I could no longer bear it. I repented of my past sins and mistakes," Hugo says, pulling me back to our conversation.

His face turns rueful.

"For months I have been wandering in search of an answer as to what to do with my life. And I soon found myself in Antwerp, when I was found by an enraged Dutch soldier who proceeded to beat me."

I swallow the bile in my throat, my mouth drying as I part my lips to speak.

"And then Ezra found you."

He nods stiffly, confirming my words.

I close my eyes against the current of thrashing emotion welling in my chest, wishing now more than ever that Ezra were by my side.

"I don't know why he chose to do it, Ruth. I know that I certainly do not deserve it. But I am grateful for his actions," he says, swallowing. "Truly, I am. He saved my life and has given me hope that I *can* be forgiven."

I nod softly, the still small voice whispering to me again as the room falls silent once more, save for the soft rise and fall of Fletcher's snoring ensuing from the living room.

Forgive, as I have forgiven you.

I know, Father; but how?

How can I forgive him and simply forget what he has done?

How can I say I forgive, even though bitterness and anger still rage in my heart? How can I ignore the person he was in the past and trust that he *has* changed, and how can I know that he will not betray us once more?

But the answer is simple: *I cannot.*

But I can, Daughter, the voice says. **I know it seems impossible right now, but it will come.**

Forgiveness, for me, is not something that simply occurs in a moment, or even in a single word. It is something that takes days, weeks, and years of time and healing before genuine forgiveness is met.

"I cannot promise you forgiveness, Hugo. Not like Ezra, anyway," I say tentatively. "But I pray that one day it will come."

"I understand," he says, nodding his head.

So we sit for a moment longer like this. No longer enemies, but still not quite friends. But at least we stand on level ground.

A few moments pass and I leave Hugo alone once more, the little Bible clutched to my chest as I retrace my steps through the sleeping house and return once more to the quiet solitude of my room.

"Oh, Andrew!" I whisper in sorrow as I gaze at the little Bible in my grasp.

May this keep you safe from harm, the engraving on the Bible's face tells me silently.

"But you didn't keep him from harm," I whisper, falling to my knees at the foot of my bed. "You took him away from me."

Why Andrew?

Andrew was fearless in the face of evil, and obedient through it all.

He was loyal until death.

"You took him away from me," I repeat softly.

CHAPTER THIRTY-THREE

ANDREW

"**I** don't want you to go," I whisper softly.

The comforting sounds of seagulls crying overhead soothe me like a whimpering child who has at last found solace. The wind whistles and the waves roar in my ear, blowing bitter tears across my cheek.

Andrew's gaze is soft as he smiles at me, his features peaceful and serene despite the zealous and daring fire that had once burned within them.

We sit side by side on the beach in Vlissengen like we used to as children, the sun casting a golden hue across the beach as it warms my bare toes in the sand.

"I *must* go, Ruth. You know that," he says. "I left you before now, but you have to let me go this time."

I shake my head, tears falling down my cheeks as I search his eyes, but they offer me no hope of his returning to me.

They are calm and certain, though they dance with a joy and happiness that I have never witnessed in them before, not in the years we spent together.

His face is bright as he smiles at me, the scars along his body left from his days with the Resistance no longer marking his flesh, and as I gaze upon my dear brother, there is no wound, hole, or scar where the bullet pierced his chest the day that he left.

"I *can't,* Andrew," I say. "I can't let you go."

He smiles a sideways sort of smile, laying a thin hand over my own.

"Yes, you can, *Zus,*" he says softly, his breath warm against my cheek. "This isn't goodbye."

My lip trembles.

"It certainly feels like goodbye," I say.

He nods, his gaze softening.

"I know. But do not trust those feelings, Ruth. They are lying to you," he says earnestly, his eyes shining. "We will see each other again. Do you understand?"

His hazel eyes meet mine, and every moment we ever shared flashes in his gaze; our earliest childhood memories on the beach playing together, traveling to Antwerp as older children, and our days helping Papa beside one another as young adults before the war, and lastly, I see his memories of his time with the Resistance, ending with the final day in Ghent.

It's all there, all twenty-four years of my brother's life on this Earth.

And I understand.

But I do not want to.

My brother is leaving me for the final time.

I shake my head.

"No, *Broer*," I say, my voice thick with unbelief.

He nods his head softly, his hand tightening over mine even as I try to pull it away.

"Yes, *Zus*. I must go," he repeats gently.

He touches a hand to his chest, where the yellow badge had once been.

Where the bullet had struck him.

The former things have passed away...

"Look at me." He smiles. "I am still here. And I will be waiting for you, Ruth. I *promise*."

"Why you?" I whisper softly.

He smiles gently.

"Why *not* me?" he asks.

A broken sob escapes my lips, and he pulls me to his side, holding me there as I tremble.

I bury my head into his shoulder, breathing in deeply the scent of the salt air that I recall from my childhood.

He sighs softly, holding me in a brotherly embrace as he whispers in my ear.

"It is well with me, *Zus*," he says.

~ ~
·

IT IS WELL WITH ME, ZUS.

I open my eyes.

The early rays of the winter sun peek into my window as dawn slowly illuminates the darkness of the starless night sky, whisking its few and faint tendrils into my room and pulling me from my dream.

"Andrew," I whisper softly, lifting my head from the foot of my bed where I had fallen asleep last night.

I do not cry out or even scream his name. Instead, I smile; a broken and tear-rent smile, but a smile, nonetheless.

Do you understand, my daughter? The still small voice whispers to me gently.

I nod.

Yes, I think I do.

The dream had been an altered memory, fabricated from the varying memories of Andrew in my mind that I have carried for so long; but I know that the dream had not come to me of its own accord.

No, it came to remind me that our stories do not end in death.

Not for those who have accepted Jesus.

Our stories live on, even after death; for we are not bound to the temporary hope of this Earth, but our lives, along with our stories, will remain in Heaven, cascading down through the ages of eternity.

Andrew had been right.

We *will* see each other again, just not on this Earth.

"Andrew," I whisper again, his name stirring old memories in my mind and emotions in my heart.

But along with the old feelings of anger at his death and grief for his loss, comes a new softer feeling: *acceptance.*

I push myself stiffly upright again, raking a hand through the untidy strands of my dark hair as I step absently to the desk where the faint morning light glints and reflects off of the metal keys of my typewriter as it sits waiting for me.

Write, Daughter.

Write what?

Your testimony, comes the swift reply. **Write the story I have given you.**

I slip silently to the door, where my small trunk still sits, harboring my few belongings from Antwerp.

Turning the old trunk onto its side and gingerly opening the brass clasp of the closure, I slip my hand inside its depths as I search blindly for the green portfolio.

My hands close over the thin book, and I draw it out. I flip swiftly through the many leaflets and documents and carbon papers within it, coming at last to the yellowing and tattered draft of my earliest newspaper column.

The title gazes back at me in the dim light, and I sigh.

The Yellow Badge.

Along with the article, I take my old green journal.

Standing once more, I step to my desk, where I slip into my chair as a shiver runs down my spine from the draft in the room, but I ignore it.

Instead, I turn to the messy ink stains and faded words of the newspaper article as I hold it up to the window to see.

My gaze flits across the words I had written so long ago at Still Waters, before the ambush and before Andrew's death.

My childhood days were filled with all manner of light. These were the days before the darkness threatened to extinguish the light and its inhabitants with it.

These were the days of menageries and childhood dreams, of long days spent in one another's company strolling on the beach in the warm glow of the summer sun...

I brush the tears from my eyes gently with the back of my hand and prop the few pages of carbon paper holding the article along the wall in front of me.

I gaze at them for a brief moment, Jack Lewis's kind advice to me circulating through my mind.

Write for someone...

I do not have to wonder who to write for, because his name comes warmly to my mind like a golden memory from my past.

Andrew.

Even if I cannot write for myself, I *can* write for Andrew.

Maya moans behind me, still safe beneath the fold of the blankets where I had left her last night.

I stand abruptly, stumbling toward the wardrobe, where I swiftly retrieve Andrew's rucksack.

A soft pain washes over my chest as I gaze at it, but I push the feelings away as I open it and reach inside, my hands feeling blindly until I find what I want. I pull it out, gazing down at it.

It is a small brown journal with tattered edges and a rather threadbare appearance, seeming as if it had been dropped in the mud and abused mercilessly during its short life.

I crack the spine, gazing inside at the few short lines of Andrew's tight handwriting that account each day he spent away from home.

Tucked within these pages, are the loose leaflets of letters that he had received from me and his commander.

I smile softly.

Andrew's journal.

Returning to my desk, I pull a fresh sheet of carbon paper into the tight grasp of the typewriter's roll, adjust its margin, and lock down the hammer as my hands hover above the keys idly and I begin to absently hum the melody to Spafford's *It Is Well with my Soul.*

My fingertips brush against the cold keys once again, and the story falls from my mind to the paper almost effortlessly as my memories form into words that begin slowly weaving the story of my past.

I write furiously until the wintry morning light dawns over the farm and the others begin to slowly arouse from their restful slumber, and even then, I write.

PART THREE

Brussels, Belgium

For everything there is a season, and a time for every matter under Heaven: ...a time for War, and a time for Peace.

ECCLESIASTES 3: 1-8

CHAPTER THIRTY-FOUR

Three months later

My heart flutters as Ezra's brown eyes drift across the pages of my story, his lips pulling into a soft smile as he reads and recalls the memories that I have written.

We sit side by side on the porch stoop, the warm early May sun illuminating the farmlands that surround us as the gentle wind stirs the pages clasped in Ezra's large hand.

It feels like a lifetime has passed since he began reading the story I have so lovingly and painstakingly written all these weeks, and I study his face as he reads.

It has been three months since the bombing, and we are all adjusting to life as it is now.

Ezra's burns have healed completely, though he still limps noticeably as the feeling in his legs has not returned to its former strength; beneath the denim trousers that he wears, I know that the burns along his legs have left their permanent vestige in the form of scars and discolored flesh, forever reminding him of the day he nearly lost his life.

In the few months that have passed, we have all returned to the family that we once were. Papa has returned to his work in Antwerp for a time, Eline and Fletcher have returned home to Oma's estate, though they visit daily, and Mr. and Mrs. Shepherd are still reeling from the loss of our beloved Still Waters.

Hugo has changed in small ways noticeable to us all as we all learn to forgive him and turn to face the future and the hopeful end of this horrid war.

At this moment, as Ezra and I sit on the porch, I can hear the lively chatter of the others eluding from the open windows as they prepare for breakfast at the dining table.

A moment passes as I think, and Ezra lays the final page down in his lap.

I steal a glance up at him.

"Well?" I ask softly, almost afraid of the answer.

He nods softly, swallowing as he meets my gaze.

"It is good, love. Truly," he says.

I smile, my cheeks flaming as my spirit brightens.

"Do you think so?"

"Yes." He smiles. "But it isn't finished."

I raise my brows in surprise.

"It isn't?" I ask, glancing down at the last page he had read.

The page that stares back at me is the closing scene that had almost killed me to write: Andrew's grave.

Ezra smiles softly, following my gaze to the sheaf of paper in his lap.

"It is a beautiful story, Ruth. But you cannot leave the ending this way. Not there," he says gently. "Not with death."

My heart sinks at his words.

Not with death.

Not with Andrew's death.

I sigh.

"It took everything I had to write that scene. I'm not sure I could go on any further," I say.

Ezra nods, understanding written across his face.

"I know. And I am proud of you; I know this could not have been easy to write. But I believe that the rest will come in time," he says softly, his gaze daring. "This is your testimony. This is the story that God has given you, and it doesn't end in death."

I smile at him.

"No, I suppose it doesn't," I say.

He returns my smile, his gaze falling back to the manuscript as he leafs through the beginning chapters of *The Yellow Badge.*

"I remember it all so well, Ruth. Being at Still Waters, I mean. And reading this makes me long for those days spent there, in the early days of this war when we were all together and less damaged than we are now." His gaze is wistful as he returns it to me, his voice tender as he speaks, "It feels as if we were just children then. Children forced to grow up too soon."

Children forced to grow up too soon.

He had joined the Resistance.

I was arrested and imprisoned.

We were all left to somehow survive and preserve our freedom.

I nod, leaning on his shoulder.

"We were," I say thickly as I clutch the sheaf of the unfinished story to my chest. "But we survived."

"By God's grace, yes we did," he whispers, pointing down to the manuscript and reading its title. "*The Yellow Badge.*"

He smiles softly as he thinks for a moment, leaning closer to me as his gaze travels to the land around us.

The fields surround the small house on every side, green grass beginning to rise from the earth as the snow finally leaves us until next winter, and the magnolia tree and the Dutch tulips are beginning to bloom along the hillside of the eight crosses on the hill, where both Oma Edwards, Bram Hendrik, and six other men are buried. To the left of the large barn is a wide plateau of unearthed dirt that has been freshly plowed and tended, and beside that, the horses and chickens roam in the shady green pastures.

"*This* is our life now, Ruth. The yellow badge is gone, and so is Still Waters. And we are certainly no longer children." He smiles wistfully.

A small laugh escapes my lips at his wry and obvious words.

"I know some of us still carry the weight of the badge, and the burden of our pasts is heavy," he says thickly, "but this is life after the badge."

After the badge.

I steal a glance at Ezra, an idea forming in my mind.

Perhaps he is right.

Maybe the story doesn't end there.

"So, what about the future?" I ask tentatively, nodding my chin toward the manuscript. "For the *story,* I mean."

Ezra smiles, his eyes brightening as he understands my meaning.

This story.

Our story.

"Well, um, yes. Let's see. I suppose a wedding will be needed first," he says, glancing at the ring on my hand. "As soon as your father returns and your mother is brought home safe."

I nod, my cheeks growing warm at his words.

"And then we will settle down here, Ruth," Ezra says after a moment of silence as he gazes at his palms.

I follow his gaze and notice that the callouses have grown few and far less visible in his few months of recovery.

"And we will tend this land just like Pa used to. He wouldn't want me to, of course. But I am." He smiles wistfully, memories of his father rolling through his mind. "I want to grow the herd and re-establish what he and Mama built all those years ago when I was a child."

I smile softly at him, laying my hand into his open palm.

He smiles, his fingers folding around my hand.

"It won't be easy," he says.

"Nothing in life is," I reply softly.

He laughs, shaking his head.

"No, I suppose not," he says softly.

We share a smile, our gaze meeting as we sit together talking of the future just as we had at Still Waters; though the future seems closer than it had been in those days, and much happier if spent by one another's side.

I have led you beside Still Waters, now I will make you lie down in the green pastures, the voice says in my ear suddenly, almost causing me to jolt forward.

God led us to Still Waters three years ago, where we all met and became the family that we are today. Still Waters is where Ezra and I first met, and this story began; and now it is gone.

But *He* is making us a new refuge, and making us settle down here, in these green pastures.

"Green pastures," I whisper wistfully, after a moment of deep thought.

Ezra raises his brows.

"What?"

I turn to him.

"That is what we will call this place," I say, smiling. "*Green Pastures.*"

He is silent for a moment, running a hand absently over the stubble on his chin.

A soft smile pulls at his lips.

"I like it," he says after a moment.

His gaze is wistful and rueful all at once, and I know that he is thinking once again of his parents, who will never see their one and only son so gallantly carry on their legacy.

"Green Pastures," he murmurs, testing the name out with a smile. "*The Lord is my Shepherd, I shall not want. He makes me lie down in green pastures.*"

He wraps an arm around my shoulders and pulls me close, his mood somber and tender as we sit in silence.

The wind rustles through the leaves gently as the faint murmuring of the radio broadcast that Mr. Shepherd is announcing the morning news, and the vivacious laughter of Mrs. Shepherd and Eline can be heard.

I sigh with contentment.

"Good Heavens!" Mrs. Shepherd says suddenly from inside.

And then, glass shatters.

It pierces through the morning air with a sharp cry that startles me, pulling Ezra and I from our planning and dreaming as we glance at each other.

We stand quickly, rushing to the screen door and over the threshold of the house.

"Mrs. Shepherd?" I ask as I step into the kitchen, Ezra on my heels. "Is everything alright?"

The scene that I am met with is quite normal; nothing seems out of place or out of the ordinary.

Mr. Shepherd sits at the head of the table, Maya on his right, and Hugo on his left; Eline and Fletcher sit in silence as they gaze at the small radio in front of Mr. Shepherd, as Mrs. Shepherd stands upright at the counter, her eyes wide as the remains of the poor cup she had dropped lay shattered across the floor at her feet.

I step to her swiftly, gingerly stepping over the glass as I lay a hand on her forearm.

"Quiet, dear. Listen," she says, nodding her head to the small radio that sits speaking on the table as everyone turns to listen.

Mr. Shepherd twists the small knob, and the broadcaster's voice rises higher.

"...this is the day of celebration and long-awaited freedom from our enemies! Rejoice, you Dutchman! You have fought a brave battle, and we are now free. Many fear it isn't true and doubt what the intelligence sources are telling us..."

Static overcomes the man's voice for a moment, shattering through the room before clearing once again, and I lean closer to listen.

"...while today we celebrate, Nazi Germany is crumbling beneath the heavy blow dealt to them. Yes, it has just been confirmed by German radio broadcasts in Berlin. As of yesterday, April 30th, Adolf Hitler, chancellor and dictator of Nazi Germany, is dead!"

CHAPTER THIRTY-FIVE

"...ACCORDING to a German intelligence source, Hitler was found in his personal study with a gunshot wound in his right temple. He shot himself with his own pistol..."

We stare at one another in stunned silence, our faces flushing as smiles tug at our lips, though doubts arise in our hearts almost immediately.

Hitler is dead.

I swallow.

Is it true?

It cannot be true.

Can it?

I want to laugh with joy over the news and shout it from the housetops.

Hitler is dead!

The war is over, and the enemy is at last dead, gone to a place where he can no longer torture us and his beloved *Reich* will collapse in his absence.

We are *free* from the clutches of Hiter and his ruthless Nazi followers, and free from the persecution and authority they once held over us.

But with these feelings of joy and happiness, come doubts, anger, and questioning as I feel the overwhelming sensation to cry.

Can it all truly be over?

If the war is declared over just at the death of this one man, then what was it all for?

Why did we go through such persecution and reproach all this time for it to come to a close like this?

What have all of our men died for?

What have these past five years of turmoil and bloodshed been for if it can all be dissolved in the moment the enemy's leader dies?

What have we been fighting and striving all this time for, if a war so fierce and unending as this one could end in a second?

But the answer is simple; it cannot.

Though Hitler is supposedly dead, and the war may be declared over in the coming days, the war is far from over.

No, it will live on in the hearts and minds of its victims and survivors—in the dreams, nightmares and memories that were rooted during the world's darkest hour.

The radio blares on, but we do not hear a word the man says. No one speaks.

Ezra stands thoughtfully in the doorway we have just come through, his eyes wide as he gazes absently at the radio.

Hugo sits calmly at the table, his face no paler than usual as he gazes questioningly at us all around him, obviously uncertain as to how to take the news of his former leader's death.

"Praise the Lord, the enemy is dead!" Fletcher says, smiling brightly at the rest of us as we struggle to form our own reactions to the news. He laughs softly as he says, "The vile man is gone!"

Maya looks around at us all, simply not understanding the meaning of the radio broadcaster's words.

"What's the matter?" she asks suddenly. "Who is gone?"

I press a finger to my lips.

"Quiet, little goose," I tell the little girl gently. "Just a moment, and we will explain."

Eline glances at me.

Is it true? her gaze seems to say.

Mr. Shepherd sits in thoughtful silence at the table, his fingers arched over his plate as his face pales, and his eyes grow distant. His wife, meanwhile, stands clutching my hand tightly in her own, her eyes hopeful as her flushed cheeks color with life once again.

She glances around as if waking from a dream, catching sight of the glass on the floor.

"Oh, Ezra, I am so sorry. It seems I have broken one of your mother's cups," she says suddenly, releasing my hand and bending to collect the broken fragments.

I stifle a laugh at her strange words as I reach for the straw broom propped in the corner near the cellar door.

Ezra shakes his head, stepping forward.

"That's quite alright, Mrs. Shepherd," he says, his voice soft and almost breathy as he takes a seat by Mr. Shepherd's side, folding his arms and cupping his chin in his hand thoughtfully.

Silence fills the room as Mr. Shepherd turns the radio off and I help Mrs. Shepherd sweep up the broken pieces to the delft blue cup she had dropped in the excitement of the moment.

"Are we certain that it is true?" Eline asks softly, glancing from Fletcher to Mr. Shepherd. "Do we really believe that a man like Adolf Hitler would just fall without a final attempt at destroying us?"

"It was his final attempt, dear," Fletcher tells her. "His men, those *Mofs,* began fighting the Soviets over two weeks ago in Berlin as a final attempt at gaining power. He knew that his end was coming, but he was too much of a coward to face it."

Hugo shifts in his seat uncomfortably, his eyes flashing as his gaze rests on the table in front of him.

Coward.

That is what I had called him the day he betrayed us.

Though he has proven his loyalty and repentance over his past actions and we have all learned to slowly forgive him, we cannot forget our pasts, and therefore, there remains tension and distrust.

I suppose there always will be.

"I'm not certain that I believe it's true either, Fletcher," Ezra murmurs softly as I rake the glass into the waste basket beneath the sink. "I pray so, but I just cannot help wondering if the Germans aren't just pulling the wool over our eyes."

I nod absently, joining them at the table.

"They have certainly done it before," I say softly, slipping into an empty chair.

What if he is right?

What if Hitler is truly still alive?

Eline grimaces.

"And they could do it again," she says.

Ezra sighs softly beside me.

"They could have only done it under false pretenses, knowing that they would soon be defeated, and are truly ushering him to safety using the underground tunnels," he says.

A soft shudder runs down my spine at his words.

I turn to Mr. Shepherd, stepping toward the table.

"What do you make of it, Mr. Shepherd?" I ask him, glancing down at the large loaf of sweet bread that sits in the center of the table.

He shakes his head slowly, looking up at me over his small spectacles.

"I don't know," he says softly as he drums his long fingers against the table, his gaze traveling across the table as he falls once more into thoughtful silence.

A small smile crawls onto his face a moment later, forming the familiar lines and wrinkles into his kind face.

"I certainly hope and pray that it is true; that man has done so much evil that if he is gone, I cannot say I am sorry that he is."

Fletcher raises his coffee cup in the air in a sort of informal toast.

"Hear, hear!" he says.

A soft laugh circulates around the table as he downs the rest of the bitter black liquid.

"But if he *is* dead, does that mean that the war is over?" Mrs. Shepherd asks the question we are all thinking as she begins passing out pieces of the sticky sweet bread.

Mr. Shepherd nods from the head of the table.

"Well, that depends on how swiftly Nazi Germany will dissolve without Hitler leading them. We can pray that it will fall quickly, so therefore declare the true end of this war."

Declare the true end of this war, my mind repeats his words silently.

And I pray that they are true.

~ ~
.

"HAVE YOU HEARD about Seth Larkins and Miss Eliza?" Mrs. Shepherd asks softly, her cheeks growing red as she gossips.

Eline lays down the pair of denim trousers that she is working on in her lap.

"I have not, but do tell," she says, smiling.

I shake my head at the gossip they share, smiling as I drown out their conversation and return to my typewriter that is set before me as my fingers poise over its keys, driven by the task of an article for the newspaper written solely on Hitler's death.

It is late in the afternoon now, and the men are working in the fields as Eline, Mrs. Shepherd, and I sit together at the dining table, the two of them mending garments while I stare at my typewriter, my stomach churning with quiet relief and joy as I write the words I have longed to write for so long.

The enemy is dead!

Since the radio announcements on the broadcast this morning, rumors have circulated through town and through the Resistance groups and intelligence airways—rumors of both celebration and doubt over Hitler's supposed death.

"Ruth?"

I glance up at Eline, my fingers stilling over the metal keys.

"I'm sorry, yes?" I say, glancing from Eline to Mrs. Shepherd.

Mrs. Shepherd laughs at me softly.

"You truly weren't listening to my story, were you?" Mrs. Shepherd asks, her thick fingers swiftly mending the woolen sock in her palm and returning it to its former glory.

My cheeks flush and I smile softly.

"No, I wasn't," I say truthfully.

Eline smiles, shaking her head at me as she returns once more to the trousers in her lap.

"I swear, Abram must cut holes in these trousers on purpose, just for the pleasure of watching me sew them back up again. This is the third time I have sewn up a hole in the left knee." She sighs, gazing down at her work.

I watch as the two of them skillfully and swiftly mend the garments, my mind returning to the days I spent in the seamstress cell.

I had sewn so many Nazi uniforms during my time in the barracks, and was forced to do so for so long, that I can no longer hold a silver needle between my fingers without trembling all over.

My fingertips burn as if being pricked and I rub them absently over the fabric of my skirt.

Mrs. Shepherd watches me as she sews, her brows raised.

"I couldn't help but overhear you and Ezra talking on the porch this morning, Ruth. Can I assume that you will need a dress soon?"

Now it's my turn to raise my brows as heat crawls into my cheeks and I laugh softly as she gazes at me in a motherly fashion.

I nod.

"Yes, I suppose you can, Mrs. Shepherd. Ezra and I hope to be married as soon as we can, when Mama and Papa have both returned," I say, blushing furiously.

Eline smiles at me, her eyes shining.

"But what will you wear?" she asks. "Silk and lace is rationed these days, and expensive if you can find them."

"Honestly? I was just going to wear the green dress you all gave me for my birthday a few years ago," I say, running my finger lightly over the newspaper draft still tucked into the typewriter's roll.

Eline shakes her head.

"You cannot wear green, Ruth. It must be white," she says with a droll look. "You are welcome to wear my dress, though it may be a bit long for you."

I smile softly.

"Thank you, Eline, but I cannot use your dress. You are a dear for offering, but it wouldn't feel right if I did. Your dress was perfect for you, and special; I do not want to take that from it," I say softly.

Mrs. Shepherd muses quietly.

"My dress was left in Still Waters," she says softly, her face somber as she thinks. She turns to me, her eyes brightening. "What about your mother's dress? Dirk and I attended her and your father's wedding, and I do recall that she was quite a picture in a simple ivory gown."

I nod softly, closing my eyes as I try to recall the old grainy photograph of my parents' wedding day from my memories.

I remember the image well, for I had gazed at the old photograph many times as a child; the dress was made of a simple ivory rayon, with soft ruched sleeves and a lace-adorned skirt that fell to her calves in soft layers.

"I'm afraid I wouldn't do it justice, Mrs. Shepherd," I murmur softly.

Mrs. Shepherd sighs dramatically.

"Oh, pish posh. You would be absolutely captivating in her dress, dear. And I am certain your mother would want it no other way than for her only daughter to use her wedding dress," she says.

I smile, glancing shyly at her.

"I suppose you're right," I say, tucking a loose strand of dark hair behind my ear as memories of my dear mama come rushing through my mind with a strange vibrancy. "But I believe her dress is at home in Vlissengen."

Eline smiles, an idea forming in her mind as she and Mrs. Shepherd share a glance.

I narrow my eyes at them.

"What?" I ask, smiling.

Eline smiles sheepishly, picking up her sewing once again.

"You could go to Vlissengen and have a simple ceremony there," she suggests.

"You mean a beach wedding," I say, smiling softly at the thought. "I would have to ask Ezra, of course. But I would like that."

Vlissengen.

I haven't been home to Vlissengen since I visited Andrew's grave a year and a half ago, and only briefly then.

I nod gently, turning back to the typewriter in front of me and the half-finished article awaiting an ending.

And with these thoughts dancing through my mind, I begin to write once more.

~.~

AT LONG LAST, OUR enemy is dead!

Shall our freedom taste all the sweeter because of this most glorious and long-awaited news?

Hitler is dead!

Rejoice, all you lands and peoples! For his grueling clutches are no longer held upon us.

Because of Hitler, our men have known the horror and the honor of facing the enemy in broad daylight, and the valorous glory of being put out of action by enemy fire.

And we—the civilians, families, and laymen—have fought a knavish, crafty, lying adversary, whose criminal behavior, driven to a degree of extreme cruelty, went beyond the limits of the most beastly insensibility.

Our men faced soldiers in uniform, and we all faced the phantoms dressed with the filthy cloak of Hitler's Nazi regime, who had nothing but crime and torture as an object and aim.

But alas, all of this is over.

For Hitler is dead!

R.M.D.

CHAPTER THIRTY-SIX

Dust flies as wheels churn down the narrow road headed toward the farmhouse.

I cannot see the origin of the noise or the dust, but I can hear it from where I stand in the field, surrounded by horse pastures.

"Do you hear that?" I ask no one in particular.

The first field that has been plowed inhabits a small plot of land near the barn, while this one is directly behind the grain silos, broad and rich with red clay dirt as the large plow churns the dirt up and casts clods and rocks to the surface.

Anouk and Hans, two large sorrel-coated plow horses, have been harnessed up and burdened by the load of the heavy plow they pull behind them, Hugo leading the horses forward as Ezra follows behind guiding the plow.

"Ho! Stop there, Hugo," Ezra calls to Hugo, he and the pale German working together to plow the field.

At Ezra's bidding, the horses stop abruptly, pawing anxiously at the ground with their white feathered hooves as their master stands back, gazing at the field that surrounds us.

For a long distance, it is fields and beyond the red dirt, green horse pastures.

Ezra nods.

"It is good," he says, satisfied.

He turns to the horses, his gait slow and stiff as his left leg hinders him, but he doesn't utter a complaint as he begins swiftly releasing the plow from their harness.

I step to his side as I wade through the large rows cut in the dirt, stopping short by Hans' heaving side.

I begin absently stroking Hans' thick neck, gazing at his face.

With a broad forehead, thick-set jaw, soulful brown eyes, and flared nostrils, Hans bears the customary ginger colored coat, with a white blaze traveling from the center of his forehead down to his muzzle.

Both the horses are tired and breathing heavily, sweat forming along their sorrel coats as their tense muscles relax from the day's hard work.

"Good work, my friends," Ezra tells the horses, a small smile pulling across his face.

I smile softly, turning my ear back toward the road.

Somewhere in the distance, the sound grows closer.

What is it?

Or, *who* is it?

Gooseflesh raises across my arms.

Ezra bends and releases the final strap that keeps the horses bound to the plow, straightening swiftly and turning to me.

"Ruth, take Hans," he says to me, mopping his brow with a dirt-stained hand. "Hugo, you take Anouk. Take their harnesses off and let them go. They may rest for today."

Hugo and I do as he says as Ezra prepares to finish the day's work, leading the large horses out of the dirt fields and to the grass, where we begin to undo the straps and buckles of their harnesses, freeing them of the burden entirely.

But as the horses roam away from us to the promised reward of green grass, the noise grows so close it echoes across the fields.

"Do you hear that?" I ask again, turning to face the house.

"Hear what?" Hugo asks softly, rubbing the dirt from his thin, bony hands.

"Listen," I murmur, squinting through the trees that line the narrow road leading to Green Pastures.

There, traveling swiftly toward the house, is an automobile.

An old army jeep.

My heart pounds as dread is pumped into my veins.

No, I think, panic rising in my chest as the memory of the day Andrew's troop came to pay their respects.

It had been a cold day in late November when an army jeep not unlike this one had pulled up, loaded down with the heavy burden of Andrew's entire troop. I knew already that Andrew was gone, for Ezra wrote to me as soon as he heard, but on this particular day it had become reality.

Commander van Branteghem walked up the steps of the porch with all the grace and refinement an experienced war hero could, his face downcast as he met me at the door, Andrew's rucksack in tow.

Memories of all the times I had seen him with that rucksack had filtered through my mind; from the day he left me on the beach in Vlissengen, to when he returned during the ambush, and even when he left me here at Green Pastures for the final time, the rucksack had been with him then as well.

It had hit at that moment, as I stood gazing at the solemn and sorrowful faces of Andrew's comrades, with such fierceness that my brother was not with them, and he wouldn't be coming back.

The sharp caterwaul of the automobile wakes me from my memories as it pulls to an abrupt stop at the porch stoop.

I glance over my shoulder, catching sight of Ezra as he too, gazes at the vehicle. His face pales as he absently wipes the red dirt from his hands onto the thighs of his trousers.

He joins me and Hugo where we stand gazing at the jeep, dread seeping into each of our hearts.

"Who could that be?" Hugo asks softly.

Ezra shakes his head gently.

"I don't know," he murmurs. I shrug, laying my hand on his forearm as the three of us begin trudging through the fields toward the farmhouse.

Two men in uniform disembark from the vehicle, one heavy-set and the other tall and blond, squinting at the three of us in the field.

"Pik!" the larger man calls, "is that you?"

Ezra steps forward.

"Yes, Commander," he says, his spine stiffening as he marches toward his former commander, a soldier once more.

Lars smiles at us as he waits beside the commander, leaned up casually on the side of the jeep, his arms crossed.

Commander van Branteghem smiles, his blue eyes dancing as he offers Ezra a thick, meaty hand.

"I am certainly glad to see that you have recovered, Pik." Commander smiles, his eyes dancing across Ezra's face and down to his scarred legs.

His eyes travel to meet my gaze, and he nods in greeting, winking sheepishly at me.

I smile softly, raising my brows.

What is his game?

I steal a glance at Lars, shooting him a questioning look.

Lars shakes his head, smiling smugly.

Ezra smiles wryly as he shakes his commander's hand, his voice almost rueful as he speaks.

"A bit slower than I once was, but I am still breathing, Commander," he says as Lars embraces him like a brother. Ezra laughs softly as he claps Lars on the shoulder, his gaze flitting between the two men.

He is about to speak when Oma Edward's black Minevra jostles down the narrow road.

"It looks like Eline and Fletcher are here," I say, smiling.

Ezra nods, turning his bright eyes from the familiar automobile to the commander.

"What can I do for you gentlemen today?" he asks.

The commander smiles, running a hand absently over the breast pocket of his uniform.

"We are here on official business, Pik. Do you mind if we go inside, perhaps, to discuss these matters?" he asks, glancing over his shoulder at the house.

Official business.

What does that mean? I ask myself. *Are they sending him back to Antwerp?*

Dread churns in my stomach.

Ezra nods, stealing a swift glance at me.

I can see a soft anxiousness in his eyes as he stands somewhat rigidly.

"Yes, of course," he says.

~ . ~

"TEA?" MRS. SHEPHERD says, offering the newcomers a pot of fresh tea as she sets the tea tray down on the coffee table in the living room.

"Thank you, ma'am," Lars says, smiling graciously as he slips the hat from off his head and pours himself a cup.

Mrs. Shepherd nods happily and strides quietly to where her husband sits in his chair near the hearth.

She brushes past me and pats my knee gently as I sit beside Eline on the sofa, gazing into the kitchen, where Ezra and Commander van Branteghem speak in low voices.

Fletcher hovers anxiously beside the sofa where Eline sits, his gaze following mine into the kitchen.

Lars smiles at me from across the room, stirring sugar into his tea.

"Don't look so worried, Miss DeVos. Ezra has been discharged. He isn't leaving again," he says flatly, though kindly.

I raise my brows.

"How did you know what was worrying me?" I ask softly, my spirit lifting at his words.

Lars smiles, shaking his head.

"The women are *always* worried about that, Miss. I have seen that look on my mother's face many a time as a child when my father left for the great war," he says softly, nodding toward me and Eline as he slurps his tea in a boorish manner. "Besides, Andrew always told me that you were one to worry."

A sudden laugh escapes my lips at my brother's name.

"He did, did he? Well, I suppose he wasn't lying; I worried about him every day he was gone," I say, smiling softly as I stand and step toward the tea tray.

Lars' eyes widen and he reaches into his pocket.

"Ah, that reminds me," he says, offering me a small letter. "Your father sent this to you, Miss DeVos. He wished to come with us when he heard that we were coming, but he had several other business matters to attend to, and he couldn't leave right away. He sent one to you as well, Mr. Shepherd."

I take the letter he offers me, gazing at the familiar neat Dutch lettering across its front.

I haven't heard from Papa in nearly three weeks.

"Thank you," I murmur softly, taking my tea and the letter and returning to my seat.

Lars gives the second letter to Mr. Shepherd, who takes it and gazes at it thoughtfully for a moment before opening it, Maya sitting on his knee and acting as if she too were reading the letter.

Sipping my tea, I eagerly open Papa's letter, my gaze falling on the few short and neat lines he has written.

My dearest Dochter,

I am sorry I have not written to you these past few weeks.

The last bomb fell on Antwerp in late March, as you know, but the school is still harboring any and all lingering soldiers and homeless folks who have nowhere else to go. I have spent the last two or three weeks tending to the people like a shepherd would a flock, and I believe that my work here is at last coming to a close.

I plan on leaving here soon. With any luck, I hope to arrive in Brussels on Monday.

I have written to Dirk as well, personally asking him to pick me up at the station, if he can be spared for a moment.

As you know, Bergen-Belsen Concentration camp was liberated earlier last month, and with Hitler's death, I pray that your mother will return to us soon.

I have been in correspondence with my good friends with the intelligence network, but no word has come from your mother yet.

Pray for her safe return, Ruth.

I know that you will; you have been for a long time now.

I heard of Ezra's honorable medal—tell him I am proud of him and am glad that all those countless hours we stood over him were not in vain.

Lastly, Dochter, I am proud of you.

I never said just how proud I was to have a daughter who so willingly followed in my footsteps and voluntarily gave of herself to care for wounded strangers even after she faced death in the eye herself.

I guess you got your daring courage from your mother, for I am not so bold.

It is because of this that you remind me so much of your mother and Andrew.

I miss your brother more with each passing day.

Oh, my son!

Will the pain ever go away and cease to haunt me?

I suppose not, but I know that he is waiting for us, Ruth.

I will see you soon, Dochter.

Your loving Papa

I smile softly at Papa's sober words, my heart heavy but my spirit lifting swiftly as I slip the letter back into its envelope.

I glance up to meet Mr. Shepherd's gaze as I catch him watching me, his eyes shining happily.

He knows that my father is coming home.

"If I may ask, whatever is this 'official' business that you two are here on?" Mrs. Shepherd asks Lars, pulling me from my thoughts as she stands smiling down at the young man.

I answer for him, glancing down at Papa's letter.

Honorable medal.

"Ezra is getting a medal," I say, smiling at my own words.

Fletcher straightens, a smile pulling across his face.

"He is?" he wonders aloud.

Lars sighs, running a hand over his face as he gazes at the seven of us still seated in the room.

"Hush! You aren't supposed to know that," he scolds me, stealing a glance into the kitchen.

Satisfied that no one is listening, he straightens and faces us once more.

"Let's just say that Ezra is being rewarded for his *valorous* actions this past February."

He nods toward Hugo, who sits at a distance in the corner.

Hugo looks away, distrusting the rebel soldier.

I am about to ask what he means when heavy footsteps elude from the dining room, telling of the approaching men and we all quieten down.

I sip my tea casually.

For some reason, my stomach churns anxiously as Ezra gazes sheepishly at us as he follows Commander van Branteghem into the room.

I raise my brows gently at him, holding his gaze.

He shakes his head softly in response, smiling as his cheeks flush a soft pink shade.

Fletcher stands behind Eline's chair, raising his hand to his forehead in a salute, which Ezra swiftly returns.

Commander van Branteghem clears his throat, standing gallantly before the fireplace.

"I would like to perform an informal, though official, award ceremony before you all," he says as he glances around at us all, ensuring that we have his attention before he begins speaking once again.

We stand in unison as the commander bids Ezra to come stand beside him.

Ezra obeys, though shaking his head at the fine honor as he stands across from the commander in uniform, Ezra himself still dressed in his work clothes, mud caked onto his work boots and dirt beneath his fingernails as his unshaven cheeks burn with boyish embarrassment at the attention he is receiving.

"Despite the recipient's desires that the award be given to someone else, I have been given the honorable task of bestowing upon him one of the highest awards that can be given in this fine country of Belgium." the commander says, his voice eloquent and somewhat dramatic.

I watch as he pulls a small case from his chest pocket, opening it to reveal a bronze medal lying on a bed of black velvet.

The commander smiles brightly, respect shining in his eyes as he gazes at Ezra.

"I informed the royal authorities of your actions, Ezra, and you have been cited several times because of what you have done for this country, and for the Resistance. I know you have faced trial after trial since joining the Secret Army, and more recently, you have faced the loss of your father. Still you have remained faithful."

Ezra nods softly, straightening to his full height as the weight of the commander's praise weighs heavily upon him, and a broad smile stretches across his face as he looks more like a soldier in this moment than if he had been wearing his uniform.

I smile at Ezra, my heart swelling with pride and admiration as Mrs. Shepherd brushes a stray tear from her cheek beside me, and Mr. Shepherd lays a gentle hand on my shoulder as Maya clutches at my skirt.

The commander gingerly picks up the small medal between two thick fingers as he lets it dangle from his grasp.

"This particular medal, Belgium's *Croix de Guerre,* is a war cross awarded to men for their valorous and virtuous acts of bravery on the battlefield. In your case, Ezra Pik, I give it to you on behalf of King Leopold the third, for your bravery on February the eighth, when you risked your own life to save your fellow man."

Hugo smiles softly in the corner of the room, gratitude and brotherly affection gleaming in his eyes as he gazes solemnly at Ezra as the memories of that day rush to his mind with a raw vibrance.

I watch as the commander pins the brass medal delicately on the left side of Ezra's chest, where the pair of golden wings had rested just a few months ago.

The four-pronged medallion extends from a small crown that hangs suspended from a small red-and-green-striped ribbon, a pair of brass drawn swords glinting in the medallion's midst as it rests now upon Ezra's chest, reminding us of all of the risk he took.

I smile at him, knowing in my heart what this moment truly means for him. He had assumed that when he was put out of action and had to pass his rank to Lars that everything he had fought for these past three years had abandoned him like the feeling in his leg had.

But today confirms that his actions were not in vain.

Ezra smiles sheepishly, shaking hands with the commander.

"Thank you, sir," he says gallantly.

The commander laughs shortly, clapping Ezra on the shoulder as he takes his hand.

"It is my pleasure, Pik. You have been a trustworthy and dutiful soldier these few years, and I am honored to bestow this medal to you today," he says.

Ezra smiles, the color deepening in his cheeks.

The room is silent as Hugo approaches Ezra first, his gaze downcast as he closes the gap between him and Ezra, his thin hand extended.

Ezra takes it swiftly, shaking it heartily as he lays a hand on Hugo's shoulder, forcing the German to look him in the eye.

No words are passed between them, for there are none at a time like this, but I can tell as I stand observing them, that unspoken understanding is passed between the two men, and all past debts erased.

I smile softly.

They part, and Mrs. Shepherd plants a large kiss on Ezra's forehead and Mr. Shepherd embraces him in his usual hospitable and fatherly fashion.

"I am proud of you, my boy," Mr. Shepherd says, a tender rasp audible in his voice.

"Immensely proud," Mrs. Shepherd adds softly.

Ezra smiles at them, his eyes shining as if he were gazing at his own parents.

"Thank you both, for everything," he says softly, his words harboring a deeper gratitude than what is expressed.

Fletcher claps him on the shoulder in a brotherly fashion.

"I told you it was an honor to serve one's country. It is something more to take a stand for your fellow man, and enemy," Fletcher says, offering us all a glimpse of his soulful side. "You did your duty well, my brother."

"Thank you, Fletcher," Ezra says, nodding gratefully.

Eline is next as she comes to embrace Ezra in a sisterly manner, clearing her throat to speak.

"A man is not defined as a soldier by the uniform he wears or the badges on his chest, but by the heart that beats beneath it," she says softly. "And it is for your actions that we celebrate today, not the medal. You did a great thing not only for your country, but for this family."

"Come now, Eline. I didn't do all that much," he replies, his cheeks flushing under the weight of the room's attention.

After a few more moments of congratulation ensues, I step to his side.

His dark eyes meet, mine, his gaze soft and sorrowful.

"What's wrong?" I ask gently.

He shakes his head smiling wryly.

"I just wish I were deserving of this honor," he says softly, glancing down at the war cross on his chest.

La Croix de Guerre.

I follow his gaze down at the medal, my fingertips grazing the cold surface of the brass, my gaze lingering on the courageous lion emblem upon the bust of the medal's reverse.

"You *do* deserve it, Ezra," I tell him softly.

He shrugs, slipping his hand into mine.

"Maybe so," he says softly, "but I didn't do anything special, Ruth. I only did what God bid me to do. And that was to love my enemy—which in that moment, meant saving Hugo."

I glance up to meet his gaze once more, holding his stare steadily as I shake my head at him, smiling.

He raises his brows.

"What?

I smile, laughing softly.

"You," I say.

"What about *me?*" he asks.

I finger the medal between my fingers as I answer him.

"Ezra, it's not the medal that counts—it's your actions upon which foundation you were given the medal. You willingly risked your life to save the life of the man who could have easily killed your entire family. I am not sure who would have the courage and faith to do that. But in your quiet and obedient manner, you did it. Simply because that is what God told you to do."

I smile up at him, my voice thick as I point to the medal.

"*That* is why you deserve this medal, regardless of the grounds that King Leopold issued it to you on. Because it was your duty to distrust your own ability, that you may rely on *Him* that is stronger than all."

He smiles softly, his eyes soft and sincere.

"Well said," he says.

I smile, flattening the medal on his chest and gazing at him.

"Besides, it looks good on you," I tease.

Ezra laughs softly, his eyes brightening at my words.

"Thank you, Ruth," he says.

He pulls me to his side, and my gaze falls to the medal one more time, placed directly over his heart—right where the yellow badge had rested over Andrew's heart for so long.

And mine.

But not anymore.

CHAPTER THIRTY-SEVEN

"L'allemagne a capitulé!" I whisper to myself, reading the headline for today's issue of *La Libre Belgique. Germany capitulated!*

Green Pastures is alive with excited chatter and giddy laughter as we rejoice over the end of this horrid war. Everyone is inconsolably happy and relieved, though somewhat apprehensive, at the prospect of our long-awaited victory.

I stand in the midst of the small kitchen, reading the newspaper again for what seems like the twelfth time today as I absently break green beans into a bowl at the counter.

Around me are the certain makings of a feast; mashed potatoes, baked potatoes, gravy, a multitude of vegetables and side dishes, roasted turkey and boulets is just the beginning of the glorious foods that are already lining the dining table.

"Eline, tell me again where you got your hands on all this food?" I ask, tucking the newspaper carefully in the china cabinet for safe keeping.

Eline laughs from her post at the oven as she watches a pair of coconut custards.

"Today is a celebration, Ruth. It deserves all this food, and we haven't enjoyed food like this since our time at Still Waters," she says, carefully avoiding the root of my question. "Besides, everyone in town was so happy today that they were practically giving food away, no matter the ration restrictions."

Mrs. Shepherd smiles at me over the pot of sugared strawberries that she is stirring.

"You read it yourself, Ruth," she says, her eyes shining happily as she repeats the words I had just read moments ago. "Germany has capitulated."

I return her smile.

Just five days after Hitler's alleged death, an unconditional instrument of surrender has been signed by the German Third Reich early this morning at Eisenhower's headquarters in Reims, France.

The news was announced late this morning over a radio broadcast, when the whole of Belgium began celebrating.

The Germans have agreed to surrender their arms, and the ceasefire will take effect tomorrow night at precisely *12:01*, thus ending the war once and for all!

I can hardly believe it's true.

Has the end come at last?

Can I be so foolish as to hope it has?

Mrs. Shepherd, Eline, and I have slaved away over our victory feast all afternoon now. Even Hugo has been aiding the food preparations in honor of the day by peeling potatoes and carving the turkey.

Ezra and Mr. Shepherd left earlier today, per Papa's request, for the train station, where they have hopefully already retrieved Papa, and are returning home from their journey.

I glance swiftly out the window, praying to find Fletcher and Eline's old black Minevra pulling into the road, but I don't.

Instead all that meets my eyes is Fletcher sitting cross-legged in the yard with Maya as the spring chicks run across his lap and the hens peck incessantly at the ground around them as Maya cackles over something Fletcher has told her.

Smiling, I turn back to face the water pump, where I fill the tea kettle and place it on the cook stove to rest until it begins to whistle.

I turn on my heel, opening the china cabinet and gazing at the blue delft and green porcelain chinaware that wait inside.

"Should I use Ezra's mother's good china, in honor of the day?" I wonder aloud.

"I don't see why not, Ruth," Mrs. Shepherd says absently as she gingerly pours the syrupy strawberries into a dish for dessert. She glances up at Hugo. "Hugo, dear, would you mind helping Ruth set the table? We will need ten places set."

Hugo nods, murmuring a swift, "Certainly."

I scrunch my nose in thought.

"Ten places? I thought there were only nine of us, counting Papa," I say, retrieving ten plates from the cabinet and offering them to Hugo.

Mrs. Shepherd is quiet for a moment as she mentally counts heads.

Her cheeks turn a soft crimson, and she smiles to herself as she turns to face Eline.

"Right you are, Ruth. My mistake, there *are* only nine of us," she says.

I take one of the ten plates from Hugo's possession and return it to its rightful place in the cabinet, retrieving instead nine bowls and a gravy bowl.

I step to the table, laying my burden down beside the wide variety of food already waiting on the table as Hugo begins placing the plates at each chair, and I follow the plates with a bowl.

I circle the table and gently set a bowl in the table setting in front of him, and he looks up at me, his eyes bright.

"This brings back memories," he says slowly, offering me a small smile.

I nod gently, understanding his meaning as the memories of the conversation between Hugo, Ezra, and I at Still Water's comes vibrantly to my mind.

It was the day he had called Ezra his *broer,* and me, *deutlich. Bold.*

It was also the day I had told him to choose a side.

"It does," I say, returning his tentative smile.

"I am on your side this time, Ruth. Truly," he says, as if in yet another desperate attempt to prove his loyalty to us. "And I think I have finally chosen well."

I smile at the irony of his words.

"I am glad to hear that, Hugo," I say.

We continue setting the table in silence as Eline and Mrs. Shepherd finish with the desserts. Several moments go by, and still Mr. Shepherd doesn't return.

Eline sets a plate of warm biscuits on the table as she turns to me, her blue eyes wide.

"Oh, dear me, I have forgotten the preserves for the biscuits," she says as the front door screeches and Fletcher and Maya enter the house. "Would you be a dear and run down to the cellar to get a jar, Ruth? I believe Ezra said he had some stored away down there."

I smile, stifling a laugh.

"Eline, I believe we will be alright without them. I don't think they will be missed," I say, waving a hand at the table before me.

"No matter," Eline says with a smile. "Would you go get some, please?"

I sigh, admitting defeat.

"As you wish," I say, reaching for the box of matches above the stove and rolling one between my fingers as I turn to face the cellar door.

Laying a hand on the cellar door, I unlock the bolt at the top and let it fall open on rusty hinges as I step inside.

I strike the match on the wall to my left, wishing the farmhouse had electricity. The tiny flame illuminates the air just enough for me to see my feet as I begin the slow descent down into the depths of the cellar, my footsteps echoing around me as the air entering my lungs grows thick and damp.

The air quality aggravates my scarred lungs, and my breath is slightly constricted as I reach the bottom of the stairs, my shoes meeting the dirt floor as I push a breath through my lips.

I wave the match in front of the various shelves of canned goods and items from days gone by, my gaze landing on a dainty jar of peach preserves.

I step forward to grab it, my foot hitting something and I nearly fall, catching myself by pressing a cold hand to the wall as I regain my balance.

I glance down, the faint tendrils of the match's flame illuminating the small trunk at my feet that I had tripped over, nearly identical to the one I carried to Antwerp, except this one is already full of belongings as it sits open on the floor.

Who has been down here? I think to myself.

I have seen the trunk before on many of my various trips to the dark depths of the cellar, but never have I opened it; but I know that it holds family heirlooms and items of specific value to Ezra.

From where I stand, I can see random documents and title deeds scattered in the bottom of the trunk, covered by a few family Bibles and even an old horse bridle.

But the thing that catches my eye is a small black velvet box, nearly like the one Ezra's medal was in.

Gently, I bend down beside the trunk and with trembling fingers, I pick up the box.

It fits easily in my palm and is soft to the touch as I finger it gingerly, prying its velvet mouth open as the hinges release rigidly, and I peer inside.

It is empty.

No jewels or gold meets my gaze, but only a small scrap of white paper that has been carefully folded and placed in the bottom upon the velvet cushion, as if compelling me to read the message inscribed on it.

I squint at it in the faint light, struggling to make sense of the small Dutch writing.

My dearest Son,

I give these to you now, for I no longer have a use for them except the memories that they bring to my mind.

I pray that you may find a use for them in the years to come, Ezra.

Remember that two are better than one, but a threefold cord is not easily broken.

Love, Pa

I straighten, a soft sigh falling from my lips.

It is a note from Ezra's father.

Upstairs, I can hear the faint screeching of the screen door, followed by heavy footfalls and familiar voices.

I close the box abruptly and return it to the trunk, straightening myself swiftly as I reach for the can of peach preserves from the shelf and lurch for the stairs just as Ezra calls down to me.

"Ruth?"

"Coming!" I call, my voice echoing strangely in the damp darkness.

My match goes out just as I approach the stairs and I am forced to wade through the thick darkness unaided and nearly blind.

I climb toward the light in the kitchen coming from the door, my hands grasping the cold walls on either side of me as I meet Ezra at the top.

Clean-shaven and dressed in mended trousers and a starched shirt, he smiles brightly at me, causing my heart to flutter.

I smile at him.

"What took you so long?" I ask, teasing.

He ignores my question smiling.

"I have something for you to see," he says, taking my hand and pulling me from the dark stairwell and into the kitchen, where the entire Still Water's clan stands gazing at me expectantly.

My heart rate quickens as my cheeks flush scarlet.

I eye everyone wearily, and Eline nearly laughs from sheer excitement as Mrs. Shepherd avoids my gaze altogether.

I notice quickly that Papa is not with them.

I narrow my eyes at them, turning to face Ezra.

"Ezra," I say tentatively as I attempt to pull back from his grasp, "what's going on? Where is Papa? "

His gaze softens but his smile only grows as he holds my hand fast in his own calloused one.

He steps closer to me.

"Your father is fine, Ruth. I promise. He is in the living room," he says, his voice firm and yet gentle.

Then why is everyone acting so extremely strange? I want to ask, but don't.

Instead, I nod hesitantly.

"Trust me," he says, pulling me gently forward as he places a firm hand on my shoulder blade and ushers me over the threshold.

I surrender to his hold, and he leads me gently through the kitchen and silently into the living room, his face soft as we turn the corner to find Papa standing at the fireplace, his eyes damp and shining as his gaze lands on me.

I gasp, tears welling in my eyes as my breath is stolen from my lungs, and Ezra helps me take a step forward.

It is not for Papa alone that I begin to cry, but the broken figure that he holds to his chest.

I recognize her immediately.

She is my own aged and broken reflection.

She is the remnant of the person from my memories.

"Mama?" I whisper softly, my voice nearly breaking.

With a pitifully shorn head and malnourished body, her pale skin is stretched tightly over defined cheekbones, and her large, hazel eyes soften as they lock with my gaze, recognition flushing each of our eyes as tears begin to create trails down our cheeks.

She reaches for me with thin arms, emotion welling up in her eyes as her thin lips part to speak.

"Oh, my *dochter!*"

Just the sound of her voice is enough to nearly break my heart, and I come to her, my feet moving almost mechanically as I step from Ezra's side toward her.

I gaze at her deformed and deprived bodily state, an almost feral look passing her gaze as she watches me. Her hands are cold to the touch as I clasp them eagerly, searching her eyes through the tears in my own.

"You're alive," I say, stroking her thin cheek gently with my fingertip, just as she used to mine as a child.

She nods, smiling softly at me as she pulls me to her chest.

"Yes, *schat.*" she whispers into my ear.

Schat.

Treasure.

Oh, how I have longed to hear her say that!

I wrap my arms around her, burying my face into her chest as a broken sob escapes my lips. I feel almost as if I am a child again, running back into the safe and protective embrace of my mother, though now I am a grown woman, and we are all three damaged and altered.

Her body is so thin and brittle, so deprived and dehumanized by the German's cruelty that I can feel her ribs through the thin garment she wears, and I can see along her limbs the marks and vestige of the starvation and beatings that she has endured all these months.

She is like a fragile flower that I fear I will crush if I hold on too tightly, but I am afraid I will lose her again if I let go.

I glance up from her shoulder at Papa.

His eyes are glassy as he gazes at Mama and I, love and sorrow etched into the lines of his face.

I offer him a small smile, and he returns it as he cups my cheek in his warm hand.

"God has brought you both to me at last," he says thickly, wrapping his free arm gently over Mama's shoulder and pulling the both of us to his chest.

And for a moment, it is as if nothing has ever happened.

And I am their daughter once again, just as I have always been.

It has been over three years since we were together, but it feels as if a lifetime has passed and I have aged twenty years; and even now I can feel the void of my brother in our midst.

Andrew.

If Andrew were here, our family would be complete.

I am still here, his voice says in my memories from Eline and Fletcher's wedding day as he and I spoke before Ezra took me to dance.

And in some ways, I know he is still here.

I can see him in myself, in Papa and in Mama; he meets me in my dreams and in my memories, he comes to me in the most profound ways, in the strangest of places, and at just the right time when I need him the most.

But more than this, I know my brother lives.

No longer there with me, but in Heaven, where we shall all be called home one day.

And so, for tonight, I will be content with this partial reunion and restoration of my family as the three of us hold on to one another as we mourn Andrew's death for the first time as a family, and we offer our praise to God our Father for seeing it fit to bring us back together again.

~ ~
.

AS IT TURNS OUT, everyone knew of Mama's homecoming, save for me.

Apparently, Papa had informed Mr. Shepherd of his secret in the letter he sent him by way of Lars, and so requested that he and Ezra be the ones to come pick him and Mama both up from the train station.

Even Maya knew, which is why she and Fletcher stayed out in the yard to prevent either of them from telling me the secret of my mother's liberation and return.

Ezra had known, but was forbidden to tell me, and so wishing to further impress my parents, he kept the secret dutifully and without slipping.

Papa had been working tirelessly to get in touch with Mama at Bergen-Belson again, and when it was liberated in the middle of last month by the British allies, his chance came.

And so, here they are tonight, sitting happily beside me at the table as we laugh at Fletcher's stories and try our best to leave our pasts behind us.

"I cannot believe that you all knew, and yet no one told me," I say once again, smiling at the lot around me.

Mrs. Shepherd smiles.

"I wanted to tell you so bad, dear. Trust me. But Dirk swore me to secrecy." She laughs, laying a hand on her husband's arm.

Mr. Shepherd smiles gently at me, laughing.

"You still came right close to telling her, you know, Mrs. Shepherd," Eline says brightly, referring to the plate incident from earlier.

Mrs. Shepherd scoffs.

"Nonsense." She smiles.

I laugh softly as Mama pulls me to her side once more, pressing her cold lips to my cheek.

"What matters is that we are all together again," she says.

Soft murmurings of agreement arise from the table.

"And so it is, my dear," Papa says, gazing lovingly at Mama's pale face, the same look in his eyes that I remember from my childhood.

I smile softly, turning to Ezra.

He meets my gaze, his eyes dark as soft shadows dance in his brown irises, a sad smile pulling at his lips.

I do not have to ask what he is thinking, for I already know.

He is thinking of his own parents who, unlike mine, are no longer here.

My heart jolts with sharp pain as I realize that he will never be able to experience a reunion like the one I just have.

Valerie Pik passed away unexpectedly early in the war as her health quickly declined, leaving Ezra to care for Jozef and his weak mind alone.

And now Jozef has been taken from Ezra as well, executed at the hands of the Nazis.

I shake my head, swallowing.

"Ezra, I'm so sorry—" I begin.

He smiles softly at me, his eyes glassy.

"No, Ruth. Don't be sorry," he whispers gently, his eyes filling with light and love as he gazes at me, and then my parents. "The Lord gives, and the Lord takes, remember?"

I nod, smiling.

I remember, and I know that he is right.

"And He *has* given," he says, his eyes turning back to me, blazing with a light that wasn't present a moment ago. "He has given me all of them. He has given me you."

I smile softly, leaning my head on his arm.

And so, the following two hours are spent in one another's company as we laugh and smile together and it is almost like old times, save for the few absent folks that are still missed in the clan.

But, it is nearly perfect all the same.

And it is later that night, as everyone lies sleeping in their own beds, that I am still awake.

I stand in the doorway of my room, gazing at the scene before me.

Mama lies sleeping soundly in my bed, her thin chest rising and falling beneath the security of many woolen blankets, her pale face calm and tranquil for the first time since she was captured.

Papa sits snoring softly upright in the chair by her bedside, his head pressed against the side of the chair's neck, his hand draped across the bed and clasped tightly into Mama's.

I sigh contentedly as I stand gazing at my sleeping parents, the current of unbreakable love between the two of them evident even after all this time apart.

I smile softly.

God had given them to each other.

And now He has brought them together again.

He has brought *all* of us together again.

CHAPTER THIRTY-EIGHT

Mama grips my arm tightly, her knuckles flashing white as she stumbles feebly at my side.

Her breaths are short and forced, her skin so pale and cold that it is nearly frightening, and she is so dangerously thin that I fear a strong wind may do her in, but even so, she smiles softly at the land around us, content to be by my side and away from the horrors of war.

Today is the day of our victory! Or, tomorrow, rather.

The past two days have been spent in blissful celebration as people all across Europe, from my beloved Belgium all the way to the outskirts of Italy, rise in a chorus of victory over the Germans.

Church services, street banquets, and parades of all sorts imaginable ensue in the streets of not only Brussels but in France, England, and even in America as well.

In Antwerp, the cathedral bell rings five times over the broken, desolate, and utterly demolished streets, one ring for every year the war has tormented us.

Allied flags are raised once again in the streets as chanting civilians gather once more, celebrating our victory just as they had our liberty a mere nine months ago when the British allies first captured Belgium from the clutches of the Nazis.

From late morning even until the last hours of evening as dark settles across the world, the celebrations continue as we all seem to hold our breaths until the moment time stretches beyond one minute past twelve tonight, when the war will at last be over.

Mr. Shepherd and Fletcher left earlier this morning to go to town and witness the joy of the celebrations and will hopefully return home soon with any news for us still at Green Pastures.

Mama and I walk arm in arm up the hill with the eight crosses, the warm May sun shining down upon us in all its golden glory as a gentle breeze stirs through the leaves in the trees and through the rustling grass at our feet, gorgeous yellow tulips blooming across the green fields as far as my eyes can see.

Valerie Pik's roses are blooming, as well as the gardenias, and as the wind blows gently across my face, I swear that I can smell the lovely fragrance even on the hillside.

I smile softly.

Neither of us talk as we slowly make our way up to the eight graves that inhabit the tree line beneath the flowering magnolia tree, my mind wandering back to this time two years ago when I watched the Resistance bury the fallen men.

Mama stumbles and nearly falls as her thin legs buckle beneath her, causing me to lurch forward to grab her as I help her stand upright once again.

"Are you getting tired, Mama? We can go back now," I say softly, searching her weary, though smiling, eyes.

She shakes her head.

"No, not yet. I have missed the sunshine," she says, attempting to take another step as I stop her.

"No, Mama, you need to rest," I say firmly, ushering her toward the magnolia tree. "Come, sit."

She begrudgingly obeys and I help her ease herself down onto the carpet of green grass beneath the magnolia tree as she leans her back up against its young trunk.

"I'm not a feeble old woman, Ruth," she says with a sigh, though the smile that pulls at her lips tells me that she is only teasing. "Not yet anyway."

I smile softly as I sit down gently beside her.

"I know, Mama," I say, glancing at her pale face, "but I worry about you."

I study her face, searching her features for any hint at the human I used to know.

Her skin is so pale and her beautiful brown hair that once fell in soft curls at her jaw is no longer there, now replaced with a short brown fuzz that is just beginning to grow since her liberation from the Nazi camp.

But I can look closely into her hazel eyes, and I still see the traces of my dear Mama from long ago—I can see the familiar softness as well as the bold blazing look that I have so often seen in my own eyes, and Andrew's.

No matter what has passed since we were last together, she is still the same person I ran to as a child.

Her hazel eyes are shining softly with a tender and knowing look as I hold her gaze, and she takes my hand into her own.

"I know these past few years have been hard, Ruth." She smiles gently. "And they have changed you, I can tell. The war has changed us all."

She shakes her head, her gaze traveling to the field below us as the late morning sun illuminates her cheeks with a warm blush.

"But not all change is bad."

I lean my head against the trunk of the magnolia tree, white blossoms falling around us and in my lap.

A small songbird lands on a thin limb of the magnolia tree, his tiny head swiveling as it seems to look at me.

The bird is often seen as a symbol of freedom and liberty—freedom from all entanglements and snares that attempt to hinder it from flying...

I smile softly at the reminder that the bird serves.

"I suppose not," I say, my mind wandering over all the changes in my life.

I can see it all so clearly, the hand of change and of God in my life in these past three years, from the moment I first stepped foot into Still Waters Inn, until now, where I sit at Green Pastures.

I smile.

"Isn't it funny how day by day, nothing changes, but when you look back, *everything* is different?" I whisper, closing my eyes as the sun warms my face.

Mama laughs softly.

"I've been wondering the same thing myself," she says, her voice tired and soft.

We fall silent after that as the sun shines brightly on the hillside, illuminating the eight wooden crosses that rest in a solemn row to my left, where I can still see upon each the carved initials of each of the seven fallen Resistance men, the one on the far end being that of our dear Oma Edwards.

On the one closest to me, I can read the faint *B* and *H* that marks it, standing for none other than my dear friend, Bram Hendrik.

Below his grave, at the very foot of the hill, is where Andrew and I had spoken shortly after the funeral service for the seven men.

There is something different about you, Ruthie, he had told me that day.

How so? I had asked.

He had, of course, simply been teasing me about Ezra, but I know that his words went deeper than that.

He had seen something shift in me, something that was different from when he left me behind at Vlissengen.

And now I know what it was.

My heart had been breaking.

You will not remain broken, the still voice whispers to me.

Mama glances at me, studying my wistful face as I am carried off into tender daydreams and memories.

"Are you alright, Ruth? You've gotten awfully quiet," she says softly, her eyebrows arched.

I nod, glancing at her as I lean on her arm.

"Yes, Mama," I say. "I think I am."

And I smile as the black Minevra rumbles up the road, a cloud of dust rolling behind it as it harbors with it the hopeful news from Brussels.

~.~

WHEN MAMA AND I return to the farmhouse at noon, we are greeted by Fletcher as he calls out from the living room.

"Churchill is declaring the end of the war!" he says, his voice rising to the ceiling and throughout the house as he stands his post at the upright radio in the living room of Green Pastures.

I raise my brows, my heart quickening at his words.

Churchill?

"Truly, Fletcher?" I ask, ushering Mama gently into the living room where she takes an empty seat on the sofa beside Papa, Mr. and Mrs. Shepherd sitting on the sofa opposite them.

Fletcher nods as Hugo joins him at the radio, Hugo's pale face coloring with hope.

"Truly," Fletcher says, twisting the black knob of the radio as Winston Churchill's eloquent voice rises through the room. "Listen."

"Yesterday morning at two forty-one a.m. at General Eisenhower's headquarters, General Jodl, the representative of the German high command and of Grand Admiral Donitz, the designated head of the German state, signed the act of unconditional surrender of all German land, sea, and air forces in Europe to the Allied expeditionary force, and simultaneously to the Soviet high command..."

Ezra steps through the door, the incessant screech of the screen door drowning out the radio as he and Maya enter the house.

"For Heaven's sake, do be quiet!" Fletcher says as he sits anxiously on the armrest of Eline's chair, trying in vain to listen to the broadcast.

Eline and I share a quick glance, stifling a laugh at the two men.

Ezra looks taken aback as he steps to my side, his eyes bright and smiling.

"What did I miss?" he whispers in a low voice into my ear.

I turn to face him, smiling.

"Churchill has just stated that Germany has signed the unconditional surrender," I whisper softly.

I seat myself gently on the floor at the radio's foot, listening quietly to the words eluding from it as Maya crawls into my lap.

"Hello, little goose," I murmur, stroking her plaited hair playfully as I adjust the ribbons tethered on each braid.

She giggles softly, and I hush her quickly before she disturbs the broadcast, and therefore, Fletcher.

Ezra sighs softly as he sits down beside me, uttering no other word as he smiles at the room, but a moment passes, and I feel him slip his hand into mine.

I smile at him.

The ten of us settle in silently after that as we gaze at the radio intently, my heart hammering with the soft and poetic words of the English Prime Minister.

"Today this agreement will be ratified and confirmed at Berlin... Our dear Channel Islands will be free tomorrow. Hostilities will end officially at one minute after midnight tonight, on Tuesday, the eighth of May, but in the interests of saving lives the ceasefire began yesterday to be sounded all along the fronts.

The Germans are still in places resisting the allied troops, but should they continue to do so after midnight they will, of course, divest themselves of the protection of the laws of war and will be attacked from all quarters by the Allied troops.

The German war is therefore at an end!

After years of intense preparation Germany hurled herself on Poland at the beginning of September 1939, and in pursuance of our guarantee to Poland and in common action with the French Republic, Great Britain, the British Empire, and Commonwealth of Nations declared war against this foul aggression.

Finally, almost the whole world was combined against the evil-doers who are now prostrate before us. Gratitude to our splendid Allies goes forth from all our hearts.

We may allow ourselves a brief period of rejoicing, but let us not forget for a moment the toils and efforts that lie ahead. Japan, with all her treachery and greed, remains unsubdued. The injuries she has inflicted upon Great Britain, the United States, and other countries, and her detestable cruelties call for justice and retribution.

We must now devote all our strength and resources to the completion of our tasks both at home and abroad.

Today is our day of victory!
Long live the cause of freedom! God save the King!"

We sit in stunned silence for a long and somewhat painful moment, gazing at one another as his words resonate in our hearts and register in our minds.

The German war is therefore at an end!

"It's over," I say softly, tears stinging my eyes as my gaze travels wistfully across each face in the room.

My heart pounds in my chest and Ezra stiffens beside me, a sigh falling from his lips.

Slowly, everyone nods and bows their heads in solemn agreement, none of us quite sure what to do with ourselves.

This war has taken so much from us; the hardship and toil that we have all endured these past five years still burden us all heavily, and as I look around me, I see the loss we have been dealt displayed wearily across each of our faces.

For Mama, Papa, and I, it is the loss of our dear Andrew, and the darkness of the Nazi's cruelty that still haunts us each.

For Ezra, it is the loss of his father Jozef, and the shadowlands that still torment his gaze.

For Mr. and Mrs. Shepherd, it's the weight of watching their newly formed and woven family torn apart by a young man they'd grown to love as their own son, and it's the memories of their time under Nazi interrogation that I see sometimes written upon their faces.

And it's the utter destruction of our beloved Still Waters.

Maya lost both of her parents.

Hugo lost his way.

And for Eline and Fletcher, they lost Oma and for a time, each other.

For five years we have fought this war, and all this time we have been waiting for this very moment.

And now that it has finally arrived, I simply do not know what to do.

I want to cry and scream for all the loss that seems to be in vain, as well as laugh with joy at our victory and freedom.

I suppose it all would be acceptable.

Mrs. Shepherd smiles softly at me, her blue eyes shining with tender understanding.

She stands abruptly.

"Why don't I go make us some good strong coffee?" she offers gently, turning and striding swiftly into the kitchen.

Eline clears her throat softly, leaning on Fletcher's arm.

"So, what do we do now?" she says gently, asking the question that we are all thinking, though no one dared ask for fear of the reply.

As if by instinct, we all turn to face Mr. Shepherd, who through it all, remains the head of us.

Mr. Shepherd smiles softly, his bright blue eyes shining with the same aged tenderness and fatherly affection as always.

"We wait until one minute past midnight tonight, I suppose," he says softly.

"And then what?" Hugo says, his gaze steady as he paces by the radio that still murmurs.

The room is silent for a moment until Papa speaks.

"We must wait and see where God leads us next," he says simply, his gaze traveling away from Hugo and resting wistfully on Ezra and me as he holds Mama gently to his side.

I smile softly.

Ezra nods softly at Papa, as if catching some unspoken meaning in my father's words.

"This day is a new beginning. For all of us," Ezra says, his gaze dancing briefly over mine as he smiles at me.

A new beginning.

I nod as his words ring in my heart, and he turns away to look at the many faces around the room.

Fletcher raises his cup of simmering black coffee in the air.

"I'll drink to that, Ezra," he offers lightly, his voice light though his face is thoughtful.

We laugh softly at his weak attempt at humor in the midst of the hurt as Mrs. Shepherd begins passing coffee around the room, the glorious scent of the black liquid filling the room.

"Thank you." I smile at the dear red-headed woman as she offers me a cup of coffee just the way I like it, with sugar and cream.

"You are very welcome, dear," she says to me with a smile as she passes a second coffee to Ezra and a glass of milk to Maya. "No coffee for you, child. You'll be up until midnight."

Ezra smiles.

"I think we will *all* be up until midnight now, Mrs. Shepherd," he says, sipping the black coffee in his hand. "I don't think anyone will want to sleep knowing that it will be over when we wake."

And so we decide to sit up and wait for the blessed hour to arrive as the scent of coffee and cinnamon hangs thickly in the air and the house is filled with sounds of the radio, laughter, and music as the sky darkens outside and the clock ticks on in its usual slow and incessant manner.

"Do you remember the day we all met at Still Waters?" Eline asks, smiling brightly as her eyes grow wistful.

"I do." I laugh softly, the memory coming back to me so warmly and vibrantly it brings tears to my eyes. It had been a warm day in June when I first arrived at Still Waters, uncertain and alone after Andrew's departure and Mama's capture.

Ezra nods gently beside me.

"I certainly do," he says wistfully. "It was just after Pa was captured, and Oma Edwards had told me about Still Waters. She said that I could seek refuge there. And I did." I lean my head on Ezra's shoulder as he sighs ruefully.

Eline meets my gaze from across the room, smiling softly at the gently spoken reminder of the feisty and quick-witted old woman that will forever be missed in our company.

"I remember the night I came," Hugo murmurs softly, his voice apprehensive as he steals a tentative glance at the rest of us.

Mr. Shepherd smiles, his blue eyes flickering gently over Hugo's as he remembers the night as well.

Ezra laughs softly, his eyes dancing merrily at the memory that comes to mind.

"You mean the night we all gathered for dinner and Fletcher told us that ridiculously embellished, yet valiant, story about the bullet in his hip?" he asks, giving Fletcher a teasing and knowing glance.

A small laugh escapes my lips as I recall the distant memory of dinner at Still Waters.

Hugo smiles, nodding as he glances at Fletcher.

"Yes, that would be the one," he says.

Fletcher scoffs playfully.

"That was not ridiculous, and it wasn't a story. It was true," Fletcher says, placing his hands on his hips as the room laughs gently at him.

"Was it, Abram?" Mr. Shepherd asks, his brows raised in a teasing manner as his lips pull into a broad smile.

Fletcher's cheeks flame, and he turns to face Eline.

"Mostly," he says quietly, "but it *was* amusing."

Mrs. Shepherd cackles.

"So it was," she says.

A moment of silence passes as we all seem to lose ourselves in memories of the past.

Ezra glances at me.

"Do you remember the day that we met?"

I smile, my cheeks growing warm as I recall the memory fondly.

"I do. I came just after Mama was arrested," I say softly, Mama meeting my gaze from where she sits with Papa, smiling tenderly at me.

I return her smile, turning back to Ezra.

"Mr. Shepherd introduced me to all of you, and I believe that you were the last one to speak to me. I don't think you said more than three words to me, either." I laugh softly, squeezing his hand playfully.

He smiles, his cheeks flushing pink.

Fletcher snorts softly.

"Now look at him," he says in a droll manner.

I laugh softly, glancing around the room at each individual that makes up the former Still Waters clan, my eyes landing on Maya, who lies on her back with her head resting in my lap.

I smile gently.

"It's hard to believe that was three years ago now," I say softly, shaking my head in quiet disbelief.

Time, I have learned, is a sly thing; it slips into being without our noticing, and it is only when we face it from behind that we see what vast changes it has wrought.

I see them now as I look at each familiar face around me.

We all nod in solemn agreement.

"It is, dear." Mrs. Shepherd sighs softly, her eyes smiling benevolently around the room as she clasps hand with Mr. Shepherd.

Mr. Shepherd smiles, his countenance brightening as an idea forms in his head.

He glances at Ezra.

"Say, Ezra, what about a song at the piano?" he asks, standing from his seat beside his wife. "For old time's sake, and in honor of the day."

Ezra nods, standing stiffly from the floor beside me.

"Certainly, Mr. Shepherd," he says, stepping gingerly toward Valerie Pik's piano as he glances down at his stiff left leg.

My heart sinks as I watch him.

Even tonight, his leg still bothers him from the bombing accident.

I suppose it always will.

He sighs, forcing his leg to work as he sits down at the piano's bench, his spine straightening as he smiles lovingly down at the ivory keys.

"What song would you like to hear?" he asks, absently flipping through sheet music that had once belonged to his mother.

The room is silent.

" *Wilt Heden nu Treden,* perhaps?" Mama suggests, her voice rich with a Netherlandish Dutch accent.

We gather together.

I smile softly, and Papa nods.

"That would be quite fitting. It is, after all, an old hymn of thanksgiving while celebrating victory," he says.

Perfect, I think to myself.

Ezra nods, plucking two sheets of yellowing music from the stack and propping them up on the piano's ledge.

"Everyone please stand," Mr. Shepherd says with a glance around the room.

We obediently stand from our various seats around the room, everyone gathering at the piano-side, just as we would have at Still Waters on Sunday morning.

Ezra catches my eye, smiling at me as his fingers poise over the keys.

I smile in return, my insides warming as memories persist in filtering through my mind.

"Is everyone ready?" he asks.

"Yes, *Mastroe,*" Fletcher says, his voice rising above the rest.

Ezra shakes his head but utters no reply as his nimble fingers softly strike the keys and the graceful melody soon fills the house.

I close my eyes as I let the melodious current carry me away, and the voices of everyone present rise as one into a beautiful tapestry of celebration, though Fletcher's voice rises loudest of all, terribly out of tune as he belts the lyrics.

"We gather together to ask the Lord's blessing;
He chastens and hastens His will to make known;
The wicked oppressing now cease from distressing.
Sing praises to His name, He forgets not his own.

Beside us to guide us, our God with us joining,
Ordaining, maintaining His kingdom divine;
So from the beginning the fight we were winning:
The Lord was at our side—the glory be thine!

We all do extol Thee, Thou leader triumphant,
And pray that Thou still our Defender wilt be.

Let Thy congregation escape tribulation;
Thy name be ever praised! O Lord, make us Free!"

And so for the rest of the day, we celebrate.

We remain in the living room with one another as we laugh and reminisce over the past three years we have all been together, and over the last five years of darkness and loss.

We eat a warmed-over dinner of last night's feast, sing hymns, and dance to Glenn Miller as night begins to fall outside.

And midnight remains on the horizon.

CHAPTER THIRTY-NINE

I open my eyes with a jolt as I begin to nod off again, my head pressed against Ezra's shoulder where we sit side by side at the piano, facing the room around us.

It has grown dark outside the window, casting us all into darkness as we sit together by the warm illumination of oil lamps and candles.

I lift my head, brushing the weariness from my eyes.

I glance at the grandfather clock.

11: 46.

I sigh softly.

"Almost there," Ezra murmurs softly, smiling at me in a teasing manner. "Try not to fall asleep yet, or you'll miss it."

I smile wryly, straightening in my seat on the piano bench, my backside growing numb.

"No promises," I say, fighting a yawn.

Coffee and cinnamon hang thickly on the air around us, mingling with the scent of the cold ash that rests in the hearth as the Glenn Miller Orchestra plays softly from the record player, the record I had given Ezra for his birthday rotating in an incessant circular motion as *Stairway to the Stars,* my personal favorite, eludes from it.

I smile, the song stirring fond memories in my mind.

Maya had not lasted much longer after the clock struck ten and now lays snoring peacefully beside Mrs. Shepherd on the sofa, her little chest rising and falling as we continue to laugh and converse amongst ourselves in a fleeting attempt to keep each other awake until midnight arrives.

Fletcher paces anxiously by the radio, his uneven gait casting an odd echo throughout the house.

"Abram, dear, why don't you sit down?" Eline asks, smiling up at her disquieted and impatient husband.

"Because," Fletcher says, "I am afraid I may fall asleep and miss it."

Ezra smiles softly, his gaze resting on the record player.

"I'll wake you when the clock strikes twelve," he says jokingly.

Fletcher shakes his head.

"No, it will only be a minute now," he says.

"Nine minutes now, to be precise," Hugo murmurs vaguely from the corner of the room.

I yawn softly, brushing my palm across my face as weariness settles over me once again and I absently hum the melody as Ray Erbele croons the soft lyrics, the music rising to the rafters as Papa begins to nod off, resulting in frequent nudges in the ribcage by Mama to keep him awake.

Mr. Shepherd sits gazing at the open Bible in his lap, the pages fluttering gently as his blue eyes scan the words thoughtfully.

"My own papa read this passage in Ecclesiastes every New Year's Eve as the family stayed up until midnight," he says after a moment, "and I would like to read it to all of you tonight. No, it is *not* New Year's Eve, but it *is* the eve of our victory and freedom, and new beginnings."

Ezra silently reaches for the record player, lifting the needle as the record slows in pace and the music falls flat, casting the room into silence as we all turn to face Mr. Shepherd.

Mama elbows Papa, and he snorts as he jolts awake.

"I'm up," he says sleepily.

"Quiet, honey," Mama says to him. "Dirk is reading."

And with the room's attention upon him, Mr. Shepherd begins to read, his soft voice rising crisp and clear through the room.

"*For everything there is a season, and a time for every matter under heaven:*

A time to be born, and a time to die;

A time to plant, and a time to pluck up what has been planted;

A time to kill, and a time to heal;

A time to break down and a time to build up;

A time to weep, and a time to laugh;

A time to mourn, and a time to dance;
A time to cast away stones, and a time to gather stones together;
A time to embrace, and a time to refrain from embracing;
A time to seek, and a time to lose;
A time to keep, and a time to cast away;
A time to tear, and a time to sew;
A time to keep silence, and a time to speak;
A time to love, and a time to hate;
A time for war, and a time for peace."

I smile softly, his words carrying me back to the countless times he had read from his black Bible to us all at Still Waters.

Around me, everyone smiles as we all understand the meaning of his words, and all of us take something away from this passage and bury it deep within our hearts.

A time for war, and a time for peace.

His words cast light upon the dark crevices of the past and brightening horizon of the future ahead, and I can feel the familiar threads of the light taking root once more in my soul, reviving my spirit as I forget my weariness.

"Amen," I whisper softly.

He looks up from the page and meets my gaze, his blue eyes shining in the dim light of the room.

He smiles at me, his gaze traveling to the grandfather clock.

And suddenly, as if told to do so, the grandfather clock rings, casting its enchanting twelve-note melody through the house as it reminds us of the hour.

My heart jolts.

It's midnight.

We have only one minute to go.

Hugo turns the radio on with a swift flick of his thin wrist, and the familiar Antwerpen radio broadcaster's voice eludes from it.

"We have one minute to go folks!" he says happily, his voice cutting through the static that stirs from the speakers.

Mr. Shepherd smiles.

"The hour is at last here. We may have a moment to spare," he says with a glance around the room. "I think I will ask Ezra to pray over us all tonight, if everyone approves."

"I think that would be quite acceptable, Dirk," Papa says, smiling softly.

"Agreed," Fletcher says with a smile from across the room, his eyes shining with respect at Ezra.

Ezra raises his brows, a soft pink coloring his stubble-lined cheeks.

I smile at him, love and pride swelling in my chest.

Mr. Shepherd turns back to Ezra.

"Ezra, would you like to pray over our *new beginning,* as you have rightfully put it?"

Ezra nods, smiling across the room at the middle-aged man.

"Yes, of course," he says. "Will everyone rise in honor of the moment?"

Silence ensues for a moment as the room obeys his wishes, standing all over the room, joining hands and bowing heads.

I offer him my hand as I stand beside him, and he takes it as he clears his throat and bows his head.

His voice is deep and thick as he begins.

"Lord Jesus, it has been five years since war has crushed our world and sown the seeds of desolation and death everywhere. We have seen our dear country of Belgium violated of her independence and our freedom. We have watched as millions of men have fled from the threat of the invader. We bore the pain of seeing our army defeated by the number and strength of Enemy arms and were forced to capitulate. We saw thousands of our own brothers and sisters held captive as prisoners of these dark forces. Again, we watched as our country was pillaged and reduced to extreme poverty as the enemy grew rich from its vile and dishonest gain. We have known all along that the anguish and worry we experience only grows day to day."

He pauses for a moment, swallowing as he sighs softly.

I steal a glance at him.

He is staring at the floor, his dark eyes dancing with shadows as he recalls everything that has befallen us in these past five years of war.

I give his hand a gentle squeeze as I close my eyes, and he begins again.

"And we do not know, O Lord, what tomorrow will be, nor the day after. But we do not revolt, O Jesus, against these trials. You have given us victory over our enemies tonight, and Lord let not the loss of these past five years be in vain. Help as we face this new beginning and guide us in the days to come. Let our first words tonight be a word of courageous acceptance, and freedom. Amen."

The room is silent for a brief moment as we all open our eyes to gaze at the clock, just as the large hand approaches the first minute past midnight.

One more second...

12:01.

"It's over!" Eline breathes softly.

"Hear hear!" Fletcher cheers, wrapping his arm around Eline.

"Alas, the war with the Germans has come to a fierce and certain close! The ninth of May has dawned. Rejoice, people of Belgium. Rejoice I say!" the radio broadcaster exclaims excitedly.

I laugh softly as I gaze at the cheering, clapping, and celebrating persons around me, the laughter and joy of the moment rising in my chest swiftly.

This is the moment we have labored toward for five years—and this is the moment that Andrew dreamed of while fighting with the Resistance.

Now it is finally here.

The war is over!

Relief, joy, peace, and reminisce collide in my heart, but I smile all the same.

I turn to catch Ezra gazing at me, his eyes blazing as he smiles at me in such a way that I have never seen before.

"What?" I ask, raising my brows.

He shakes his head sheepishly, wrapping his arm around my shoulders as he leans closer to me, and presses his lips to my cheek.

"Will you marry me now?" he whispers in my ear.

My cheeks flush with a warm blush at his words, and I smile up at him, searching his gaze.

"What?" I say softly, smiling. "I believe you already asked me once. I haven't changed my mind."

His brown eyes shine brilliantly as he laughs softly.

"I'm glad to hear that," he says, "but that isn't what I am asking. Not exactly."

I raise my brows, bidding him to continue.

"I told you before that God would bring us together. We have been waiting all this time, and the war is over now. Your parents are home—there is nothing more to wait on," he says.

I smile softly, understanding his meaning.

"Have you asked Papa?"

"Yes."

"And?"

Ezra steals a glance over my shoulder at my parents.

"He approved. Your mother did as well," he says, turning back to look at me, his eyes soft, "and I think we both know what Andrew thought of the matter."

I laugh softly.

"Yes, we do," I say, leaning into his hold as I hold his gaze and we both fall silent for a moment.

Ezra raises his brows at me.

"Well?"

I smile radiantly.

"I thought you would never ask," I say.

CHAPTER FORTY

Vlissengen, The Netherlands

The four pale green walls of my childhood bedroom stare back at me, reminding me of all the hours I spent writing at the small desk in the corner and reading by the window, or simply gazing out at the ocean.

I gaze out the window now, the lively chatter of the women around me distant as I gaze wistfully at the choppy blue-green waters I have known all my life and my keen eyes follow the seagulls as they soar with the wind, seeming to greet me like old friends.

I smile contentedly.

Hello, sea, my heart whispers softly.

"Ruth, dear, are you ready?" Mrs. Shepherd calls from the other side of the dressing screen, pulling me from my distant thoughts.

"Just a moment, Mrs. Shepherd. She is nearly finished." Eline laughs softly behind me as she nimbly cinches and ties the ribbon at the back of my torso, and my breath catches softly.

I glance down at my dress.

Soft ivory rayon covers my torso in a ruched manner, falling from my waist in a pleated skirt embellished with lace that falls all the way to my feet.

The capped sleeves flutter about my forearm, the dainty lace that trims them tickling the flesh of my arms as I adjust the small teardrop diamond pendant at my collarbone.

The dress is Mama's from nearly thirty years ago when she and Papa married in Antwerp.

Now I am wearing it.

I glance at myself in the mirror hanging on the wall, catching sight of a pale-skinned, wide-eyed young woman who, only a few years prior, had been a young girl.

With pink cheeks, high cheekbones and large hazel eyes, I smile at my reflection, and the woman in the mirror flashes the customary DeVos dimples.

"You know, Maud, it is truly remarkable how God works," I hear Mama say from the other side of the screen, where I know Mrs. Shepherd is making final adjustments to her own dress. "One day I am standing at the train station waiting to find my daughter, and five days later, I am at her wedding."

Mama laughs softly.

"I have missed so much," she adds ruefully.

I can almost hear Mrs. Shepherd's soft smile as she lays a gentle hand on Mama's thin shoulder.

"I know *exactly* what you mean, Judith. Believe me," she says kindly.

I smile softly at their conversation, tugging gently at the dainty earrings hanging from my earlobes.

"Alright, look at me," Eline says to me, and I turn to face her.

She smiles at me happily, her blue eyes shining bright with sisterly love as she clasps her hands together giddily.

She is dressed in a becoming pale yellow dress, the daffodil yellow skirt falling just below her knees, and her seemingly untamable curly hair has been tamed for today's event, swept away from her face and off her shoulders by a simple barrette at the back of her neck.

"You look beautiful, Ruth," she says, wrapping her arms around my shoulders and pulling me into an embrace.

I smile softly despite the color that I can feel warming my cheeks.

"Thank you, Eline," I say into her hair, closing my eyes as I hold her tightly, "I don't know what I would do without you."

She laughs softly, pulling away.

"Oh please, all I did was tie a simple ribbon," she says, brushing moisture from her eyes.

I laugh softly, narrowing my eyes at her teasing.

"You know what I mean," I say.

She nods, smiling.

"I do," she says softly, her gaze wistful, "and I thank God that he gave me a sister like you. I always wanted a sister, and now it feels like we are, though not by blood. Or marriage."

We share a soft smile.

"Well, you are ready now; let's see how your mother looks," Eline says after a moment, taking my hand and pulling me from behind the dressing screen, saying, "Here she is."

I step out to face my childhood bedroom, where Maya lies lazily on her stomach on my bed, and Mama stands by the bedside while Mrs. Shepherd helps her into the stunning sage-green dress Eline made for her.

My mind immediately returns to my childhood spent on the beach, when Mama would wear her green muslin gown, her brunette hair fluttering in the wind and she held my hand fast in her own as we waded through the cool waters.

She smiles at me now, brighter than she had that day on the beach in my memory, tears forming in her soft eyes.

"You look absolutely wonderful," she whispers.

Eline had quickly fashioned Mama a dress to wear for today, and the result is a beautiful, soft sage-green dress that is cinched at her thin waist, as the garment covers her thin shoulder blades and torso in a flattering manner that seems to disguise her malnourished form; her pale cheeks are colored by life and love and happiness, her eyes shining with so much vibrancy, she almost looks like the Mama I knew as a child.

Mrs. Shepherd smiles behind her, dressed in a shirtwaist dress that mimics the color of Mama's, though slightly darker to contrast beautifully with her stark red hair.

Mrs. Shepherd smiles brightly at me.

"Oh, Ruth! Look at you," she says, her keen, motherly gaze traveling quickly over my ensemble. She narrows her eyes as if thinking. "But you need one last thing, dear."

I raise my brows, smiling.

"I do?"

She nods wordlessly, reaching behind her to the small vase of yellow roses resting on the nightstand that Mr. Shepherd had sent up earlier.

With thick, nimble fingers, she quickly plucks the thorns from a single, near perfect, yellow rose, before stepping softly toward me.

"Bend your head, dear,"

I do so, dipping my chin softly as she gingerly tucks the rose into a fold of my dark hair behind my ear. My hair falls in its natural loose state, falling around my face and down my back.

With a few last adjustments, Mrs. Shepherd smiles at me.

"Now then," she says, stepping back to admire her work, "what do you think, Judith?"

Mama smiles at me, her eyes wistful and soft.

"Oh, *schat,*" she breathes softly, placing a thin hand on her chest as her gaze travels from my face and down the dress, and then meeting my gaze once again.

She brushes a hand across her cheek.

"Oh, Mama," I say softly, stepping forward and wrapping my arms around her small shoulders. "Don't cry."

She laughs softly.

"I'm sorry, *Dochter.* I told myself I wouldn't, but I have failed." She smiles. "I have missed far too much, and I never knew my girl was so strong and bold until we all had to face what we have. And I never thought I would see this day."

She glances around the room at Mrs. Shepherd, Eline, and Maya.

"I am *so* proud of you. "

She cups my cheek in her cold palm, and I smile as gooseflesh is raised across my limbs at her touch.

"Thank you, Mama," I whisper, my voice soft and thick.

She nods and pulls away.

"No more tears." She laughs to herself as she brushes her cheek once more and turns to give herself a once-over in the mirror, and I can't help but notice the painful grimace that crosses her face as her gaze lands on the shorn head in the reflection.

Her gaze falls down to the pleated skirt of her dress, her eyes wistful.

I smile softly, turning to the little girl lying on the bed, memories of my own time spent in this room at Maya's age filtering through my mind.

"Are you ready, little goose?"

Dressed in a pleated pale gooseberry dress with matching hair ribbons that I had woven into her hair half an hour ago, Maya nods, sliding from the mattress and to the floor.

She smiles at me.

"Yes," she says. "I want to see the beach!"

The three of us laugh softly.

"Just a moment, child, and we shall see the beach," Mrs. Shepherd tells her.

A knock at the door makes my stomach churn.

Eline opens it, finding Fletcher and Hugo waiting on the other side in the hallway.

"Is everyone ready?" Fletcher asks, stealing a glance over his wife's shoulder into the room.

Eline smiles.

"Yes, Abram, I believe that we are," she says, taking his arm.

The men enter the room hesitantly, stopping short in the doorway as they both gaze at me.

My cheeks flame.

Fletcher smiles brightly and Hugo clears his throat, his gaze meeting mine as Mrs. Shepherd takes the arm he offers her.

"Your father is waiting for you outside, Ruth. He has asked to speak with you before the ceremony begins," he says softly. "He is waiting by the sea oats."

I nod, my cheeks growing warm as I smile.

Papa.

Mama gives me a knowing smile.

"I will find him, Hugo. Thank you," I say gently, gazing at the steel-faced German.

Hugo nods stiffly, a genuine smile pulling at his lips as his eyes shine.

"Of course," he murmurs.

Fletcher smiles across the room at me, his eyes shining with a softness that I do not often see.

"One last thing," Fletcher says.

He pulls something from his pocket, perhaps a handkerchief.

"Ruth, the *pilot* gave me this to give to you," he says, offering it out to me.

I step toward him, and he lays it gently in my palm.

It *is* a handkerchief, but there is something inside of it.

I glance up at him, surprised by the soft weight of it in my hand.

"What is it?"

Fletcher shrugs.

"All Ezra told me was that it belonged to his mother, and I was to give it to you," he says with a soft, knowing smile that suggests to me he knows more than he lets on.

I smile at him, reaching for a small, folded piece of carbon paper that I had folded and tucked beneath the vase of roses earlier.

I hold it out to Fletcher.

"Give this to him, please,"

He scowls lightly, his eyes smiling at me.

"What am I, a messenger?" he says, pocketing the note as he gives me a brotherly smile. "I will make certain that he gets it."

I smile.

"Thank you, Fletcher," I say, memories of the day at the Dossin Barracks when I had given him that "last" letter to Ezra resurfacing in my mind.

He nods, still smiling as he turns to Mama.

"I will walk you out as well, Mrs. DeVos. Hugo will take Mrs. Shepherd and Maya."

Mama smiles, taking Fletcher's free arm as they prepare to leave me. She squeezes my hand gently.

"I love you, *schat,*" she says softly.

I smile, my stomach churning with silent anticipation.

"I love you, Mama," I say softly.

And with that, Fletcher leads both Mama and Eline out the door, followed by Hugo, Mrs. Shepherd, and Maya.

And I am alone.

My heart hammers softly as I wait.

I absently sit down on the foot of the bed.

I gaze down at the curious yellowing handkerchief in my trembling hand, stroking the worn lace edging as I open its many folds to reveal what waits inside.

My heart beats softly.

Lying on a bed of silk, is a small dainty gold bracelet.

Smiling to myself, I pick it up carefully.

The thin and delicate chain is made of yellow gold, with a single green, emerald baguette greeting me on its chain.

Green, I think softly to myself.

I pull a small, rolled note from the handkerchief as well, my eyes immediately recognizing Ezra's handwriting upon it.

Dearest Ruth,

This bracelet belonged to my mother when she was young. I never knew it, but she had hidden this away several years ago for her future daughter-in-law, if I should have chosen to ever marry.

I know by now that green is your favorite color. Why my mother chose a green emerald, I do not know, other than that God must have guided her to do so.

She would have simply loved you, Ruth, I know it.

I just wish you could have met her, and Papa.

Today will be hard without them by my side, but I take comfort in knowing that we will soon be joined as one today, and you will be by my side until God calls us home.

I told you once that I wanted to strive by your side.

But the words do not capture my meaning strongly enough.

I want to live, work, fight, and remain by your side until my last breath; but even then, we will not be parted in death.

This is a new beginning for us, a beginning free of war and bloodshed.

I cannot promise you a life free of toil and hardship, for I know that they are certain to come to us.

But to love you, to cherish you, protect you from harm, and to walk with you all my days is my desire, Ruth.

We have faced so much in these past three years since we first met, and God has carried you and I through so much darkness that I am certain he will lead us and guide us as we embark on this road called marriage.

Are you ready, love?

Yours, Ezra

I glance out the window, my gaze searching for and finding the small gathering on my childhood beach of Vlissengen, where Andrew and I had spent our days with one another.

I smile softly at Ezra's words.

"Yes, I am ready," I say softly.

CHAPTER FORTY-ONE

EZRA

The soft murmurings of the crashing waves whisper to Ezra's hammering heart, somehow calming it.

His deep eyes gaze at the blue depths of the churning ocean as he scans the golden shoreline, his mind wandering back to the last time he stood on this beach; the day he took Ruth to visit Andrew's grave.

That day had been dark and heavy to bear, veiled in the cloud of grief as he watched Ruth struggle with her brother's death.

He had watched her heart break.

But today is different.

Today holds a bright and vivacious light, and even as his stomach churns with nerves and his hands tremble slightly in his pockets as he stands patiently waiting, he knows that today's burden is a good one. A worthy one.

It's the day he and Ruth have been working, waiting, and praying for for so long now.

"Here come the others," Mr. Shepherd says from beside him, his gaze resting toward the house, where the various persons of the Green Pastures clan approach them from the sand dunes. Mr. Shepherd smiles softly at Ezra. "Are you ready, *Zoon?*"

Ezra nods, smiling softly.

Son.

He meets Mr. Shepherd's gaze.

Over the past three years since Ezra arrived unannounced on his doorstep, Mr. Shepherd had cared for him like his own. He became a father to Ezra when he had lost his own.

"I am, Mr. Shepherd. Just a bit nervous, that's all," he says, shifting his feet in the sand.

"Nerves are good, Ezra," he says, his voice serious and soft as he smiles almost sheepishly, his gaze traveling to Ezra's left leg, where the bomb has left its permanent mark. "They show that you can feel."

Ezra laughs suddenly, understanding the hidden meaning behind Mr. Shepherd's words.

Mr. Shepherd laughs softly, laying a gentle hand on Ezra's shoulder as they fall into a brief moment of silence before Mr. Shepherd speaks once again.

"I thought we were going to lose you that day Ruth called me, Ezra. You have no idea how worried Maud and I were. And I *know* that Ruth was worried. I never heard such fear in her voice as I did on that day," he says gently, shaking his head.

Ezra runs a hand over his cheek, sighing softly.

"I know," he says, his voice steady and clear.

He gazes back out across the waves, the vague and dark day of the bombing coming to his mind. His memories of that day are marred by pain, intense burning, and an incessant ringing in his ears.

He recalls his conversation with Ruth that night.

Just don't leave me, okay? she had asked him, her voice soft and almost fearful.

I'm not going anywhere, Ruth. Not until the Lord bids me home, he had whispered in return.

Her question was not a surprise to him, for at that moment, he *felt* he was going home.

But God had other plans for them.

A small smile pulls at his lips.

Mr. Shepherd watches him carefully, his Dutch blue eyes shining with fatherly affection as he reflects Ezras smile.

"But look at the two of you now," he says, seeming to know Ezra's unspoken thoughts. "God has been faithful."

"He certainly has." Ezra smiles as the clan joins them, Fletcher leading the way.

Mrs. Shepherd steps from the crowd first, the wind blowing through her bright red hair as she embraces Ezra in a motherly fashion.

"Ruth is ready, and she is a vision," she says into his ear as she pulls away and looks him over. Her eyes brush over his uniform swiftly before studying his face.

She smiles her approval.

"Well, don't you look handsome," she says.

Ezra laughs softly, his cheeks brightening at her strange, albeit sincere, comment.

"Thank you, Mrs. Shepherd," he says, smiling as he holds the older woman's gaze.

Her blue eyes dance as she smiles.

"I am proud of you dear," she says, adjusting the medal on his chest.

Ezra nods, finding his supply of words quite gone as he watches the dear woman turn and join Judith and Eline as Fletcher steps toward him.

Fletcher strides causally to Ezra's side, his gait stiff as he struggles through the sand at his feet, his eyes dancing merrily.

"I come bearing a message," he says, digging in his trouser pocket and retrieving a small note that flutters in the wind. "From the *auteur* herself."

Ezra raises his brows.

"Oh?" he says, taking the note as he glances up at Fletcher, smiling as he unfolds the note, neat words covering the entire page.

Fletcher snorts.

"Leave it to Ruth to write you a book at a time like this," he teases.

Ezra smiles, his gaze lingering over her words.

Fletcher smiles at him, his gaze knowing as he studies the younger man.

"You seem rather calm for a bridegroom," he observes with narrowed eyes. "I was a mess when Eline and I married."

Ezra laughs softly, glancing up at him over the fluttering letter.

"I know, my friend. I was there," he teases lightly, smiling at Fletcher. He motions toward the letter. "Thank you for bringing this."

Fletcher nods, bowing gallantly.

"My pleasure, *Commander Piloot,*" he says with one final tease before he claps Ezra's shoulder in a brotherly manner. "I am happy for you two lovebirds. Honestly, I'm not sure what took you so long."

"Perhaps the war?" Ezra offers, teasing.

Fletcher laughs, and the two friends share a smile.

"Well, it's nearly time. I see Ruth and her father now," he says, giving Ezra one last smile. "Don't get cold feet now."

Ezra smiles.

"I won't," he says assuredly.

Fletcher laughs before he turns and traipses across the beach.

Ezra shakes his head after him.

He turns back to the letter, his gaze landing on the lovingly written note within, Ruth's familiar cursive sprawling neatly over the page.

My dearest Ezra,

There are so many things I want to say to you that I fear I will run off this page.

I suppose I have a whole lifetime to tell you, now don't I?

There have been several times since we met that I thought we would lose each other.

I could bear the darkness of the barracks and face the snarling Germans alone, but when you nearly died in the bombing, that was something I could not face.

I didn't know how.

I thought that God was slowly taking you away from me. I had thought for a brief, though painful, moment, that you had reached the end without me.

When I gave Fletcher what I thought was my final letter to you, I thought I had reached the end of my life. I knew that if I got on that deportation train, then I most likely would never come off alive.

But Fletcher told me something that day as I gave him that letter that I still remember.

"None of us are promised tomorrow."

I began to understand that day that my life is a vapor. I am a flower quickly fading, here today and gone tomorrow. I am a mere shadow, a toss of the ocean, and a whisper in the wind.

We all are, for we are only mere humans.

Our futures are no more certain today than they were in those days, Ezra.

But I know that every tomorrow that the Lord lets me live will be spent by your side, and I consider that the greatest privilege.

I am ready to face this life with you, whatever shadowlands that we may be forced to walk through.

We will do it together.

My hands are trembling as I write these last few words to you.

May we run into rivers unknown and valleys below, if that is where He is calling. May we stay planted in lands and riverbeds, no matter how dry if that is what He asks of us. May we live these lives in complete surrender, for they were never ours to begin with.

May we walk ever beside one another, wherever He leads.

With love, Ruth

CHAPTER FORTY-TWO

The wind blows my hair gently across my face and the sand greets my feet like an old friend as I approach the tall figure of my papa as he stands with his back to me, facing the pale stone in the midst of the sea oats.

Andrew's grave.

My shoulders fall slightly as I stop short behind him, the sand at my feet keeping my steps silent as I study Papa.

He looks so much like Andrew, it is almost painful to look at him as he stands gazing at the grave, his face solemn and wistful. The wind stirs his graying brown hair and his patient and glassy eyes gaze at the words engraved upon the small stone placing, his thin cheeks taut.

I follow his gaze to the stone, but I do not have to look at it to know what it says; I know it by heart.

Do not be afraid of those who can kill the body but cannot kill the soul.

I sigh softly, glancing up at the sky for a moment.

Andrew is not in that grave, I know.

He no longer inhabits the Earth like the rest of us do, but even now, on my wedding day, I can hear his boisterous laughter ringing with the wind.

I am still here, he had told me in the dream.

I smile softly, the wind pricking gooseflesh across my arms as I clear my throat.

"Are you ready, Papa?" I ask, my voice soft as it collides with the force of the wind.

Papa turns.

He is wearing beige dress trousers and a pressed green button-down shirt tucked in at his waist, with new suspenders crawling up his thin shoulders.

His eyes soften as he smiles at me, and I step to his side.

"Oh, *Dochter,* you look *schitterend,*" he says, kissing my cheek, slipping back into our native tongue of Dutch.

Wonderful.

He tips my chin up to meet his tender gaze.

"No, I am not ready. But the question is, are you?"

I smile, nodding.

"I am, Papa," I whisper softly, my eyes filling.

"As long as you're sure." He laughs softly, patting my hand as he holds it clasped in both of his own.

A small laugh escapes my lips as I hold his gaze, my eyes flickering over his face and noticing the age that now inhabits it.

Worry lines have left their marks upon his forehead and silver lines his temples as his ever-patient eyes smile happily down at me.

He clears his throat audibly as he swallows, his gaze traveling to the beach ahead of us.

"I have spoken with Ezra on several occasions and am quite certain that he is a decent and godly man. And he cares for you deeply." He pulls his eyes away from the beach and turns back to me, smiling softly. "Just promise you won't forget one thing."

I smile softly, blushing furiously as I nod for him to say what I know he will.

"*Jij bent de dochter van de dokter,*" he says with a smile.

I laugh softly, remembering the words he had told me so long ago.

You are the physician's daughter.

He offers me his arm, his eyes smiling.

"I am my father's daughter," I say softly, wrapping my arm through his and leaning my head against his shoulder, just as I had so many times as a girl.

He laughs softly.

"Yes, you are," he says.

He kisses my forehead softly, and his gaze falls gently to the grave at our feet.

I follow his gaze.

And with one final look at the stone, Papa and I face the wind and walk arm in arm through the dunes and to the beach, where I can see the whole Green Pastures family waiting for us.

The waters thrash against the sandy shoreline as the seagulls converse above my head, and the breeze stirs through my dress skirt as the sun casts a glorious golden hue across the dunes and upon the small ceremony that is about to begin.

Papa and I walk forward through the sand, and I can see Fletcher standing with Eline as she, Mrs. Shepherd, and Mama have all three been reduced to tears, though they promised they wouldn't.

Maya makes a face at me from where she stands with Hugo, her eyes wide and happy as she watches the scene before her, though I am certain she doesn't know what it means.

Mr. Shepherd stands at the head of the clan with his old Bible in one hand as his other rests father-like on Ezra's shoulder.

Ezra smiles gently at me as the wind tousles his caramel hair across his forehead, causing my heart to flutter as our eyes meet.

Clean-shaven and striking, he is dressed in the simple beige uniform of the Secret Army, as is customary for soldiers, with only the single war cross medal and pair of golden wings resting solemnly on his chest, directly over his heart.

I hold his gaze as Papa and I take the final three steps, and Papa releases his hold of my arm, and I take the last step alone to join Ezra in front of Mr. Shepherd.

Ezra extends his hand out to Papa.

"Thank you, sir," Ezra whispers to him softly.

I smile softly at the two of them as they clasp hands.

Papa nods softly, his gaze soft as he meets Ezra's gaze, gingerly laying my right hand into Ezra's left palm.

"Take care of her," he says.

Ezra nods.

"I will."

Papa smiles, pressing his lips to my forehead one last time before turning and joining Mama with the others.

Ezra turns to face me.

We smile at each other, and I can feel a strong blush take root in my cheeks as he takes my other into his own, a look of such sincere gaiety and love shining in his eyes that it takes my breath away.

Mr. Shepherd clears his throat, gaining the attention of both Ezra and I, and the on lookers surrounding us.

A deep silence settles over us all, and it seems as if the winds still and the seagulls are silenced in honor of the moment.

My heart is pounding in my chest, drumming persistently, though not from fear or anxiety, but from sheer happiness.

Mr. Shepherd smiles at Ezra and I like we are his own begotten children, his eyes shining with such a burning look of relief and satisfaction at the sight of the young couple he had nurtured and guided for these past three years.

"We are gathered here today to witness the union of Ruth Muriel DeVos, and Ezra Christiaan Pik—a union that we have all secretly suspected for quite some time now," Mr. Shepherd says, addressing the group as a soft laugh arises from them, and I blush furthermore. "These two have faced a lot in these past three years leading up to today, and the journey has been hard-fought thus far. But alas, here we are."

His fatherly voice breaks several times as he speaks, but it only adds to the beauty of the simple ceremony and pricks the tears that threaten to fall down my cheeks as my heart is warmed by his words.

He opens his hands up, as if motioning toward us, I on his right and Ezra on his left.

"Let us begin," he says, cracking the worn spine of his old black Bible, the wind fluttering the wrinkled pages.

"*Love bears all things, believes all things, and endures all things,*" he reads, his voice rising crisp and clear. "*Love never ends.*"

Many waters cannot quench love, the still small voice whispers to my heart, and I remember His words from the day I was loaded on the deportation train at the Dossin Barracks: **Neither can the floods drown it.**

Mr. Shepherd glances at Ezra.

"Ezra, the rings," he says, smiling warmly.

Ezra smiles softly, his hands trembling as he opens his palm to reveal two golden rings, one larger than the other.

They had belonged to his parents for twenty-five years, and Jozef had given them to Ezra after Valerie's death.

Wordlessly, Ezra gives me the larger of the two, and I finger it between my trembling thumb and forefinger.

I smile, a silent tear rolling down my cheek.

Ezra notices, and he smiles as he takes a step closer to me, taking my left hand into his.

He pushes a shaky breath from his lips as he begins to speak in a voice so soft, I am certain that no one else hears his words save for me.

"Flesh of my flesh, and bone of my bones; with this ring, I thee wed," he whispers softly, his own hand trembling as he slips the dainty golden ring onto my finger.

I stare at my hand in wonder for a moment before glancing up to meet his gaze.

We share a soft smile.

I take his left hand, feeling the warmth of it as I slip the gold band over his ring finger.

"Flesh of my flesh, and bone of my bones; with this ring, I thee wed," I repeat the vow softly, my voice surprisingly steady and clear as I smile at him.

The next few seconds of speech are lost to me, as my heart flutters happily in my chest and I hold Ezra's steady gaze, and the next thing I hear is Mr. Shepherd.

"I now pronounce you, Man and Wife," he calls happily. "You may kiss the bride!"

Acclamations, clamor, applause, and general merriment of all sorts arise around us as Ezra leans closer to me, and cups my cheek in his hand.

He strokes my cheek, his eyes questioning.

I smile radiantly, and our lips meet as we kiss in sight of everyone.

And as we pull apart a long moment later, I am far too happy to notice everyone's gaze upon us.

"God has brought us together," I whisper softly.

Ezra smiles at me.

"He has at last," he says.

CHAPTER FORTY-THREE

Four months later

Over the course of the months following our small wedding, Ezra and I adjust to life as husband and wife as we face life side by side, at a rhythmic and peaceful pace.

Several changes are wrought by the changing of the seasons, as May fades into June, and June into July and the spry heat of August has its final hoorah before September brings the cool breath of autumn to us once more.

The vast and assorted array of thriving crops expand across the fields and pasturelands as far as my eyes can see, simply a prelude to the abundant harvest we will prayerfully have in the coming days.

We had worried that the harvest wouldn't a be a good one this year, since it was late plowing and sowing as the war came to a close around us, but as the old saying goes:

Prepare the distaff, and the Lord will provide the flax.

Several young yearlings now roam across the pastures, new additions to the herd that Ezra had purchased at the sale in hopes of reviving the bloodlines of Jozef Pik's herd from days gone by.

My eyes follow a particular black yearling colt, the one Ezra has taken to calling Solomon for his handsome build and docile spirit.

I smile softly out the glass pane of the kitchen window as I observe such changes, sighing contentedly.

Green Pastures flourishes, as does the family that inhabits it.

The dreams still wake me most nights, though not with the frequency and violence they once had, and the flashbacks only come at moments when I least expect them.

Some nights, I still wake up screaming and it is all Ezra can do to calm me once again.

I suppose the dreams will never truly go away.

I have noticed over the past few months of our marriage that Ezra fights with past memories as well, though not in the same way as I do.

His struggles come in the form of quiet moments of distant thought and silent rage; there have been many times when I have found him on his knees in our bedroom, his lips moving fervently though no sound escapes them as he pleads with his Heavenly Father.

But slowly, with one another's help, we are healing.

I step away from the window absently.

I walk quietly through the kitchen, and into the hall, where I stop to stare at the new photograph hung in the hallway across from the Pik's family portrait.

I often find myself gazing at this picture when I think back over the changes in my life, gazing at the familiar sideways and charismatic smile of my brother that has been timelessly captured within the frame.

The void Andrew left behind is still tender and vacant, and I often find myself glancing over my shoulder to look for him, or I will sometimes hear his voice when it is only the wind in my ears.

It is at these times that he feels closest to me.

Last month, a Netherlandish government official came to Green Pastures, and it frightened me nearly to death.

But it was a young soldier who had been sent with a medal that the Secret Army, on behalf of the Royal Family of The Netherlands, had issued posthumously to my brother, and it now hangs suspended on the wall beside his picture.

The *Verzetskruis,* or Dutch Cross of Resistance, is an award for valor and bravery in the Netherlands.

The medal is a gold cross set upon a blazing star with the inscription reading on the cross' limbs:

Trouw tot in den dood.

Loyal to Death.

Andrew *had* been loyal unto his dying breath.

Loyal to the Resistance, loyal to the cause of our country, loyal to the DeVos legacy, and firstly, loyal unto God.

I smile softly at his picture before turning on my heel and retracing my steps back into the kitchen.

I sigh softly as I sink into the chair at the dining table, my gaze lingering over the cold keys of the typewriter before me as I press a warm cup of tea to my lips.

I had begun the morning on the fervent endeavor of writing but have lost myself to the spiraling sight of change all around me.

So much has happened, I do not even know where to begin.

Mama and Papa returned to Vlissengen not long after Ezra and I married, for they missed home, and the salt air is good for Mama as she continues to recover from the deprivation and dehumanization that she endured all those long months in Germany.

Papa has not returned to active medical work yet as he watches diligently over Mama, though I can tell that he is itching to get back to his old line of work and aid in the rebuilding of our country as he would offer medical aid to all who needed it.

Eline and Fletcher returned to Antwerp for a short trip in July to visit the children we had cared for at the *Koloniale Hogeschool*, and to the shock of us all, returned to Brussels two weeks later as the proud Mama and Papa of three adoptive children.

Twin three-year-olds James and Julia, and eleven-month-old Henk prove to be a handful and the secret joy of us all, and now take up all of Eline's time and energy these days as she has become the perfect little mother goose.

Fletcher got a job as a banker in Brussels to support his family, but after only three months, he gave it up and came to work with Ezra at Green Pastures.

For several weeks, Mr. and Mrs. Shepherd have been staying with Eline, Fletcher, and the children at Oma Edwards Estate on the hill as a small house is being built for them on a small plot of land Ezra has given them, which will hopefully be completed in the days to come before winter.

Since Maya lost her family during the war, Mr. and Mrs. Shepherd officially adopted Maya, deeming her a true Shepherd after all these years without children.

As for Hugo, he drifts between us all, though he has of late taken residence in the barn here at Green Pastures, where he works side by side with Ezra every day, along with Fletcher.

I can see, with my quiet observations of the three men each day as they toil in the fields with the horses and gardens, the sincere brotherhood and newfound camaraderie between them.

Hugo has shocked us all with his loyalty and transformed ways since we first found him again at Antwerp after the bombing; he is no longer the man who had ruthlessly betrayed us so long ago, and by the grace of God, he has been forgiven.

I suppose some traitors *can* mend.

Of course in the midst of the family that inhabits our beloved Green Pastures, discord comes and goes, but ultimately, peace and prosperity reigns.

The land flourishes in peace as well, the warm hue of its glorious and hard-won beams shining benevolently down on all the world, but not just Belgium alone.

Last month, the Americans defeated the Japanese by dropping not one, but two, atomic bombs upon the enemy land, thus ending the war entirely and completely.

And after five years of war, the world is at last free from its evasive arms and nasty tendrils, and light shines once more.

I sigh softly once more, raising my fingertips to the typewriter before me.

The warm rays of the late morning sun reach in through the window where I had just stood, illuminating the small and tidy kitchen where I sit, and resting on the manuscript sitting on the table to my left.

I turn my gaze back to the blank piece of paper before me.

After, I write simply, the single word staring back at me as the ink dries upon the carbon paper swiftly.

After what?

But before I can answer my own unspoken question, a faint knock at the front door steals my attention.

I frown.

Who could that be?

My heart pounds softly in my chest as I stand from my chair and make my way into the vacant and still living room.

I brush gently past the piano, my fingertips grazing the ivory keys where Ezra had left the lid open last night.

I step toward the window, peering out at the yard from behind the lacey curtains that flutter at either side of the window pane.

My breath catches.

An unfamiliar automobile sits in the yard, the sun glinting off its chrome features as its inhabitants stand waiting on the stoop at the door.

I begin to absently adjust my skirts and brush the ink stains from my hands, though only smearing them helplessly across the cloth of my dress as I reach for the door knob.

I open the door to reveal two men facing me.

The first man is younger and dressed in fine clothes, while the man that stands feebly beside him is withered and worn, his face ashen and aged as he gazes at the green pastures around the house as he leans heavily on a cane.

I raise my brows softly.

"Hello. Can I help you?" I say.

The younger man speaks first, nodding graciously at me.

"I am so sorry to bother you, ma'am," he says, extending a dark hand out to me. "I am Peiter Rhams—I work with the former Intelligence network of the Resistance."

"It's lovely to meet you," I say tentatively as I plaster a small smile on my face, my gaze traveling from the younger man to the older, who stands with his back to me. "I am Ruth Pik."

The old man stiffens as I speak, and I swear I can see a broad smile brightening his entire face. He laughs softly to himself, closing his eyes, and breathing deeply, almost as if deeply pleased with something.

I turn to Peiter Rahms.

"Is he alright?" I ask softly, concern lining my voice.

Pieter Rahms smiles at me.

"Yes, ma'am, he is. His mind just slips every now and then." He pauses for a moment. "May we come in?"

I nod, concern and compassion for the old man stirring in my chest as I step aside.

"Of course," I say cordially with a wave of my hand. "Do come in, please."

Peiter Rahms smiles gratefully at me, laying a hand on the old man's shoulder.

The man turns to face me, brown eyes meeting mine as they dance merrily across my face.

My heart jolts with faint recognition.

It can't be, I think to myself.

"You've got some nice bloodlines, Mrs. Pik." He laughs softly.

I raise my brows at the curious old man.

What does he mean by that?

"I'm sorry?" I ask gently.

He smiles.

"The horses, I mean," he says, nodding toward the yearlings out to pasture.

I smile, a small laugh escaping my lips as I nod.

"Yes, thank you, sir. That is my husband's doing," I say as Peiter Rahms guides him over the threshold and into the house. "Come, sit. I'll get you some tea."

I step into the kitchen as the old man steps in the doorway, stopping for breath as he murmurs something to himself about the living room being familiar to him. A moment later, he follows me into the dining room, his wooden cane pecking methodically against the floor along with his shuffling footsteps.

It can't be, my mind repeats as I turn my back to the guests and pull two of Valerie Pik's teacups down from the cupboard, filling them each to the brim with the hot liquid from the whistling kettle on the stove.

Behind me, the old man sighs audibly as he sinks into a chair, Peter Rahms sitting tentatively beside him.

I offer a cup to Peiter Rahms, who takes it gratefully.

"Thank you, ma'am," he says.

I nod.

"My pleasure," I say, lifting the second dainty cup as my gaze travels to the old man. "So what can I do for you two gentlemen today?"

The old man looks up at me, his dark brown eyes familiar behind the mask of age and dementia, his lips curling into a soft and genuine smile as he takes the tea I offer him.

"I am looking for my son," he says to me, his voice thick and steady.

And familiar.

My heart nearly stops.

It's him.

I sit down in the chair beside him, wiping my hands absently on my skirt.

"Your son?" I ask, tears pricking my eyes as hope builds in my chest.

The old man nods, a look of gleeful knowing shining in his old eyes as he reaches out an aged, wrinkled, and calloused hand, and takes my hand into his.

"I take it that you know him?" he asks, his once baritone voice raspy as he smiles wryly at me.

I laugh softly.

"Yes, I know him," I say, blushing. "He is my husband."

I meet the old man's gaze, seeing in him all sorts of familiar features and movements that remind me of Ezra.

"Jozef, isn't it?" I ask him softly.

Again, he nods, smiling at me so brightly I fear it hurts him.

Jozef Pik.

Peiter Rahms clears his throat.

"Is your husband home, Mrs. Pik?" he asks me, nodding softly to the old man in our midst.

I smile softly.

"Yes, he is. He is working in the barn," I say.

But the words are barely out of my mouth before the front door opens, and Ezra calls out to me.

"Ruth! Are you alright?" he calls from the living room, his voice alarmed as his heavy footsteps echo through the house, growing closer.

I stand swiftly from my seat.

"There he is now," I say softly, giving Jozef a gentle glance as I step quickly into the living room.

Ezra stops as he sees me, relief dawning in his brown eyes.

"I saw the car pull in, and I was worried for a moment that it was either the Germans or another official," he says, taking my arm.

I do not think our perpetual fear of the Germans will ever fade.

Dirt covers his hands, crawling all the way up his forearms and falling from his boots onto the floor and leaving traces along my arms as he grips me.

I smile softly at him.

"I'm fine, love. It wasn't a German," I say to him as I greet him by the door, my heart fluttering excitedly. "But you do have a guest."

He raises his brows.

"I do?" he asks, searching my eyes. "Who is it?"

I want to tell him so badly, but I refrain from doing so as I smile somewhat sheepishly up at him, taking his hand into my own as I step toward the dining room.

He narrows his eyes at me as he falls into step beside me.

"Ruth," he says, as if to begin questioning me on the matter, but as we turn and enter the kitchen, he understands my silence.

Ezra's eyes widen, and his grip on my hand tightens.

"Pa?" he breathes softly, doubt and disbelief evident in his astonished voice.

Standing upright at the dining room table, with withered form and trembling limbs, Jozef Pik faces us, his warm brown eyes meeting the identical ones of his son.

"Hello, Son," Jozef says, taking a trembling step forward with the aid of his cane as he smiles tentatively at Ezra.

Ezra struggles for words, and for a long moment, no one speaks.

Peiter Rahms stands from his chair, smiling at me as he steps past us.

"I'll give you all a moment alone," he says in a respectful manner.

I nod.

"Thank you, Mr. Rahms," I say gratefully as the kind man leaves the room, and I turn my focus back to Ezra and Jozef.

They stand staring at each other silently, neither of them knowing what to say.

Like father, like son, I think to myself.

Wordlessly, Ezra rushes to his side, offering his arm out to his father, and Jozef takes it for support.

I smile softly as I watch the two of them embrace somewhat awkwardly as they are reunited after three years apart, and I can see the tears shining in Ezra's eyes as he grips the feeble hands of the man he had looked up to all these years.

The man he had been told was dead.

"They told me the Germans had—" he starts softly.

"Executed me?" Jozef asks, smiling softly at his son as he nods sorrowfully, "I know, my boy. But after months of interrogation and questioning, I learned that if I acted the fool, they'd either let me go, or kill me. They nearly *did* kill me. But thanks be to God above, for here I am."

Ezra shakes his head, dumbfounded.

"I don't know what to say," he says, softly, running a hand over the stubble on his chin.

Jozef smiles, winking in my direction.

"You always were a boy of few words, Ezra," he says softly, turning to his son. "Why don't you start by introducing me to your young wife here?"

Ezra's cheeks brighten at his father's words as he lets a breathy laugh fall from his lips, and I can see a weight lift from his shoulders.

He turns to face me, smiling softly as he offers me his hand.

I step forward and slip my hand into his.

"Ruth, this is my father, Jozef," he says with a soft smile. "Pa, this is my wife, Ruth."

CHAPTER FORTY-FOUR

For the next week, the land flourishes and comes to life as we gather together to revive and restore Green Pastures to her former glory; the tulips have long faded as the soft breeze stirs the long limbs of the windmills on the hilltops in the distance, seeming to watch over the various persons toiling in the fields below.

Every morning and evening, under the command of Ezra and the keen eye of his father, we set to work.

The rolling hills and expanding pastures of Green Pastures are alive with the various persons of the clan as the men work tirelessly in the fields and we women drift from our duties in the house and to the fields, as Eline and Fletcher's children and Maya's chickens run across the yard.

The work is hard and tiresome, and by the end of the day, we are all dirty, tired and worn—but smiling and satisfied with the work of our hands.

"Well, it looks like the boys are finished," Mrs. Shepherd says one evening in early September as the men finish the day's work, gazing out the kitchen window at the late evening sky as we prepare dinner.

I follow her gaze, my eyes landing on Ezra, Hugo, and Fletcher as the three of them trudge through the fields toward the house as evening settles over the land, and the day's work is complete.

"And so are we," I say, turning to face the small cake on the counter that will serve as the final course of the evening.

I lift it from the counter and balance it carefully on my forearm, stepping gingerly toward the screen door that stands openly inviting us into the warm evening air.

I glance at Mama, who sits gazing wistfully out the window. She brushes a hand across her cheek as she watches me.

"Are you alright, Mama?" I ask her softly.

In the past few months she has gained back most of her strength and her color, though her body is still whisper thin and brittle in appearance.

She scowls softly at me, though her eyes are tender.

"Yes, my *schat*," she says, smiling softly as she shakes her head at me, standing from her chair as she gives me a keen look. "You, on the other hand, look tired."

I smile softly.

I *am* tired.

The past few weeks of work on the farm have been hard, making my back stiff and body sore as I still battle most nights with dreams that keep me awake.

"I am alright, Mama," I say assuredly. "I promise."

Mrs. Shepherd smiles sheepishly as she loops her arm through Mama's, and the two walk out the door murmuring to each other like old friends.

I step out onto the porch after them, where I am greeted by the scents of hay and our dinner of roasted chicken, as well as the vivacious cackles of James and Julia as they play in the yard chasing chickens under Eline's gentle care as she holds Henk clutched to her chest.

While James and Julia resemble Eline with their Dutch blue eyes and little heads of tousled blond hair, little Henk has been blessed with the faint whispers of red hair that rivals Mrs. Shepherd's in its vibrancy.

"*Tante Rutte!*" James calls to me, leaving his sister behind as he runs on thin legs to meet me.

Aunt Ruth.

I smile down at him, lifting the cake above his head as he reaches for it.

"Not yet, *Neef*," I tell him with a laugh. "We must eat dinner first."

Nephew.

Eline smiles at me as she falls into step beside me, Henk resting on her hip as her daughter follows behind her in a docile and well-behaved manner.

I smile at the quiet little girl.

"How is my little *neef* today?" I ask, my gaze falling to the shy little boy in her arms, his large brown eyes gazing at the world around him as he clutches at his mother's dress.

"Tired and hungry." Eline laughs softly, smiling contentedly at her children as they frolic around us.

I smile softly, my heart beating with a new longing.

"Aren't we all?" Fletcher asks from behind us, smiling charismatically at his wife and children as he arrives for dinner, accompanied by Hugo. "I am famished."

"You are dirty," Eline tells him as he attempts to kiss her cheek, laughing at the dirt that covers his boots and the bottoms of his trousers, along with the hole he has busted once more in the knee. "Go clean yourself."

Fletcher smirks gently, stealing a kiss on Henk's little redhead before Eline swats him away and he turns to the twins as they begin arguing with one another.

"Settle down, *kinderen,*" he says softly, bending to their height. "What is the matter?"

"James is a troublemaker," Julia says indignantly, placing little fists on stout hips.

Fletcher fights a laugh as he gazes steadily at his daughter.

"And what did James do?"

Julia leans closer to him, mumbling something in his ear that I cannot identify as words.

Fletcher holds her gaze, smiling softly.

"Do not worry, my little one," he says, his gaze rising to Hugo. "Even the worst troublemaker can mend. I've known one that could."

I suppose even a traitor can mend.

Hugo nods gently, his eyes softening as he understands Fletcher's simple, yet profound words.

He looks down at his once pale and thin hands that are now calloused and tan from the work Ezra has given him to do these past few months.

A small smile pulls at his lips as Fletcher smiles brightly at him.

Eline and I share a soft smile.

Laughter rises over our heads, breaking the moment as our attention is drawn upward.

I squint against the sun in the direction of the sound, placing my hand to my brow.

Up in the oak tree beside the barn, tucked on one of the limbs, is a small, brown-headed and barefoot girl.

"Maya!" I call to her. "Get down from there. It's nearly time to eat, you silly little goose!"

"Coming!" comes the reply as the girl nimbly climbs down from her position and to the ground, landing on her feet as she trots happily into the barn with Mama and Mrs. Shepherd.

I smile after her, shaking my head.

"Where is Ezra?" I ask as I turn to Hugo, glancing behind him.

"He is finishing up in the fields. He is headed this way now," Hugo says nodding toward the fields behind the house as Ezra is the last to leave them. Hugo motions toward the cake I still hold. "I can take that to the table if you like, Ruth?"

I nod, smiling my gratitude as he takes the dessert from me.

"Thank you, Hugo," I say, tucking a loose strand of dark brunette hair behind my ear as the wind blows it gently across my face. "I will wait for Ezra and then we can eat."

Hugo nods, turning as he, Eline, Henk, and Fletcher continue toward the barn, followed shortly by James and Julia.

Ezra's gait is slow and stiff as he walks toward me, and I notice the tense burden on his worn shoulders as the weariness of work and toil is written across his face.

As he comes closer, I can see the dirt that has caked on his boots and trousers, and the fields have left their vestige upon him by the traces of dirt I can see along his forearms, beneath his fingernails and over his brow as he rakes his hair from his tired face.

"Looks like our fathers are getting along capitally." He smiles, nodding his chin ahead of us toward the barn, where Papa and Jozef stroll aimlessly in deep conversation with Mr. Shepherd as they follow the others inside the barn.

I smile, nodding with satisfaction.

"They are," I say, falling into step beside him, slipping my hand into his as I study his face hopefully. "You are finished for the evening, I hope?"

He nods.

"I am." He sighs softly, smiling contentedly at the land around us as he reaches into his breast pocket, brandishing a small piece of scrap notebook paper.

He smiles. "I nearly forgot."

He offers it out to me, his fingertips leaving whispers of red dirt on its once white surface.

I meet his brown gaze, arching my brow questioningly.

He nods and I take it, squinting down at his familiar handwriting.

Klein Brothers Publishing House

19, Rue de Flandre

Brussels, Belgium

I look up at him, my eyes searching his again.

"What's this?" I ask.

He smiles softly, a small laugh escaping his lips.

"It's a publisher, love," he says wryly, "for your manuscript."

The blush in my cheeks deepen, and I shake my head.

"Oh, Ezra, I don't think I *could* publish the manuscript," I say, sighing softly. "It's far too personal and deep to make public. Besides, you said yourself that it was unfinished."

Ezra nods, smiling.

"I did, Ruth. And the proper ending will come in time," he says, his arm tightening around me, "but your story was good. It deserves to be told and heard."

I chew my lip, a small thread of hope taking root in my heart.

I glance up at him, my brows raised.

"Do you honestly think so?"

He nods, his dark eyes soft and knowing.

"I do, but it's up to you. I'll support you either way." He falls quiet for a moment. "Just remember that this is your testimony. You mustn't squander that; but you can't ignore it either. God gave you that story as a testimony for a reason."

He smiles, giving my hand a gentle squeeze.

"Perhaps you are meant to share it."

I smile at him, the familiar boldness stirring in my chest as I nod.

Perhaps I am, I think to myself.

"Are you two *coming*? Some of us would like to eat this evening," Fletcher asks dramatically, breaking into our conversation as he smiles drolly at us from inside the barn.

Ezra smiles at him, shaking his head.

"Yes Fletcher, we're coming," he says, meeting my gaze.

I laugh softly.

And so, Ezra and I walk hand in hand into the old horse barn, where everyone has already gathered around the large makeshift table the boys set up this morning in the middle of the aisle between the horse stalls where Ezra's *Fokker C.V.* has been hidden, and now sits out in the field awaiting its pilot.

A cloth has been spread over the worn boards of the table, and now sits covered in a vast array of foods from the harvest, with a large roasted chicken as the centerpiece.

We are greeted by the usual lively chatter and overall dysfunctional chaos and conversation of mealtime, with three different conversations being carried out at once as Julia squeals.

"James, do *not* pull your sister's hair again," Eline warns her son as Fletcher returns to his seat beside her with an exasperated, though content, sigh.

"The harvest has been a good one. The crops are abundant, and the herd is flourishing," Jozef says softly to Papa. "I am proud to see that I have trained my son well."

Jozef smiles at Ezra, and Ezra's cheeks grow red.

"Hugo and I did the majority of the work, you know," Fletcher says, his voice rising higher than the others as if to ensure that Ezra will hear him. "Ezra sat in the shade all afternoon."

I laugh softly, and Ezra shakes his head at him as we step through the barn doors.

He smiles at Fletcher, his brows raised in a teasing manner.

"Telling stories again, are we, my friend?" he says.

Fletcher shakes his head.

"No, not stories. Just facts," Fletcher says, smiling in an equally teasing manner.

Two seats remain at the table's head, and Ezra and I take them, sitting down unnoticed on the bale of hay that is used in place of chairs as the chorus of laughter and conversation ring around us.

Mama smiles at me from her seat to my left, where she sits beside Papa.

She lays a thin hand over mine.

"We made it, *Dochter*. We went through the Slough of Despond, and this is the other side," she says, referring to a book I recall her reading from my childhood.

The Pilgrim's Progress.

I smile wistfully at her, my mind wandering to the fever dream I had while on the deportation train.

"I just wish Andrew were here with us," I say softly, my voice low so as to not arouse attention to my brother's absence.

Andrew.

Oh, how I wish he were here tonight!

But even so, it is well with me.

Mama nods, sighing.

"I know. I have been thinking a lot about him today myself," she says, her eyes somehow both sad and blazing all at once. She swallows gently. "But it pleases me immensely to know that his sacrifice was not in vain, though it pains me greatly."

I smile, her words familiar to my ears.

Papa meets my gaze, his brown eyes soft and knowing.

"No sacrifice comes without pain," he says, his gaze travels around the room. "But God has given me peace and consolation in you all."

Mama nods as Papa takes her hand, her gaze following his to the people gathered around us.

I smile softly at them all, my stomach tightening as I think of what it has taken for us all to be here together tonight.

I gaze around at each familiar face, my mind wandering back over everything we have faced and fought together for all these years. Upon each of us rests the scars of our pasts, some visible on our physical bodies while we harbor hidden ones in the depths of our hearts.

We will carry these scars with us for the rest of our lives, and looking back, I can see with open eyes that they are all part of a story that God will use, for they tell of His love toward us each.

And as I look at the scarred and wounded people around me tonight, I see my family, both by blood, marriage, and woven in.

I smile.

This is *my* family.

There are a few persons that are no longer present, and their absence is felt heavily, but even so, we are still the family that God has woven into a beautiful tapestry of conquering grace.

Ezra sighs softly beside me, drawing my attention to where his gaze rests on Mr. Shepherd as he sits silently observing the lot of us around him, smiling wistfully.

He smiles at Ezra and I, and I notice a slight hint of light in his eyes as he gazes at the faces around us that causes my mind to drift back to our time in the Dossin Barracks.

It was our duty and honor to serve you in our home...

These are the words he had told Fletcher and I when I had asked why he and Mrs. Shepherd decided to hide us at Still Waters—though we were strangers and runaways.

Mrs. Shepherd gazes at me, her lips pulling into a soft smile as if she has heard my unspoken thoughts.

Now their home no longer stands, and we cannot go back to those days at our beloved Still Waters. But by the grace of God, we are all still together tonight, at Green Pastures.

Mr. Shepherd nods at Ezra and I, smiling as he takes Mrs. Shepherd's hand.

Do you understand, children? His gaze seems to say.

I smile softly in return, glancing at Ezra.

His eyes are shining happily as he smiles at me.

He understands.

And the murmurings soon come to a close as Ezra stands at the table's head beside me, gazing at the face of every person present as a silence and stillness falls over us.

I smile as my heart beats softly with understanding.

Green Pastures is our home now; and it is our greatest duty and privilege to serve this family in it, just as Mr. and Mrs. Shepherd had done for us all at Still Waters.

"Let us pray," Ezra says gently.

Everyone's gaze travels to the head of the table where Ezra has just risen beside me, and Mr. Shepherd nods at him once again, smiling at him with pride and respect.

"Everyone rise from your seats and bow your heads," Ezra says, offering me his hand.

I take his extended hand and rise along with everyone else at the table, closing my eyes and bowing my head as I grip his hand tightly in my own.

Ezra clears his throat, and begins to pray, his voice thick as it rises to the rafters of the barn and to the heights of Heaven.

"Lord, as our Shepherd, you have led us all these years. Our foes have been many since the days when you first led us all together, and it has not been an easy road leading up to this moment, as you bring us all together once more. We faced the valley of death, and we lived in the shadow of darkness, but even then, you were there."

Gooseflesh raises across my arms as tears sting my eyes at his words, soft-spoken and eloquent for a man of such few words.

...faced the valley of death...

"Father, you lead us all beside Still Waters, and that is where you formed us. But now you have brought us to this place of abundance at Green Pastures, where you will make us lie down and find the rest we've longed for through these five years of war. I can see your hand so clearly upon us all tonight, Father. I pray that it remains steadfastly with us as we face the coming days ahead."

He pauses for a moment, his hand tightening around mine, and I lean my head against his shoulder as he finishes the prayer.

"You have been faithful, O Lord, in the past; and I know that you will continue leading us all our days. You have taken away and given again. Bless this harvest and bless the lives of everyone you have gathered together tonight, now and forevermore." He pauses for a moment, taking a shaky breath before whispering, "Amen."

"Amen," Mr. Shepherd says, nodding his head as his eyes shine with approval.

"Amen," the table murmurs in soft agreeance as the effect of the moment is not lost on anyone save the children, as all faces are turned toward the head of the table.

"Good boy!" Jozef says, clapping his withered hands as he smiles at his son.

I lift my head and smile at Ezra, nudging his shoulder gently.

"That was lovely, Mr. Pik," I say close to his ear, teasing him softly.

He laughs softly, his hand tightening over mine.

"Thank you, Mrs. Pik," he whispers back, smiling gently at me as his warm gaze causes my heart to flutter in my chest.

Hugo clears his throat, gaining our attention as he bends to lift his glass in the air.

"I would like to propose a toast," he says, waving it in front of him as he smiles, gazing at the barn and surrounding land around us. "A toast to Green Pastures and all her inhabitants, may the Lord ever keep us from harm."

He pauses for a moment, his gaze meeting mine for a brief second as he speaks again.

"And to freedom and forgiveness, for I know I have received far more than I deserve."

I smile softly, nodding at Hugo.

Forgiveness is no easy task. It is messy and complicated, and a burden that is heavy to carry.

But somewhere deep in the crevices of my heart, I have forgiven Hugo, though the memories that haunt me of his betrayal will never truly fade, and the scars along Ezra's leg will forever remind me of when Hugo's life nearly cost him his own.

But, the past cannot be helped, and we must keep our gazes on the horizon ahead of us.

"Hear hear!" Fletcher says, sharing a sober glance with both Hugo and Ezra.

Eline smiles softly at me from across the table as Henk pulls her hair and James steals a blackberry from off the cake.

I stifle a laugh at the rebellious child, my attention stolen away once again as Mr. Shepherd clears his throat to speak, his gaze soft and his voice raspy as he lifts his glass.

"To you, my children," he says, smiling brightly at all of us, his adoptive children, as his eyes fill with fatherly affection. "May the Lord bless you, and keep you. May His face shine upon you as we face this life ahead, and may He give you all His peace. And may He bless us all, and the generations to come."

A small smile pulls at my lips.

"Amen!" Papa says, lifting his glass with his old friend as we smile at one another. "Now, let's eat!"

"Agreed," Fletcher says, smiling drolly as he bends to help Julia fix her plate.

Ezra steals a soft smile at me, and I return to my seat as he leans closer to whisper something in my ear.

"So, about this story..." he says, his breath warm against my skin. "How does it end?"

I smile, shrugging slightly.

"I suppose we will just have to wait and see, won't we, love?" I ask, understanding the hidden meaning behind his words.

Our story thus far has not been an easy one.

But through it all, God has been with us.

He knew before our days began that from our first breaths we were all broken, and that at our first step, we were wandering; he knew before we were born what our days would hold, and he knew before the world began each hardship and trial we would endure.

He wrote with his own hand every twist and turn of the plot, and he chose to weave in the bitter with the sweet.

All along, God knew my story.

And I know just how it will end; it all ends with us, with Him.

Ezra nods softly, seeming to understand my unspoken thoughts as he gazes intently into my hazel eyes.

"I suppose we will." He smiles at me, bending his neck and kissing me gently. He holds my gaze steadily for a moment before he turns to face the table, saying, "Now, who will carve the chicken?"

And with that, dinner begins.

The food is passed around as voices rise with the silverware as darkness settles over Green Pastures and the song of the night crickets begin their soft serenade in the fields and valleys below.

Here is where we remain for the rest of the evening, laughing and dining in one another's company like we have so many times before; and prayerfully, as we will in the days to come.

Issue #751   La Libre Belgique   1950

FIVE YEARS LATER

Brussels, Belgium

"Behold, I am making all things New!"

REVELATION 21:5

EPILOGUE

Klein Brothers Publishing House

I gaze at the typewriter resting absently on the polished desk before me, my fingers twitching as my heart beats softly in my chest, and I lift my chin with purpose.

"Do you know, Mrs. Pik, what the going royalty rates are these days?" Herman Klein asks me from across the desk, his green eyes meeting mine through the spectacles perched on the bridge of his nose.

Herman Klein, my publisher at *Klein Brothers Publishing House* in Brussels, is a genuine and honest man acquainted with the most beloved and widely acclaimed authors in Belgium.

I nod, smiling winsomely at him as my stomach churns.

"I do, and I believe that eight percent is perfectly fair," I say with a certainty that I do not feel.

Mr. Klein sighs, a genuine look of concern passing over his face.

He stands suddenly, turning his back to me as he opens a cabinet along the wall behind him, his nimble fingers flipping through various manuscripts and drafts before he finally pulls one out.

"It is, Mrs. Pik. But for a well-known and beloved author. Not an unpublished authoress such as yourself," he says, laying the sheaf of paper down before me beside the typewriter and motioning toward it pointedly with his hand, palm-side up.

I smile down at it, its title meeting my gaze.

The Yellow Badge.

My heart beats softly as I finger the worn and ink-stained manuscript.

"I know that you have a family to provide for, Mrs. Pik. I understand. But this is risky. Dangerous, even. This is a major investment," Mr. Klein says as he returns to his seat, his fingers forming an archway as he thinks.

I smile at him.

"A lot of things are dangerous, Mr. Klein," I say softly.

But that doesn't mean we avoid them, I add silently in my heart.

He sighs once again, softer this time as he meets my gaze, his antique eyes beaming at me from behind his glasses.

"This industry is not an easy one to navigate, and it is oftentimes unfair. But I will try everything in my power to help you, ma'am. You have my word," he says.

A slight smile pulls at my lips.

Mr. Klein sighs once again, setting his jaw as he leans forward.

"Seven and a half percent—I am afraid I can do no more," he says, offering his hand out to me as he makes his final offer.

I chew my lip, narrowing my eyes slightly.

After a moment, I smile.

"Done," I say, taking his hand and shaking it in agreement.

He beams at me, his green eyes dancing.

"Excellent, Mrs. Pik," he says, standing once more. I watch as he opens the drawer of his desk. "I received your first printing from my bookbinders this morning, ma'am."

He pulls a small book from the depths of the drawer, offering it out to me.

My heart pounds at the sight of it as I watch my fingers fold around its cloth-covered spine, relishing the feeling of the weight of it in my grasp.

Bound in a deep green cloth covering its face, the title glares back at me in gold foil, and a small star is stamped beneath the words.

I feel a small smile pull at my lips.

The Yellow Badge.

And at the bottom, it reads the author.

Ruth De Vos Pik.

"It is quite a story, Mrs. Pik," Mr. Klein says to me.

I nod, smiling.

"It is," I say.

~ . ~

I GAZE AT THE BOOK in my hand.

My fingers press against the small yellow badge that has been impressed into the cloth as the current of memories flood my heart and mind.

The yellow badge had been used as an instrument of shame and reproach, at least it had been for me.

But for Andrew, it had been so much more.

It had been a call to action, a symbol of courage and valor in the face of persecution and opposition, and a burden that he bore gladly even though he knew the consequence.

And in hindsight, I understand.

I smile softly at the little book

For Andrew.

Andrew has been gone for seven years now, and it feels like just yesterday we were children running across the beaches of Vlissengen.

I clutch the book to my chest as I turn my face to the glass window pane, where snow is falling once again outside, covering Green Pastures in a blanket of white as the sky is covered in a veil of thick clouds that reflect the color of the earth below.

The evening sun casts a warm hue across the tranquil landscape of undisturbed snow as it combats the snow clouds to shine for a brief moment; and for that moment, something catches my gaze.

My heart rate quickens as I lean closer, my breath fogging up the pane.

But when the glass clears, it is gone.

I sigh softly, shaking my head.

A soft moan arises behind me, pulling my gaze from both the book and window as I glance over my shoulder at the small crib in the corner of the room.

Valerie.

Sitting the book down on the desk, I step softly to the crib's side, where I gaze down at the small whimpering baby lying in her crib as she is aroused from her sleep too soon by the force of dreams.

When she was born, Ezra and I feared that we would lose our Valerie Jozefin.

She had been silent, and so small and frail that I believed in my heart that her days on this Earth would be few. And since then, little has changed; her white cheeks are thin, and her body far too small for a one-month-old.

But with every prayer that is whispered over her and with each day that passes, I see a faint shift in her small body.

A shift that gives me hope.

I see the new color in her once pale cheeks, I feel the rising strength in her tiny limbs, and I see the blazing boldness in her large eyes that she inherited from me.

I smile down at my little daughter, gingerly lifting her from her blankets and cradling her to my chest as she sighs softly in my arms.

"Did you have a dream?" I murmur to her softly, pressing my lips to her cheek. "I have dreams too."

Dreams that will never leave me, no matter how many years may pass.

Valerie whimpers and cries softly, her arms thrashing lightly as I begin to hum a soft melody to her that stirs the well-known chords of my heart.

"And Lord, haste the day when the faith shall be sight,
The clouds be rolled back as a scroll;
The trump shall resound, and the Lord shall descend,
Even so, it is well with my soul!"

Once she is settled in my arms, I lift my eyes back to the window, where something had caught my eye just a moment ago.

My breath catches.

A man dressed in a yellow plaid shirt stands gazing back at me, the snow falling all around him as his boots are nearly buried, and his smiling hazel eyes meet mine for a moment.

Yet his face is unclear, as if I am looking at him through a fogged mirror, but still recognition dawns on me as my heart pounds.

"There you are, love," says a thick baritone voice behind me, and it takes me a moment to realize that it is Ezra and not my brother's voice as I turn to find Ezra standing in the doorway of Valerie's nursery.

He smiles brightly at me, his eyes soft as they land on Valerie.

"How is my little *dochter?* I heard her crying," he says, stroking her pale pink cheek tenderly as he steps to my side.

"It was only a dream," I say softly as he wipes a single tear from our daughter's cheek, "but it still upset her."

Ezra smiles wryly, his eyes meeting mine.

"Like mother, like daughter," he says.

I smile softly.

He takes my hand, nodding toward the kitchen, where the vivacious voices of the Green Pastures clan can be heard as we gather to celebrate my twenty-eighth birthday.

"Everyone is waiting for you. It is *your* birthday, you know," he says, his eyes bright. "Andrew is about to begin eating *Slagroomtart* without you."

I laugh softly.

Just then, a soft voice calls out from the hallway, accompanied by swift footsteps as our son, four-year-old Andrew Christaan, calls for Ezra.

"Papa!"

Ezra smiles.

"We are in here, *Zoon,*" he says, his voice soft so as to not upset Valerie.

A moment later, a short and ruddy-cheeked little boy appears at the door, where Ezra lifts him into his arms.

"What is it, Andrew?" I ask softly, smiling as I wipe a curious smear of cream from his chin.

While Andrew had inherited most of Ezra's Dutch features, like his sharp nose, broad shoulders, and caramel brown hair, he had inherited my wide hazel eyes.

And as he smiles at me now, he flashes the familiar dimples that he shares with me, and also the sideways grin that had belonged to his uncle Andrew.

"*Oom* Fletcher just told me a story about how you fought the Germans," he says, his blazing hazel eyes shining with sheer curiosity as he turns to Ezra. "Is it true, Papa?"

Ezra and I smile softly at each other, a look of knowing passing between us before Ezra turns to gaze into Andrew's young eyes, smiling tenderly at him.

"I believe that is a story for another time, *Zoon,*" he says.

In my experience, I have learned that some stories carry us on a journey far from home.

But for other stories, such as mine, it is only at the journey's end that we realize that all along, the story was leading us *home.*

I smile at our children.

I pray that they will never face the horror and the darkness that we had too, or fight such ruthless enemies as the Germans. I hope with every fiber of my being that they will never know why I wake up screaming at night, or the fear that still grips both Ezra and I at times when we least expect it.

I pray that our son will never face the fighting that Andrew and Ezra had to endure, and I beg God to keep him from the same call of sacrifice that Andrew had been.

One day, they will run across the fields of Green Pastures just as Andrew and I had growing up on the beach in Vlissengen.

One day, when they are older, Ezra and I will tell them the story of our pasts and what God carried us through; we will tell them of their uncle who fought and died for the peace that will guard their futures.

One day they *will* face the inevitable darkness of this world.

For as long as there is light in the world, darkness must abide as well.

But for this moment, as I cradle Valerie in my arms and Andrew is perched in Ezra's strong hold, they are safe.

I turn to face the window once more.

The man smiles at me, his lips pulling into a soft sideways grin as he lifts his palm and waves to me, his hazel eyes meeting mine once again as he gazes at my small family.

"*Broer,*" I whisper gently, my voice so soft I can barely hear it.

I smile softly at him, tears filling my eyes.

I blink them away, and he is gone.

Goodbye, Andrew.

It is only a trick of the imagination that I see him at all, but I know that I will see my brother again face to face.

For our lives and stories are not bound to this Earth, where pain, sorrow, and loss will always be; no, there is only peace and joy where I am bound, and *that* is where Andrew is, waiting for me.

My gaze falls down to the small green book that still rests on the desk, my mind wandering to all the memories of Andrew that have been written within its pages.

The yellow badge gleams a vibrant shade of citrine, reminding me of where this story began eight years ago.

And as this story comes to a close, I look away from the badge as Ezra takes my hand, and I lean my head on his shoulder as the four of us turn to join the others.

I smile softly.

This is my story.

This is my testament of the battles fought and won and lost; this is the story of light in the midst of darkness.

This is my life.

After the badge.

GLOSSARY

Auteur- Author

Broer- Brother

Dochter- Daughter

Deutlich- Bold

Oma- Grandmother

Oom- Uncle

Jude- Jew, a person of Jewish heritage or origin

Kliendochter- Granddaughter

Kinderen- Children

La Libre Belgique- The Free Belgium- the illegal underground clandestine newspaper of the Dutch Resistance published in both World War 1 and World War 2.

Mof- *German.* A slang word used by Dutch and Flemish individuals to describe and address their German enemies. It is also a way of expressing Dutch resentment and hatred for Germany's occupation.

Slagroomtaart- A traditional Netherlandish sponge cake covered in whipped cream and fruit usually used to celebrate birthdays.

Tante- Aunt

Vriend- Friend

Zus- Sister

Zoon- Son

AUTHOR'S NOTE

This novel has been the hardest thing for me to write, only because I know that the story has at last come to a close.

I will be honest with you; I did *not* want to write this sequel. Every bone in my body dreaded the thought of writing a sequel to my beloved *The Yellow Badge*.

It was my sister Caitlyn, my editor and co-dreamer, who persistently and incessantly brought up the subject of a sequel.

An idea I quickly shot down before it could get very far.

The story was finished. Or so I thought.

It was only while doing some unrelated research that I stumbled upon an Ernest Hemingway quote that got me thinking.

"All stories, if continued far enough, end in death. And he is no true storyteller who would keep that from you."

At first, I used Hemingway's words to justify my hard-kept resolution to *not* write a sequel, even after the first one ended in Andrew's death.

But then the Holy Spirit came along and showed me the falsehood in that quote for us believers.

For the truth is, if you have found salvation in Jesus Christ, then your story does *not* end in death.

And so, neither should Andrew's—or Ruth's.

So, it was then that I finally surrendered to continue the story.

And thus, through months of thought, prayer, and research, a sequel was born.

Throughout this story, we dance around the end of the war for months, but we do not reach a declared end until closer to the end of the book.

So it was in real life.

When allied British Troops were led through the streets of Antwerp and Brussels at the first of September in 1944, along with other major cities in Belgium, the citizens rejoiced.

They gathered in the streets, danced, sang, and chanted around their valorous liberators as all Nazi personnel were led away, or killed, as all German belongings and Nazi Reich tokens were thrown out into the streets and burned.

And so, for the next month and half, the people of Belgium lived in blissful hope of the end of war as they all tried to return to normal life.

Until in October, on Friday the Thirteenth, when the first of many V1 flying bombs and V2 rockets began pelting the city of Antwerp.

It is during this time that Ezra is summoned back to duty with the Secret Army as the Resistance, stronger than ever before, continues to fight the Germans.

After the liberation of Belgium in September, the war issues of *La Libre Belgique* under the masthead *de Peter Pan,* dissolved. In its place rose the regular form of the newspaper that we see today by the same name.

In *After the Badge,* Ruth is offered a true job as a journalist for this reformed paper by Paul Struye, one of two men who revived the illegal paper after the invasion in 1940.

Ruth takes it, and is sent to Antwerp on assignment, where she and Eline are faced with unimaginable destruction as they offer their aid to the Secret Army at the *Koloniale Hogeschool.*

According to historical accounts, there is nothing confirming nor denying that the Resistance gathered the sick and wounded at the university, but before the liberation, it is said that the school was the stronghold of the Resistance.

So, it is not a stretch of imagination that the Resistance would still resort to carrying out their work after the bombardment began in the school.

During the six-month bombardment of Antwerp, the city was destroyed and utterly devastated; at the close of the bombings in

March 1945, the city was left unrecognizable as its streets and homes were nothing more than mere rubble and its people had either fallen as victims of the bombs or left for safe country.

It is while here that Ruth joins the Resistance to serve the fallen Resistance men, allied soldiers, and civilians, and is finally reunited with her beloved Papa, as well as where she meets Jack—known famously as C.S. Lewis.

C.S. Lewis was mentioned in *The Yellow Badge,* and while there is no factual reason or account that he was in Belgium during WWII (he in fact was not), I felt that him having a cameo in *After the Badge* would be the perfect addition to Ruth's story that also brought us back to where we began.

I also want to include that the broadcast talk that is included earlier in the story is not my own, but C. S Lewis's.

Titled *The New Man,* this particular broadcast was his final radio talk on Christianity that originally aired on March 21st, 1944.

Due to a shortage of tapes and recording supplies, most of Lewis's talks were taped over and lost, save for this one. You can still find and listen to original audio of this single surviving recording of this broadcast.

As for Ezra's incident and Hugo's return, this particular scene has rather personal ties to it for me.

The story that Ezra willingly risked his life for Hugo is not just a novelty or a cliche but is actually inspired by my own grandfather's actions in the Vietnam War.

My grandfather risked everything to save a comrade who attempted to flee in the face of a bomb, which I believe later resulted in the comrade's death and my grandfather walking away with serious wounds.

Later on, my grandfather was awarded with the Purple Heart, a US medal given to servicemen who were wounded or killed in the line of duty.

And so, in *After the Badge,* Ezra is awarded the *Croix de guerre,* or War Cross.

The War Cross of Belgium is a small bronze medal in the form of a Maltese cross with a pair of drawn swords beneath a central medallion poised in its center bearing the image of a lion rampant.

The medal was generally given to cited individuals during WW2 for bravery or good conduct on the battlefield, though a few select and cited units received one as well.

The Bergen-Belson concentration camp in Germany is infamous for its inhumane living conditions and the illnesses and diseases that its inmates had to endure. Though what may be most widely known about this camp is that it was where Anne Frank and her sister Margot died of typhus in early 1945 before the camp was liberated by British allies in April of the same year.

It is in this dark and vile camp that I chose to put the fictional character of Judith DeVos, Ruth's mother.

For the whole of the story up until her return home, Judith is never seen in the present moment, save for Ruth's memories and her fever dreams on the train to Auschwitz.

And when she and Ruth are at last reunited, she is only a shadow or a mere whisper of the person in her memories. Her body is malnourished and deformed, thin and brittle; they had shaved her head, as they do all inmates at death camps, and her skin had drained of all color, leaving it a pale and pasty white.

Perhaps one of my favorite moments is this one, though. Where Judith, Nathaniel, and Ruth are together for the first time in the entire story. It is a tender moment where we learn just what the Jews of their day went through, and what it took for them to be reunited.

After the end of the bombardment and the advancing of the liberating allies came the final blow to the Nazi Third Reich that brought an end to the war.

Hitler's death.

After months of fighting, the Germans were finally losing their footing in the war and Hitler knew that his time of power was coming to a close.

So on April 30th, 1945, Adolf Hitler was found dead in the *Fuhrerbunker* in Berlin, where he and his wife of one day had committed suicide.

According to witnesses, Hitler shot himself in the right temple, with his own pistol.

The world rejoiced as the news was announced by German radios the next day, May 1st; but with the joy and celebrations, doubts and fears arose as well.

There was no literal proof that Hitler *was* dead. And the people had been lied to and fooled by the Germans' trickery far too many times to willingly believe such news.

It seemed impossible that the power-hungry and manipulative man that had caused them to suffer for so long would flee from defeat by taking his own life like a coward.

And even today, in 2024, his death and suicide are believed to be "alleged." No one knows for certain how, when, or if Adolf Hitler died on April 30th, 1945.

I suppose we will never know, but his death remains the object of speculation.

Nine days after Hitler's alleged death came the long-awaited and hard-won day of victory as the war with the Germans came to a close.

On May the seventh, Germany signed an unconditional instrument of surrender in Reims, France. It stated that the surrender would take effect at one minute past midnight the next day, on May the eighth.

A second document was signed the next day, declaring the same conditions.

On the morning of the eighth, just hours from the surrender, British Prime Minister Winston Churchill gave his infamous victory speech to the British people, which I have included in this history for more historical dimension.

Shortly after, as the world seemed to hold its breath for the moment when the clock struck midnight and the final minute of occupation, the war came to a close and marked May the eighth for all time as Victory in Europe day (V.E. Day).

For days, the people across the globe celebrated in various ways as they began living in victory for the first time in over five years when Germany invaded Poland in 1939.

The final thing I want to touch on in a historical sense is the Dutch Cross of the Resistance that our dear Andrew received posthumously.

The *Verzetskruis* is a decoration of valor in the Netherlands, both Ruth and Andrew's birth country.

It was awarded to individuals in recognition of courage and valor shown in resistance against the enemies of the Netherlands, and in most cases, the sacrifice made in maintaining the freedom and liberties of the country.

The medal is in the form of a bronze cross set upon a flaming star with an image upon its face of the Dutch Resistance slaying a dragon (the Nazis).

The cross' limbs bear upon them the inscription of *Trouw tot in den dood,* Loyal to death.

On the reverse of the medal is an image of a chain being torn in two, symbolizing not only the Dutch victory from German bondage but also Andrew's victory over death.

~.~

I WROTE THIS BOOK with the same goal as the first one:

To testify of God's love and guidance of his people through the years, from generation to generation.

As I said before, my faith is very important to me, and it is the very reason you hold this book in your hands right now. Without my faith to carry me through and guide my words, I would be lost, and my stories would lack purpose.

And just as with the first one, God has been the only thing that carried me through this sequel with my sanity and belief intact, as well as my faith stronger now than before.

For Ruth, this is not an easy story to tell, and it broke my heart as I faced Andrew's death through her eyes, and was left reeling with the questions of *why?*

Ruth, I think, represents the very human side of us all; she is a very real character struggling with grief and bitterness, as well as confusion and doubt as she is faced with the unimaginable darkness of evil.

But the beauty of faith is being able to ask questions while still choosing to believe that God is carrying us, and that no matter the outcome, he is good.

Such is the faith I wanted to portray.

Ezra remains the voice of faith and certainty even as he faces the blunt force of war; and his faith is stronger still as he is faced with his enemy and is given the choice to save and forgive.

I absolutely love the closing scenes of the epilogue, where we see Ruth and Ezra together and we see the goodness of God in the close of their story.

We see, also, Andrew one final time.

Andrew is not really there, of course; he is merely a memory that gives the readers one last glimpse of our three main characters together again.

The reason I chose to weave Andrew into the epilogue this way is to prove that our stories *don't* end in death.

As Ezra told Ruth, *"This is the story that God has given you; and it doesn't end in death."*

For those who have been saved by faith in Jesus Christ, our stories do not end in the grave. No, our lives continue in Heaven, where our stories and lives remain throughout the ages of eternity.

And so it was for Andrew, Ruth, and Ezra.

So it is for me.

I hope you have found the truth of the Gospel woven into this story.

And I pray that you will not let this history fade away, nor let it be forgotten; for in the past we find traces of God's faithfulness in history, and they point to His faithfulness for us, in the future.

But most of all, I pray that you have found that light *can* shine in the darkness, and I hope that in these pages you have come to know the love of God.

For this is the very reason I have written these things.

*These [things] are written so that you may believe that Jesus is
Christ, the son of God, and that by believing you
may have life in his name.*
John 20:31

A.R.C.

ACKNOWLEDGEMENTS

I would like to begin this acknowledgement by thanking all the people in my life who read the first book, first—their enthusiasm and feedback are priceless to me.

This book would not be possible without the constant support and persistent encouragement from my sister Caitlyn, who remains my steadfast and loyal editor, and co-author. As always, Caitlyn, thank you for sticking with me through it all, even when it seemed no one else cared; I thank God for you.

And I would like to thank Laney, my tech-savvy and artistic sister who never fails to create a cover that strikes my fancy even when I have no clue what I want.

Thank you to Mama and Daddy for putting up with my 'author' moments where I could focus on nothing else but the story, and for also being patient when I spent our entire vacation fretting over the plot of this sequel.

Thank you, Mimi, for being so honest and enthusiastic with your review of *The Yellow Badge;* and thank you for loving it as much as I do. I hope you love the sequel just as much.

To my entire reading group who has grown larger than I can count now, I thank you each and every one.

And once again, I cannot end this acknowledgement without saying a final thank you to all who actually lived this story and made it possible for me to tell it by the published accounts of World War 2.

Thank you all—soldiers, nurses, writers, Resistance workers, pilots, Jews, Germans and prisoners.

It has been the greatest honor and privilege to tell your story of battles fought, won, and lost.

ABOUT THE AUTHOR

Since early childhood, Addison Crissone has dreamed of becoming a published author—crafting many stories, poems, and blog posts with the passion of telling others about Jesus Christ.

Addison lives in the mountains of western North Carolina with her family, and her mini-Aussie, Millie.

You can visit Addison and check out her other work at:

https://addisoncrissone.pubsitepro.com/

www.ingramcontent.com/pod-product-compliance
Lightning Source LLC
Chambersburg PA
CBHW020344010826
48973CB00005B/1263